Herbert Maxwell

The Honourable Sir Charles Murray, K.C.B.

A memoir

Herbert Maxwell

The Honourable Sir Charles Murray, K.C.B.
A memoir

ISBN/EAN: 9783337412128

Printed in Europe, USA, Canada, Australia, Japan

Cover: Foto ©Raphael Reischuk / pixelio.de

More available books at **www.hansebooks.com**

THE HONOURABLE
SIR CHARLES MURRAY, K.C.B.

𝔄 𝔐𝔢𝔪𝔬𝔦𝔯

BY THE

RIGHT HONOURABLE

SIR HERBERT MAXWELL

BART., M.P., F.R.S., ETC.

Γηράσκω δ' αἰεὶ πολλὰ διδασκόμενος.
—PLUTARCH, *Solon*, c. 31.

WILLIAM BLACKWOOD AND SONS
EDINBURGH AND LONDON
MDCCCXCVIII

PREFACE.

IT is sometimes said, perhaps not without reason, that in these days we are over-fond of compiling biographies, and that a man ought to have touched a definite degree in the scale of achievement, distinction, or merit before the public are invited to peruse his memoirs. It may be so, though some difficulty might be found in fixing that degree. It is not probable that the world is too full as yet of personal annals. He who is most grateful to Tacitus for the too brief narrative of his father-in-law, Cnæus Julius Agricola, and for the light which it throws on the extension of the empire of Rome, as well as for the information it conveys of personal traits and social habits, will be most apt to sigh over the absence of all record concerning consuls and generals less famous than

b

Agricola, but perhaps of integrity and energy not inferior to his.

The British Empire, far exceeding that of Imperial Rome in extent and population, possesses many characteristics in common with it, and British rulers have many lessons to learn, even at this day, from Roman precedents. The personal characters and habits of the men charged with the conduct of our affairs at foreign Courts have a vital bearing on the stability of our empire : when one of these has united to the office of diplomatist the parts of scholar, traveller, courtier, and sportsman; when he has added to the natural advantage of birth in one of the oldest houses of our aristocracy, a charm of manner and conversation which endeared him to all his acquaintance; when he has lived far beyond the average human span in constant intercourse with the most cultivated minds of his country, and maintained throughout the high ideal of a Christian gentleman,—then I think that no apology will be exacted for preparing a brief record of his years.

It must be confessed that this has been attempted under many disadvantages. Sir Charles Murray, like many of us who have less to record, sometimes began to keep a journal, but seldom persevered for more than a few days. In vain his friends urged him in later life to undertake writing out the reminiscences with which his mind was so plentifully stored. It was not till he had passed fourscore years that at Lady Murray's earnest request he was persuaded to commit to paper a personal narrative. The book is now before me— a promising quarto—alas! all but the first twenty pages remain blank. In the last year of his life, when penmanship had become too great an effort, he was induced to begin afresh, dictating the record to his niece. This also came to no good: it is perhaps the noblest natures which have least taste for autobiography — talking of themselves.

Unwilling that the events of such a good and actively useful life should pass utterly into oblivion, Lady Murray has committed to me the task of gathering out of the scattered papers which remain something like a connected narrative. In attempting this I have been confronted with the great disability of not having known personally the subject of the memoir, nor has it been possible to repair this in any appreciable degree by the help of Sir Charles's most intimate friends, nearly all of whom have passed away. To some of those who knew him in his later years—his son, Mr Charles Murray, M.P., Mr Reginald Smith, and Mr Reginald Lucas

—I am indebted for much assistance, and offer sincere thanks. But no writer ever felt more keenly than I do that—

> "None can truly write his single day,
> And none can write it for him upon earth."

Such as it is, this sketch of Sir Charles Murray's long life is offered in the hope that it may afford interest, not only from his own character and work, but from his association with leading men and a distant past.

HERBERT MAXWELL.

Monreith, 1898.

CONTENTS.

CHAPTER I.

LINEAGE, PARENTAGE, AND EARLY DAYS (1806-1822).

The House of Moray—Childhood—Samuel Rogers—Letters
from S. Rogers—The home at Glen Finart—Paris after
Waterloo   1

CHAPTER II.

SCHOOL-TIME AND HOLIDAYS (1815-1822).

Eton—Edinburgh society—Lord Eldon—Fonthill—William
Beckford—Neighbours at Hamilton—Sport in Arran—The
old style   36

CHAPTER III.

LIFE AT OXFORD (1822-1830).

At a private tutor's—Letter from Fraser Tytler—John Henry
Newman—An escapade—All Souls—A poet's prescription—
A lawyer's prescription—Letter from Lord Brougham—
Hon. Henry Murray   52

CHAPTER IV.

TRAVELS IN EARLY MANHOOD (1830–1834).

A tour in Germany—Visit to Goethe—Correspondence with Carlyle—Unsuccessful contests—A leak !—A disabled ship —Detained in the Azores—Nugæ—Washington's tomb— American correspondence—The evils of slavery—Tour in the West   71

CHAPTER V.

ADVENTURES AMONG THE PAWNEES (1835).

Lexington—The wild West—American hospitality—The Paw- nee village — A quarrel between brothers — Red Indian character—Pawnee dandies—A cruel horse-master—The " medicine-tube"—Alone in the wilderness—Finding their way home—The Kansas once more—Inhospitable weather —On their old trail   96

CHAPTER VI.

AMERICAN TRAVELS CONTINUED (1835–1837).

The Irish in America—Cuba in 1835—Lake Otsego—Murray's ' Travels '—The fate of the Red Men—Chateaubriand's opin- ion—Author and publisher—Sir Charles Vaughan's letters— Miss Elise Wadsworth   125

CHAPTER VII.

POLITICS, LITERATURE, AND COURT LIFE (1837–1838).

Letter from S. Rogers—Murray accused of turning Tory—Elec- tioneering experience—The poll for Lanarkshire—Journal at Court—Confidential correspondence   .   .   .   148

CHAPTER VIII.

JOURNALS, ETC. (1838–1844).

Geological news—Delicate negotiations—Successful diplomacy
—Letters from Lord Douglas—Journal at Court—The Czar's
visit to England—Political forecast—Official espionage   . 165

CHAPTER IX.

LITERATURE AND DIPLOMACY (1844–1848).

The 'Prairie Bird'—Fraser Tytler's 'History'—Fraser Tytler's
letters—Murray's literary gifts—Enters the diplomatic service—Death of Lady Dunmore—Mohammed Ali—Massacre
of the Memlooks—Mohammed's treachery—Mohammed's
method of rule—Harriet Martineau—Murray as a slave
purchaser   193

CHAPTER X.

MARRIAGE AND LIFE IN THE EAST (1849–1857).

Murray's first love—The song of Ah-to-menō—'Horizons
Célestes'—Letter from Fenimore Cooper—Service in Egypt
—First hippopotamus in England—Appointed to Persian
Mission—Persian affairs—The Shah's letters—The Persian
imbroglio—War with Persia—Letters to his brother—
Persian treaty of peace—Murray's defenders in Parliament
—Mistaken economy—Antelope hawking—Voyage on the
Euphrates—Persian journal—Sadr Azem   .   .   . 231

CHAPTER XI.

DRESDEN AND COPENHAGEN (1850–1867).

Second marriage—The Schleswig-Holstein difficulty—Specula-
tions about heaven—An Italian's *equivoque*—Letter from J.
L. Motley—Solvency of United States—Hans Andersen and
Stirling Maxwell—Appointed Minister at Lisbon   .   . 285

CHAPTER XII.

LISBON AND RELEASE FROM SERVICE (1867–1882).

The throne of Spain — Dom Fernando — Spanish intrigue—
Wanted, a king—Overtures to Dom Fernando—Letters from
Lord Lytton — Letters from Sir W. Stirling - Maxwell—
Murray retires from public life — Purchase of Oaklands
Hall—Letter from Hon. Mrs Norton—Letters to his wife
—Letter from Dean Stanley 302

CHAPTER XIII.

HOME LIFE (1882–1892).

Letters to his wife—Correspondence—Philological discussions—
Last visit to Dunmore—Early recollections—Rogersiana—
Letter from Cardinal Manning—Letter to his younger son . 337

CHAPTER XIV.

LAST YEARS (1892–1895).

Nearing the end—Some perplexing letters—Note on the Ash-
burnham Collections — Two French journalists—Sâdi and
Shakespeare — Incidents in Egypt — Biblical criticism —
Criticism of Professor Drummond—Problems of religion—
The Athanasian Creed   354

INDEX   375

LIST OF PORTRAITS.

THE HON. CHARLES AUGUSTUS MURRAY   *Frontispiece*

THE HON. MRS MURRAY   .   .   . *Facing p.* 238

THE HON. CHARLES AUGUSTUS MURRAY ⎫
    AT THE AGE OF FIFTY-SIX   ⎬ *Between pp.* 286 *and* 287
THE HON. EDYTHE MURRAY ⎭

THE HON. SIR CHARLES AUGUSTUS MURRAY, K.C.B. *Facing p.* 354

THE HONOURABLE
SIR CHARLES MURRAY.

CHAPTER I.

1806–1822.

LINEAGE, PARENTAGE, AND EARLY DAYS.

In primitive times, and in the earlier stages of the history of every nation, the convenient expedient of surnames to denote the members of separate families was not adopted. The utmost that was done was to distinguish between individuals bearing the same personal appellative by mentioning their father's name, as in the case of the two apostles—James the son of Zebedee and James the son of Alphæus,—or in that of the four kings of ancient Alban, all named Constantine, and distinguished in the chronicles by the patronymics of Mac Fergusa, Mac Cinaeta,

A

Mac Aeda, and Mac Cuilen—the sons, respectively, of Fergus, Kenneth, Hugh, and Cullen.[1] Sometimes a "to-name' was added to the personal name, denoting the office, calling, or some characteristic or peculiarity of the individual; and to these, as well as to patronymics, may be traced many of the surnames in use at this day, having been adopted as the common designation of members of one family when, about the fourteenth century, the increase of population in this country, and wider intercourse, rendered surnames of some sort a necessity. But with the growth of feudal institutions, involving the personal possession of lands which had hitherto been held in common by the clan or sept, well-to-do persons came by a natural process to be known by the name of their territorial possessions.

Thus when Freskin, a Frieslander or Fleming, became possessed of extensive lands in the east of Scotland in the twelfth century, he required no second name to distinguish him among the Norman and Anglian magnates with whom it was the policy of David I. to replace the Celtic toiseachs. But his son, having received the baptismal name of William, was not so easily to be recognised. The Norman Conquest had

[1] Synchronisms of Flann Mainistreach, an Irish MS., A.D. 1014-1022.

brought that name into such fashionable repute
that in 1173 Sir William de St John and Sir
William Fitz Hamon gave a dinner-party at the
Court of Henry II. to which only knights bearing
the name of William were invited. No fewer than
one hundred and twenty guests sat down to
table. So William the son of Freskin having
great possessions in the province of Murmhagh [1]
or Moray, it was natural that he should become
known officially as Gulielmus de Moravia, and
familiarly as William of Moray.

From this William of Moray the Scottish
houses of Tullibardine and Abercairney trace their
descent. William Murray, second Earl of Tulli-
bardine, married, first, in 1602, Cecilia, eldest
daughter of Sir John Wemyss of that ilk; and
second, Lady Dorothea Stewart, eldest daughter
of John Stewart, fifth Earl of Athol. On the
decease of this earl without male issue the earl-
dom reverted to the Crown; but John Murray,
eldest son of the Earl of Tullibardine and Lady
Dorothea, afterwards obtained a new grant from
Charles I., whereby in 1629 he became first Earl
of Athol of the house of Murray. He was suc-

[1] Pronounce "Muragh" — a Gaelic compound, signifying land
beside the sea. The Manx word *mooiragh* is used at this day to
denote "a waste by the sea," and there are several seaside farms
in Lowland Scotland called Morrach.

ceeded by his son John, who in 1676 was created
Marquis of Athol. He married Lady Amelia
Stanley, only daughter of James, seventh Earl
of Derby, by his famous countess, Charlotte de
la Tremouille. The marquis's eldest son, John,
was created Duke of Athol in 1703; his second
son, Lord Charles Murray, Master of the Horse
to Queen Mary, having been raised to the peerage
in 1686 by the titles of Lord Murray of Blair,
Moulin, and Tillymott, Viscount Fincastle, and
Earl of Dunmore. Fourth in descent from this
earl came George, fifth Earl of Dunmore, born
in 1762, and created a peer of the United Kingdom in 1831 as Baron Dunmore of Dunmore.
He married on 3rd August 1803 Lady Susan
Hamilton, daughter of Archibald, ninth Duke of
Hamilton, by whom he had three sons—Alexander Edward, who succeeded him in 1836 as
sixth Earl of Dunmore ; Charles Augustus, the
subject of the present memoir ; and Henry An-
thony, afterwards Rear - Admiral in the Royal
Navy.

Charles Augustus Murray was born on 22nd
November 1806. Prince Augustus Frederick,
Duke of Sussex, sixth son of George III., stood
sponsor to him, being his uncle by marriage with
Lady Augusta, daughter of the fourth Earl of

Dunmore. The earliest historic allusion to the child occurs in a letter to his mother, then Lady Susan Fincastle, from Samuel Rogers. It is a long letter, for in those days letters had to be made to compensate for heavy postage by being filled in every corner of the large sheets with news of every description. Here is an extract from it :—

Samuel Rogers to the Countess of Dunmore.

"WOOLBEDING, *November 8th*, 1807.

"I hope the little boys are growing all day long —they have now, you know, nothing else to do. What an age it is since Mr M.[1] threw his little round person into the sofa in Berkeley Square ! He and his brother Charles together must now be more than a match for the turkey-cock, and must by this time be learning to dance, ride, and flirt with the ladies, as men of fashion ought to do. . . . Pray kiss them both for me, though Mr M. has now, I daresay, no recollection of any of us. . . .

"You are so kind as to ask after my poem. It was in the press the other day, when, as good luck would have it, a fire broke out at the printer's, and consumed it among other precious MSS. Perhaps you will ask how I have spent the summer —in visiting about, I believe. I could almost wish I had gone to Tunbridge, if it was but to see Mary Godfrey's *pas seul* upon the Pantiles."

[1] Alexander Edward Murray, afterwards sixth Earl of Dunmore.

The Same to the Same.

"St James's Place, *May Day*, 1808.

"I saw a young man yesterday who has just spent a month with Madame Potocki while Lord D. was there (who is now gone, he says, to Vienna). By his account she is a very beautiful woman of fifty, her children are cherubs, and she lives in a style of magnificence of which we have no idea. *Apropos* of cherubs, so Mr Murray is no longer one—he is a man grown, it seems, and buttons his coat and wears his hat as fiercely as other men. Well, I shall never forgive him if he loses a look he had once—but that is impossible. And his little words, 'No, mama—Yes, mama—How d'ye do, horses?' are they as sweet as ever? As for his brother-Cupid, your picture of him makes me mad to see him; but whenever that great event takes place, we shall meet, alas! like two strangers from distant planets. Poor little M. himself must have now no more remembrance of our friendship than of those he contracted some years ago in a pre-existent state. Pray, what is his father the Laird about just now? Is he walking deck or is he climbing a mountain? Is he draining or planting, or enclosing or damming or building? Everybody I meet has received a letter from him as long as the road to Edinburgh. Seriously speaking, I do believe he never vouchsafes a line but to Lady Barbara, who is as proud of it as Lucifer, and if it was not for you who give signs of life now and then, we might conclude he had gone to explore Africa or the moon, or anything else."

The friendship between the Fincastles and Samuel Rogers was very close and enduring. The following notice of the poet occurs among the fragmentary notes which Sir Charles Murray, at the repeated instance of his family, began to put together in his eighty-sixth year :—

" One of the earliest things that I can recollect, when I was, I suppose, six or seven years old, was a visit from a very dear and old friend of my parents—Samuel Rogers, the poet—who has himself recorded that visit in some very pretty lines, which have since been reprinted in the well-known volume called ' The Pleasures of Memory.' "

At that time Lord and Lady Fincastle rented a lovely place, Glen Finart, on the northern shore of Loch Long, in Argyleshire. The Highlands had not come into fashion yet, though the tide of tourists was shortly to begin to flow—the ' Lay of the Last Minstrel' having been published in 1805. But so far, whatever curiosity people might have to explore the mountainous west was severely kept in check by the physical difficulties of travel. To realise how complete was the seclusion of Glen Finart in those far-off days, one has to remember that there were no steamers on the Clyde. Access to civilisation lay through the port of Greenock, which could only be reached from Loch Long by rowing or sailing boats.

In this delicious isolation the Fincastles used to spend their summers, returning to their house in Lower Berkeley Street for the London season, which, by the rational and enviable disposal of fashion, was then held in the winter months. There was also a short season at Tunbridge Wells in autumn, where they went sometimes. Rogers kept Lady Fincastle well informed of what went on in her absence in social and literary circles, and some of his tattle refers to well-known people. Some of his letters are dated only with the day of the week, but others it is possible to quote from in chronological order.

Samuel Rogers to the Countess of Dunmore.

"WOOLBEDING, *November 8th*, 1807.

"This is a very pretty place : a river runs along a narrow valley, overhung with woods, and above these rise the South Downs, which in hazy and cloudy weather, though you won't believe it, affect to look like people of consequence, I had almost said like some of your mountains. But pray how do you pass your time?—in longing to return among us, I hope ; but you *will* come in the spring at all

events, I know you will; for what will become of
me when I have nobody to walk with, nobody to
call upon? I saw a very pretty picture in St
Martin's Lane the other day, but you are now out
of harm's way, and are in no danger any fine morning of an inundation of Saints, Angels, and Holy
Families. . . . I hope the harp is now standing out
of its green baize. How do the zephyrs of the north
agree with it?—not so well, I hope, as those of the
south. You must have heard much of Casimir; he
is a prodigy and his notes are wonderful, but he
wants a something which I doubt whether he will
ever acquire. Pray do those who have it keep
it all to themselves?—I suspect they do. . . .
The Berrys are gone to Strawberry Hill, but
Lady Donegal has no thoughts of leaving town
till August. T. Moore[1] is again among us, and
sings as sweetly as ever; his new songs are very
pretty. *Apropos* of voices, Susan B. is returned
in great perfection. It made some very extraordinary flights last Monday evening. So a new
lover has appeared above the horizon there.
Guess—perhaps you know—or perhaps there is
nothing in it; but if fixed and melancholy looks,
short sighs, and continual silence mean anything
—I daresay you know whom I mean, Lord G. L.
The lady does not appear to answer any one of
the signals, but his sisters, particularly Lady H.,
lay a strong siege. Lady H., as Knight says,
makes love much better than her brother. . . .
Lady E. and the Blakes are roosting again in St
James's Place. Lady E. has been ill, but is now

[1] Tom Moore, the Irish poet.

revived, and the world gives her a suitor, Mr
Elliott. He is always there, and there are strong
symptoms of it. Their house is small and dark,
and contains themselves, a dog or two, a little
girl, a cat, and a pair of turtle-doves. So that
nothing goes on but barking, crying, laughing,
mewing, and cooing all day long. Honoria looks
handsomer than ever—the Holy Roman, just as
she used to do. Lady Clifden [1] is shut up with
a cold, and receives visitors every evening from
nine till twelve. Caroline [2] is really growing
almost pretty. Lord Clifden [3] is busy in planning
repairs in Hanover Square. T. Hope [4] has bought
a house, Deepden, near Dorking, once belonging
to the Duke of Norfolk. It is large, with but
little land round it, in a very pleasant country.
She is still very low and far from in health.
There are two whole lengths of her in the Exhibition, one with the little boy. We had our
Academy Dinner yesterday, and I wished for Lord
Fin. . . . Heigho! when will you stop your cur-
ricle to give me another gingerbread-nut under
the old paling? [5] I *have* read 'Corinne,' and like
it with all its faults. The Frenchman is delightful. Have you read 'Marmion'? One thing is
so revolting—the walling-up of Constance; no-

[1] Lady Caroline Spencer, daughter of third Duke of Marlborough.

[2] Died unmarried in 1814.

[3] Second Viscount; died in 1836.

[4] Thomas Hope, Esq., author of 'Anastasius,' &c. His third son,
the late Right Hon. A. J. Beresford Hope, M.P., succeeded by the
will of his stepfather, Viscount Beresford, to the estates of Bedge-
bury in Kent and Beresford Hall in Stafford.

[5] At Tunbridge Wells.

body here will believe it. Do you? Every miss
insists on her appearing again, and I really believe
many expect her to revive in a second part. I
praised it to the Duchess of Gordon,[1] and found
I was wrong; she shakes her head whenever I
mention it. She grumbles on still, and will to
the end of the chapter. Columbus[2] thanks you
for all your kind inquiries; he shall wait quietly,
he says, for your return. So Mrs Radcliffe has
come to life again with a novel in her hand.
Aren't you dying to read it? Mr Cholmondeley
has let his house here, and calls himself a country
gentleman. Mrs C. is now at Brighton on account
of the little girl, who is thought to be in a poor
way. Poor Lady Donegal and her ophthalmia!
She entertained three or four leeches every day
while it lasted. The Shaftesburys are making
magnificent preparations. The plate Lord S.
bought at Naples for £300 is the handsomest
I ever saw—three vast dishes and three ewers
richly sculptured like the shield of Achilles, with
battles, processions, &c. I saw it at Rundall's
yesterday. The Spencers, as you know, have left
town and let their house, and their absence casts
a damp upon everything. What a pitiful worthless thing money is! and yet who can do without
it? S. is now at Lord John Townshend's, and
Mrs S. is at Brighton. Lady Elizabeth Loftus is
nursing her little boy in Wimpole Street, and is
very happy."

[1] Jane, daughter of Sir William Maxwell of Monreith, a celebrated
wit and beauty; died in 1812.

[2] Rogers published his poem 'Voyage of Columbus' in 1812.

The Same to the Same.

"I am resolved for the future to fire no more broadsides at friend or foe. A little small - shot now and then—that I am up to — but a formal sheet of quarto paper confounds and annihilates me.   Not that I would have others follow my example—I acknowledge my weakness with confusion of face—pray encourage me by your conduct to better things. So you have been basking, I hear, under the Rock, while we have been freezing into icicles. Your gaieties at Hamilton I heard much of from Lady O., but your *vie privée* in the Glen — to me far more interesting — I can only get from yourself.   Now pray don't think of playing the Nurse (a character, I own, you must fill to perfection) at Hamilton or Edinburgh, but pray, pray keep your word and come at Easter to London - town. Remember two years are long enough in all conscience — a few more such fits of absence and where shall we all be ? What are you doing ? are you reading the 'Corsair,' the 'Giaour,' Miss Edgeworth, or Mme. de Staël ?   Mme. D'Arblay's novel begins as a novel should : 'It was in a dark night in the month of November.' But when are we to have it ? Nobody knows.   What a world is ours ?   And what is to happen next ?   'C'est le commencement de la fin,' says Talleyrand, and so it seems. 'I know him,' says Lucien, speaking of his brother ; 'I always said he would blow the bubble till it burst.'   All

talk of peace one way or another, and all are
preparing to visit Paris, and that great ice-house
Switzerland, and the Eternal City, and the firework at Naples—in plain English, to leave home
and go abroad. So pray come in time, for I will
of your party and no other. As to Fin, how he
must triumph in the fulfilment of all his predic-
tions! and how small we shall all feel before him!
My summer was passed I don't know how—in
other people's houses at Hampden, Bow-wood,
Bulstrode, Woolbeding, Althorpe, and Middleton:
I am now at home, and against you arrive, I shall
write over my door 'Accommodation for Private
Families.' Remember I have three very decent
chambers, and there are excellent hotels in St
James's Street to receive my overflowings. As
for Charles and Henry, I have a coal-hole just
to their taste, and the river is at hand for Fin
the less. I would send you my budget of news
—such as it is; but perhaps the news of to-
morrow will contradict it all, and Lady Donegal
is now giving it to you in a much better manner.
So pray remember me very affectionately to the
chief and his two sons (Johnson and Crib), and
believe me to be, ever and ever yours,

"SAMUEL ROGERS."

The Same to the Same.

" LONDON.

" Lady Donegal came from Tunbridge to Davis
Street on Thursday last, and in a week goes to
Lady Shaftesbury for a month. Lady Chatham

has just given up the house. Lady Ellenborough
is now at Brighton, and stays there till after
Christmas. She is said to look very ill. Lord
Warwick has been among the *agrémens* of Tunbridge this summer! Souza has been constant to
Worthing. Spencer has spent the best part of
his summer at Gilwele. His spirits are not as
they used to be, and I wish we could remove
the cause with all my heart. I confess I am not
very sanguine with regard to Drury Lane. So
Susan Beckford has accepted Lord Henry Petty,
and Lady Donegal Lord Mount Edgcumbe! How
entertaining the newspapers are just now! The
Clifdens left Tunbridge on Saturday; Lady C.
was in her old house, it seems. Mrs Spencer
looks better than ever she did, and exhibits her
Tunbridge donkey every morning in a kind of
car or cart that runs on three wheels—she looks
for all the world like a sorceress in a pantomime.
The day has turned to rain, and how do you think
Mr and Mrs Spencer are employed at this moment?
—in playing at battledore and shuttlecock in my
room! I can hardly write for the noise. What I
have written I don't know, and I have not the
courage to read it, but I know you will take it
all as it is meant, and believe me when I assure
you how sincerely and gratefully I am yours,

                              "SAMUEL ROGERS."

   "Pray kiss them both for me, though Mr M.
has now, I daresay, no recollection of any of us.
   "How did you bewitch Caroline Chinnery?
Her friendship for you is a passion. She dreams

of nobody else, but she can make others dream of her, for she used to play her harp every morning under my window between seven and eight o'clock.

"Poor Mrs Hope was greatly affected by the loss of her mother. Mr H. was travelling in Devonshire at the time, and when he returned, as he did instantly, to Ramsgate, he found her confined to her room: they are now at Gatton. She knows nothing of the Criticism in the 'Edinburgh Review'; he told me he should not mention it to her, he knew it would vex her so. He affects to carry it off, but I can see he is hurt by it. . . . Mrs Spencer desires her best love to you. 'I wish, I wish she was coming back,' were her words on the stairs just now. Once more adieu. I have still a thousand things to say, though at first I thought I had nothing."

The Same to the Same.

"St James's Place, *May Day*, 1808.

"I have really held my tongue so long I don't know how to speak or what to say. You know a mother, and so do I—Mrs Bouverie—who looks up her girls when they have a letter to write, and I wish I had an old housekeeper who would do me the same kindness. *You* would suffer much by it, and the other day you had a great escape. M. Godfrey was all fire and fagot at your long silence, and in the true spirit of knight-errantry I had just resolved to redress her wrongs, when an epistle arrived and saved you from a packet as large as a mortgage-deed. If I have not assailed you sooner it is not for want of a Flapper. M. G.'s first question, morning, noon, and night, in parks and streets and crowded assemblies, is, 'Have you written to Lady Susan?' Their description of Tunbridge last year is most provoking. Can you believe it was delightful? I never will. Viotti offered to go if I would, and yet he swears he will never enter the doors in Berkeley Street till your harp is again in the drawing-room. We were very sorry to hear you had all been ill."

The Same to the Same.

"LONDON, July 12th.

"A thousand thanks, my dear friend, for your kind letter, and a thousand more to your divine Susan [1] for all her kindness. Many a time in the dead of the night have I addressed a letter to her, but it was all gone before daylight, and twice have I taken up a pen for the purpose, but my evil genius prevailed, and I was called off by a knock at the door, and his sudden appearance in the shape of some dandy. The other day I said to Spencer, 'How is it that all our old friends have dropped away from us one by one?' 'Not the Dunmores,' he said; 'they are still as much our own as ever.' . . . The Lansdownes are once more among us, and full of Italy. Lady Jersey is at Paris, and Lady Orford established at Calais. She was in London for a few hours the other day, but I did not see her. Why did you not come this spring? We have had Talma, and Crabbe the

---

[1] Lady Susan Hamilton, Duchess of Newcastle.

poet, the Waterloo Bridge and the Sapient Pig. Lord Webbe paid us a long visit, and was my great comfort. To-morrow I set off for Paris for three weeks with Lalla Rookh: if I am not surfeited there or drowned by the way, you may perhaps see me notwithstanding—I do not despair—but at all events I will write to the Lady of the Glen. God bless you and yours."

The Same to the Same.

"ULLESWATER, *August* 13th, 1812.

" Pray, where are you at this moment ? I am sitting at an oak table in the little village of Patterdale, the lake in full view, and all the world out a-haymaking up and down the valley, not excepting the King himself—for you must know Patterdale is a kingdom, and has a king of its own ! He is now without coat or waistcoat on the margin of the lakes, attended by their Royal Highnesses the Princesses, while the Reverend Rector, in the same cool costume, is in solitary dignity (unattended even by his clerk) tossing about his own hay in the churchyard—and such a churchyard !—the only things to be seen in it are a yew and a sun-dial, not so much as a stone being there. The Rector's father and grandfather sleep side by side under the green turf.

" Now, pray, pray tell me what are your motions and by what signs you are to be found ; and pray write me a line (if but a line) as soon as you receive this, directed to me under cover to the Earl of Lonsdale, Lowther, Penrith, Cumberland.

B

The Same to the Same.

" Many, many thanks for your kind letter, which I have this instant received. To tell you the truth, I have been hovering on the frontiers of this kingdom till I thought I could catch you in yours, and am now in a very strong part of a very strong and well-garrisoned Border castle. You mentioned the beginning of September as the best season for my incursion, and it is my intention to spend a week or ten days here and then travel night and day till I arrive in the Glen, where I certainly wish to make my first and principal *séjour*, as, to deal plainly with you, you are the people I mean to quarter myself principally upon. On the 5th or 6th of September, therefore, you may depend upon seeing me, or perhaps sooner, if I thought you were at home. To make sure, I shall direct this letter to Hamilton, from which, of course, it will be forwarded if you are gone. I hope you have received one which I addressed to the Glen about a fortnight ago."

The Same to the Same.

"HOWICK, *November 12th*, 1812.

" Could I send you as many thanks as there are miles between us at this moment, I could not tell you half I feel; so I will say nothing and only proceed to relate that I went on to Edinburgh when I left you, and after staying three days there (one of which, a very brilliant one, was spent at Roslin), I continued my journey to Dunbar, where I passed two more, and then to Howick, where I still am, and where I have been made happy by your letter. I was rejoiced to hear that the sick were better, and hope you found Charles and Henry well and jumping for joy. Pray give each of them a kiss and a blow for me, and tell them I mean to get very strong against I meet them again in battle. Pray also remember me very affectionately to F. You will not perhaps believe me when I say so— but it is not the less true for that, and say it I must—that I left you with a heavy heart. Had I found Mary and her little Court in Holyrood—had I supped now and then with her and Rizzio there in her little chamber any night but *one*—I might have heard very sweet music, not, however, I am very sure, such as would have pleased me half so well ; and as for the kindness with which it was given, like everything else—on that and other sub-jects I will be silent, for I know you have both of you your reward. Kindness is like mercy ; it is twice blessed—it blesseth him that gives and him that takes. I am very sorry indeed that vile visitor of yours still continues to torment you, but hope you are now as well as I mean to be. Just now I have the very worst of colds. Thank you again and again for what your good nature has led you to say of a voyage now as familiar to everybody as one from London to Gravesend."

The Same to the Same.

"LONDON, *February 26th*, 1813.

"Upon my return from the North Pole I found your letter upon my table, and a most welcome welcome it gave me. It told me you were all well and had not quite forgot me, and it came from you —from Glenfinart and by the packet from Ardentinnie Point, that packet which I have watched so often on its way along the opposite shore. Heigho, the scene is changed, but I flatter myself *I* am not —at least my heart tells me so, and it has not often deceived me, though we are told ' it is deceitful above all things.' *There* are you at this moment after a game at play with Charles and Henry on the carpet, sitting at the tea-table in peace and quiet, the Thane unplaided and exploring with curious eye the columns of his newspaper, the harp by the closet door, and a book of travels lying open on the sofa. Here am I, on the other hand, dressing for a dinner at Lord Stafford's, where I shall meet nobody I shall wish to see—and at a loss to say whether I shall conclude the evening at Lady Barrington's waltzing-party or Lady Davy's conversazione, from either of which I shall be sure to return tired and not sleepy, stuffed in body, starved in mind. So Miss Berry is writing a parallel between the manners of the age of Louis XIV. and our own. 'Miss B. writing upon manners indeed!' says her friend Lady Spencer. Lyttelton is a most attentive wooer and much mitigated, though his dialect is as extraordinary as ever.

' Tip us your daddle,' was his introductory speech
the other day to Lady Sarah before dinner. He
seems, however, as far as I can judge, a little
under awe of Lord S.   Lord M. leaves London in
April.   Lady Loudon is assembling her *cortége*,
and some bouncing young ladies from the north
are already under her roof.   Indeed their dinner
resembles very much what I should conceive to be
in an Indiaman.   I am very sorry that Moore has
no appointment under Lord M.   So, *entre nous*,
the Lady behind Grosvenor Place Chapel has a
new lover, and I most sincerely wish you joy upon
the event, though it gave some disturbance to a
friend of ours, and I believe was the cause of a
gravity which I could not account for at Hamilton.
The new favourite, as you must have heard, is
the *Childe*.   Lady C. L. is in sad retirement at
Brocket; it began at Cheltenham.   As I am a
little in the secret (I am sure with no wish of
mine) I should say nothing about it.   At Howick
I passed a fortnight, and I flatter myself we
parted with mutual regret.   I then proceeded
with all alacrity to Castle Howard and Crewe,
and arrived in this wicked town with as little
emotion as if I had left it the day before.   *Little*
Fin is growing fast out of his name, but his
countenance is the same as ever, and so is his
voice.   Indeed, except in height, I never saw a
boy so little changed.   When I asked him what I
should say, he said, 'Give my love to papa and
mama, and Charles and Henry, and tell them I
am very well and very happy,' and so I daresay
he has told you himself.   Lady Donegal has had

a violent cold and inflammation, but is now about
again.   Waltzing is again in fashion, and to be
at Mrs Hope's to-morrow and at Lady Cowper's
that day week.   Now, have not I shown my forbearance, not yet to have scolded you for your
cruel, cruel determination against us?   It has filled
us all with sadness, and if you could but hear the
lamentations, you would think us amiable if not
attractive.   Above all, it is the greatest affliction
to me, and what to do I don't know, as every year
I grow worse and worse, and see clearly that I
must soon renounce all my acquaintance and live
only with such friends as will endure me.   Farewell!   Pray mention me once a-day at least to
Charles and Henry, for I believe I shall break my
heart if you stay away till they have forgotten
me. . . .   S. R.

"Mrs Hope has put off her waltzing on account
of the bursting of a blood-vessel in her ear—they
say from excessive boring; but after what passed
at Hamilton I like nothing of the kind.   Pray
remember me to Lord Webbe, if with you.   I shall
envy him his conversations under the sunny rock.
How I like Lord Archibald's manliness in Parliament!"

The Same to the Same.

"London, *July 12th,* 1825.

"Well, as I threatened you with another line,
I must keep my word with myself, whatever it
cost you; so pray mount your donkey and set out
with me last August, and embark with me on the

1st of September in the Psyche packet. To be
serious, I have done a great deal since we parted
at the Temple of Concord.

"The Hopes in less than a month start, bag and
baggage, for Italy. When shall we all meet again?
Poor Mrs Spencer is still in a very dangerous way,
I fear. She is in Curzon Street, but I have not
yet seen her. The Berrys go in a day or two to
Tunbridge, and the streets are almost as empty as
those of Pompeii. You see I have not travelled in
vain; all my similes, I promise you, shall henceforth and for ever be drawn from the kingdom of
Naples. What strange times we live in! What
times indeed, as Jekyll says, must those be which
Wraxall calls his own! I dined the other day in
Grosvenor Place, and was treated with *primavera*
and a thousand delights. If Angus is beautiful,
his sister is half divine, so the race is in no danger
of being lost. London has swarmed with poets
this spring. Moore only was absent, who has
actually sold his poem for three thousand pounds.
What do you think of Lord Aberdeen's marriage,
and of your own discernment? The little girl who
looked so glum in a back drawing-room in Meri-
vale may charm dukes and dandies yet unborn
before she dies. Lady Jersey still sits up, nor do
I believe she ever means to confine herself while
there are people in town to talk to. Her evenings
are now the only things going, and last every
night till two in the morning. Lord Erskine is
in Paris, the gayest of the gay. What a strange
assemblage of people was at Rome! Lady West-
morland's doings and Ward's sayings eclipsed the

Pantheon and the Coliseum altogether. Of the Princess of Wales, and Lady Orford, and King Murat, and my dearest best friend the Archbishop of Tarentum, on whose table at dinner were regularly served up every day his two living cats, . . ."

And so on,—all the passing incidents which make up the fabric of life and friendship. Some passages, indeed, in these letters seem to betray a deeper, warmer feeling than friendship, as if in the past Rogers had nourished hopes which had never been fulfilled. The suspicion of this is suggested by the opening sentence of one of the earlier letters quoted from above :—

"Well, write I must though I have nothing to say, but that you are almost always in my thoughts, as indeed you are. Day after day have I resolved to tell you so, but I was really at a loss how to begin, and now I will, whatever happens. Here am I in my bed-chamber at Woolbeding, and Spencer [1] is at this moment sitting in the

[1] William Spencer, a poet little remembered now, but once very popular for his *vers-de-société*. He was a constant visitor of the Fincastles, and Sir Charles Murray has left in one of his note-books an account of how Spencer's best-known poem — *Beth Gelert* — came to be written : "He was travelling in Wales with his wife and another lady, whose name I forget, and they arrived at Bettws-y-Coed, at the foot of Snowdon, associated with the name of Beth Gelert. Mrs Spencer and her lady friend agreed they must contrive to make the poet write a ballad connected with the legend. They managed to get him into a room on the upper floor of the little inn, and, throwing open the little window, called his attention to the

next room (I hear his solitary step), where I have just spent a very pleasant half-hour in talking about your Ladyship, among other people."

And here is a significant sentence from the same letter :—

"Do you know, I have often thought since that I did very wrong in leaving town before you, and many a time have I wished to recall the two or three days you spent there after I was gone, but (shall I own it?) at the time I was rather glad than otherwise. I shall never wish to survive those I love best, and though I was unwilling to acknowledge it myself *then*, I almost felt the thing like an escape. Pray remember me most affectionately to Lord F. I little thought I should ever have found such a friend so late in the day. You, I know, I can tell what I feel about him, for you will understand me ; but I can assure you, my dear Lady Susan, my eyes often fill while I am thinking of his kindness to me."

And again—

"So S. [Spencer], I find, is writing to you to-day,

beauty of the view that it commanded. Meanwhile one of them procured from below a sheet of paper, pens, ink, &c. Having placed these utensils surreptitiously in the room, they ran to the door and locked it from the outside, and then they called to him, telling him that he should have no luncheon, or meal of any kind, until he had written a ballad illustrative of the local legend. But, finding that he could not induce them by any entreaties to open the door, he set to work to write the ballad necessary for his liberation."

and our letters are to bear each other company in the Falkirk bag. Over many a hill and valley will they travel together, but mine, if it had its choice, would have taken its flight alone, from motives too selfish to mention. I must use his seal, for I have made a holy vow not to wear mine till I have bought a chain for it. Alas! alas! I lost one but last week from Lady Elizabeth's ribbon."

Eighteen years later, after returning from a trip on the Continent, the same allusion may be traced:—

"I sailed on the Lake of Geneva, visited Ferney and Gibbon's terrace, and the rocks of Meillerie and the Isle of St Pierre, walked on the sea of ice, gathered grapes to the guitar in an Italian vineyard, and ate ice by moonlight in St Mark's Place at Venice. I passed half an hour at Petrarch's tomb, and Tasso's, and Ariosto's, and Raphael's, slept in the convent at Vallombrosa, saw a nun take the veil, exchanged a word or two with the Pope, toasted a muffin on Vesuvius, wore a mask in a carnival, and wandered at sunset in the temples at Pæstum, and I brought back with me the same heart I went out with, filled with the same remembrances, the same affections, and the same ardent wishes for the same people, whatever they may think to the contrary. Yes, the letters on the rock may grow dimmer and dimmer, and wear out altogether, but there are some impressions that *never* can!"

Long afterwards, when Rogers was growing old, the expressions are as tender as ever. The allusion in the postscript is to the "Cupid" of 1808, then on a voyage to America :—

"*May* 1834.

"A thousand, thousand thanks for a letter which at once made me sad and merry at heart. Why have a few scratches made by a goose-quill or a bit of steel such a strange effect upon one? Yes, come I must and I will. As poor Warwick Lake used to say, 'When shall we set off?' If health is mine and health is yours, in July I hope at farthest; but I will write again and feel your pulse about it. How could that be done, would Mr Shandy say, 'when so many hills and valleys and rivers are between us'? Yes, it can be done, and I know it from the effect—a certain thrill that came when I broke the seal of a certain letter. Remember me very affectionately to the Thane, and believe me to be, yours ever and ever,

"SAMUEL ROGERS.

"*P.S.* — Poor Charles. He is now on the Atlantic. Well, he wears a talisman that makes everybody love him, so I don't care if he escapes shipwreck."

The latest of the letters in the little packet before me can only be read in the light of those that went long before :—

"I need not tell you what I felt when I broke

the seal of your letter. Not that I *broke* the seal,
for it told me at once when and where I found
two friends—the best—the kindest—the truest—I
ever found or shall ever find—on this side of the
grave ! May God eternally bless you !   S. R.

   "*January* 18*th*, 1837."

It is true that Rogers was very ugly—so ugly
that Sydney Smith rather coarsely advised him,
when having his portrait painted, to be taken
in the attitude of prayer, with his hands over his
features. But who knows what depth of feeling
may have been masked by that cadaverous countenance ? A Greek profile is not an indispensable
index to a tender heart.

The visit paid by Rogers to Glen Finart, referred to by Charles Murray in his notes, was
paid in 1812.

"You once asked me," he wrote to Lady Fincastle, after his return to England, "if I kept a
journal in the Highlands. I will now own to you
I began one, and as you expressed some curiosity
on the subject, I will punish it as it deserves, not
after the fashion of Barbe Bleu, but in a way perhaps little less severe. My diary ends providen-
tially with the first day, and here it is."

Here follows the poem afterwards published in
' The Pleasures of Memory,' beginning—

" Blue was the loch, the clouds were gone,
 Ben Lomond in his glory shone," &c.

Neighbours at Glen Finart were few and distant. Some of them must have afforded a delightful contrast to the crowded acquaintanceship of London.

" I remember very well," writes Sir Charles in his notes, " a visit we had from an old Highland laird named Fletcher of Bearnish,[1] who lived about fourteen or fifteen miles over the hills between us and Inverary. His manners were very primitively rough, and his stock of English was very scant. He paid a morning visit, and the drawing-room door was thrown open just as my mother was in the middle of a piece that she was playing on the harp. Of course she got off the stool on which she was playing to come and meet him, but, in a very uncouth way, he led her back towards the harp, intimating that she should go on with what she was doing. As a matter of course, he had never seen a harp before, and, after she had played a few bars, he put his hand upon her wrist, and, drawing it away, said, ' Thank ye, my lady, I only wished to hear what kind o' noise she made.' Lunch having been announced, of course he was invited to go into the dining-room, and he looked, with some surprise, at the display of fruit on the table. We had no hothouse fruit at the glen, but a supply was sent every fortnight

---

[1] In a duplicate memorandum he is mentioned as the Laird of Auchnashalloch.

from Dunmore Park, where my father had no
house, but an excellent garden. After he had
despatched the solids, he pointed to a dish on
which there were three or four very fine peaches,
and he said, 'What kind of an apple is yon?'
So my mother told him that we called it a peach,
and he said, 'Well, I'll just tak yen to taste.'
He accordingly took a peach and stuck half of
it into his mouth, and bit hard into it. The
juice ran out of the sides of his mouth, and he
said, 'Oh, it's a gran' apple; but siccan a pip
as it's got!'"

Ardgowan, the beautiful home of the Shaw
Stewarts, on the Clyde, was not very far distant
from Glen Finart by water, and the Murray boys
spent much of their time there.   Sir Michael
had three daughters—little girls—to whom the
three brothers promptly betrothed themselves.
Dis aliter visum.   Margaret, the eldest, became
Duchess of Somerset; Catherine married Captain
Osborne of the 6th Inniskillen Dragoons; and
Helenora, the youngest,[1] married Sir William
Maxwell of Monreith.

Sir Michael's second son, Houston, made a
great impression on Charles.   He died in 1875
as Admiral of the Fleet Sir Houston Stewart,
G.C.B., leaving a son, also Admiral Sir Houston
Stewart, G.C.B., whose son, Houston, gave high

---

[1] Mother of the compiler of this memoir.

promise of winning similar honours in the third
generation, but met an early death in 1884 when
serving with the Naval Brigade in the Soudan.

Lord Fincastle succeeded his father as fifth
Earl of Dunmore in the spring of 1809, but as
there was no house in the fine demesne of Dunmore Park, they continued to live at Glen Finart
till it was time to send the boys to Eton. Stirring
times they were, though the echoes of Waterloo
sounded faintly in lonely Loch Long. The following letter to Lady Dunmore from her indefatigable correspondent, Rogers, is one of many
that must have been eagerly perused in that
eventful year :—

> " *October* 13*th*, 1815.
> *At breakfast, with grapes and peaches and*
> *strawberries almost as delicious as yours.*

" I made a vow I would write to you from
Paris, and write I will though I have little to
say. I spent the 14th at sea between Dover
and Calais, and I wish you could have seen
Frederick North in his banyan, and attended by
his Athenian, distributing lavender-water among
some Irish ladies who were expiring very loquaci-
ously in the cabin. My journey lay through
Arcadia. The first day was Sunday, and the
church bells came over the hills from every
quarter, and before almost every post - house
there were children dancing and singing in the
road for the chance of a *sou*, nor did I see a

tent or a soldier until I came to Amiens, where
the English officers were preparing a *fête* for the
ladies.   At Breteuil I asked the price of pigeons
in the market, and they were 2d. apiece; no sign
of famine, you will say.   Here are soldiers everywhere, and strange it is to see English uniforms
at the corner of every street.   A poor fellow
in a jacket accosted me the other day in a
Babylonish dialect.   At last I said in despair,
'Are you an Englishman?'   'Thank God I am,
sir,' he answered very briskly.   The Bois de
Boulogne is full of English tents.   As you drive
through it, it looks like a fair, and sorry am I
to say that the axe is very busy in their hands.
I have been called off to the window by a shout
—it was the good King bowing from the balcony,
as he came from mass, to his loving subjects.
Some say he will stay—Lord Kinnaird thinks
he will go with the first wind after the Allies.
The Comte de Mosebourg gave the most splendid
balls and dinners at Naples.   He was Secretary
of State under Murat.   Going into Vary's, I found
him dining at a table there in the crowd, and he
lives in a *troisième* in one of the darkest streets
in Paris.   Such are the changes in this world.
I sat down in the *café* near him, and who should
tap me on the shoulder but Lady Caroline Lamb.
She had come in alone, and her freaks here are
as wonderful as in London.   I am myself just now
enrhumé, but my windows console me a little for
my confinement.   They command the Tuileries
and the Tuileries Gardens, full of statues and
orange-trees, and groups of loungers and news-

paper-readers. I hope, however, to be released
to-morrow, and to see Talma and Mlle. Mars in
the 'Partie de Chasse de Henri IV.,' as I deny
myself Mlle. Goselin's dancing in 'Psyche' to-
night, and the 'Pia Valeuse,' which last has now
run 85 nights, drawing francs and tears innumerable. The theatres seem not to have been painted
since the Peace of Amiens—all are dingy, but
the acting admirable. The *cuisine* is certainly *en
décadence.* So at least say the judges. The
Gallery is now, alas! full only of pedestals and
picture-frames—the swallows are literally on the
wing there—and it looks like an auction-room
after a sale. A scene of still greater confusion
is the Austrian Barrack, where the Venus, the
Apollo, the Transfiguration, and a thousand precious things, are huddled together. They say the
French show no feeling, but the melancholy groups
assembled in the Place de Carrousel to gaze at the
Venetian horses for some days before they were
taken down by our engineers, and those now assembled round the Column with the same sad pre-
sentiment, would affect even F. a little. 'They
won't rob us of everything,' said an old gentleman
to me in the crowd; 'they would take away the
city of Paris if they could!' There is a caricature
of the Duke of Wellington in circulation with great
moustaches, inscribed M. Blucher, and I fear we
are growing very unpopular. My reading, alas! is
confined to plays and farces, which I read before I
go to the theatre, because they talk so damned fast
there, as Dangle says in the 'Critic,' that I can't
understand a word they say. I was very agreeably

surprised to find in the Rue de Grenelle a very delightful English family the other day, and theirs is the only house I have been in—Mrs Ann Scott and her son and daughter—and who do you think I introduced there but Glasserton Stewart under a magnificent pair of whiskers. He came with a King's messenger from Turin to see the Gallery, but it has vanished like the Palace of Aladdin, and he came only to empty walls. He returns next week to Florence. He was at Genoa when Lady Jane Montague died, and at Naples he saw the last of poor Eustace, events that have thrown a shade over our Italian town. As I came out of Rochester, who should be driving into it but poor Lady Shaftesbury; but we were both driving so fast that I had only a glimpse of her, though I made what noise I could. I dined with Lady Barbara just before her confinement. I have said so much about nothing, I have no room for real things. I am not sure I should like to see the parting between you and Charles [1]—strange it is, as you observe, that a mother's nerves should be strung to quiver for people so passionately fond of enterprise and danger, and that all her business should be to prepare them for leaving her. Ever and ever yours, S. R."

His next letter comes the following year, deploring business which prevented him coming to Glen Finart :—

"I have a line from Lord Byron : he is on the

[1] Who was just going to school.

Lake of Geneva, and, like another St Preux, was nearly cast away the other evening under the rocks of Maillarie. He has read 'Glenarvon' and finished another canto of 'Childe Harold,' and a smaller poem or two, and sets off for Italy immediately. Madame de Staël has also written three vols. for you. The two first are on France, the last on England."

CHAPTER II.

1815–1822.

SCHOOL-TIME AND HOLIDAYS.

THE journey to Eton from Dunmore was a formidable affair for young Charles, who never,
to the end of his life, succeeded in going to sleep
in a carriage. The fastest travelling from Dunmore to London occupied three days and two
nights, and, on account of his inveterate sleep-
lessness in a coach, the boy was generally sent
by the Leith smack to the Thames. In Edinburgh he was taken in charge by his father's
estate agent, Mr Tait, and formed a close friendship with his two sons, of whom the second
afterwards became Archbishop of Canterbury.

Eton boys of to-day perhaps do not realise
the ease of transit they enjoy—eight hours from
London to Edinburgh in a saloon furnished like
a boudoir—though they may regard somewhat en-

viously the large inroads which the old-fashioned travelling sometimes made on the school-time. On one occasion the smack in which Charles, bound for school, embarked at Leith, was blown over to the coast of Norway, and it was a fortnight before she landed him again, not in London, but in Leith!

Notwithstanding such impediments as this to consecutive study, Charles Murray acquired a pretty turn for Latin verses, the making of which was really nearly all a boy could learn at Eton in Keate's day. Sometimes the exercises were varied by practice in English verse; and once a-week an afternoon was devoted to what was called an *extempore*, though the subject was set at 2 P.M. and the lines (which were not to exceed four) had not to be shown up till two hours later. On one occasion the subject set was Horace's *Insanire omnes*. On this a very shy, quiet boy, whom nobody suspected of capacity for a·joke, sent in the following stanza :—

> "Old Horace says 'All men are mad,'
> And so they are, I think. Egad!
> Surely the man *must* be a fool
> Who sends his son to Eton school."

Charles's elder brother, Lord Fincastle, was also

at Eton, but afflicted with great shyness, especially with ladies. Charles, who never suffered
from that complaint, has left on record his device
for curing him. The two lads were at a party in
the house of Sir Michael Shaw Stewart in Edinburgh, a town which was famous for gaiety in the
early part of the century.

"I wished to make him known to a very pretty
young lady, with whom I was myself talking, and
I hit upon a device for removing the usual for-
mality of an introduction. Accordingly, before
performing that ceremony, I said to my brother,
'Miss —— is very pleasant in conversation, but
she is very deaf;' and a few minutes afterwards
I went across to her and asked her if she would
let me introduce my brother. Upon her saying
that it would give her very great pleasure, I said,
'I should warn you that he is very deaf.' After
this I performed the introduction, and went to
the farther part of the room to watch the result.
As I expected, I saw him approach his mouth
to her ear and shout out something, probably an
insignificant remark. She was startled, but in
making her reply also put her mouth very near
to his ear, and shouted a few words in answer.
Both seemed very much surprised, but before long
one had occasion to say, 'You needn't talk so loud,
I'm not deaf.' 'Oh, I'm very glad to hear it, but
my brother told me you were very deaf.' Then
she said to him, 'He told me the same of you!'
The result was a hearty laugh, the absence of all

shyness, and in a few minutes they were laughing at the mischief-maker, who had obtained his object."

Edinburgh society, though small, was very lively, and the literary activity of certain coteries has perhaps had no parallel in a town of equal size. Jeffrey had steered the 'Edinburgh Review' to a brilliant position; Lockhart and John Wilson between them had launched 'Blackwood's Magazine' to the attack, with a memorable display of fireworks; the Waverley Novels, not yet avowed by their author, were confidently attributed to one hand after another. Charles Murray preserved notes of some of the incidents which amused him at the time. Some of the stories invite repetition, though this may possibly not be the first time they have appeared in print :—

"A certain Scottish peer had long desired to obtain the honour of the Order of the Thistle, one of which happened to be then vacant. For a considerable time he canvassed all the persons whom he thought likely to have it in their power to assist him in attaining his object. He was very sanguine of success; but while the Law Court was sitting at Edinburgh, of which Harry Erskine was a member, intelligence came in to the effect that Lord S. had been unsuccessful. As soon as the report was read to the assembled

advocates, Harry Erskine wrote two lines on a
slip of paper and threw it over the table to one
of his brother-advocates. The two lines proved
to be in reference to Lord S. as follows :—

> " ' When he heard the thing was settled,
>   Not being thistled he was nettled.' [1]

"There were some amusing incidents occurred
when, between the year 1820-30, King George
IV. took it into his head to pay a visit to Edinburgh, and, by way of rendering himself popular,
he dressed himself in full Highland costume on
the occasion of his receiving the Provost and
the Bailies in state. These worthies had been
informed that, after the reading of their loyal
address and receiving his Majesty's gracious reply,
they were to retire, kissing hands as they withdrew. Accordingly they defiled, as they went
out, kissing their own hands to their astonished
Sovereign."

[1] Another impromptu by Henry Erskine is preserved in these
notes. A case on which Erskine was engaged was being tried by
Lord Cringletie, who, in mitigation of the offence of which the
defendant was accused, referred to the force of circumstances under
which he had acted, and more than once quoted the proverb,
"Necessity has no law." Erskine passed a slip of paper to his
neighbour with these lines pencilled on it :—

> "Necessity and Cringaltie are suited to a tittle,—
>   Necessity has no law, and Cringaltie has little."

The English equivalent to this story may be found in Samuel
Rogers's 'Table-Talk': "Dunning (afterwards Lord Ashburton) was
stating the law to a jury at Guildhall, when Lord Mansfield interrupted him by saying, 'If *that* be law, I'll go home and burn my
books.' 'My lord,' replied Dunning, 'you had better go home and
read them'!"

King George's visit was the cause of some inconvenience to Lord and Lady Dunmore. Queen Anne had bestowed on the first Earl of Dunmore a suite of apartments in Holyrood Palace, which had remained in the family as a possession by what Scottish lawyers call "tacit relocation" ever since. On this occasion the king, probably with an eye to future sojourns in the Scottish capital, caused the apartments of the Duke of Hamilton, Hereditary Keeper of the Palace, to be added to the royal suite, and bestowed on the Duke the rooms previously occupied by the Dunmores.

The new house at Dunmore had just been completed from the designs of Wilkins of Cambridge, who was also the architect of Lord Rosebery's new house at Dalmeny. At the last-named place constant sociable gatherings took place, at which many Edinburgh and other notables assembled from time to time. Among these appears the name of Lord Chancellor Eldon, then a very old man, whose pleasantries seem to have been rather of the bludgeoning, Johnsonian type.

"One of the numerous Dundases—well known in the neighbourhood of Edinburgh—had the preceding year exhibited a collection of pictures which he had lately purchased in Germany, previous to their being transferred to his private residence.

It happened that one of the guests at Lord Rosebery's table mentioned his intention of visiting the
Continent for the purpose of making some addition
to his own collection of paintings, and he asked
Lord Eldon if he could give him any suggestions
as to where he had better begin his search.   Lord
Eldon replied, 'I think he had better go to Dusseldorf.'   'And why to Dusseldorf?' said the in-
quirer.   'I think you might find something good
there, as our friend Dundas went there last year
and bought all the d——d trash in the place.'"

This Mr Dundas shared the passion which distinguished James IV. for amateur dentistry.   It
was said that whenever his wife engaged a new
housemaid or kitchenmaid, Dundas used to offer
her a sovereign to be allowed to draw one of her
teeth.

"Lady Rosebery, who was a sister of Lord
Lichfield's, a handsome person, and an excellent
hostess, was very fond of playing the harp as an
accompaniment when singing.   One favourite song
—a Russian air with Russian words—she played
and sang so frequently that I can remember the
words to this day.   On one occasion when she was
singing it a Russian *attaché*, who happened to be
sitting next to me, whispered to me, 'Does Lady
Rosebery understand Russian?'   I replied, 'Certainly not; but why do you ask me?'   'Because,'
said he, 'the words she is singing are most atroci-
ously improper.   Somebody ought to tell her.'

"I need scarcely add that I took the earliest opportunity of doing so, and the song was never repeated."

Much of Charles Murray's early recollection is connected with Hamilton Palace and visits to his uncle there. The Duke of Hamilton [1] impressed him as a fine specimen of the old grand school, retaining not only the manners of a bygone court but some of the peculiarities in dress. He continued to wear a wig, tied with a ribbon behind, long after that fashion had been discarded.

"Of the Duchess I hardly trust myself to write, so gifted she was with talents of various kinds, but most of all in music. She had a magnificent voice of three perfect octaves, and her scientific knowledge of music was as remarkable as was her intuitive feeling. I may add that many of her gifts above alluded to were inherited from her father, William Beckford of Fonthill Abbey, one of the most extraordinary men in some respects that it has been my chance to meet in life. Before he was twenty he had written in French, and published, the oriental novel of 'Vathek,' which was for many years to be found in almost every drawing-room in England or France. Some literary pirate having published—of course without authority—a translation of it, Beckford published his English version of it. In respect of music I do

[1] Ninth duke, died in 1819.

not know whether he ever knew a single note, but I have often seen him sit down at the piano and play a succession of the wildest and most extravagant unpremeditated compositions.

"I remember on one occasion an article had lately appeared in one of the magazines describing the nature of the sovereign succession in Thibet, and how the spirit of the dying ruler was supposed to pass into the body of his successor. Beckford, taking the bass and sitting beside his daughter at the piano, said in French (which he always spoke to her), 'Now, Susan, we'll suppose that the Grand Lama is just dead, and that his spirit has passed into the body of a little child. Now we'll have the scene.'

"A remarkable performance ensued. There they sat at the piano together, the father and the still beautiful daughter, whose face, like her soul, was all music, he making the most grotesque faces in the world, as he suggested in a single word the successive changes of his piece — she playing the tenor and he the accompaniment on the bass notes of the instrument. First was a solemn dirge for the death of the old lama—then a march intended to describe the procession of grave senators and sages to the assembly where the successor to the deceased prince was to be proclaimed—then a solemn strain describing the discussions and divinations of the assembly—then a grand chorus announcing the result and the proclamation of the infant successor. All this was improvised without any other guide than an occasional glance at one another, while their duet, expressive of a whole series of incidents, continued without a hitch. Presently Beckford, breaking off, remarked to his daughter, 'À présent, à toi!' Upon which, after a solemn pause, she began a soft solo in the treble, which she presently accompanied with her voice, singing, 'Le Grand Lama vient de dire ta-ta!'[1]

"I may here add a humorous little story that the Duchess herself related to me, connected with her girlish days at Fonthill Abbey. There were several peacocks and peahens that used to promenade about the lawns and terraces adjoining the house, and her father took it into his head to learn and practise in a back-room of the house the shrill cry of a peacock. He knew that when the peacock on one side screamed loud, another peacock on the opposite side of the house generally screamed in defiance. One morning, when he felt pretty sure that he had learnt his lesson correctly, he went out, and hiding behind a cedar-tree, he gave his peacock cry: to his great delight, the peacock on the opposite side of the lawn screamed defiantly. Immediately after this, which occurred just before breakfast, he came into the breakfast-room, saying with triumph to his daughter—

"'And, Susan, the other peacock answered me!'

---

[1] "In the evening Beckford would amuse us by reading one of his unpublished works ; or he would extemporise on the pianoforte, producing the most charming and novel melodies (which, by the bye, his daughter, the Duchess of Hamilton, can do also)."—Rogers's Table-Talk, p. 217.

" To his great annoyance, instead of congratulating him on his success, his daughter only burst
into a loud fit of laughter. Rather provoked at
this, he said—

"'Well, I think you might have congratulated
me !'

" And then, though still hardly able to speak
for laughing, she said—

"'Why, papa, *I* was the peacock that answered
you !'"

Lord Eldon figures characteristically in these
reminiscences of Hamilton Palace. Phrenology
was a fashionable craze for some years, and
among those most bitten with it was a neighbouring laird, Mr Hamilton of Dalzell,[1] a very
old gentleman. Sitting opposite to Lord Eldon
one night at dinner, and fixing his eyes on the
great lawyer, Hamilton suddenly asked him—

" Have you ever read Dr Spurzheim's two great
volumes on phrenology ? "

" No, sir," replied Lord Eldon, "and I'd be
ashamed to own it if I had."

Which cast rather a damp over the discussion
in which Hamilton was burning to engage.

" In the earlier part of this century the article
which we call the 'dessert-spoon' was not known
in Scotland : the two houses in which it was first

---

[1] Father of the present Lord Hamilton of Dalzell.

introduced were Hamilton and Dalkeith.   Before
that, there was no spoon known between the table-
spoon and the teaspoon.   Bearing this in mind,
we proceed to the following incident.   A rough
country squire, dining for the first time at Hamilton, had been served in the second course with a
sweet dish containing cream or jelly, and with it
the servant handed him a dessert-spoon.   The laird
turned it round and round in his great fist and
said to the servant—

" ' What do you gie me this for, ye d——d fule ?
Do ye think ma mooth has got any smaller since a
lappit up my soup ? '

" At one of these dinners there was a Russian
prince, whose name I forget, and who sat on the
right hand of the Duchess.   At the close of the
first course a servant brought round a plate on
which were a dozen little square pieces of toast
with a delicate morsel, apparently of meat, upon
each, which he elicited from the Duchess to consist of the inside of a woodcock, and considered
a great delicacy.   Unconscious that the plate
was to go round, he took it from the hands of
the servant, placed it before him, and deliberate-
ly ate up the whole of it, saying that he found it
excellent ; but he ascertained that the delicate
meat upon the toast was not termed in polite
circles the ' stomach,' but was called the ' trail.'
Whether that particular dish or any other disagreed
with his digestion I know not, but it happened
that the same night, a little before midnight, the
Duke heard the footsteps of his guest walking up
and down in the passage adjoining the rooms in

which they both slept. The Duke lit a candle,
opened his door, and went up to his guest, and
inquired whether he was suffering any pain? and
the latter replied—

"'Yes, I have got a very bad pain in my *trail*.'"

Walter Scott was one of the acquaintances
whom Charles Murray made at Hamilton. He
left the poem *Cadzow Castle* as a memento of his
visit, little dreaming, perhaps, how famous the
whole neighbourhood was to become by his pen.[1]
Henry Brougham and Chief-Justice Denman are
others of note whose names appear.

"It was during one of these visits to Hamilton,
Brougham and Denman being both guests at the
time, that my uncle asked me to go over to Lanark
and show them an establishment that was then
making a great sensation in Scotland. I allude to
the Educational Institution of the well-known Mr
Owen. He was one of those visionary individuals
who held that the human mind and human character in childhood were perfectly free from vice of
any kind, and that a careful education could mould
the youth of both sexes into a state of perpetual
innocence. The establishment was upon a large

---

[1] Cambusnethan, in the immediate neighbourhood of Hamilton,
is the original of Tillietudlem Castle in 'Old Mortality.' The crowds
of tourists who visit it at this day take their tickets, not for Cambusnethan, but for Tillietudlem—perhaps an unrivalled instance of the
power of a novelist to influence the prosaic details of railway management.

scale; and the pupils, boys and girls, took their lessons together between the ages of seven and seventeen. Owen was a plausible fellow, and described his system and his course with great volubility to the two distinguished lawyers above mentioned. I watched them during the interview, and I could see that Brougham listened to his explanations with considerable interest, while Denman d——d Mr Owen from the first as a complete humbug. I regret to be obliged to add that a few years later the fact of half-a-dozen of the girl pupils proving *enceinte* caused Mr Owen to be driven out of the place by the indignant population. I may add that, curiously enough, I found the same charlatan, Owen, in the United States, conducting a school near Philadelphia, but I never heard any more of his success or failure."

Shooting, in the first quarter of the century, had not become the arduous, semi - professional business with which we are familiar; nevertheless, Charles Murray used to bring out his flintlocked "Joe Manton" with as much pride and as much confidence that it was a perfect firearm, as any modern youth can feel in his two or three hammerless breechloaders fitted with ejectors and all the latest improvements. Nowhere had he a finer field for its exercise than in the Isle of Arran, that princely possession of the Dukes of Hamilton, and space must be found for his eulogy on a gamekeeper of the old school :—

D

"The kennels, which contained somewhere between fifteen and twenty pointers and setters, were under the charge of old George Croll, whom I have always considered the most perfect dog-breaker I ever knew. The greater part of his system of dog-breaking was done in the kennels themselves, which were admirably clean and roomy. The whip seemed to me to be almost unknown in his system, and when he opened the door and entered, the dogs all flocked round him, wagging their tails with joy and affection. But the moment he raised his arm pointing upwards, every dog lay down immediately in the spot where he was, and when he let them out for a run, whether they ran near or far, as soon as he whistled and beckoned, every dog immediately lay down where he was. There was one dog whose remarkable sagacity has remained imprinted indelibly on my memory. It was a small smooth pointer, called 'Peter'; of course it had been exercised with the other dogs along the roads or the sea-shore, but it had never smelt a grouse or been taken out on the hills till the day that George Croll took him out with me to see what he would do. I may mention that rain had been falling and the ground was wet, and consequently most of the birds were on foot. We had scarcely been on the moor five minutes before we saw Peter going very slowly forward and trembling with excitement. George Croll encouraged and patted him, but could hardly get him to advance, and at last he said to me, 'The birds have been here, but they are on foot, and running before us.' With difficulty we persuaded

Peter to go on, his master patting him all the time, and after a few minutes the covey rose, out of shot, before us. This was a very hard trial. We continued our walk over the moor, and then Peter, after a few turns to the right and left in search of a fresh scent, came again to a point; the same thing recurred, the birds were restless, and got up out of shot. Peter seemed to think that the birds were making fools of us, but he went off to the right as fast as possible, described a half-moon till he got three or four hundred yards in front of us, and then came slowly traversing the ground towards us. Thus, if there were any birds, Peter had got them between him and us, and, sure enough, he had out-manœuvred the grouse, for he had got them between. They rose and came over my head, and I killed a brace—the first grouse that ever had been shot to Peter."

It is vain to sigh for the old leisurely kind of shooting. Men with breechloaders cannot be got to give a dog time to exercise his wits : they walk on without a pause after a shot, and the dogs, which have the same faculties and sagacity as of yore, have no chance of bringing them into play. But it is pleasant to get a glimpse of moorland sport as it was before the days of flurry and big bags.

CHAPTER III.

1822–1830.

LIFE AT OXFORD.

AFTER leaving Eton in 1822 Charles Murray spent two years at a private tutor's preparing for Oxford. It was to this tutor, the Rev. Mr Hichings, vicar of Sunninghill, that he gratefully ascribed the strong love for the classics which he maintained through life. But the reminiscences which he began to put together in 1892 had been carried little further than his school-days when he died in 1895. A few notes of his life at Sunninghill, a few stories of his college companions, and still fewer of his own doings at Oriel College, Oxford, form the only semblance of a consecutive narrative of the time after he ceased to be an *alumnus* of the redoubtable Dr Keate at Eton. The only fellow‑pupil at Sunninghill of whom he has left any mention is Henry Hope of the Deepdene.[1]

"He was a good sort of lad, quick-tempered, and very ugly, owing to a large, ill-shaped mouth. For some time I took to calling him Boccaccio, which rather pleased him, as he knew it to be the name of a distinguished author; but on one unlucky day he took up an Italian dictionary that happened to be lying on the table, and in turning over the leaves he came to '*Boccaccia*—a wide, ugly mouth.' In a moment of rage he threw at my head a beautifully bound book that he was reading: I ducked my head, and the poor book went into the fireplace behind my chair. This did not improve his temper; but the incident had no further consequences, except that I never called him by the great Italian's name again."

Murray's favourite amusements at Sunninghill were walking, and driving the London coach. His pedestrian powers must have been somewhat remarkable. On being invited to Deepdene, the home of his friend Henry Hope, he walked over there in time for luncheon, a matter of some five-and-twenty miles.

Letters from Patrick Fraser Tytler (already distinguished as a man of letters, though his prin-

[1] Uncle of the present Mr Philip Beresford Hope. He was afterwards one of Murray's opponents on the hustings of Marylebone. Both of them were beaten.

cipal work, 'The History of Scotland,' did not appear till five years later) show that Charles Murray at the age of seventeen, just before he went to Oxford, had already given evidence of ability beyond the common. Tytler was fifteen years his senior, yet he wrote to him as a man does to his intellectual equal.

P. Fraser Tytler to the Hon. Charles Murray.

"MOUNT ESK, BY LASSWADE,
July 26th, 1823.

"MY DEAR CHARLES, — Notwithstanding your pathetic appeal in the words of Penelope—'nil mihi rescribas, attamen ipse veni'—*ipse* is sincerely sorry to say that at this moment he cannot come to Dunmore. This is to him the more sad since nothing could have given him more real pleasure, Dunmore being delightful always, and not the least so when it is illuminated by your sallies, whether classical or diplomatic, in your character of Charles Murray the scholar, Charles Murray the *chargé d'affaires*, or, to sum up all, Charles Murray the madcap. But to be serious and to come to my reasons. I have the misfortune to have a sister who is just going to be married, and till that solemn event has taken place I cannot leave this cottage of ours. Lord Dunmore may recollect perhaps that I once sent him some views in the Himalaya range of mountains in India : they were the production of my cousin

James Fraser, who was then the partner of a
mercantile house at Calcutta.   He has been a
great traveller, and is an uncommon fine fellow,
and having returned with a sufficient, though not
large, fortune, is about to marry my youngest
sister, to whom he has been attached since his
youth up for ten years.   There's patriarchal and
primitive constancy for you.   Mercutio, whose
heart, I take it, is a riddle in all senses, both
physically and morally—*at jam satis et plusquam
satis de matrimonio.*   I like to leave the subject, for
I am an abandoned literary bachelor, fond of my
own fireside, my old books, my own private comforts, and what I believe is the most fatal symp-
tom of all, I have thoughts of taking into
keeping (no impropriety) a teapot, and making
my own tea at a little table in the library—this
is what may be called innocent profligacy.   Perhaps you would like to know what I am about;
but first, before I give way to egotism, let me say
that I saw some letters and read some verses of
a certain young scholar when I was last at Dunmore
which gave me the greatest pleasure, and that
with the talents which are possessed by this
anonymous individual, and the ardour for classical literature which he seems to enjoy, it will be
entirely his own fault if he does not, one day,
distinguish himself in no common way.   Indeed,
seriously, Charles, I look to see you very high,
and the more that I am at Dunmore, the more
keenly do I anticipate the delight which your
success will give to those who love you best.

  " I have lately been reading a good deal upon

a very interesting subject—the revival of Greek
letters in Italy, in the latter part of the fourteenth
and beginning of the fifteenth century. There
is a fine chapter in the last volume of Gibbon
upon the subject, and something in Roscoe's Life
of Lorenzo de Medici and Shepherd's Life of
Poggio, but for full information you must go to
the original authors themselves, whose names are
too long and too hard to come in here. This I am
now attempting, and it has opened a scene of
literary genius and exertion of which before I had
formed no conception. It is delightful and wonderful to see old Homer, and Euripides, and Æschylus
wakening from their long sleep of seven hundred
years and resuming the lyre, and re-civilising the
barbarians of these dark ages."

Murray has left a few notes about his early
Oxford days which do not give one the idea of
very sedulous study. His tutor for several terms
was Newman, and it is strange how completely
that gentle, thoughtful mind failed to secure the
affection of these terrible youngsters.

"He never inspired me, or my fellow-under-
graduates, with any interest, much less respect:
on the contrary, we disliked, or rather distrusted,
him. He walked with his head bent, abstracted,
but every now and then looking out of the cor-
ners of his eyes quickly, as though suspicious.
He had no influence then: it was only when he
became vicar of St Mary's that the long dormant

power asserted itself, and his sermons attracted hundreds.[1]

"I well remember one trick we played him. I was up to him for Greek. At lecture he was quiet, and what I should call sheepish; stuck to the text, and never diverged into contemporary history or made the lecture interesting. He always struck me as the most pusillanimous of men—wanting in the knowledge of human nature; and I am always surprised, and indeed never can understand, how it was he became such a great man. I never heard him preach.

"We were a merry set of youngsters, fond of singing late into the night over suppers. The songs were not classical, but, I am ashamed to say, generally very noisy. They disturbed Newman, who liked quiet; but instead of coming himself and asking us to be earlier and quieter, he sent a porter, whom *we* sent to the devil. It showed either his cowardice or his want of humanity. If we were noisy, we were all of us gentlemen, and not one of us would have rebelled if he had spoken to us himself. As it was, he stuck up a big bell outside his room, about twelve feet from the ground. At nine o'clock or so, if we began to shout, he pealed this bell to summon the porter to tell us to be quiet. This was too much. I

---

[1] In his recent memoirs of Cardinal Manning, Mr Purcell quotes him as having remarked of Cardinal Newman: "I never was, like Newman, a student or a recluse. Newman, from the beginning to the end, was a recluse—at Oriel, Littlemore, and Edgbaston; but I, from the beginning, was pitched head over heels [*sic*] into public life, and I have lived ever since in the full glare of day" (vol. i. p. xiii).

said I'd have the bell down; the others all chaffed me, and said I shouldn't. It was impossible to do it alone, but not one of them would join me. At last Lord Malmesbury's brother, Harris, a lieutenant in the navy, who was up on a visit, volunteered, and we laid our plans. Next night we brought a ladder and a pickaxe. The fellow had had the bell fixed in with nails some five inches long, and we took it in turn to hold the ladder and to pick at the nails. Of course Newman *must* have heard us, and if he had been anything of a man, he would have come out of his room and caught us red-handed; but he was too pusillanimous for that, and we were allowed to finish our work in peace, so far as he was concerned. Unluckily for me, though, as I was coming down with the great bell and its fixtures in my arms my foot slipped, and I fell, spraining my ankle. Of course next day there was the devil of a row, but no one was sent down. No one was put on his honour to say who was the culprit, and Harris left for his ship. The old Dean—Tyler—my tutor, and a great friend of mine, came and sat by my bed where I was kept 'by an accident,' and I saw by the twinkle in his eye that he knew all about it, but he kept his counsel, and as it was the end of the term the thing blew over. But Newman never put up his bell again."

Si peccas, pecca fortiter—a classical maxim to which undergraduates of those days acted up with some spirit. One of Murray's Oxford friends was

Lord Edward Thynne, son of the second Marquis of Bath, and afterwards M.P. for Frome, a very handsome but dissolute young fellow. He and Murray, having been "gated" for some minor offence, determined to eclipse it by a more heroic one, and bet that they would ride to London, sixty miles, and back in one day. Having arranged for relays at Henley and Maidenhead, they started from Oxford about 8.30 A.M., changed their clothes at a hotel on arriving in London, mounted two hacks, and trotted off to the Park, where they saw many friends. Then they dined quietly at a club, saw the first act of a play at some theatre, and, allowing themselves three hours to cover the sixty miles in returning, galloped off at nine o'clock.

"It was a pitch-dark night, and tearing down Henley Hill we shouted to each other, 'Are you all right?' 'Yes; he's not down yet—expect he will be in a minute;' but no! we arrived back at the College gate three minutes to midnight, and were received with vociferous cheers by our friends, who were waiting supper in case we got back. I regret to say one of the horses ridden by Thynne— a much heavier fellow than I—died from the effects of the pace."

Fragmentary notes remain of other and less creditable episodes and escapades. These were the days when most youngsters of breeding thought it necessary to qualify as "bucks" and men of "the *ton*" by the rapt of bell-pulls and door-knockers. Sidney Herbert [1] had been a companion of Murray's at Eton, and to him Murray, on leaving Oxford, left a large collection of these objects, among them—Newman's bell! But during his undergraduate days he excelled also in athletics of a less spasmodic order. He was an ardent tennis-player; he won the chief prize in the University—a silver racquet—and retaining it against all competitors for three years, became the possessor of it for ever. "This," he wrote shortly before his death, "is the only incontestable distinction that I can claim to have achieved in my long life."

There are many traces, also, of more scholarly tastes than these. The ink has wellnigh faded away in Murray's earliest commonplace book, but it is still possible to decipher verses in Greek, Latin, and English, of which the following alcaics —a rendering of Milton's ode to Echo in "Comus" —written at the age of nineteen, may stand as a single example of many, though the author has scribbled a note to the effect that none of these

[1] Afterwards Lord Herbert of Lea, and father of the present Earl of Pembroke; died in 1861.

verses are "worth the trouble of transcribing, much less of printing":—

"O nympha dulcis, nympha recondita,
Dulcissima Echo! tardiflui tenet
Quam ripa Mæandri virescens
Aeriâ redimita conchâ,

Valle in reductâ quam violaria
Odora pingunt, purpureum decus,
Quâ tristis infaustos amores
Nocte tibi Philomela deflet.[1]

Dic si latescunt, par ubi amabile
Narcissinæ queis forma simillima,
Dic si latebras his cavernæ
Floriferæ, dea, præbuisti.

Vocale numen, terrigena! o preces
Ne sperne nostras, sic doceas nove
Elata, sic sedes deorum
Dulcisono resonare cantu."[2]

After he had been more than two years at Oriel, Murray passed from Newman's care, and Dean Tyler then became his tutor. He got on better with him, and formed the ambition to be elected a Fellow of All Souls. A vacancy occurring there before he was twenty-one, he spoke to Tyler about it, who said it was out of the question, because Murray had not even looked at Theology or Logic.

[1] *Plangit* would surely sound better than *deflet*.

[2] Many years later, in 1840, Murray sent these verses, with two or three alterations, to Dr Hawtrey of Eton, who said he preferred Sapphics, and returned a version in that metre.

"The Dean went every day for long walks, and
I said to him, 'If you will allow me, sir, to accompany you on your walks, I could learn logic from
you then.' He agreed, and that was how I learnt
all the logic I ever knew—I never opened a book.
The schools came off, and I went up merely to
pass. This I did, and the examiners were kind
enough to offer me a 4th class honour, which I
refused, as I said people would only say, 'He went
in for honours and only managed a fourth.' When
my age was objected to I claimed my privilege as
son of a Peer, and I was elected. In those days
the reading colleges said of us (at All Souls)
—*Bene nati, bene vestiti, moderate docti.* This is
changed nowadays so far as the learning goes,
but I doubt if, socially, All Souls has gained much
by it."

About this time Murray seems to have contemplated taking seriously to literature, for there is
a letter (with a characteristically long postscript)
to him in 1826 from Samuel Rogers, whom he had
consulted on a projected poem on Trajan's pillar.

—"Two of a trade, my dear Charles, can never
agree; but *we*, I hope, shall be an exception to
the rule. Read Eustace Forsyth, and all the
travellers on the subject, not forgetting Kotze-
bue, who has published his travels and is very
poetical in his prose when he visits those cities
of old. With every five grains of Pompeii mingle
three of Vesuvius, and with so much of the com-

bustible as you have in your composition, you will be sure of a rocket that will leave all the rest below.—Ever yours,   SAMUEL ROGERS.

"*P.S.*—Goethe in his Life visits Vesuvius, and I think Pompeii. In Dr Clarke's Memoirs there is also a very lively account of the mountain. When you have read these and also Gray's lines, 'Nec procul infelix se tollit,' &c., take two or three strides up and down your room, and the work will be done in a twinkle.

"*Mem.*—Let it be at early dawn, at the hour Milton rose for the purpose, and after an early going to bed and spare fast. 'Spare fast, that oft with gods doth diet,' is a far better friend on such an occasion, whatever some may say to the contrary, than the very best champagne, sweet or dry. There is a poem written six years ago, which I have rather run through than read, but which has some strong tempesta-kind of painting in it. It is called 'The Last Days of Herculaneum,' and was published, I believe, by Baldwin. If you read it, throw it aside before you begin.

" It is unnecessary to remind you of Pliny's two letters on the subject."

It is difficult to discern in the fragmentary notes and shreds of correspondence which have been preserved, any definite purpose for the disposal of his life, either on the part of Charles Murray himself or of his parents.

The following rather remarkable letter, written in 1828 by Lord Brougham to Lady Dunmore, seems to indicate a destiny that was contemplated, but never fulfilled, though the precepts may remain of service to others. Although Murray began to read for the Bar with Mr Nassau Senior, he never practised.

Lord Brougham to the Countess of Dunmore.

"Now you of course destine him for the Bar, and assuming that this, and the public objects incidental to it, are in his view, I would fain impress upon you, and, through you, upon him, a truth or two which experience has made me aware of, and which I would have given a great deal to have been made acquainted with earlier in life, from the experience of others. First, that the foundation of all excellence is to be laid in early application to general knowledge is clear; this he already is aware of: equally so it is (of which he may not be so well aware) that professional eminence can only be secured by entering betimes into the lowest drudgery, the most repulsive labours, of the profession. Even a year in an attorney's office, as the law is now practised, I should hold not too severe a task, or too high a price to pay, for the benefits it must surely lead to. But at all events the life of a special pleader I am quite convinced is the thing before being called to the Bar. A young man whose mind has once been imbued well with general learning and acquired classical propensities, will scarce sink into a mere drudge— he will always save himself harmless from the dull atmosphere he must live and work in, and the sooner he enters it, the sooner he will emerge from it, and arrive at eminence.

"What I wish to inculcate, especially with a view to the great talent for public speaking which your son happily possesses, is that he should cultivate that talent in the only way in which it can reach the height of the art ; and I wish to turn his attention to two points. I speak on this subject with the authority both of experience and observation. I have made it very much my study in theory ; have written a great deal upon it which may never see the light, and something which *has* been published ; have meditated much and conversed much on it with famous men ; have had some little practical experience in it, but prepared myself for much more than I ever tried, by a variety of laborious methods — reading, writing, and translation, composing in foreign languages, &c., &c.; and have lived in times when there were great orators among us,—therefore I reckon my opinion worth listening to ; and the rather because I have the utmost confidence in it myself, and should have saved a world of trouble and much time had I started with the same conviction of its truth. The first point is this, the beginning of the art is to acquire a habit of easy speaking ; and in whatever way this can be had (which individual inclination or accident will generally direct, and may safely be allowed to do so), it must be had. Now I differ from all other doctors of rhetoric in this : I say let him first of all learn to speak easily and fluently, as well and as sensibly as he can, no

E

doubt, but at any rate let him learn to speak; this is to eloquence and good public speaking what the being able to talk in a child is to correct grammatical speech. It is the requisite foundation, and on it you must build; moreover, it can only be acquired young, and therefore let it by all means, and at any sacrifice, be gotten hold of forthwith. But in acquiring it every sort of slovenly error will also be acquired. It must be got by a habit of easy writing, which, as Wyndham said, proved hard reading; by a custom of talking too much in company; by debating in speaking societies with little attention to rule, and more love of saying something at any rate than of saying anything well. I can even suppose that more attention will be paid to the matter in such discussions than to the manner of saying it; yet still to say easily *ad libitum*, to be able to say what you choose, and what you have to say, this is the first requisite, to acquire which everything else must for the present be sacrificed.

" The next step is the grand one—to correct this kind of easy speaking into chaste eloquence; and here there is but one rule, which I earnestly entreat your son to set daily and nightly before him —the great models. First of all he may look to the best modern speeches, as he probably has already— Burke's best compositions, as 'The Thoughts on the Cause of the present Discontents;' 'Speech on American Conciliation,' and 'On the Nabob of Arcot's Debts'; Fox's 'Speech on the Westminster Scrutiny,' the first part of which he should pore over till he has it by heart; 'On the Rus-

sian Armament,' and 'On the War of 1803,' with
one or two of Wyndham's best, and very few, or
rather none, of Sheridan's.   But he must by no
means stop here if he would be a great órator ;
he must at once go to the fountainhead, and be
familiar with every one of the great orations of
Demosthenes—I take for granted he knows those
of Cicero by heart.   They are very beautiful, but
not very useful, excepting perhaps the 'Milo' or
the 'Pro Ligario,' and one or two more ; but the
Greek must positively be the model, and merely
learning it, as boys do to know the language,
won't do at all.   He must enter into the spirit
of each speech, thoroughly know the positions of
the parties, follow each turn of the argument, and
make the absolutely perfect and most chaste and
secure composition familiar to his mind.   His taste
will improve every time he reads and repeats to
himself (for he should have the fine passages by
heart), and he will learn how much may be done
by a skilful use of a few words, and a vigorous
rejection of all superfluities.   In this view I hold
a familiar knowledge of Dante next to Demosthenes.

"It is in vain to say that imitations of those
models won't do for our times.   First, I don't
counsel any imitation, but only an imbibing of
the same spirits.   Secondly, I know from experience that nothing is half so successful in these
times (bad though they be) as what has been
formed on the Greek models.   I cite a very poor
instance in giving my own experience ; but I do
assure you, that both in courts of law and Parlia-

ment, and even to mobs, I have never made half so
much play (to use a very modern phrase) as when
I was almost translating from the Greek. I composed the peroration of my speech for the Queen
in the Lords after reading and repeating Demosthenes for three or four weeks, and I composed
it twenty times over at the very least, and it
certainly succeeded in a very extraordinary degree, and far above any merits of its own. This
leads me to remark that though speaking without
writing beforehand is very well until the habits of
easy and fluent speech are acquired, after that he
can never write too much : this is quite clear.
It is laborious, no doubt, and it is more difficult,
beyond comparison, than speaking off-hand, but
it is necessary to perfect oratory, and at any rate
it is necessary to acquire the habits of correct and
chaste diction ; but I go further and say, even to
the end of a man's life he must prepare, word for
word, most of his fine passages.

"Now would he be an orator or no ? In other
words, would he have almost absolute power of
doing good to mankind (in a free country) or
would he not ? If he wills this, he must follow
these rules."

From all which it is clear that Brougham held
that if poets are born, orators must be manu-
factured.

Charles Murray's younger brother, Henry, was
a sailor, and on the occasion of his return to sea,
Charles, still an undergraduate, writes somewhat

enviously of the midshipman's active life, and betrays little relish at his own prospect of a legal career :—

Hon. Charles Murray to his Brother.

"ORIEL COLLEGE, *Sunday* [1829 ?].

"MY DEAR HARRY,—As it is decreed that we are not to meet again before your departure for the other world, we must wish one another good-bye as well as we can per post ; and, in truth, although it is not agreeable that we should not meet, yet I believe it is just as well that it should be so, for however melancholy it is writing to bid farewell, it is not quite so sad as uttering the word in person ; and you and I love one another too well to need any reiteration of expressions of affection ; so you must suppose me now shaking your great mutton fist as cordially as I possibly can. . . . I have been trying to think what sort of animal you will be when I see you again ! 'Monstrum, horrendum,' &c., you will be six feet four, the head of a bull with a capacious grog-dish in front ; in fact I expect to see you a young Sir F. Livingstone, and you will find me a blear-eyed, pale-faced, threadbare-coated pedant, or else a snivelling, sneaking, smirking lawyer, with papers and deeds in the home view, fees in the background, and a full-bottomed wig in the distance. Oh Harry ! how some of the old Murrays and Atholes would start at this ; but such is the state of the world, and we younger brothers must salt our own porridge or nobody else will do it for us. So take care of yourself, my honest fellow, and take my advice, while you are a drudge, make the most of it, drudge to some purpose, for you can have but little fun in your present situation; so get all the good you can out of it first, and then you will have time to enjoy yourself when you have got out of it."

CHAPTER IV.

1830–1834.

TRAVELS IN EARLY MANHOOD.

THE broken records which enable us to trace the boyhood and youth of Charles Murray down to the time when he took his degree in 1830, cease altogether for some years after that. The few who still remember him at that time speak of the extraordinary charm of manner which he possessed, his magnificent physique and handsome countenance. With the capacity for enjoyment afforded by perfect health and a sociable disposition, with the means of indulging it without any necessity for labour of hand or head, this young Fellow of All Souls might have drifted down the easy tide with other light - hearted voyagers, tennis-playing, shooting, dancing—only conspicuous among his comrades for the ease, sometimes the elegance, of his society verses.

What wonder if his purpose of reading for the Bar faded into the background, and that till the age of three-and-thirty he lived as a man about town for half the year, and spent the other half in field-sports and other rural delights. There is evidence in some of his note-books that Murray sometimes looked back with regret to the years so pleasantly squandered: witness the following reflection on Charles Darwin, made when the writer was within sight of the end :—

" Of all the scientists who have ever lived, few have equalled Darwin in the laborious industry with which he carried on his investigations, even employed on subjects that might have seemed of secondary importance, when compared with those which led up to his great work on the 'Origin of Species' and others by which his name has become immortalised. He spent eight years in examining, describing, and classifying one species of insect, the *Cirrhipedæ* (Barnacles), and yet his labours embraced the whole field of geology, physics, botany, &c., and this is more surprising that throughout nearly the whole time that these labours continued, they were constantly interrupted by bad health, attended by such pain and weakness as to compel him to suspend them."

One sentence in a letter written to a friend when he was twenty-seven shows his opinion on work in the pursuit of science. "I trust that I shall always act as I now feel and think, that a man who *dares* to waste one hour of time has not discovered the value of life." It is humiliating to remember how many young men of his then age and standing in life are busily employed in devising means for *killing* that time which he considered so precious !

Luckily Murray's nature was too strenuous, his habits too active, to allow the enervating round of fashionable life to become a habit with him. He was no doubt inspired to exert his natural faculties by frequent intercourse with leaders in letters and politics, not only at his father's house, but at that of Samuel Rogers, at whose celebrated breakfasts there was always a place reserved for Charles Murray. And so it came to pass that in 1830, when travelling in Germany to acquire the language, although unfurnished with any written introduction, he was able to secure the attention of Goethe, then Prime Minister of the Grand Duchy of Weimar. A meeting which made so deep an impression on the young traveller's mind had best be given in his own words, which have been preserved in the following memorandum :—

" Having passed the night at Weimar, I ordered

the horses to be ready to continue my journey; but before starting I told the landlord that I was most anxious to see the great poet of Germany, who was then Prime Minister at the Court of Weimar. He told me that a similar wish was frequently expressed by travellers from every country passing through Weimar, but that the Minister never acceded to it, excepting in the case of persons bringing him letters of introduction from great personages or intimate friends. Nevertheless, I would not give up my object without making an attempt to attain it, so I sat down and wrote a note to the great man, the contents of which I need not record here, even if I could remember them. Suffice it to say that they were as persuasive as I could make them, and with my note in my hand I drove to Goethe's house. Having gained admittance, I requested the servant who opened the door to take my note to his Excellency. While he was executing this commission, I looked around the entrance hall, where a bust of Byron occupied a prominent place opposite the door, and awaited anxiously the result of my audacious attempt. To my great surprise and joy he returned saying that he was instructed to conduct me to his Excellency's study. When I entered it he was sitting at his writing-table. I will not attempt to retrace here a portrait of the great poet's features. They are too well known from existing pictures, busts, and prints to require it. I need only say that, although upwards of eighty years had left their indelible traces on his countenance, it was still one of the most striking that had ever met my eyes. Rising from his seat, he gave me his hand, and with a good-natured smile, which put me at my ease at once, and satisfied me that he had not taken offence at my unauthorised note, he motioned to me to be seated, and asked me what was my object in visiting Germany. After a few minutes' general conversation he pointed to a large volume lying before him on the table, and said—

"'It is curious that when your visit was announced to me, I was engaged in making a few notes on your Old English literature. Is that a subject that has ever engaged your attention?'

"To this I was fortunately able to make an affirmative reply, as I had not long before, when at Oxford, spent some time in the study of Anglo-Saxon, and was, moreover, well up in Chaucer, which enabled me to elucidate a few old words and phrases which he had marked as requiring explanation. This circumstance evidently gave him pleasure, and he asked me whether I could not defer my departure for a day or two, adding that his daughter-in-law, Madame de Goethe, had a few friends coming to her in the evening, and that he should like to introduce me to her and to them. It is needless to say that I gladly acquiesced; and I spent two days agreeably in Weimar, passing half an hour of each morning with Goethe, and the evenings in the salon of Madame de Goethe, where I met all the best of Weimar society. On the third morning, when I went to take leave of the poet, after thanking him for all his kindness to me, I ventured to ask if

he would complete it by writing for me a stanza
which I might keep as an autograph memento
of my visit.   After a minute's reflection he wrote
for me the following quatrain :—

> " ' Liegt dir Gestern klar und offen,
>   Wirkst du heute kräftig treu ;
>   Kannst auch auf ein Morgen hoffen,
>   Das nicht minder glücklich sey.'

"I must add, alas! that after my return to
England I put away this autograph so carefully
that, on coming back from the United States,
where I spent the years 1834-5-6, I never could
find it again, though the stanza was indelibly
engraven on my memory. In 1869, nearly forty
years after my visit to Goethe, never having
met with the above quatrain among his published works, I sent the stanza with a note to
Carlyle, asking him whether it was to be found
among Goethe's printed works.

"This note elicited the following reply :—

·5 CHEYNE ROW, CHELSEA, *Nov.* 23, 1869.

DEAR SIR CHARLES,—Your agreeable letter from Lisbon
found me yesternight, and I was happy to be able to throw
some little light on your Inquiry. The Goethe quatrain,
given you in those interesting circumstances, and afterwards
lost, has hung here in facsimile of Autograph, attached to a
lithograph portrait of Goethe, for about forty - five years
now, and always regarded as one of the Penates of the
House. Where this lithograph Portrait was got I cannot
now recollect, but I think it must have been from Ham-
burg in 1826—as the readiest attainable Portrait of Goethe
—and in German Printshops most probably it is still on
sale as such. It does tolerably resemble, though quite
without flattery, an earnest, patient heavy-laden old man,
cheeks hollow, upper front teeth gone, &c. Bendixen and

Vogel, names unknown to me, are Painter and Engraver. Length of the Print, epigraph and all, is about 14 inches; epigraph itself about 3 inches. It was from this portrait that I took your quatrain, translated it, printed it some-where, not as the barbarous timber-headed Editor gives it, but accurately, thus :—

> Know'st thou yesterday, its aim and reason?
> Work'st thou well to-day for worthy things?
> Calmly wait to-morrow's hidden season,
> Need'st not fear what hap soe'er it brings.

The original and your remembrance of it differ only in one monosyllable, 'frey' instead of 'treu'—important only for the rhyme—and the Hand is evidently Goethe's in good strong Roman letters—facsimile completely correct—date, Weimar, 7th Nov. 1825. Not having the Index to my Goethe's 'Werke,' the final Cotta one, I cannot at once as-certain whether these lines are in Goethe's printed works or not, though I rather think they are. If you wish it ascer-tained, I will with pleasure have that done.

If you return to London while I continue here, pray call and see the picture and me. Glad of this pleasant, unex-pected passage between us, and begging always a place in your remembrance, I remain, yours sincerely,

T. CARLYLE.

P.S.

> "ZAHME XENIEN.
>
> " Liegt dir Gestern klar und offen,
> Wirkst du heute kräftig frey :
> Kannst auch auf ein Morgen hoffen,
> Das nicht minder glücklich sey,"

is in Goethe's 'Werke,' 1828, Ausgabe letzter Hand, vol. iv. p. 337. I have had it by heart for some forty years past, as also the one opposite to it on p. 336—

> " Halte dich im stillen rein,
> Und lass es um dich wettern ;
> Jeh mehr du fuhlst ein mensch zu seyn,
> Desto ähnlicher bist du den göttern."

Both in Section 4 of 'Zahme Xenien,' at the end.—T. C.

" In respect to the sentence in Carlyle's letter in
which he states that 'frey' instead of 'treu' is
important only for the rhyme, I must state my
conviction that in the quatrain as given to me by
Goethe (and which we now know had been composed three or four years before) the second line
ended with 'treu' and not 'frey,' and with all due
deference to the high authority of Carlyle, I
venture to affirm that in that place 'treu' is better
in sense, and as good in rhyme as 'frey.' Moreover, it is more actually represented by Carlyle's
own translation, 'Work'st thou to-day for worthy
things,' where 'frey' seems a mere expletive with
little meaning.   With respect to the rhyme, any
German scholar who takes an interest in the question may easily satisfy himself that (at least in
Goethe's opinion) the one word is as permissible as
the other, for he will find in the minor poems of
Goethe scores of passages in which the diphthong
'eu' is made to rhyme with 'ei' and 'ey.' Several
of these are now before me in the 'Xenien,'
'Freude' rhyming with 'Beide,' 'Scheu' with
'sey,' 'treu' with 'vorbei.'" [1]

The intercourse thus established between Murray and the philosopher of Chelsea continued till
Carlyle's last years of decrepitude.

It was natural that the scion of an old Whig
house, not being under the necessity of working
for a livelihood, should allow himself to be drawn

[1] The disputed line is quoted by Julius Hare in 'Memorials of
a Quiet Life' (vol. i. p. 429) as ending—"heute froh und frey."

into the vortex of politics. Murray attained
manhood in the years when the Reform agitation
was approaching its height. When the last un-
reformed Parliament was dissolved in 1832, he
offered himself for election for the Falkirk Burghs,
but without success, standing second on the poll,
between a Tory and a Radical. The following
year, 1833, on a vacancy occurring in the representation of Marylebone, he accepted an invitation
to stand in the Whig interest for that borough.[1]
A "Conservative-Whig" he called himself, and
as such received at first the support of the Tory
committee against the only other man in the field,
a Radical. But his sentiments on Free Trade in
general, and the Corn Laws in particular, were
too far advanced for the Tories, who deserted
him and nominated a candidate of their own
party, Mr Henry Beresford Hope, Murray's old
companion at Sunninghill. The result of this
manœuvre was the return of an out-and-out
Radical.

After this double reverse, Murray sought con-
solation in travel. Europe was not wide enough
to satisfy his craving for adventure and extended

[1] In his notes Sir Charles states that it was in 1837, on the eleva-
tion of Mr Portman, the member for Marylebone, to the peerage,
that he first contested that seat; but I have before me his printed
address to the electors of that borough dated 1833.

knowledge; he longed to explore the New World, at that time so much more remote from the Old one than it is reckoned in our day. A question had arisen about his father's title to some property in Virginia, the deeds of which, in the fourth earl's name,[1] had been found in the Capitol at Washington. Charles Murray was therefore commissioned to visit and report on the lands. Accordingly on 18th April 1834 he embarked at Liverpool on the American ship Waverley, of 530 tons, bound for New York. There occurs a reference to his departure in a letter from Rogers to Lady Dunmore.

"The young girls of this village [London] sigh and soften their voices when they mention him, as they often do in a corner to *me*. To them he is a creature of romance, though to their mothers the most dangerous of all detrimentals."

Four years had still to elapse before the Sirius and Great Western, pioneers of ocean steam navigation, were to begin the Atlantic passage at the modest speed of eight or nine knots an hour, and the voyage which a modern "ocean grey-hound" may be reckoned to accomplish in a little less or more than six days, in William IV.'s reign depended on the direction and force

---

[1] The third Earl of Murray had been Governor of Virginia.

of the wind. In this respect the passengers on board the Waverley were unlucky beyond the average. The ship fared well for the first seven days, making her eight knots under press of canvas before a fresh easterly breeze; but on the 27th the wind shifted north-west, blowing hard, and the vessel was hove to. On the evening of May 1, the gale having passed away, Murray was playing draughts in the saloon, when a fellow-passenger, the only one who had crossed the Atlantic before, rushed up and, grasping his arm, exclaimed, " Sir, the ship has sprung a leak ! "

" I defy any writer to describe exactly, or any reader to understand, the *first* sensations occasioned by an announcement of this nature, unless he has experienced them; for each succeeding suggestion, as the mind glanced over it with the rapidity of lightning, only seemed to magnify the peril of our situation, and almost to shut out hope: we were about 1200 miles from Liverpool and much more distant from New York, a high sea running, and only provided with boats which, in a calm, might contain one-fourth of the number on board." [1]

Everything under such circumstances depends

[1] Travels in North America. By the Hon. C. A. Murray. Third ed., vol. i. p. 10.

on the nerve and knowledge of the ship's captain. The Waverley was well commanded : Captain Phillips allowed no confusion ; the pumps were set steadily to work ; all the able-bodied men on board, both crew and passengers, were divided into gangs of eight, to relieve each other at the task. But as the wind was westerly, the ship was put about and all sail was made for the nearest European port. The pumps proved wholly inadequate to cope with the leak: so poorly found was the Waverley in this respect, that only four men could work at once; and on the morning of the 3rd it was found that the water was deepening in the hold. The cargo was chiefly pig-iron, the pressure of which had started one of the timbers, so it was determined to ease the ship by heaving it overboard. Twenty tons of crockery and seventy of iron had been disposed of by nightfall. The ship's course had been altered once more for the Azores, owing to the wind having veered to the north; but in the evening a heavy south-west gale arose, with fierce hail-squalls; the sea ran mountains high. Captain Phillips declared that in twenty-two years' experience of the Atlantic he had never encountered such weather.

The pumps would hardly work, owing to the rolling of the ship; the storm-jib was blown to pieces, and the Waverley scudded under bare poles towards the north-east—a direction contrary to that in which lay their only hope of making a harbour. The condition of the Waverley was almost past hope; nevertheless she weathered that night, and during the afternoon of the 4th the wind moderated, though a terrible sea was still running.

On the afternoon of May 5th, having been seventeen days at sea, they made a sail on the weather-bow, which proved to be an East India-man bound for London. She was short of water and provisions, and having still twelve hundred miles to run, could only offer to take off a dozen or so of the Waverley's complement. Then arose some hubbub among the passengers, of whom several were ladies, whether they should stick to their disabled vessel, or abandon the voyage and return in the Lady Raffles to England. Some of them consulted Murray in their anxiety: he said that he had no hesitation, and intended to remain. A number of Irish emigrants on board—about 150 of them—crowded aft towards the quarter-deck to see how many were going to leave the ship. They were within very little of becoming un-manageable, when one of them called out, "We'll just see what the young Scotch lord does: if he stays, it's all right." Of course Murray stayed, and, after putting off some of the passengers upon the other ship, these fellows went cheerily back to the labour of pumping and heaving out cargo.

There was an anxious half-hour later, however, when the steerage passengers, aching from their hard work, began clamouring for spirits, which the captain resolutely refused. A gang of Irishmen declared they would not go to the pumps without whisky. Firearms were loaded in the cabin to protect the spirit-room. The captain of the gang, a young Welshman, floored with his fist the first of the mutineers, and the second also. He told the next that there was no hope of whisky, but that a few more minutes' delay might send them all to the bottom. They went sulkily to the pumps, but when Murray jumped down among them and set to work, they all joined in, and there was no more trouble. On the morning of the 9th they were safely off Fayal, their cargo lost, their ship disabled, but every life preserved.

It took more than a month to refit the Waverley—leisure which Murray made use of in exploring the various islands in the Azores group. Indeed there is nothing that strikes the modern reader more forcibly throughout his narrative than the tolerance of detention, and the absence of all

that hurry and fuss which seem inseparable from
the movements of latter-day tourists. The Portuguese islanders, indeed, appear to have become
rather bored by their British visitors. The Irish
emigrants especially, having quarrelled with the
boatmen in the harbour, were engaged in more
than one serious affray, and Murray himself incurred the vengeance of a Portuguese shopkeeper
by felling a dog which flew at a lady with whom
he was walking. The dog died, and his owner
vowed that Murray should die also. A friendly
townsman warned him not to go out after dark,
upon which Murray marched straight into his
foeman's shop and taxed him, through an interpreter, with having threatened to take his life.

"I said it, and I meant it," replied the fellow,
sullenly.

"In that case," replied Murray, "let me inform
you that I always carry a brace of pistols" (which,
in fact, he never did), "and the first time I
see you out after sunset, I shall shoot you."

There was no more trouble on the score of
the dead dog.

Once more afloat, towards the middle of June,
the unlucky Waverley encountered further delay,
this time from persistent calms. The ordinary
voyage from Fayal to New York was reckoned

at sixteen days, but on this occasion the ship drifted about for six weeks, during the last ten days of which the rations were limited to mouldy biscuit, salt junk, and a very short allowance of filthy water, and went into quarantine at Staten Island on 26th July — fourteen weeks and two days after leaving Liverpool. Of such were the vicissitudes of a tourist when our fourth William was king.

Murray has left a minutely detailed account of his first impressions of New York,[1] which is not without the interest of contrast to readers who know the place as it is now. Sir Charles Vaughan, British Minister in the United States at the time, received the traveller with amazement, for it was confidently believed the Waverley had gone to the bottom.

Among the *nugæ* preserved in Murray's various note-books, there are many traces of his American experience which find no place in his published Travels. Of these the following may serve as a sample. During his stay in New York he made great friends with a fair one of very tender years, on whom, by reason of the length of her hair, he bestowed the name of Absolomina. She returned his affection, and, in turn, used to call him *grand-père*. Being invited to tea in the young lady's

---

[1] Travels, vol. i.

schoolroom one evening, and arriving rather late, Murray found that she had retired to bed. As she had told him that she did not believe he could put *two* rhymes together, he left the following jingle for her on the next morning, in which it must be admitted some technical difficulties have been overcome :—

" Oh ! Lady of the flowing hair,
How could you yester-evening dare
(Having invited me to share
At nine your tea-and-toasty fare)
To court the god of slumber, ere
My foot was heard upon the stair ?
I entered—looked—you were not there ;
Around I with surprise did stare
At empty room and vacant chair,
And wondered where on earth you were.
Then came your father to declare
He'd begged in vain you would but spare
One hour from sleep.   The pretty pair,
Which, from beneath your forehead fair
Spread, with their lustre soft and rare,
For careless hearts a dang'rous snare,
No more fatigue or light could bear,
And, sinking on their ' fringèd lair,'
Forgot at once me—tea—and care.
You thought I could not rhyme !—I swear
For polished style and graceful air,
That Milton's Muse or Shakespeare's ne'er
(Shakespeare's, forsooth ! a vulgar player)
With mine might venture to compare—
So buxom, blithe, and debonair.
Of this you're now perhaps aware :
Lovely Absolomina ! Fare-
you-well, and, in your gentlest prayer
To Heaven, remember old Grand-père."

In an expedition up the Hudson river Murray
was delighted to find a fellow-passenger in Fenimore Cooper, whose acquaintance he had made at
one of Rogers's breakfasts, and whose romances of
Indian life were then greatly in vogue. Later in
the autumn he went on a shooting expedition into
the west of Virginia, encountering some original
characters, in what was then a semi-civilised district. One of these was a certain Colonel M.,
whose acquaintance he made in Leesburg, known
as the victor in one of the fiercest duels ever
fought. The colonel having quarrelled with his
cousin, a general, and equally a fire-eater, knocked
him down. A challenge was the inevitable result,
the choice of weapons being left to the colonel,
who proposed that he and his adversary should
sit on the same barrel of gunpowder, and each
apply a match to it. This was declined by the
general, as also a suggestion that the cousins
should leap hand in hand from the top of the
Capitol; but the third proposal, that they should
fight with musket and ball at ten paces, was accepted. They met; the general was shot through
the heart, while the colonel got off with a shat-
tered wrist.

British visitors to America used to be prone,
perhaps a few are so still, to look with prejudice

on an English-speaking nation who betray un-
familiar traits. Sixty years ago the remembrance
of mutual resentment was still green between the
two nations; but Murray's eager, fresh intelligence
was captivated by a great deal that he observed in
the vigorous young community. He was shocked,
indeed, at the neglect with which the tomb of
George Washington at Mount Vernon was treated
at that time, but this only inspired him to a
panegyric on the national hero.

"The memory of Washington is dear to, and
revered by, not only America, but mankind; and
mankind had a right, according to all the rules of
good taste, good feeling, and good example, either
that the illustrious dust should have been allowed
to remain in the simple mound where it first slept,
shadowed by the melancholy boughs that first
waved over it, . . . or, if it had been removed, it
should have been to a sepulchre worthy of its
name and glory. . . . To no one who has ever
lived is the glorious Periclean elegy of πᾶσα γῆ
τάφος[1] more applicable than to Washington. . . .
The fame and glory of the illustrious dead can
neither be diminished nor tarnished by the neglect
of their countrymen; but does that palliate or
excuse such neglect?"[2]

Very different such honest criticism from the
carpings of the ordinary globe-trotter; and so the

[1] The whole earth his tomb.   [2] Travels, vol. i. p. 119.

American public felt it to be when Murray's book was published, though they were not less jealous of criticism by "Britishers" in those days than they are now, as may be seen from the following letter to Murray from the President of the United States :—

"ALBANY, *August 5th,* 1836

"MY DEAR SIR,—I was highly gratified to receive your kind note, and thank you sincerely for the obliging expression of respect and friendship which it contains. The satisfaction you have received from our short acquaintance has, I assure you, been more than reciprocated on my part. Casual visitors from your country to this are unfortunately so seldom desirous of seeing things here as they really are, or at least give themselves so little trouble to do so, and the right disposition in this regard having been so marked in you, I have, I confess to you, been not a little anxious about the result of your observations. My anxiety on this account, relieved in part by the general justice and frankness of your conversation, is now entirely removed by the generous and liberal sentiments of your note. No one could reciprocate more cordially than I do your wishes for a long continuance of the friendly relations at present so happily existing between our respective countries, and you may rest assured that nothing that I can do to promote that object shall be neglected.

"Do me the favour to make my best respects to Lord Lansdowne and Palmerston when you happen to see them.

" Accept my prayers for your safe return to your friends, and believe me to be very truly yours,

"M. VAN BUREN."

This was written before the publication of the ' Travels'; but that the impression remained the same afterwards is shown by the following letter, written from Mexico by Waddy Thompson :—

" I have just finished reading of your book of travels in the United States ; and feeling that I am your debtor for the happiness which it has afforded me, I hasten to acknowledge the debt. It is greatly to be regretted that the English travellers who have written books about the United States have been for the most part of a class who could not obtain admittance (as they did not deserve it) into the better circles either in the United States or in their own country, and their books are not unfaithful pictures of what they saw. Mrs Trollope's book, for example, is a most accurate description of that portion of our society into which alone could a vulgar woman as she is obtain an admittance. From gentlemen like yourself and Lord Morpeth we have nothing to fear but just criticism, and that is really a thing not to be deprecated, more especially when administered as you have done it, in that spirit in which 'a father chasteneth his children.'

" I do not use too strong a word when I say to you that I love the man who can see everything in a foreign land as you have seen and described ours."

It was for the institution of slavery that Murray
reserved his sternest displeasure, although he admitted that "from what I had seen of the social
qualities of the gentlemen at whose houses I was
a visitor [in Virginia], I was rather gratified than
surprised to witness the comparative comfort and
good usage enjoyed by their slaves." Their
clothing, food, and lodging were suitable to the
climate and their work.

"During the days that I spent in the neighbourhood I did not see any corporal punishment;
but each overseer was armed with a cowhide;
and one, with whom I had a long conversation
regarding the detail of his occupation, informed
me that he was obliged constantly to use the
lash, both to men and women; that some he
whipped four or five times a-week, some only
twice or thrice a-month; that all attempts to
make them work regularly by advice or kindness
were unavailing, for their general character was
stubborn idleness; and that many who were
cheerful, and even appeared attached to the
family, would not work without occasional hints
from the cowhide."

This overseer believed that slave labour was
most extravagant, partly from the prime cost (the
price of an able-bodied negro being, on an average,
£150), partly from the cost of maintenance, and

partly owing to the perpetual loss by disease or accident, death or running away. He was sure more revenue might be obtained if his employer's estate were let under lease.

But it was not because of the physical hardships of the slaves, nor on account of the wastefulness of slave labour, nor yet by reason of the horrors of the ocean traffic in human cattle, that Murray declaimed most vehemently against the system. He was a staunch Whig, and the worst feature in his eyes was the necessity for keeping these creatures in the grossest ignorance, for excluding them even from the knowledge of the sentiment lying at the root of all self-improvement and self-respect—the love of liberty.

Murray spent most of the winter in Washington, and an unpublished reminiscence of his sojourn there remains among his private notes. It is, perhaps, not particularly edifying, but it serves to show the kind of frame in which his gentle, cultivated nature was lodged.

"When I arrived at Washington on my travels through America, some foolish friend of mine talked about my various feats of strength, such as bending and breaking pokers over my arm, and above all, of putting my fist through a closed door. This annoyed me rather, but the climax came one

evening at a big party. There was amongst the
guests a little Dutchman, who pooh-poohed the
idea of its being possible to put a fist through
the panel of a door, upon which my friend, who
had more loyalty than tact, grew very angry,
and made a bet that I would not only do it,
but would do it then and there. When I was
told this, I flatly refused; but they urged that
my friend would lose his money, and so forth;
so with much reluctance I went up to the lady
of the house and told her the facts of the case,
and added, 'If, madam, you are kind enough to
allow me to make this experiment, I will naturally hold myself responsible for any harm that
may be done to your door, and will send an up-
holsterer to remedy it in the morning.' She
looked rather astonished, but very good-naturedly
said I might try my hand on her door. I waited
till nearly every one had gone in to supper and
the room was almost empty; then carefully shut-
ting the door, I planted myself firmly, brought
my fist against the panel, and, as usual, through
it went, amidst great applause. Unluckily, at
that moment a footman happened to be bringing
up a great pile of plates to the supper-room,
when just as he passed the door, through came
my fist and forearm, caught him right in the
chest, and felled him and his pile of plates with
a mighty crash to the ground. You can imagine
the hideous noise. Every one came rushing out
to see what the deuce was going on, and found
me, very shamefacedly, the culprit. Next day,
to my great annoyance, all Washington was ring-

ing with the story of the rough-and-ready English cub, who came to evening parties and broke doors and knocked down footmen. Meantime the Dutchman, seeing I had so easily done what my friend had claimed I should do, turned round and declared that after all it was perfectly easy—he could do it himself. I said nothing, as his bumptiousness annoyed me. Of course it is a great deal a knack, as well as strength; but the knack must be known, as the Dutchman found to his cost. He bared his arm and hit out at the door, but the door remained uninjured, while his wrist broke instead; so he lost his money, and got a nasty arm into the bargain."

In spring Murray revisited the West, taking in his tour Richmond, Jamestown, and Norfolk. He spoke gratefully, and even enthusiastically, of the simple hospitality which he encountered everywhere. Returning in April to Washington, he started again in May for Baltimore, crossed the Alleghanies in the rope-railroad—a great marvel in those days — passed through Pittsburg, embarked on the Ohio, and came near ending his days at Cincinnati, where, being attacked by cholera, he made and forwarded his will to the British Legation at Washington — a document which he had the satisfaction of reclaiming and tearing up the following year.

CHAPTER V.

1835.

ADVENTURES AMONG THE PAWNEES.

ONCE more re-established in health, Murray, resuming his travels, sailed up the Ohio to Louisville, and, as an instance of the discriminating nature of his criticism, there may be quoted his remarks on that town :—

"Louisville is an active and thriving town,[1] but, like all the others in the West, wretchedly lighted and paved *at present*. It is necessary to mark these two words, as in this most wonderful portion of this most wonderful continent, observations of a condemnatory nature are not likely to be true for more than twelve months."[2]

In passing through Lexington he was delighted

[1] The population of Louisville at the time of Murray's visit was under 11,000 ; in the census of 1880 it stood at 123,758.

[2] Travels, vol. i. p. 184.

at meeting Harriet Martineau ; and here again one is struck by the true liberality of Murray's mind, for nothing could be more directly opposed to his profound attachment to religious doctrine, conspicuous even at this early age, than the avowed scepticism of this writer.

"This lady's writings," he says, "are too well known to require any comment on them here. I differ from many of her opinions, but nobody can deny her possession of great talent, or refuse her the merit of writing in a clear, concise, and elegant style; moreover, her conversation is agreeable, lively, and varied, displaying a mind both strong and original, a judgment very decisive, though not without prejudice, and a quickness of observation and comparison that render her an entertaining as well as an instructive talker." [1]

His host at Lexington was the celebrated American statesman, Henry Clay, then in the zenith of his reputation, although he had been twice defeated in contests for the Presidency. Murray had already heard this famous orator during a debate in the Senate, and was greatly impressed with his voice and manner, which produced on him "that most powerful of all effects—a conviction that, if provoked, the lion could roar yet more terribly." How commonly is this grace of

[1] Travels, vol. i.

oratory neglected ! How seldom does one hear a
speech delivered without the impression that the
orator is launching all the thunder of which he is
capable !

In Mr Clay's house Murray made the acquaintance of a young German called Vernunft, also on
his travels. They struck up a friendship, and remained fellow-travellers for many months. Returning to Louisville, they passed down the Ohio
to St Louis, where Murray was anxious to see
some society, with the help of General Clarke, a
well-known writer, traveller, and authority on
Indian affairs. But finding that a steamer was
on the point of starting for the upper Missouri,
Vernunft and Murray agreed not to lose this
chance of penetrating the wilderness, hurriedly
purchased an outfit for camping, and in a few
hours were on their way to Fort Leavenworth,
then the westernmost military post of the United
States. Here at last the Fellow of All Souls
encountered the chance of adventure for which
he had hitherto pined in vain.

To understand the position, one must call to
mind the vast advance of white population which
has taken place since 1835, and the dwindling to
insignificance of the once powerful and multi-
tudinous Red Indians. At the time of Murray's

tour the total area of settlement in the United
States was not much more than 600,000 square
miles ; it now amounts to more than three times
that figure. The vast stores of mineral wealth in
Missouri, Colorado, Idaho, and California lay un-
suspected under virgin forest ; the Choctaw and
Chickasaw nations blocked advance westward in
Mississippi State, though the white population had
spread up the valley as far as the present site
of Kansas city. Over the unreclaimed lands the
Red Indians still hunted and fought, no one at
that time foreseeing their approaching fate. Those
sounding floods and slumbering lakes, those tower-
ing cones and winding cañons, those immemorial
forests and flowery plains—above all, the picturesque, mysterious tribes, by describing whose
high attributes, as well as their dauntless ferocity,
Fenimore Cooper had fired the imagination wherever the English language was read — such was
the scenery and such the people among which the
very atmosphere seemed charged with materials
for adventure.

Judge, then, of Murray's enchantment when, on
the 4th July, Commemoration Day, being seated
at dinner with the officers of the fort, the arrival
was announced of one hundred and fifty Pawnees.
A dozen of their principal braves were at once

invited into the mess-room: no whisky-sodden, degraded wretches these, like the Kickapoo tribe, who lived nearest to the frontier, but unspoiled, genuine sons of the forest, in deerskin leggings, buffalo-skin cloaks, bead necklaces, and earrings. Few of these men had ever been in a white settlement before, or even seen a chair or table; yet their self-possession and intuitive tact were perfect: they shook hands all round, seated themselves at table, sipped Madeira and smoked cigars without betraying a sign of wonder or committing the slightest absurdity.

"I do not think there was a countenance among them that could be pronounced handsome, though several were pleasing and good-humoured; but the prevalent character of their expression was haughty, impenetrable reserve, easily distinguishable through the mask of frank conciliation which their present object rendered it expedient for them to wear." [1]

In short, Murray was completely captivated: a visit to their encampment brought him to the hasty resolution of accompanying these Pawnees in returning to their "nation." Vernunft required little persuasion. With some difficulty they secured the services of a lad to lead the packhorses, and

[1] Travels, vol. i. p. 210.

of an Indian who could speak excellent Pawnee, execrable French, and no English, to serve as their only means of oral communication with their Redskin friends. Besides these, there was Murray's Scots valet, who, though excellent in his own sphere, could hardly be blamed for ignorance of what was required in the backwoods.

I have said that Murray often referred gratefully in his subsequent volumes to the hospitality he received everywhere in the United States; but I am indebted to one of his note-books for a token of the kindness of his American friends at Fort Leavenworth. He, Vernunft, and the Scots valet had spent nearly a week there, and before leaving he asked the messman to render his bill, which was done in the following graceful manner :—

To six days' board	.	.	.	$0 0 0
„ five nights' lodging	.	.	0 0 0
„ feeding dogs .	.	.	.	0 0 0
„ making four bags .	.	.	0 0 0
„ washing 13 pieces .	.	.	0 0 0
				$0 0 0

For several days Murray and Vernunft rode with the Indians, always in "Indian file," in a north-westerly direction, heartily enjoying life in the open and the glorious scenery, but much disappointed in the scarcity of game, on which they relied for supplying their larder. On July 16 the course was altered west-south-west, and the long march began to tell on their horses, nearly all of which had sore backs. After riding for nearly a fortnight, they overtook the Pawnee [1] "nation," that particular nomad branch of the Pawnee Indians to which Murray's braves belonged, encamped on a wide prairie.

"Our approach excited some curiosity and interest. The families of those who had been to the fort placed themselves in or near our path; and as the husband, father, or brother came near, the little kindred group would withdraw to a retired spot and indulge those feelings of curiosity and affection which nature has implanted as strongly in the bosom of the savage as of the civilised man. I witnessed with much pleasure the meeting of *my* old chief, Sâ-ní-tsă-rish, with his wives and children, which took place under a knot of fine trees a little to the right of our path. I could read in the glistening eyes of the women, and in the glad faces of the children, that the old man was a kind husband and father; and if the features of the parties had not been so totally devoid of anything like beauty, the family picture would have been as picturesque as it was interesting." [2]

---

[1] Now written *Pani* by American ethnologists.
[2] *Travels*, vol. i. p. 230.

Murray and his attendant were accommodated in the skin tent or summer lodge of Sa-ni-tsa-rish, while Vernunft and the other attendant were hospitably lodged with another brave. There were about six hundred lodges in the village, each of which contained, in addition to its human complement, an average of seven dogs. "It is needless to suggest," observes Murray, "the grand effect of a dog-chorus at midnight in the Pawnee village!" At last he had attained his desire. Civilisation, so far as his own environment of many hundreds of miles was affected, was as though it had never been.

Though this assemblage of lodges was called a village, it was in fact no more than a flying camp, and the next morning after the arrival of the Europeans the whole affair was packed up and the "nation" resumed its march. On July 22 Murray witnessed a sight which living man shall never see again. "Taraha! taraha!" was the cry: buffalo [1] had been found some fifteen miles off, and about a thousand braves [2] mounted in hot haste and set

[1] The American buffalo (more properly bison, *Bos taurus*), which swarmed in countless numbers until thirty years ago, is now believed to be totally extinct in a wild state, the only living representatives of the species being a small herd preserved in the Yellowstone Park.

[2] The Pawnees have wellnigh shared the fate of the buffaloes. This brave nation lived at almost constant warfare with the Dakota Indians. The Delawares defeated them badly in 1823; smallpox

off in pursuit. Then ensued great and reckless
slaughter, followed by a feast which Murray was
ill able to enjoy, because the only frying-pan he
possessed had been smashed, and Indian notions
of cooking were very sketchy.

Scarcely more exciting was the cry that went
forth the same evening—"Men have been seen!"
—on a runner from the out-pickets bringing news
of a band of Arikarees, a hostile branch of the
Pawnees, noted horse-stealers. The camp stood
to arms, the braves yelled war-songs, women chat-
tered, children screamed, dogs howled; all night
long the hubbub raged, of which the enemy took
advantage by stealing twenty-two horses during
the darkness. A few nights later the camp was
again attacked, this time by a band of 150 or 200
Cheyennes,[1] but these were easily beaten off.

On the whole, however, the tribe suffered little
molestation : for their human enemies, as for themselves, this was the season of plenty—the hunter's
harvest—and all over the far-stretching west the
Red Men were busy pursuing buffalo. For a few

afterwards wrought havoc among them, and in the American census
of 1880 they were numbered at no more than 1440 all told, living on
a reservation in the Indian territory.

[1] A tribe of the Algonquin family, now numbering only some 3000.
In physique and mental powers they are said to excel most other
Indians, but they do not seem amenable to civilisation, and live by
war and hunting.

weeks the novelty and freedom of the life and the exciting sport kept Murray and his German friend from wearying for the comforts of home and civilisation.

A small band of Otoes,[1] who, though a branch of the hostile Dakotas, were friendly to the Pawnees, joined the encampment during this season, and were permitted to hunt with the nation. Their chief, Iotan, spoke a little English, and Murray became interested in him, although with his English he had contracted an unhappy taste for ardent spirits, of which the Pawnees were wholly free. Iotan had lost his nose under circumstances which form part of Indian history, and were recounted to Murray by an eyewitness. Iotan quarrelled with his elder brother, the chief of the tribe, probably about buffalo, of which the *sacra fames* embittered many friends. This brother sprang suddenly on Iotan one day and bit off his nose. True to the national etiquette, Iotan suffered no other muscle of his countenance to move, though he must have felt that his brother, in depriving him of a convenient adjunct to expression, could scarcely plead .the excuse that it was any use to himself. He went to his lodge, washed

[1] The remnant of this tribe now inhabit a small reservation in Nebraska, in common with what is left of the Missouries. Together they number less than 500 souls.

his face (an extraordinary proceeding in Otoe circles), carefully loaded his rifle, stalked his bad brother, and shot him dead. Thereafter he surrendered himself to be judged by the Council of Braves, who unanimously elected him chief in place of the defunct.

In spite, however, of the constant interest which Murray found in studying the character, the manners, and the language of this primitive people, the situation was not without its drawbacks, which became more pressing and more numerous as the sense of novelty wore off. Truth to tell, the noble savage proved far from immaculate, either in personal habits or in morals. There were certain points in each to which Fenimore Cooper had given no prominence in his romances of Indian life. To put it plainly, a Pawnee encampment, both inside and outside the lodges, with its crowded population of human beings, horses, and dogs, was indescribably filthy, and Murray offers a few graphic details as some excuse for the longing he soon felt to get back to Fort Leavenworth.

"It is not a pleasant thing to comment upon nastiness of any kind; but a few trifles, of daily occurrence, may be necessary to rescue my companion and myself from the charge of caprice.

Imprimis: every article within the lodge (including my own skin, jacket, and shirt) was covered with vermin. These insects are, as is well known, of two species—the one frequenting the hair, the other the body. The former of these are considered by the Pawnee naturalists as *Pedicularis esculentus;* for whenever the squaws are unemployed in severer labour, they enjoy a feast of this kind, gathered either from the hair of their children or of each other. For many successive weeks I have observed them pass from half an hour to an hour of every day in this manner, and they really seem to eat this filthy vermin with no small satisfaction; but I have been told by traders that they will not eat them from the heads of the whites." [1]

As for the moral character of the Red Indian, before it was affected for good or ill by contact with the white man, it is melancholy to find that in this also disillusion awaited the travellers. For the old chief, Sa-ni-tsa-rish, with whom he lodged, Murray indeed conceived a warm affection and was able to entertain genuine admiration. He relates several traits of his generous and lofty character. But as for the rest, let him, no prejudiced critic, speak in his own words :—

" Every hour that I spent with the Indians impressed upon me the conviction that I had

[1] Travels, vol. ii. p. 8.

taken the only method of becoming acquainted
with their domestic character.   Had I judged
from what I had been able to observe at Fort
Leavenworth, or other frontier places, where I
met them, I should have known about as much
of them as the generality of scribblers and their
readers; and might, like them, have deceived
myself and others into a belief in their 'high
sense of honour,' their hospitality, their openness and love of truth, and many other qualities
which they possess, if at all, in a very moderate
degree.   And yet it is no wonder if such impressions have gone abroad, because the Indian, among
whites, or at garrison, trading post, or town, is as
different a man from the same Indian at home as a
Turkish mollah is from a French barber.   Among
whites he is all dignity and repose : he is acting a
part the whole time, and acts it most admirably.
He manifests no surprise at the most wonderful
effects of machinery—is not startled if a twenty-
four pounder is fired close to him, and does not
evince the slightest curiosity regarding the thousand things that are strange and new to him;
whereas at home the Indian chatters, jokes, and
laughs among his companions—frequently indulging in the most licentious conversation ; and his
curiosity is as unbounded and irresistible as that
of any man, woman, or monkey on earth.

"Truth and honesty (making the usual excep-
tions to be found in all countries) are unknown or
despised by them.   A boy is taught and encouraged
to lie and steal, and the only blame or disgrace
ever incurred thereby is when the offence is de-

tected. I never met with liars so determined, universal, or audacious. . . . But from all these charges I most completely exonerate my old chief, Sa-ni-tsa-rish. Nature had made him a gentleman, and he remained so, in spite of the corrupting examples round him." [1]

Unsatisfactory though they were, these Red Men, from an ethical point of view, in appearance they fulfilled a very high æsthetic ideal. They were always picturesque, whether attired in gorgeously painted buffalo robes, or in blue-and-white blankets which floated behind them as they galloped, or in the extreme of Pawnee dandyism— in scarlet cloth, with glittering beads on arms and necks. Nothing seems more sensitive to corruption by contact with civilisation than the æsthetic instinct, often unerring, of primitive races. These Pawnees were absolutely unsophisticated : the only alteration they had made in their hereditary habits was the substitution, in part, of cheap Birmingham firearms for bows and arrows and spears, yet the hundred and fifty braves who had formed the deputation to Fort Leavenworth had each received the present of a common English round hat. These they considered " great medicine," and strutted about on

[1] Travels, vol. i. p. 249.

feast days wearing them, still wrapped in brown paper and string, on the top of their other finery, or, when the weather was warm, as their sole article of clothing.

Before resuming the narrative of Murray's pilgrimage, I must quote one more page from his work, containing, as it does, a picture so characteristic of these Children of the Waste :—

" The son of Sa-ni-tsa-rish was a great Pawnee dandy : we had hunted antelope and elk several times together, and I always considered him very quiet and good-tempered. He used to call me his brother ; and while we were going to or returning from a hunt, would teach me Pawnee words and phrases. He was now holding in his hand a kind of Mexican bridle, which he wished to put over the head of his horse ; but the latter, a fine, half-broken animal, backed, and would not let him approach. With the foolish violence common among Indians on such occasions, he stood directly before it, hauling hard upon the *laryette*. Of course this made the animal pull against him and back still further, when, with a sudden movement of rage, he drew his scalp-knife, sprang at the horse like a tiger, and buried the blade in its eye.

" The old chief was standing by, looking on with the imperturbable nerves of an Indian : he neither spoke a word nor moved a muscle, because the young man was grown up, and was among the warriors of the tribe ; but I could not resist saying

to him, 'That was not good.' The chief answered
gravely, 'No.' I then turned to observe the son.
As soon as he became sensible of what he had
done in a moment of passion, he was vexed and
ashamed, but too haughty to show it; and, walking to a spot about twenty yards distant, throwing
his scarlet blanket over his shoulder, he drew himself up to his full height, and there stood — a
motionless statue. The camp moved on,[1] and long
after the last straggler had left the place, I saw
him standing in the same attitude on the same
spot. The poor horse was led off by one of the
boys; and as I saw the heavy drops of blood
coursing each other down his innocent nose during
all the march of that day, while the hanging head,
the flapping ears, and the trailing limbs showed
the acuteness of his sufferings, I wished to ter-
minate them by putting a musket-ball through his
head; but it would not have been prudent to ask
permission to do so. I went on my way, sickened
with disgust at the cruelty of the young chief.
He *felt*, however, though he would not display
them, both sorrow and shame, for he kept aloof
from the band all day."[2]

By the middle of August, Murray and Vernunft
felt that they had experienced quite enough of
Indian life. They had fulfilled their purpose of
spending a few weeks in observing the Red Man
at home, and the advancing season, as well as

---

[1] This incident occurred at the beginning of a day's march.
[2] Travels, vol. i. p. 332.

sundry circumstances which had arisen, warned
them that it was high time to make a start
homewards. But Fort Leavenworth lay many
hundreds of miles to the east, across the pathless
wilderness: fresh horses were a necessity, for
which their remaining articles of exchange hardly
sufficed as a fair value, let alone such fancy prices
as the growing rapacity of the Pawnees, now
only too evident, might exact. Then a guide or
guides were indispensable, and none were forthcoming; added to which the Indians were as
jealous of any independent party traversing the
prairie at the risk of setting the all - important
buffaloes on the move, as any Highland stalker
could be of trespassers in his forests.

In short, it became apparent that the travellers
were on the brink of an awkward predicament.
Every wandering " nation" could not be expected
to be as friendly towards inquisitive whites as
the Pawnees had proved; and even among the
Pawnees signs were not wanting of a disquieting
character. Sa-ni-tsa-rish had been superseded
in command of the nation by the chief of the
Grand Pawnees—an allied and senior tribe, which
had joined forces with Murray's Indians for the
better bullying of buffaloes. This picturesque per-
sonage evidently regarded the European travellers

as promising subjects for exploitation : Murray's
" medicine-tube," or stalking telescope, was far too
remarkable an instrument to be viewed with indifference, and the grand chief soon caused him to
understand that it was extremely bad taste that
he—a white chief—should continue to lodge with
Sa-ni-tsa-rish, and offered him quarters in his own
lodge. Murray, however, excused himself, and
the jealous potentate closed the colloquy with an
angry "Ugh !" and an expression of countenance
the reverse of amiable. Other eyes had dwelt
with longing on the "medicine-tube," as well as
on Murray's fine double - barrelled Purdey rifle,
decidedly more desirable than the thirty-shilling
"trade" single - barrel, which formed the usual
artillery of a brave ; and more than once Murray
and Vernunft found themselves followed in a very
suspicious manner, when, strolling outside the intolerably filthy camp, they sought to enjoy the
balmy evening air.

An exceedingly awkward incident occurred on
12th August 1835. After interminable haggling
and disappointment, the travellers had got together
guides and horses, and started on the homeward
track the day before. Vernunft had been disabled
by a fall from a brute of a horse with which a
cunning brave had "stuck" him ; and Murray, full

H

of thoughts of the sport that opened that day on the far-away Scottish moors, set out alone to get some fresh meat. After a long walk, he descried a single buffalo grazing on a hill-top, which, by a difficult stalk, he approached within eighty yards. Just as he was raising himself slightly to take aim, the report of a rifle rang out, and a bullet hummed at what seemed a very short distance over his head. A Pawnee gentleman had been stalking *something*: whether it was the buffalo or himself, Murray could not swear to, though he had a strong suspicion. At all events, when the Pawnee, having explained how he missed the buffalo, began to reload, Murray stopped him sharply, saying that it was quite unnecessary, seeing that he himself had two barrels undischarged. Certainly this was not exactly the company in which a stranger would care to lose his way, yet this is exactly what happened. Murray was completely out of his bearings, and at nightfall had to accompany his dubious acquaintance to a small encampment of Pawnees eight or ten miles off.

"I now found myself in a very unpleasant predicament. My life, indeed, was not in much danger, because I might, probably, have been permitted to accompany these Indians to the

Pawnee villages on the Platte, where I might
have waited until some trading party should go
down the Missouri; but my condition, in this
case, would not have been very enviable. With
neither horse, clothes, nor blanket, and with a
very small stock of ammunition, I was certainly
not well equipped for a long journey and residence
with the Pawnees; neither did I think that my
own party could get on very well without me,
as Vernunft was crippled, and none of them were
hunters. So I determined to sally forth and seek
them at all risks." [1]

It was now dark, but the sky was clear, and
Murray, taking his bearings by the pole-star and
the door of the lodge, which, according to invari-
able Indian custom, faced due east, set off alone in
search of his party. He affected great confidence
before his Pawnee hosts, who believed he was
making "great medicine," but in truth his hopes
were low: he had been walking all day; he had
nothing between himself and starvation but two
or three slices of buffalo-beef hung to his belt,
nothing between his skin and the cold night but
a dirty calico shirt. By almost incredible luck,
after travelling for some hours through a hilly
tract of country he discerned the glimmer of a
camp-fire. Approaching it stealthily, lest it might

[1] Travels, vol. ii. p. 36.

come from a party of strange Indians, he found to his great relief that it was his own comrades.

But the travellers were only at the beginning of their troubles. At the close of the second day's march their Pawnee guides mutinied and refused to proceed. To punish them as they deserved would not have been prudent; they would have deserted instantly, and probably would have returned with a strong party to raise the scalps of the Palefaces. So Murray, making the best of a bad business, ordered them out of the camp, "and they slunk off, leaving us seated with great dignity and apparent ease."

The dignity may have been real, but ease was a hollow show; and the difficulties thrown upon Murray, on whom now devolved the duties of guide, may be realised from the following description of the first day's march :—

"Never since we entered the prairies of the West had we been entangled in such a labyrinth of steep, irregular, and broken ridges as those which obstructed our progress. As soon as one height was attained, another and a higher rose before us. In the ascent the packs slipped over our mules' and horses' tails ; in the descent, over their necks and ears. It was in vain that I halted my party and rode to the right and left ; I could find no practicable escape from the tumultuous and confused mass of hillocks, which were not (as is usually the case with the heights in the western prairies) in a regular succession of ridges, like the Atlantic in a gale of wind, but like the short, broken, irregular seas raised by heavy squalls from opposite quarters in the Irish Channel.

"I soon found that the shades of night would overtake us in this disagreeable situation unless I again directed our course to Snake river, which I reluctantly did, and we encamped at a place not more than four or five miles south-east from the spot where the guides had left us." [1]

To add to the hazard of their situation, a terrific thunderstorm, with torrents of rain, raged throughout the night, drenching the whole party and causing great suffering from cold, for of course they had neither tent nor Indian lodge to protect them.

"When I reflected upon the strange contrast of our present mode of life, as compared with our usual habits in society; when I reflected what severe colds are produced by sitting for an hour with wet feet, or sleeping in shirts only rather damp, and then looked upon our present party, after we had been lying for seven or eight hours without a fire and perfectly soaked through, I could not help feeling surprised, and I hope I may add grateful, for the health we had enjoyed and still preserved." [2]

[1] Travels, vol. ii. p. 52.   [2] Ibid., vol. ii. p. 53.

Perhaps even in stranger contrast than that
which their physical surroundings presented to
the native environment of these white men, appear some of the reflections which Murray noted
in his diary as they passed through his mind.
Each night as they advanced a watch had to be
set, for if any Indian horse-stealers had made
a successful raid, their situation would have been
desperate indeed. Wrapped in his buffalo robe
during his tour of duty one starlit night, this
British dandy kept himself awake by repeating
the opening lines of the 'Agamemnon' of Æschylus :—

Φρουρᾶς ἐτείας μῆκος, ἣν κοιμώμενος
   .   .   .   .   .   κυνὸς δίκην,
ἄστρων κάτοιδα νυκτέρων ὁμήγυριν,
καὶ τοὺς φέροντας χεῖμα καὶ θέρος βροτοῖς
λαμπροὺς δυνάστας ἐμπρέποντας αἰθέρι.[1]

For a week Murray guided the little party of
four (including himself) towards the Kansas river,
which it was his main object to strike. Luckily
none of the others was strong enough to dispute his ruling, for had any difference of opinion
arisen, they would almost certainly all have per-
ished in the wilderness. There was some mur-

[1] " Stretched on the ground like a dog, gazing at the starry hosts
of night, those brilliant rulers shining forth in the heavens, and
bringing to mortals the changes of summer and winter."

muring on August 20th, when the leader, on
emerging from a wooded valley, struck out in a
direction exactly contrary to that which his followers judged the right one. Murray carried a
compass, but he had become so accustomed to
guide his course by the sun that he led straight
on in a northerly direction without consulting
the instrument. He overheard his Scottish servant grumbling to the American lad, "Where
on earth is he taking us now? Why, we are
going back exactly where we came from." Murray turned and asked him to point out the direction in which *he* thought Fort Leavenworth lay.
The man did so; on which his master pulled out
the compass, and showed him that he was pointing south - west, in the direction of Santa Fé
and the Gulf of California.

It was a joyful moment when Murray, on the
following day, riding as usual some distance ahead
of the others, drew rein on a hill-top, and beheld
a long bending line of sloping woods, already
tinged with the glow of early autumn. Throwing
himself from his horse, he rendered thanks to
the Almighty, for he felt that the worst of the
danger was past. They were still in the unaltered
wilderness, soaked in every thread they wore by
persistent rain, but he felt sure that the winding

valley before him was the course of the Kansas
river, which he knew ran athwart the true line
of march to Fort Leavenworth. For some days
they had been endeavouring to follow an old
Indian trail, but this had been so completely
obliterated from time to time that when they
picked it up again they had no assurance that
it was the right one. There were also several
crossing and parallel trails. Now, however, Murray thought that they had proof of the correct-
ness of the clue to the labyrinth; but still the
river had to be crossed, and this was no simple
matter in its flooded condition.

"Of course my office of guide left me no choice
as to whether I should try and discover the ford;
though the experiment was not agreeable, as the
river was from one hundred and fifty to two
hundred yards wide, and so swollen and muddy
from the present and the late rain that it was
not easy to ascertain its depth except by sounding. I must confess that I am but an indifferent·
swimmer in a strong stream, although I did not
on this occasion feel any doubt of being able to
get across. Arming myself with a long pole, and
throwing off my jacket, I went in. I was soon
over the middle; before I got half-way across I
was up to the chest, and could not keep my feet
owing to the strength of the current; so I struck

out, swam a few strokes, and tried again for the bottom, but could not touch it. I therefore thought it better to swim till I was near the bank : I did so, and came safe to land. After a tedious search for the trail, I found it about three hundred yards below the place where I had crossed. I now entered the water again, and with some trouble made out the ford, and returned to conduct my companions and the baggage. By feeling the way carefully with my pole, and winding along a kind of ridge which appeared to be in the bed of the river, I was able to get them over without their getting wet much above the middle."

The nights of August 22nd and 23rd were the most miserable the travellers had hitherto endured. The rain descended without pause ; every stick in the forest was soaked, and their utmost exertions hardly succeeded in producing the semblance of a fire.

" Instead of a blaze, it emitted a kind of sulky, cheerless glare ; and instead of heat, a hissing, frizzing sound, with volumes of smoke. We were lying in the same clothes in which we had crossed the river, and the rain was so continuous that we were actually in puddles of water. Buffalo skins, when thoroughly drenched, are the most cold, soapy, comfortless covering that can be used ; so that I was warmer when wrapped only in my light Highland plaid than under the thickest robe in our collection." [1]

Moreover, the personal wardrobe of the party had become of a most honorary kind. Vernunft's last pair of trousers had vanished from the effect of constant riding; he had no stockings, and his nether limbs were covered only by a pair of wash-leather drawers and mocassins, while a tattered blanket thrown over his shoulders concealed all that remained of what were once jacket and shirt.

"I was sitting with an old woollen coloured night-cap on my head, a faded shirt of printed calico, . . . while my nether man was protected by a pair of coarse corduroy breeches, without drawers, and plastered to my skin with wet; grey worsted stockings full of holes, and shoes full of water." [2]

On the third day after crossing the Kansas it became apparent to Murray that they were following the wrong trail. He made up his mind that they had struck the Kansas nearly one hundred miles lower than the point where they had crossed it in the outward journey, a conclusion which was justified in a singular

[1] Travels, vol. ii. p. 85.   [2] Ibid., vol. ii. p. 86.

manner on the following day, August 25th. A
large cross-trail ran at right angles to the northerly course they were pursuing. Murray was of
opinion that it was their own trail which they
had made in the beginning of July. The American lad agreed with him, but Vernunft and the
Scotsman were of a contrary opinion. Murray
set off alone to explore it, and try to pick up
some remembered landmarks. He had not ridden
more than two hundred yards when, observing
a small white object in the brake not far from
the path, he dismounted to examine it. It proved
to be a scrap of the advertisement sheet of the
Times newspaper. He rode back with it in
triumph to his comrades, and immediately they
struck into their old trail, with lighter spirits
than they had felt for a fortnight, though nine
long days' marches still lay between them and
anything approaching to comfort.

It is unnecessary to trace their adventures
further in this place, though every page of the
original narrative is full of vigour and interest.
Picking up a brace of prairie-hens here, a badger
there, to eke out their scanty larder, for elk and
deer were hardly ever even seen, and Murray's
duties as guide left him little strength to devote

to stalking them, they arrived safely at Fort
Leavenworth on September 3rd, where they once
more enjoyed the luxury of exchanging saluta-
tions in their own language.[1]

[1] George Catlin, whose work on the North American Indians remains the standard authority on the subject, has the following note
to his chapter on the Pawnees (vol. ii. p. 25) : "Since the above was
written I have had the very great pleasure of reading the notes of
the Hon. Charles A. Murray, who was for several months a guest
among the Pawnees ; and also of being several times a fellow-traveller with him in America, and at last a debtor to him for his
signal kindness and friendship in London. Mr Murray's account
of the Pawnees, as far as he saw them, is without doubt drawn
with great fidelity, and he makes them out a pretty bad set of
fellows. . . . There is probably not another tribe on the continent
that has been more abused and incensed by the system of trade and
money-making than the Pawnees. Mr Murray, with his companion,
made his way boldly into the heart of their country, without guide
or interpreter, and I consider at great hazard of his life. . . . I
congratulate him on getting out of their country as well as he did."

CHAPTER VI.

1835–1837.

AMERICAN TRAVELS CONTINUED.

MURRAY, it might be supposed, had seen enough of the Red Men and their ways to satisfy him for one season, but his ardour and energy were indefatigable. He spent several days at Fort Leavenworth in visiting villages of Kickapoo and Powtawatomie Indians, and collecting vocabularies of their language. These tribes had become sadly debased by their intercourse with white Christians, and had exchanged most of their free, wild traits for habits the reverse of exemplary.

"I know not why it is," writes Murray, "but there is no human being (except a woman) that affects me with such inexpressible pity and disgust, when under the influence of liquor, as an Indian. I know this is unphilosophical, because it certainly is a greater disgrace and debasement to a white

man. Still, I then feel my pity lost in my disgust ;
while in the case of an Indian (although I have
lived too long among them to believe any more
tales of their innocence, simplicity, &c.) my fancy
fondly clings to the delusion of that state 'when
wild in woods the noble savage ran.'   Thus,
when I see him grovelling in the dirt, with a
helpless body and a reeling brain, and uttering
thick and half-choked sounds, I cannot help thinking, 'We have done this !—we, who boast of our
civilisation—we, who pretend to spread abroad the
refinement of art and science, and the purity of
the Gospel among the nations—we have reduced
the eagle eye, the active limb, the stately form of
our red brother to the grovelling, swinish animal I
now see before me.'   Of all the plunderers, thieves,
and landsharks on earth, there are none that
I more detest, none that will hereafter have a
heavier charge against them, than those settlers
and traders in the West (whether British or
American) who cheat the Indians of three
hundred per cent in every bargain by making
whisky the medium of purchase, knowing, as
they well do, that it leads to the degradation,
the misery, and, ere long, the extirpation of the
purchasers." [1]

Having returned to St Louis, Murray started
again to visit the lead-mines and other places on
the Upper Mississippi. Here he came in contact
with a white population before whose drunkenness

[1] Travels, vol. ii. p. 189.

and abandonment of all restraint his Pawnee friends shone as models of domestic and social virtue. He speaks of the Irish miners as a very numerous and troublesome body. Whig as he was by training and inclination, Murray was far from satisfied with the government of Ireland by Great Britain ; but he describes himself quite unable to indorse the opinion that Irish turbulence owed its origin, as many believed, to defects in the Constitution and its administration.

" It may be *partly* so ; but no more. The Irish in America—in every State from Maine to Louisiana—where they certainly are not oppressed, and are free from tithes, from heavy taxes, from ecclesiastical burthens, from want, in short from every subject of complaint and grievance in Ireland, are still the most improvident, quarrelsome, turbulent population on this continent." [1]

That these words were written more than sixty years ago does not render them less worthy of consideration now, when every grievance of which Irishmen complain, except the maintenance of the Union, has been generously dealt with in the Imperial Parliament, yet the complaints remain as bitter and as constant as ever.

At Dubuque, on the Platte, now a large manu-

[1] Travels, vol. ii. p. 179.

facturing town, then a mining village with plenty
of drinking-bars, and one small, low room where
divine service was conducted occasionally, Murray
attained some distinction by daring the bully of
the place. A tall, stout fellow, with an evil
countenance, this worthy was a great boxer, but
was not squeamish about resorting to less chivalrous methods of revenge, for he had stabbed more
than one man within the previous ten days.
Murray was sitting reading in a bar when this
fellow entered and ordered him out of his way, as
he wanted a drink. Murray calmly told him to
walk round, as there was plenty of room. The
bully looked amazed, but, to the surprise of the
landlord and his other customers, he did as he
was bid and took his dram quietly.

Murray's next experience of the wilderness was
in company with a hunting party of Winnebago
Indians; but they were bad companions, being
jealous of the white hunters, and doing all in their
power to spoil their sport, even to firing the woods
and prairies, so as to drive off the game, and,
if possible, to grill their rivals in the chase.

Christmas was spent in New Orleans, after
which Murray paid a visit to Cuba, and some of
his observations on that island are not without
interest in relation to recent events.

"The military force in Cuba is greater than I could have imagined, considering the state of its mother - country ; indeed I very much doubt whether the Queen could bring into the field as large a body of troops in Spain as her powerful deputy commands in Cuba. As far as I am able to collect, he has nearly twenty - five thousand regular troops and forty thousand militia." [1]

After exploring the island of Cuba, Murray returned to the mainland and passed some very agreeable weeks in the Southern States—ten days at Charleston were especially festive, a week at Baltimore, and so to Philadelphia, "which has always been my favourite of all the American

---

[1] Cuba was taken by the British under Lord Albemarle in 1762, but was restored to Spain by the Treaty of Paris in the following year. As an example of contrast in the method of administering colonial possessions, this Spanish colony may be compared with the British empire in India. In Cuba not only have the aborigines been completely exterminated by the conquerors, but the present native population has been deprived of political, civil, and religious liberty, the government being administered wholly by officials sent from Madrid. A population of less than a million and a half settled on an area of 45,883 square miles has been in a chronic state of insurrection since 1829.

In British India and Burmah there is a population of upwards of 240,000,000 (exactly double Gibbon's estimate of the Roman empire at the height of its power), on an area of about 1,500,000 square miles. Of these persons only 250,000 (less than 1 per thousand) are Europeans or of European blood. The policy has been to preserve perfect religious liberty, to regard race as no disqualification for political or civil responsibility, and to respect the authority of native rulers who govern peaceably and well. The British garrison consists (in 1895) of 74,299 British troops and 129,963 natives.

I

cities : there is more quiet and leisure, more symptoms of comfort, than elsewhere. It contained many of my friends, and in the beauty of its women it yields to no place that it has yet been my lot to visit." [1]

Subsequently he made a journey to the Alleghanies, once the territory of the proudest and most powerful of all the Indian nations — the Lenni Lenape, or Delawares.

" Alas ! I have seen the remnant of that tribe which once numbered its warriors by thousands. The white man has pressed and pushed them gradually westward, and their small village is now near the junction of the Kansas with the Missouri, some hundreds of miles to the north-west of St Louis. [2] In dress and agriculture they are half civilised, but in heart and spirit they are still Indians, still brave and haughty ; and being better armed than the western tribes, and more accustomed to the use of the rifle, a small party of them go annually to the Rocky Mountains to hunt, and they have given several signal defeats with unequal force to

[1] Travels, vol. ii. p. 275. At the time of Murray's visit Philadelphia numbered about 140,000 inhabitants. It is still, as it was then, the second city in population of the United States, containing about one million inhabitants.

[2] Various removals took place subsequent to this date, until in 1866 the survivors broke up their tribal organisation, accepted lands in severalty, and became civilised, prosperous citizens. The Delaware Indians now amount to not much more than one thousand souls.

bands of the Pawnees, Rickarees, and Blackfeet, by whom they have been attacked. I do not believe they would now muster two hundred warriors. Human nature cannot help giving a momentary sigh at their gradual approach to extinction." [1]

Modern travellers, rushing through the United States in Pullman cars, certainly enjoy such ease and economy of time as were undreamt of sixty years ago. On the other hand, the impressions they receive of the scenery are far more fugitive, their intercourse with the inhabitants far less intimate, than those brought about by the old system of locomotion. Murray preferred to perform his journeys on horseback, except where he availed himself of river steamboats.

"From Albany I proceeded on horseback to Lake Otsego, a distance of fifty-four miles, which I easily performed on my active nag in less time than the coach, which started at the same hour, although it had three or four relays of horses, so deep and muddy were the roads. Indeed, I have no hesitation in saying that it was far less fatiguing to ride those fifty miles than to have performed them in the stage." [2]

At Lake Otsego, once the country of the famous Mohawk Indians, he spent several days with an

[1] Travels, vol. ii. p. 308.   [2] Ibid., vol. ii. p. 323.

English widow, whose husband had built a regular
English country-house in this lovely spot, and
enjoyed himself in fishing and other sport. But
what impressed itself most on Murray's memory
was an afternoon spent with "the Walter Scott
of the Ocean," as he terms Fenimore Cooper. The
works of this once popular writer have been ousted
from the high place which they at one time shared
in the estimation of English schoolboys in common
with those of Marryat and Mayne Reid; but there
is no doubt that such degree of forbearance as the
Indian tribes have experienced at the hands of the
ever-advancing whites is chiefly owing to the
romantic interest with which Cooper invested the
Red Man by his long series of fascinating novels.
Murray had experience of the seamy side of Indian
life; yet he, too, was deeply penetrated by the singular contrast between the high intellectual powers
of this people and their rude, arduous existence.
He discerned their defects, but he also perceived
much to admire. If they were often treacherous,
mendacious, and avaricious, he recognised these
qualities as not unknown in European races; and
to some individuals among the Indians, such as
the Pawnee chief Sa-ni-tsa-rish, a lofty morality
seemed to come naturally; while as a nation they
were singularly brave, patient of pain and fatigue,

and exceedingly affectionate. So in after-years, and in a very different scene, Murray published a romance, 'The Prairie Bird,' in which he presents some of the characters he met, and describes some of the incidents which he had witnessed or heard of, in his wanderings among the Indians. This book went through many editions: it is still to be found on railway bookstalls in this country, and has proved a special favourite with American readers. But there falls first to be noticed the two volumes of 'Travels in North America' from which such liberal quotations have been made in the foregoing pages.

This book also found much favour with readers. It was first published by Richard Bentley in 1839, and dedicated to the Queen. It is interesting, bearing in mind the significance of the Diamond Jubilee celebrations of 1897, to read one sentence in the brief dedicatory epistle addressed to the youthful monarch who had just ascended the throne, containing as it does a prophecy and a prayer, both of which have been fulfilled far more literally and completely than their writer can have foreseen.

"It has been customary to clothe a dedication in the language of panegyric: I will not presume to follow the tempting precedent. Your Majesty's qualities will be attested by an Empire, and be recorded by History. Nevertheless, I trust I may venture, unblamed, to express on this occasion my earnest desire and my heartfelt prayer that your reign may be long and happy, and that Britain will hereafter look back with regret and pride on a Sovereign who blended the wisdom and energy of Queen Elizabeth with the more winning and attractive attributes of her sex." [1]

A bold aspiration about a girl of nineteen, yet one which it is impossible that events should have more amply justified.

Allusion has been made already to the appreciation bestowed by American readers on an author who passed such kindly, yet wholesome, criticism on the people among whom he was travelling. One more quotation may be made from Murray's pages, because it may be applied as usefully as when it was written to the present mutual attitude of English and Americans, and illustrates the large-minded discernment of the writer :—

"There remains one more American characteristic, frequently noticed by travellers, on which I wish, in conclusion, to offer a few observations. I allude to the national vanity with which the Americans are usually charged by English writers. Its existence and prevalence I admit; but I am

[1] At the time these words were written Murray was Master of the Queen's Household.

very far from viewing it as a heinous offence, or
as deserving the animadversion which has been so
generally bestowed upon it.   In truth, I know not
any nation that has ever been distinguished in
history, where this has *not* been a national characteristic; and certainly it has never been carried
to a greater height than in Britain.   There is not
a popular poem, or ballad, or proverb, in which our
superiority over every other people is not set forth;
neither is there a sailor in our fleet who does not
believe that one Englishman is equal to three
Frenchmen, as certainly as that three and one
make four.   Look, again, at the gallant nation
last named, and see in their drama, in their
ballads, in their proclamations, whether it is not
assumed as an indisputable fact that, of the hab-
itable earth, France is the mistress — Paris the
capital." [1]

Fifteen years later, in 1854, a third edition of
the 'Travels' was called for, in the introduction
to which Murray makes mournful reference to
the fate which had overtaken his Pawnee friends
in the interval :—

"That portion of the Journal which refers to
my residence with the Pawnee tribe of Indians
possesses a melancholy interest from the fact that
the unlucky band with whom I travelled and
hunted the bison have since been swept away
from the face of the earth.   Some years after I

[1] Travels, vol. ii. p. 303.

left them the smallpox desolated the tribe, and
while many of the warriors were prostrated by
its effects, they were attacked by their hereditary
enemies, the Dakotas, or Sioux, who, sparing
neither man, woman, nor child, completed the
destruction which the malady had commenced.
Many years will not elapse before the other
Indian tribes on the North American continent
will melt away like the snow in spring; and it
is more than probable that before the termination
of this century not a single bison, nor a single
descendant of the Red lords of the soil, will remain
between the Mississippi and the Pacific.[1]   The
philanthropist, the philologer, the antiquary, and
the lover of the romantic, may sigh over the hard
necessity of civilisation, which seems destined to
overwhelm in oblivion all records of these interesting tribes; but the onward march of the Anglo-
Saxon with the rifle and steam, and commerce in
his train, will not be stayed.   Before long the
fierce and warlike Dakotas and Blackfeet, Up-
sarokas and Comanches, whose tomahawks have
drunk the blood of their enemies for centuries past,
will either be destroyed altogether or be reserved
for the still harder fate of cringing submissively
at the feet of the once-despised Paleface, like the
half-civilised Indians on the banks of the Mississippi, and occasionally shooting a deer or a wild
turkey, to be exchanged for a bottle of that whisky

---

[1] This foreboding has been fulfilled literally in the case of the
bison; but the Indians, though they have greatly declined and de-
teriorated, still numbered over 400.000 in the United States and
British Possessions when the census was taken in 1880.

which is known among the wilder tribes of the Far West by the name of 'fire-poison.'" [1]

The volumes of Travels were very well received, as indeed they deserved to be, for to this day they remain a vivid and accurate picture of scenes which can never be witnessed again. Here is testimony from another American traveller, François Réné, Vicomte de Chateaubriand, in a letter to Charles Murray's cousin, the Princesse de la Tremouille :—

"PARIS, 20 *Avril* 1841.

" J'ai commencé à lire avec le *plus grand* plaisir les travels de l'Honorable Ch. Murray, que vous avez eu la bonté de m'envoyer. Tout le monde, quoiqu'en dise votre extrême politesse, a le droit d'écrire après moi ; d'ailleurs, comme vous le remarquez, madame, l'Amerique a changé de face depuis mes voyages ; il n'y a que mon Itineraire à Jerusalem qui ressemble encore à ce que j'ai vu, parceque dans l'Orient l'homme et la terre sont immobiles."

Labourdonnais having read this letter, returned it with a shrug, observing, " C'est le seul ouvrage qu'il aura lu avec le plus grand plaisir qui n'est pas écrit par lui-même ! "

No sooner did the 'Travels' prove a success than the time-worn question of division of profits

[1] Travels, vol. ii. p. 2.

arose. How it was decided there is no means of
knowing now, but a letter from Fraser Tytler,
the historian, explains the nature of the controversy :—

P. Fraser Tytler to Hon. Charles Murray.

"I have received and read with care the two
agreements with your Bookseller. Nothing, I
think, can be clearer than the First—on the important point of the *property* of the 'Travels'
being *yours,* after Bentley has either printed and
sold off, or *declined* a second Edition. And since
the first Edition is now out of print, he must
give you a direct and definite answer on the
point. Whether the reprinting some sheets with
a new Title-page, a pious fraud not unfrequently
resorted to by bibliopolists, be called a new Edition
or no, the case is not altered as to his obligation
—either to publish a new Edition himself, or, by
declining it, to set you free, that, if you think fit,
you may publish it elsewhere.

"By the agreement the *first* Edition was to run
to 1250 copies : price to be paid, £300. The 2nd
Edition, according to Mr Bentley's option, was to
be either of 1000 copies, price £200, or of 750
copies, price £150, or of 500 copies, price £100.
But it having struck Mr B. that perhaps it would
be a better speculation to make the First Edition
1500 copies instead of 1250, there is a Memor-

andum I see added in which you permit him to print, if he pleases, 250 copies more, which are to be accounted part of the First Edition, and for which, on the sale reaching to 1450 copies, he is bound to pay you £50 in addition to the £300.

"Now what I want you to tell me is—Whether *he did this*, and whether you have *received from him* £350? If the book *is* out of print, he most probably has done it. What I suspect he did (and I believe under the memorandum he was entitled to do it) was that at once he threw off an edition of 1500, and that not selling the last part of them very readily, he got you to correct some little errors or misprints and, printing a new Title-page, called it the 2nd Edition. In any case he is bound, the book being out of print, to give a decided answer to your letter — accepting or declining a new edition.

"As to the second agreement—it is equally clear that you have sold the whole property of the little 'Prairie Bird'[1] for Four Hundred Pounds—which I regret, and beg you never to do with any other feathered fowl again — for she may, and I have little doubt she will, prove a Phœnix, and then Bentley will have the profit of her melody, instead of you,

"'Who imp't her wing, and sweetened all her songs.'"

The 'Prairie Bird' did not appear till after a considerable change had come over Charles Mur-

[1] Murray's Indian romance.

ray's prospects. The following extracts from letters written to him by Sir Charles Vaughan contain the only references I can find to a certain event which, though it receives no mention in the 'Travels,' was the most important episode in which he bore a part. Vaughan was a Fellow of All Souls, and had been British Minister at Washington when Murray first went to the United States, but had returned to England before the latter brought his wanderings to a close. The first three extracts are from letters sent out to Murray in America :—

Sir Charles Vaughan to Hon. Charles Murray.

"ALL SOULS, *4th November* 1835.

"Our election terminated late last night, when we chose Mr Francis Hastings Doyle[1] (a candidate I recollect in 1832); Mr Grimstone, a son of Lord Verulam and member of Parliament for St Albans; Mr Howard, Lord Suffolk's son; and Mr Charles Harris, Lord Malmesbury's son. We had fifteen candidates, amongst whom there was a son of Lord Talbot's and a son of Lord Harris, who commanded in India; Mr Dean, a son of the Commissioner of Excise; Mr Ridley Colborne. These are the only names likely to be of any interest to you. . . .

"I have had the greatest difficulty in answering the thousand inquiries made of me about yourself.

---

[1] Afterwards Sir Francis Doyle, Bart., Professor of Poetry in the University of Oxford, 1867-77; Commissioner of the Customs, 1869-83.

I have told them of all your hairbreadth escapes *per mare, per terras*, your average of game, twenty buffaloes a-day brought down by your own rifle, your hunting excursions in the prairies—the treachery of the Pawnees—the singular acuteness which you discovered in striking the Missouri. I was then questioned about your excursion after gold-mines in Virginia—of which I told them I knew nothing."

"Dover, *5th March* 1836.

" The weather was bad yesterday at sea and not very good to-day, but we hope to get over to Calais to-morrow morning.

"Your letter, which I received before I left London, did not appear to be written in good spirits, nor did it contain any satisfactory information about your future views. I wish you well in for diplomacy : you will not be happy till your way of life is decided upon and entered upon, and do not let your spirits be depressed by your disappointment at New York ; you must shake that off, or you are not in a state to enter manfully in pursuit of usefulness and fame—so much for the twaddle of a sexagenarian celibate."

"London, *27th April* 1836.

" As to political news from England, you will obtain that from better sources than such as are accessible to me. Never was the country in a more prosperous and flourishing condition. The new Poor Laws have mended greatly the condition of the agricultural part of the population,

and since the meeting of Parliament the expectations of increased power on the part of the
Conservatives have been completely disappointed.
The session of Parliament has been distinguished
by great application to business, by judicious conduct on the part of the Administration, and the
decided junction of Lord Stanley and Sir James
Graham with Sir Robert Peel has not made any
serious impression. I see no reason why you
should not congratulate yourself upon your absence from England during the last year or two.
When you return you will be able to form a
very correct judgment of the state of political
parties, and take up your public career in the
path most congenial with your own feelings and
your old connections. I venture to predict that
you will not hastily recede from the Whigs. As
for myself, I have been so much a stranger in
my own country that the asperities of party are
so offensive to me, that I am a Whig in the
company of Conservatives, and a Conservative
in the society of Whigs, in all cases, all times,
and all occasions detesting the Radicals. . . .

"I have been passing the Easter holidays at All
Souls : our party varied from eight to seventeen—
a rubber at whist every evening—good fellowships
expected, as a heavy fine was paid on a lease renewed. I hope that you will save your sealings,
as I proposed when College offices were disposed of
that you should be named *cus. ioc.*—*alias* keeper
of the jewels, and you were accordingly registered.
The College is being repaired ; .they are removing
decayed stone from the tower of the staircase lead-

ing to my rooms, and facing it with bath stone, and not before it was absolutely necessary. . . .

"The tranquillity of Oxford has been lately ruffled owing to Lord Melbourne having appointed Dr Hampden Regius Professor of Divinity. The leading divines amongst the resident members have publicly declared that the doctrines which he preached in some Bampton Lectures are not orthodox. Dr Hampden replies that there is a wide difference between the Apostles' Creed, which contains only facts from the Holy Scriptures, and the scholastic deductions from those facts contained in the Nicene and Athanasian Creeds." [1]

"ALL SOULS, 17th December 1836.

"It has been agreed to celebrate on the 10th of February next the foundation of the College, on that day four hundred years ago. We are to have service in the Chapel at eleven o'clock, and a grand feast in the Hall, and all those who have been Fellows of the College are to be invited to attend. You must come up on that occasion, as it was observed that it would be impossible for any actual Fellow within the three kingdoms of England, Scotland, and Ireland to absent himself on that occasion. . . .

"I do not at all like the complexion of your last letter. It seems that all your pleasing dreams of future life will be disagreeably dissipated by the late change in your political and pecuniary interests.

[1] Dr Hampden was twice formally censured by the University of Oxford for heterodox doctrine—in 1836 and in 1842.

It is very natural in that case that you should fall back with intense interest upon the object of your regard in the United States. Remember, however, that is not the state of mind in which a man ought to come to a final decision. Ninon de l'Enclos used to thank God every night for the good sense with which He had blessed her, and prayed for protection against the follies of her heart : distrust your judgment in worldly concerns when the heart is troubled."

"63 CURZON STREET, MAYFAIR,
13th January 1837.

" I received this morning your confidential letter of the 10th inst. I like exceedingly your chance of getting into the Diplomatic service, and I am sure that you ought not to hesitate one moment about taking the Secretaryship of Legation at Washington, if your friends can by any possibility secure it for you. As to your diffidence about accepting the appointment because you have not gone through the business of an *attaché*, the art in being a good *attaché* consists in diligence and discretion, in learning to cipher and decipher, and in writing a good hand. I think that you will soon begin to wish that you were in some profession. I am of opinion that political life should be taken up as an appendage to the law, the army, the navy, or diplomacy, and then you will always have more than one string to your bow. But nothing surely could meet your wishes more completely than returning to the United States in an official capacity which will leave you to your speculations in land and love during three or four summer months. I do not enter into your feelings about Buchanan :[1] you cannot take from him that which he has so little chance of ever obtaining. He will go with me to Constantinople, and the difficulty is to agree upon the title he is to have in the Embassy. Lord Palmerston will not be in town till to-morrow evening. . . . In short, my advice to you is, seize the Washington Secretaryship if you possibly can. But do not, until you are gazetted, relax in the slightest degree in your exertions to get into Parliament. The better your prospects in the burgh you allude to, the more likely are you to get the diplomatic appointment ; and you have plenty of time to turn about before any dissolution of Parliament can take place. If I pick up any rumours about your appointment by Lord Palmerston, I will write to you. If your name is mentioned before me, as being likely to be so named, I shall be prepared to give you a good hearty lift by swearing that it would be the appointment of all others agreeable to the Americans.

"I dined with your friend Rogers yesterday— what a good house, and what a good dinner, and what a good man ! "

"42 CURZON STREET, MAYFAIR,
21st January 1837.

" I am really distressed to find myself obliged to tell you that I cannot execute your commission of seeking an interview with Lord Lansdowne, and explaining to him your wishes and views. In the first place, I hardly know him ; and in the next, I

˒ [1] Afterwards the Right Hon. Sir Andrew Buchanan, G.C.B., Minister at St Petersburg, &c.

K

cannot venture in any shape to appear, directly or indirectly, as a solicitor for a friend who is a candidate for employment under Lord Palmerston, because he has kindly permitted me to interfere with his patronage in the Mission upon which he did me the disinterested service to appoint me, by allowing me to take Buchanan with me. It is not many days since I was obliged to tell my old friend Sir Hurford Jones, who wished me to get Lord Palmerston to allow his son to go with me as an *attaché* to Constantinople, that I could not open my lips upon the subject to Lord Palmerston, who had already allowed me to rob him of one appointment. Besides, I do not think that Lord Lansdowne would think that you had made a prudent choice of a friend to communicate with him, when you send me to him, at best considered but a doubtful friend of the Administration, in preference to a host of powerful connections which you have. Again, Lord Palmerston would sturdily resist the presumption of a *ci-devant* Minister in the United States venturing to tell him who should be employed there. I do heartily wish not only for your sake, but for the interests of our Mission at Washington, that you were there as Secretary of Legation, as I hear that my successor shuts himself up, shows no disposition to mix with the Americans, or do anything but save money. . . .

" I am not surprised at the decision which has been sent you by the family in America. I never knew an offer made by an Englishman to an American, that the separation from the family and country was not made an almost insurmount-

able difficulty. Two or three years' residence in
the United States as Secretary of Legation might
remove that difficulty, by removing the father in
the course of nature ; but you may rely upon it
that the fortune of the daughter would be made
contingent upon her remaining in America. You
are not in a state yet to endure the cold and
heartless counsel of a sexagenarian bachelor like
myself, or I should tell you *never mind !* you are at
perfect liberty once more to set your sails and take
a new departure for some other port."

The reference in the last paragraph quoted,
and in other parts of these letters, is to Miss
Elise Wadsworth, daughter of a wealthy American gentleman, with whom Charles Murray had
fallen deeply in love while a guest at Geneseo,
Mr Wadsworth's country house near Niagara.
The young lady returned his passion ; but owing
to circumstances which will be more fully explained hereafter, Mr Wadsworth not only
refused his consent, but strictly forbade his
daughter to hold any communication with her
lover. His commands were obeyed ; but in following Murray's fortunes henceforth, it must be
understood that he remained unwavering in his
attachment, true to his plighted troth, though,
apparently, without the faintest hope of ever
realising his dream.

CHAPTER VII.

1837–1838.

POLITICS, LITERATURE, AND COURT LIFE.

VAUGHAN's advice to keep political work as a second string to his bow was not disregarded by Murray, and circumstances soon arose which made it for a time the first. Here is a glimpse of what had been going on in the fussy, crowded world while he had been working off superfluous energy in the solemn backwoods and lonely prairies of the West :—

Samuel Rogers to the Countess of Dunmore.

"HOLLAND HOUSE, *December 6th,* 1834.

" When I arrived I found the world in a hubbub! Six Ministers dined at Holland House on the Friday and dispersed, not knowing they were out of office. At night Lord Palmerston called at the Treasury and asked if Lord Melbourne was re-

turned from Brighton.   He was shown in, and
he found Lord Melbourne just alighted and in
his travelling-cap, sitting in a large room, his
room of business, with two candles just lighted
on the table. 'What news?' said Lord Palmerston. 'News!' said Lord Melbourne in his bluff
manner; 'read that,' and he put into his hand a
paper giving a summary of what had passed. A
Cabinet was summoned to meet at twelve on
Saturday, but till then few of them knew it but
from the papers. And who sent it to the papers?
It is believed to be H. B.,[1] who had seen Lord
Melbourne after Lord Palmerston had left him.
If you only read the 'Globe,' you can know little
of the vagaries of Brougham, which fill the 'Times'
and the 'Courier'—but perhaps you do best to
trouble yourselves little about such matters. . . .

"To return to politics—the long and short of
the matter I believe to be this. The K. is very
honest, but very ——. The two persons he looks
up to most are Lord Grey and the Duke, and not
having one, he calls in the other—not that he dis-
likes Lord Melbourne. The Church reforms in
prospect and the mountebank tricks of the Chancellor have certainly had something to do with
it. B. had drawn him into a long correspondence
through Sir H. Taylor; he thought he must answer
his Chancellor, though heartily sick of it, and it
wore him out: but Peel will be here in a day or
two, and we shall know more. If the fair Eliza
comes to town, I hope she will acknowledge me
in public places. But I thought she was to em-

[1] Lord Brougham.

bellish Paris. I am delighted to think that
Charles is going on well. . . . I have been here
for some days, and living with ex-Ministers, but
they have now nothing to tell us. Some say there
will be a dissolution immediately and some say not.
Peel, I should think, will in the first instance try
to make a mixed Ministry, and sound Stanley—
but we shall soon know."

On returning from America in 1836, Murray
found himself accused of having altered his political opinions, which gave rise to the following
correspondence with Lord Stanley :[1]—

Hon. Charles Murray to Lord Stanley.

"DUNMORE, *September 21st*, 1836.

" MY DEAR LORD STANLEY,—Since my return to
this part of the world I have been much plagued
(as every one must expect to be who has ever been
seen upon electioneering hustings) with reports respecting my proposed canvas of one or two seats for
Parliament, and with other rumours regarding my
opinion, &c., &c. Among these the most current is
that I am turned Tory, and it is founded mainly
upon a sentence in a letter of mine quoted by you
in the House of Commons. It is desirable both
for the preservation of my character for consist-
ency, as well as in the event of my wishing hereafter to embark again in politics, that I should
have the means of contradicting these absurd

---

[1] The "Rupert of Debate," afterwards fourteenth Earl of Derby.

reports, and I regret that I omitted to keep a copy of the said letter, which I would certainly have done had I suspected that it would rise up in judgment against me.   However, it is possible that you may have preserved it : if you have done so, pray send me either it or a copy.   As far as I can remember, I simply stated that I had gone out to America an opponent of universal suffrage and vote by ballot ; that all which I had there observed had confirmed this opinion,—that I had gone out and remained still a good Whig, &c.   This, as far as I can remember, was the substance of my letter, and if you will forgive me for troubling you on a matter which has probably almost escaped your recollection, I shall be obliged if you will confirm or correct as far as may be in your power my present impressions of what I then wrote."

Lord Stanley to the Hon. Charles Murray.

"BALLYHISTEEN, *October 1st*, 1836.

" MY DEAR MURRAY,—I am almost ashamed to see your handwriting again, never having written to thank you for your very long and interesting letter from America, which letter, I am sorry to find, has been the means of putting you to any inconvenience.   I have a copy of it, but not here, nor can I get at it until I go up to town, as it is locked up among my papers there.   I think, however, on reference to the Mirrors of Parliament you will find that in quoting your authority on the subject of the ballot, to which alone I referred, I quoted it, without naming you, as that of a person who had invariably entertained Liberal opinions (at least what used to be considered Liberal opinions at the time I was speaking), and I am quite certain I let fall nothing which could imply a suspicion of your having been in the smallest degree inconsistent. I doubt if I showed your letter to any one ; but I recollect a remarkable expression in it, in speaking of the ballot and universal suffrage, 'that if you had come out a *Radical*, what you had seen might have made a Tory of you—having come out a Whig, you still remained one,' or something to that effect. When I return to town I will look out the letter and send you a copy, and I hope we are not the least likely to have any occasion for canvassing before that time."

Murray has left an account of his third and last disappointment in attempting to enter Parliament :—

"On returning from America my first visit was to my uncle, the Duke of Hamilton. It was a short time before a general election—my uncle, Lord Archibald, had just died. He had represented the county of Lanark for thirty years in the Whig interest—moreover, he had made me heir to his very small possessions ; so when I reappeared at Hamilton, a number of the leading gentry met together, and after talking over the matter, came to me to say that they would gladly give me their votes if I would contest the election ; that I was a very suitable person, and with the

Duke's influence and Lord Archibald's name to back me up, my election was a certainty. I told them that of course all depended upon my uncle. He, however, did not care to incur the expense, and refused his consent, though it was represented to him that it would be a great pity to allow such an important seat, held so long by the Whigs, to go over uncontested to the Tories, which it would undoubtedly do, as the leading men who had asked me to stand would give the Tory candidate their votes rather than have a possible Radical. My uncle was firm; so I, burning to get into the House, determined to have a venture on my own account. I made my inquiries, and found there was a likely seat going at Lichfield.

"Without saying a word to any one, I went down and got hold of some of the head tradesmen, &c., who made up the greater part of the influential voting population. I presented myself to them, and on counting noses carefully, I saw I was pretty safe. Then and there I organised committees, agents, &c., and set the whole machinery going, congratulating myself mightily that I should owe my seat to no one. Meantime Lord Melbourne had been informed of the state of affairs in Lanark, and wrote to the Duke a most urgent letter, saying the Duke had always held himself before the world as a staunch Whig; that now the moment, and a most important one, had arrived for giving a proof of his assertions and doing his party a real service, surely he did not mean to fail them, and so forth. This so worked on the Duke that ten days before the General

Election he wrote off to me, telling me of the pressing letter he had received from Lord Melbourne, which had finally prevailed upon him to change his mind, and that I was therefore at once to go north and do all I could to keep the seat.

" You can imagine my anger and dismay.

" I wrote a very sharp letter back to my uncle, telling him in so many words that owing to his shilly-shallying all the principal voters had engaged themselves elsewhere, and that I had practically won a seat for myself. I received an answer to the effect that it was my duty to do my best for Lanark, that he felt sure only a few of the leading men had gone over, &c. I was in a great rage, but did the only thing that seemed possible under the circumstances — viz., I called all my committees at Lichfield together, put the case before them, said if they held me to my word I was bound to them ; if not, and they were good enough to trust me so far, I would supply another man, who, though he was not over-clever, and would not make speeches for them, could be relied upon to vote straight. They behaved splendidly, regretted my having to leave them, but quite understood the state of the case, and accepted my offer of a substitute. And this is the most amusing part of the story : Alfred Paget was the man I had in my mind — a sporting fellow with no ideas about politics. . . . But his family had property near Lichfield, which gave him a *raison d'être*, as it were ; and, moreover, his family were staunch Whigs, so I knew Paget would never vote for the Tories. He was yachting at the time, and had no idea in the world of what I was doing with his name. But the long and short of it was that they elected him, uncontested, and he never did an hour's canvassing, nor had his electors ever set eyes on him, and he.hadn't a notion he was a candidate for Parliament till he found himself elected.

"I was thus free to go and make the best of what I felt was a very thankless task in Lanark; so, saying good-bye regretfully to Lichfield, I made my way there. I had enough to do in the few days left me. I rode all over the country, forty or fifty miles a-day, speaking at five different places in twenty-four hours,—organising a campaign in a little over a week, that ought to have lasted months. I worked harder in those days than ever in my life before or since; for although I felt it was only a forlorn-hope, still, once in for it, I grew keen and fought with a will. My uncle and aunt were in Italy, and I lived in a corner of the Palace at Hamilton. On the night the poll was to be declared, I gave a dinner to my staunchest adherents; and whilst at it, a messenger arrived, having ridden post-haste to tell the result, which was that I had been elected by one vote !

" My friends hurrahed, drank my health, and made the devil of a noise. As soon as I could make myself heard, I said, 'For heaven's sake, don't be too sure !—this is a deal too close to be pleasant.' And sure enough, in a little while a second messenger galloped up to the Palace, covered with mud, having ridden as hard as he knew to try and stop the first report, for the truth was, I was *beaten* by one vote.

" It was about the most aggravating thing ever known, as it was so clearly a case of throwing away a good cause by shilly-shallying. I had a try to make a double election of it; for it turned out that one of my uncle's most important tenants had gone in to record his vote, and was told his name had been struck out as 'dead.' In vain he protested he was wholly alive. The sheriff, or whatever the man is called who sits by while the votes are recorded, ruled that all mistakes had to be rectified before the day of the poll, and his vote was not allowed; nor was I able to get this judgment reversed.

" So ended my attempts to gain a hearing at St Stephen's.

" But my efforts were not unrewarded. Lord Melbourne, on hearing the story, was so sorry for me, and sympathised so much with me, that he looked about to see if he could not give me some non-political appointment. There was a vacancy as Groom-in-waiting, which he offered me. The Queen had just come to the throne, and there was a kind of romance about so young a girl in such a position, and I gladly accepted. I only filled the post for about four months, as then I pushed to the top of that tree and was made Master of the Household, which position I filled for nearly seven years."

Some passages in a journal which Murray began and kept diligently for nearly three weeks are worth reprinting, containing, as they do, original observations about those early days of Queen Victoria's reign which must always possess a pathetic interest for her subjects : [1]—

"WINDSOR CASTLE.

"*Sept. 6th*, 1837.—Drove my American ponies down from London, astonishing the natives with their uncommon speed, and with the slight, spider-like appearance of my carriage. Arrived at two o'clock. Made my way to Lord Cunynghame (Chamberlain) and Lilford (Lord - in - Waiting); placed myself with them in the corridor through which her Majesty was to pass in descending to mount her horse. Here I was presented and kissed hands, after which I joined the cavalcade, consisting of twenty - five or thirty equestrians, and we made a promenade about the Great Park for two hours. There was little or no form or ceremony observed as to precedence. The Queen rode generally in front, accompanied by the Queen of the Belgians and King of do., the Duchess of Kent, and now and then she called up Lords Cunynghame, Wellington, or Melbourne to ride beside her. Her Majesty's seat on horseback is easy and graceful, and the early habit of command observable in all her movements and gestures is agreeably relieved by the gentle tone of her voice, and the natural playfulness with which she addresses her relatives or the ladies

[1] The whole journal, so far as it extends, has already been printed in the 'Cornhill Magazine.'

about her. I never saw a more quick or observant eye. . . . I had some conversation with
the Duke of Wellington upon national character,
chiefly that of the English and the German.
His opinion of the latter I found to be very
high, as was also his estimation of the domestic
policy of Prussia. On the subject of emigration
from this country to America, I do not think
his views so enlightened as I should have expected. . . . During the evening her Majesty
conversed with her principal guests. She also
played two games of draughts with the Queen
of the Belgians, both of which she gained. . . .
There was a whist-table consisting of the Duchess
of Kent, the King of the Belgians, Duke of Wellington, and Lilford. . . .

"*Sept. 7th.*— . . . We rode out at half-past
three, and my pony Blackbird excited much admiration by his speed and action. The Queen
asked me his origin, history, name, &c., and
laughed very much when I told her that I had
christened his black companion Jim Crow. Her
countenance when smiling is most delightful to
look upon, so full is it of simplicity and cheerfulness, while there is always a something inexpressible which would check familiarity and
annihilate impertinence.

"The Duke of Sussex arrived before dinner.
. . . After dinner a whist-table was made, at
which I made my *début* as a player: the party
consisting of the Duke of Sussex, the King of
the Belgians, and the Duchess of Kent. We
changed partners several times, the two former

playing a middling game : the Duchess is not a
good player, but she laughs so good-humouredly
at her own blunders and losses that no partner
could get angry with her at shilling whist.

" When our table broke up, I went and stood
over our young Queen, who was playing draughts
with the Queen of the Belgians : it was a very
long game, and had reached a very important
crisis. I got so interested that, when her
Majesty made one very bad move, I groaned
audibly : she looked over her shoulder, and laughed
very much when she saw me. She asked me more
than once what she ought to play, and I told her,
perhaps wrong ; and more than once I fear I spoke
when I was not asked. . . .

" *Sept.* 9*th.*— . . . We rode out at four, and
as the King and Queen of the Belgians were of the
party, we went rather slow. . . . Our Queen's
manner to King Leopold is most respectful and
affectionate ; indeed her manner to every one
is perfectly winning and appropriate, and her
countenance lights up into the most agreeable
and intelligent expression possible. . . . After
dinner the usual whist-table was set, the only
change in the party being the Duke of Cambridge,[1]
who arrived to-day. He talked all dinner-time
without ceasing, and not less constantly during
the whist-playing. I never heard such a continued flow of spirits and words ! . . . The
Lord Chancellor, Melbourne, Palmerston, Albemarle, &c., were of the party this evening. . . .

" *Sept.* 11*th.*— . . . At dinner I had a very

[1] Son of George III.

interesting conversation with Baroness Lehzen, who has been for many years her Majesty's governess and preceptress. I know nothing more creditable to herself and to her illustrious pupil than the fact that one of the first acts in her reign was to secure and retain her preceptress in an honourable situation about her own person. Her Majesty treats the Baroness with the most kind and affectionate confidence, and the latter tells me that she has carefully copied every letter of *private* correspondence with her young mistress, both before and since her coming to the throne, but that, since she has been a Queen, her Majesty has *never* shown her one letter of Cabinet or State documents, nor has she spoken to her, nor to any woman about her, upon party or political questions. As *Queen* she reserves all her confidence for her official advisers, while as a woman she is frank, gay, and unreserved as when she was a young girl. . . .

"*Sept.* 17*th.*— . . . After dinner her Majesty played chess with the Queen of the Belgians. On this occasion her Majesty put my counsel in requisition from the beginning; and alas! I ate more dirt than on the preceding night. Whether it was that my thoughts wandered too much from the game to the interesting young person playing it—to her position, her destinies, her future—or that I really am a very bad player, I know not; but sure am I that I recommended two or three successive blundering manœuvres to her, and subjected her to a most complete defeat. . . .

"*Sept.* 18*th.*—This morning their Belgian Majesties took their departure, and I am sure that our Queen's regret and grief at the parting was sincere. She has a quiet esteem and affection for her uncle; and his young queen being nearly her own equal in rank, station, age, &c., rendered her the only companion with whom she could *entirely* lay aside the Queen and ' play at will her virgin fancies.' . . .

"*Sept.* 20*th.*— . . . At four we rode in the Great Park. The Queen was mounted on Emperor, a fine chestnut horse, very spirited, and, on one account, not fit for her to ride. As Lord Melbourne's steed was fidgety, I proposed to lend him Blackbird and take his curveting animal instead. As Blackbird could not speak, the change was effected, although he had two or three stone more to carry; but Lord Melbourne was enabled to ride by the Queen and talk quietly to her."

In his novel *rôle* of young courtier, Murray has committed little of *le dessous des cartes* to this fragment of journal, which ends abruptly with the month of September. But that he found it as needful to steer a careful course among the rivalries and jealousies of the British Court as he had learnt to do among the lodges of the Pawnee braves, may be understood from some of his correspondence at this period. If this narrative were one of the days of Queen Elizabeth, many of these letters might be printed in full, and be found entertaining reading; but

as yet most of them must be treated as forbidden fruit. Readers of Charles Greville's gossip will be aware that the position of the young
Queen in the first years of her reign was not
without its difficulties and risks. The domestic
history of her immediate predecessors had not
been altogether exemplary. To break with the
traditional laxity of the English Court, and
to set up a standard of social life loftier and
purer than anything hitherto attempted, or even
imagined, called for the exercise of tact and
resolution in a degree which few people could
have expected to be at the command of a Princess not yet out of her teens. Yet a grateful
nation, and all the world besides, know that
these qualities were forthcoming, and that the
thing was done.

Among the friendships which Murray formed
at Court, none seems to have been more intimate
while it lasted than that with Lady Mary Stopford,[1] lady-in-waiting to the Queen's mother—
the Duchess of Kent. It was brief, indeed, for
Lady Mary died in 1839, but the alliance was
very close, and directed against the encroach-
ments of a certain Court official, whom there is
no occasion to name, but whose identity may

---

[1] Daughter of the third Earl of Courtown.

easily be fixed by anybody who has studied the
domestic annals of the time. Lady Mary wrote
constantly to Murray during the times of his
absence from his official duties; and while there
is plenty of evidence of those heart - burnings,
anxieties, and competition for place and favour,
from which no Court ever can be free, she betrays no eagerness on her own account, but only
for the young Queen—that she may be protected
from the machinations of interested schemers;
and for Murray — that he may obtain the ad-
vancement which Lady Mary believed not only
that he deserved, but that it was to the advantage of the Royal household he should obtain.

One amusing feature in these letters is, that
all the principal characters about the Court are
referred to under pseudonyms. Lady Mary herself signs Judy Iscariot, to "puzzle the post-
office," as she explains; the Queen is called Niké;[1]
Lord Melbourne wears the transparent disguise
of "the Great M."; Murray is addressed as "the
Good M." or "M. minor," and so on. Lord Palmerston's visits and his endless stories were always a source of amusement in a circle more
replete with worth than with wit. But even

---

[1] The Greek Νίκη, equivalent to Latin *Victoria*.

at this distance of time it would strain, if not break, confidence to print letters intended only for one pair of eyes. They are made up of just such easy, careless, loyal gossip as a clever girl might write to a man not much more than her own age, whose heart, as she well knew, had been committed to the keeping of another — a knowledge which defended their intercourse from the inevitable restraint which would have loaded their pens and lips under different circumstances.

CHAPTER VIII.

1838–1844.

JOURNALS, ETC.

It is a trite observation that the reign of Queen
Victoria synchronises with a period of progress
and change such as the world has never before
seen. People were scarcely conscious at the time
of the magnitude of the operations which were
beginning to take place. The first railway connecting London and the provinces was opened in
1838, connecting the Metropolis with Birmingham,
and in the four succeeding years the chief existing
trunk lines of Great Britain were begun. Had
Murray foreseen the extent of the revolution thus
initiated in the habits and environment of our
people, he would certainly have made some notes
at the time, for he had a quick, observant mind
and a ready pen. But such observations and
speculations as he committed to paper must have

been written in letters to friends, hardly one of
whom now survives. Here and there among his
papers occur fleeting allusions to the new modes of
travel, as, for instance, in the following extract :—

Samuel Rogers to the Countess of Dunmore.

"LOWTHER, *Sept.* 10*th* [*c.* 1841].

"I set out the day after you were so kind as
to call, and arrived in the evening at Lancaster,
the giant that had transported me so far not
having crushed me in his impetuosity or scalded
me to death. There I found, or rather was found
out by, the little Duchess of Buccleuch, who had
travelled all day in my *tail*, and if I can contrive
it, I will pass a day or two at Drumlanrig before I
return. But my only purpose in coming was once
more to visit a brother versifier, Wordsworth, and
also these old and kind friends. Alas ! I found
him sitting for his picture, and here I am waiting
for him, day after day."

Physical science was in full movement; the
venerable diluvial theory in geology was just
beginning to yield to systematic research. Here
is an early mention of glacial action :—

Dr Buckland to Hon. Charles Murray.

"OXFORD, 17 *Nov.* 1840.

"Allow me to present you with a true statement of the condition of the world which smashed

my Hyænas and Elephants, and immediately preceded the appearance of existing species upon our
Planet. I have recently been going over much
of Scotland, and find everywhere the Remains of
Moraines and scratches on the hard Rocks which
formed the Bottom of the Glaciers—those which
Sir T. Hale attributed to Diluvial Action. For
Diluvial we must read Glacial, and the facts
remain intact. I inclose a copy which I will
thank you to present in my Name to H.R.H.
Prince Albert."

Other letters from Dr Buckland inform Murray
of the latest discoveries of fossil remains, notably
the *Megalornis* of New Zealand.

During his life at Court, Charles Murray was
able to be of some service to his friends. Here
is a letter announcing promotion to his brother
Henry :—

Hon. Charles Murray to Lieut. the Hon.
Henry Murray, R.N.

"BUCKINGHAM PALACE, *June* 29, 1838.

"With unfeigned hearty pleasure I announce
to you that you *are made.* I saw Lord Melbourne
yesterday afternoon at the Coronation, when he
said to me, ' Well, Mr Murray, I have made out
your brother's commission.' Says I, 'A thousand
thanks, my Lord; pray give me your hand to
shake.' When that was over I wished to sound
him upon a subject which you have once or twice

touched sorely upon, so (having him well jammed
up in the Abbey among feathers and diamonds
and coronets where he could not move) I went on,
'I trust, my Lord, he will do no discredit to your
kindness.' His answer was, 'I am sure he will
not—*he is an excellent officer,*' and one or two
more sentences in the same strain. Your promotion will be published in a few days. How or when
you are to get this scrawl I know not; but I hastened to tell my mother, who came to my rooms at
the Palace to see the procession and fireworks : she
wept tears of joy. In the evening, after dinner, I
went and told Lord Melbourne, adding a few words
of thanks for the kind interest he had taken in
your prospects: his answer was, 'I am very glad
he has got it, and he deserves it, for he's a *devilish
good officer.*' I give it to you in his own words.
They have postponed to you on this occasion,
therefore if you have any political bias put it in
your pocket; keep and raise the high character
you have got, serve the Queen and the Government of your country faithfully, and with God's
blessing I may yet live to drink a glass of Madeira
with Admiral Murray! I have no time to add
more, except that the Coronation went off admirably, and that our loved and honoured Sovereign
went through her part of the ceremonial with all
the modest grace and dignity for which she is
distinguished. God bless you, my dear Commander — I have not written so long a private
letter for a month!"

Murray was, not long after, engaged in the fortunes of another relative—his cousin, the Marquis

of Douglas—in a far more delicate business than mere promotion. It seems that the Princess Mary, youngest daughter of Charles, Grand .Duke of Baden, having a romantic admiration for Scotland and the Scots, and hearing that Lord Douglas was reputed one of the handsomest men, not only of that nation but in Europe, had set her heart on becoming his wife. Overtures were made on the part of her Royal parents with the view of arranging a marriage. From a worldly point of view, no alliance could have been more brilliant : the circumstances also were somewhat romantic, and the Duke of Hamilton greatly desired that his son should at least accord the lady an interview. But Lord Douglas had views, perhaps reasons, of his own. He stoutly refused at first to entertain any proposal, or even to wait upon the lady. The following extracts from one side of a correspondence will indicate how Charles Murray's services were enlisted, and how, apparently, he succeeded in overcoming his cousin's reluctance to yield himself prisoner :—

Tenth Duke of Hamilton to his Nephew,
Hon. Charles Murray.

"HAMILTON PALACE, *October* 29th, 1839.

" I have received, my dear Charles, your letter, with its enclosure, intended to be sent to my son.

I almost wish it had been sent to him without my having heard anything of the matter. You must know (even better than I can) what effect any communication of yours may have upon Angus's conduct. He requires to be treated with great caution and judgment, and is not easily to be directed. What effect the style of letter you have written may produce I cannot tell, but I have been cruelly and painfully wounded to think that my son would not even gratify me so far as to *see* the person in question, without any obligation of any sort being annexed to such a measure. I make no difficulty in declaring that I am most anxious that he should inform himself of the family, the person, the character, &c., &c., and before he objects to what might possibly be most desirable. If, upon further investigation, difficulties or disagreements arise, let him retire out of the field. This is all I have sought for: if you can obtain it you will, I think, do him a great service. You are the best judge how far you can interfere, with effect, in so delicate a piece of business.

"I am obliged to you for the part you have taken in this business, and you see it in its proper light. The prospect is too flattering for any sensible man to turn away from without giving it a thought. . . .

"*P.S.*—You might be sure that I should have returned you your letter, as, after the part I have already taken, it would be quite out of the question that anything should be forwarded by me or through my means."

Lieut.-Colonel Stepney-Cowell [1] *to Hon.*
Charles Murray.

"SENIOR UNITED SERVICE CLUB,
Nov. 2nd [1842 ?].

"MY DEAR SIR,—So perfectly do we coincide in
our views in conducting the matter I am interested
about, that immediately on reaching town I wrote
to the Duke to tell him I had been down to you,
as a relation and friend of Lord Douglas, to enlist
your interest with him on our behalf, as I conceive
no step should be taken in the matter without the
Duke's knowledge and approbation. But as he
has failed with his son, how far forwarding your
letter to the Marquis through his father's hands
is advisable, you know best. I hope you will not
be easily discouraged at a rebuff, but will return
to the charge. If it were possible for you to see
him, it would be far better than writing, should
the reply to your letter prove unsatisfactory. A
young, good-looking, elegant, highly accomplished
lady of the oldest royal house in Europe, whose
mind is filled with a German enthusiasm for Scotland and the Scotch, and who has heard Lord
Douglas's appearance, manners, and qualities much
and favourably spoken of—this lady, with the consent of her royal parents, throws down the glove
to the Marquis — surely chivalry and courtesy
should make him take it up, as in so doing he

---

[1] Afterwards Sir John Stepney Cowell-Stepney, having taken the
additional surname of Stepney by royal licence in 1857, and having
been created a baronet in 1871. He died in 1877. He seems to have
acted as plenipotentiary for the royal house of Baden in this matter.

binds himself to nothing, any more than the lady.
He is only asked to look upon her! and as the
Duke said to me in Portman Square, 'Had it been
my case as a young man, curiosity would have induced me at least to pay the lady a visit.' I will
keep Lord Douglas's refusal in my hands as long
as in decorum I decently can, in hopes of a change
in his views, which I still hope, through your
means, may be accomplished. At the same time,
I need not tell you that royal personages do not
like to be kept waiting. Pray let me hear from
you, and do your utmost. The Duke is most
anxious. Her family approve, and there are other
circumstances I am not at liberty to name, which in
every way would render the thing most desirable.
Address to me to Mannheim, should you not hear
before I sail, which will be on the 7th inst. . . .

"*P.S.*—Should the Marquis consent to a trip on
the Continent for a week to look about him, let
him come to me at Mannheim, and I will then go
on with him to where the family in question may
be. The Hereditary Grand Duke of Russia will
be at Darmstadt the latter end of this month,
and *fêtes* will be given. No one will remark the
Marquis's travelling in the neighbourhood of the
Princess."

The Same to the Same.

"BROOKS'S CLUB, *November 5, 1842.*

"I have just heard from the Duke, who approves of the step I have taken in requesting you
to use your influence with Lord Douglas to get

him to consent to an interview with the lady I spoke of, and goes on to say, 'You may easily suppose that I am inclined to catch at any circumstance that may lead to such a result,' and further adds to me, 'You did most properly and judiciously in requiring that, in any communication made to the Marquis, neither your name nor mine should appear. Perhaps the flutter of youth may succeed ere long to the solidity of the man,' &c., &c. I now must leave the rest to you. I certainly wish, were it possible, that you could see Lord Douglas, but of course you will act for the best."

The next letter shows that the forces combined against Lord Douglas prevailed, and that he had bowed dutifully to his fate :—

The Marquis of Douglas to the Hon. Charles Murray.

"LONDON, 3rd *Jan.* 1843.

"MY DEAR CHARLIE,—I leave town to-morrow morning for Scotland, and write you these few lines before starting to consult you upon a subject which interests me very much. As you know, I am now in this country making preparations for my marriage. I feel most anxious to have an opportunity of paying my respectful homage to the Queen before I return to Germany. I am on every account anxious to perform this duty, both from my own feelings of dutiful loyalty, and also by the express desire of the Grand Duchesse de Bade. Having been most cordially received by all the illustrious relatives of my *fiancée*, nothing could enhance my satisfaction so much as the countenance of my own Sovereign. I am perfectly aware that, not being a Peer, I have no *right* to ask an audience; and as at this time of the year there are no *levées* or ordinary occasions on which I could pay my respects to her Majesty, I feel that under the circumstances I cannot well apply through any official channel. I have therefore written to you as a cousin to inquire whether there is any course you could suggest by which the above object might be attained without any breach of etiquette or the slightest appearance of intrusion on my part. . . .

"I repeat again that I am most anxious to pay my loyal homage to the Queen, but have too much of the *old spirit* of my ancestors to wish to *force* myself even upon the Queen of these realms."

The next letters were written after the marriage had taken place at Mannheim, and are chiefly taken up with commissions to buy horses for the young couple :—

"VENICE, *March 26th,* 1843.

"I am very sorry to hear that there is such difficulty in getting together a team of brown horses. However, it is not to be wondered at, if there are so many amateurs of good taste who share my admiration for brown. If you think it possible to procure five very nice bloody (as dealers say) bays, for road-work at this time of the year, when people are all looking out for horses, I am of opinion that you had better buy for me. . . . You are, however, a better judge of this, as I am a perfect novice and a regular ignoramus with regard to carriage-horses, jobbing, &c., &c. Do what is best, my dear coz; I trust in thee. . . . Mind you get some nice ponies for my Sposa, otherwise she will never forgive you. She desires to be remembered to her (as yet unknown) cousin."

"VENICE, *April 8th,* 1843.

"I have just this instant received your letter of the 29th, my dear Charlie, and am glad to hear that in spite of the *low tone* of your last letter in horse - dealing matters, you have succeeded in buying me three brown horses. I trust, with the aid of my coachman, you will be ere long enabled to buy the other two. . . . I never, as you know, liked London much, even in my dissipated bachelor days. I assure you now, as a shady and respectable member of society, I do not think my liking for town will be at all increased. You will be glad to hear, my dear coz, that my wife and I have not yet pulled each other's ears, and we enjoy Venice, its gondolas, its pictures, and its recollections of days gone by, with renewed pleasure every hour. By the bye, Marie begs me to tell you that *your* ears stand a chance of being pulled (I shall not say by whom) if you do not get her three very nice ponies."

"MANNHEIM, *November 5th,* 1843.

"Will you be kind enough to call at Barker's,

the coachmaker's, and desire him to commence building instanter a Chariot Dormeuse for me, with a seat behind and a hood over the said seat. . . . Of course I wish the carriage to be as good as can be made—the colour dark blue and the inside lined with crimson. . . . I cannot say how happy I feel at the prospect of devoting my life to the object of my choice—you will agree when you see and know her. Farewell, my dear Charlie." [1]

In 1844 Murray made another spasmodic attempt to keep a journal. It records some events in the visit of the Emperor Nicholas to England :—

"*June 1st*, 1844.—Memorable day and memorable month in the history of Queen Victoria's Court ! About 5 P.M. the King of Saxony arrived. . . . I had not much time to attend to his Majesty, being ordered to go down to Woolwich to consult Baron Brunow about the arrangements for the reception of his Imperial master, the Autocrat of All the Russias. Poor Buckingham Palace ! daily abused as being totally unfit to lodge its habitual inmates, and now doomed to take in an Emperor and a King extra, with all their agreeable accompaniments of valets, jägers, trunks, imperials, uniforms, Cossacks, and interpreters !

" I found Brunow sitting with Benkhausen,

---

[1] The eleventh Duke died in 1863, and his widow in 1888.

the Russian Consul, at the 'Ship,' in 'the worst
inn's worst room.' He was not in a good humour,
for the mutton-chops were tough, and melted
butter was cold, and the cold butter hot, and
he had the dismal prospect of sleeping in that
vile posada far from the consoling embraces of
Madame B.

"Having transacted what business I had to do,
I returned to my duties at the Palace, and at the
usual hour went to bed. I was awakened out of
my first sleep by the noise of some one walking
about my room. 'Who's there?' I called, sitting
up in bed. The intruder continued to grope his
way in the dark. 'It's me,' he replied. 'Who's
me?' 'Ah, Murray! it is Brunow; the Emperor
is come.' 'Where is he?' 'At my house, and
here is an autograph letter from him to the
Prince.'[1] Having promised to deliver the illustrious despatch as early as possible, I *congédie'd*
my diplomatic disturber, and in ten minutes fell
asleep and dreamt of emperors and kings as plenti-
ful as cauliflowers.

"*June 2nd.*—At half-past eight I waited on the
Prince in his dressing-room and delivered the
letter. I had learned that the Emperor was to
attend his chapel at 10, whilst our Queen's church
service was at 12. The question now arose how
the great visitor was to be received and presented.
After a few minutes' deliberation the Prince said,
'As the Emperor has thought fit to surprise us,
we will pay him off with his own weapons: order
round a carriage and my equerry to attend me as

[1] Prince Albert.

M

soon as possible ! At a quarter-past nine we were
in the carriage and drove to Ashburnham House.
Great was the confusion and surprise occasioned
by the Prince's unexpected arrival, but the Gor-
dian knot of the diplomats was fairly cut : the
ceremonies of the presentation were dispensed
with, and the Emperor embraced the Prince
heartily at the foot of the stairs in the hall, after
which he led him into his own room apart. During their confab I renewed my acquaintance with
Count Orloff, who had been in England with the
Hereditary Grand Duke, and whose Herculean
figure now showed decided symptoms of increasing
embonpoint. From him I had scarcely time to
gather the names, rank, office, &c., of the different
parties whom we were to lodge in the Palace, when
the Emperor came out, leading the Prince by the
hand.

" I had not seen his Majesty since my visit to
Ems in 1840, where my first view of him had been
under circumstances very unfavourable to the dignity of his appearance, for he was riding a jackass,
with the Empress at his side, and a small tail of
courtiers in the rear. Now, he seemed to me, like
his favourite Orloff, to have gained in *embonpoint*,
and to have lost some of the hair from the top of
his head, but was still a noble, princely-looking
man of six feet three inches, and every inch a king.

" His countenance is remarkable for its straightforward, open expression of features ; at the same
time there is a roving, restless movement of the
eye, indicative of a spirit rather unquiet and observant than suspicious. . . .

" I had little leisure to observe what passed during the remainder of the day, my time being taken up in endeavouring to make twenty servants, who could speak neither English, French, nor German, understand our groom of the chambers and his assistants as to the locality of their respective master's rooms.

"*June 3rd.*—Moved to Windsor Castle—which was transformed into the Tower of Babel, the Emperor and his suite having brought with them eight or ten more servants than had been mentioned in the paper given to me by Orloff. All these fellows wanted to have rooms close to their master's; and when some of them found that they could not be lodged in the Castle, and others that they would be 100 yards distant, they sputtered and swore and jabbered in every discordant dialect of the Lithuanian and Slavonic tongues. After preparing a grand state bed for the Emperor, we were shown by his first valet a great sack, seven feet long by four broad, which we were requested to fill with clean straw, that being the only bed on which his imperial limbs ever reposed. Half-a-dozen of his Majesty's servants bivouacked in a large adjoining room, which was fortunately unoccupied, where they spread on the floor 150 packages and slept among them, some serving for beds and others for pillows, according to their size and shape. It wanted twenty minutes only to eight when I got them all stored away, with the exception of two whiskered *feldjägers*, who grumbled incessantly while I remained; so I ordered a servant to look after them and bring them what-

ever they might want, and I went to my room to
dress.   I had not been there five minutes before
the Prince sent for me to receive instructions about
marshalling the guests for dinner.   This was not
a very easy process, there being upwards of fifty,
many of them of high rank; nevertheless it went
off pretty well, and the table in the Waterloo
Gallery never looked better since it was a table.
I had placed about the person of the Emperor one
of the Queen's principal pages, named Kinnaird,
who had attended him when he visited this country
in 1817, and whom he had not seen for twenty-
seven years.   When the Emperor entered the
luncheon-room this day at two with the Queen, the
Prince, and the King of Saxony, Kinnaird was
standing behind the chair appointed for him.   The
Emperor fixed his eye upon him for a moment and
said, 'I remember you very well; you attended me
when I was here before.'   'I had that honour, your
Majesty;' on which the Emperor walked across the
room and shook hands with him.   Kinnaird was
'dumfoundered,' and it may be imagined he had
various jests and jokes to hear from the other
servants below stairs, who declared that they
should now be afraid to touch a hand that had
been shaken by the Czar's.   The evening was dull
and formal enough, and the Royalties retired about
eleven.

"On entering his apartment the Emperor observed Kinnaird, whom he desired to come in and
shut the door, after which he carried on the following conversation with the astonished page: 'Kinnaird, many years have passed since I was last

here; I was very young then, and we saw some
merry scenes together. I am now a grandfather.
I suppose you think I am a happy man because I
am what people call a great man, but I will show
you wherein my happiness consists.' So saying the
Emperor opened a travelling-desk, and showed to
the page miniature portraits of the Empress and
the Princesses. 'There,' said he—'there are the
sources of all my happiness—my wife and children.
Perhaps I ought not to say so, but there is not a
better nor a handsomer young lady in St Petersburg than my daughter the Princess Olga. These
are the sources of my happiness.' With these
words the Emperor closed the box and permitted
Kinnaird to retire, who was so astounded and taken
by surprise that he could scarcely speak, and when
he related to me the above particulars the tears
stood in his eyes. It was too much for him to be
thus made the depository of the private feelings
of the Czar, and the man was really overcome
by it.

"*June 4th.*—After breakfast, went up to the
Grand Stand to prepare for the reception of the
Royal Party. Never saw the Ascot Tuesday so ill
attended, although the weather was fine and there
was an Emperor besides a King in prospect. The
reception of the Royal Party was, like the attendance, meagre. It did not appear to me that there
were more than three or four thousand persons
present, and people never make a 'good noise'
unless they are in large masses, so the cheering
sounded flat and feeble. After the third race (for
a gold vase) the Emperor, the King of Saxony,

and the Prince went suddenly down upon the
course to look at the winner, without giving us a
moment's notice of their intention; and though
there was an ample force of police upon the field,
it was soon evident that there were not enough on
the spot to repress the universal curiosity 'to see
the Emperor.' They ran and jumped and pressed
forward with such uncontrollable violence that we
were soon fairly mobbed, and had almost to fight
our way back to the stand. The police made
every exertion to keep the crowd off from the
Emperor and Prince, who were close together, but
the poor King of Saxony was for a minute jostled
and separated from them. . . . In the evening I
went down for half an hour to see the Etonians
start for their annual regatta, and regretted being
compelled to return to hot rooms and gold plate,
instead of accompanying the 'lusty youth of
England' to Surley Hall. Even into the short
time that I stayed I found means to crowd many
dreams and remembrances of early days; and as
one of the rowers, a fine stout lad of seventeen,
jumped up behind a barouche to receive a kiss
from his lovely sister before getting into his boat,
I looked at him with a feeling of sadness mingled
with envy, and rode away to the Castle to join in
festivities to the gaudy splendour of which my
heart was ill attuned. How it did ache that
evening! How often has it ached at that table!
But its unknown and unnoticed yearnings have
been smothered in military music, frivolous talk,
and champagne. It does me no good to record

or dwell upon them, so I will lay down the pen for to-day.[1]

"*June 5th.*—We had a review this morning of the Household regiments, two batteries of artillery, and a regiment of infantry. The sun was very hot and the ground very hard, and the whole went off with the usual quantum of glitter, noise, dust, admiration. There was, however, one *contretemps* which occasioned no little comment afterwards. The Queen was present herself, and had brought the little Prince and Princess with her, it having been distinctly arranged by the Duke, the Commander-in-Chief,[2] that on this account the artillery guns were not to be fired. By some mistake on the part of the aide-de-camp a contrary order was given, and bang, bang went the heavy guns at no great distance from the Royal carriages. The Duke was furious, and stormed at the aide-de-camp and the artillery in a most violent manner. When the Prince tried to pacify him by saying it was doubtless a mistake, he replied, 'It is very good of your Royal Highness to excuse it, but there should be no mistakes : military orders should be punctually obeyed, and, by God! so long as I command the army they shall be obeyed!' The Emperor was astonished, and the suites looked at each other with blank faces, while the artillery were ordered off the manœuvring-ground. Not the least amusing spectacle of the

[1] The reference, of course, is to Murray's attachment, apparently hopeless at that time, to Miss Wadsworth.

[2] The Duke of Wellington.

day was W., 'the wicked Earl,' who had transformed himself into an aide-de-camp, and, clad in a
very fine yeomanry uniform, galloped to and from
the Duke with messages, orders, &c., whilst the
real aides-de-camp remained unemployed behind
him, not knowing whether to laugh or to be angry
at the noble volunteer's *dienstfertigkeit*. . . .

"*June* 6th.—There was an attempt made by a
mad or hot-brained Pole to enter the Emperor's
room. This object he purposed to effect by per-
sonating a tailor from whom a pair of trousers had
been ordered for his Imperial Majesty. He offered
Snip a large sum of money if he would allow him
to deliver these in his stead, and the latter, sus-
pecting something wrong, found secreted about his
person a long thin knife or stiletto. This incident
did not tend to diminish our anxiety or sense of
responsibility for the personal security of our Imperial guest, and in spite of the frank and princely
agrément of his manner and the gaieties to which
his visit gave rise, I, for one, wished him with all
my heart safely back again on the other side of
the Channel.

"*June* 7th.—Returned from Windsor to Buckingham Palace, and was again devoured by the
Cossacks, Uhlans, &c., of the Imperial suite. Such
a packing and unpacking I never beheld : three
royal *cortéges* moving at once from the same house,
besides about a score of private carriages leading,
made the great quadrangle look like a barrack-
room or the marching out of a regiment. . . .

"*June* 8th.—Sightseeing during the day and
the Opera in the evening. At the close of the

first act there was a cry for 'God save the Queen!'
which was received with a burst of applause so
loud and unanimous that the whole *corps drama-
tique* had nothing for it but to come forward,
dressed as they were, and obey. It was really
a very fine sight, for the house was crowded to
excess and every creature in it stood up, so that it
looked like one enormous animated mass, impelled
by one spirit, and that spirit which is nowadays
becoming very lifeless and unfashionable in all
ranks of life—loyalty.[1]

"After the Queen had acknowledged the oft-
repeated cheers by curtseying to the several parts
of the house, the orchestra struck up at once the
Russian hymn, on which the Queen led forward
the Emperor, who bowed his acknowledgments to
the house, and, stooping over her Majesty's hand,
kissed it with much grace and dignity.

"*June 9th, Sunday.* — This morning we were
all very busy again with preparations for the
Emperor's departure, and I had several interviews
with Count Orloff and Baron Brunow on the subject of the *cadeaux d'usage* to be left by his
Majesty. It was rather an awkward matter for
me to speak of (although I was desired merely to
give a memorandum of the presents that had been
given by the King of Russia on his visit), because
my own name appeared on the list : however, I put
myself down on the second class or *boîte à chiffre*,
which was a modest untruth, the King having

[1] Perhaps no more direct testimony than this, read in the light of
the later years of her reign, could be borne to the extent of the
Queen's personal influence in attaching all classes to the Crown.

given me a snuff-box with his portrait. Orloff
showed the list to the Emperor, who approved it
throughout until he came to my name, when he
said, 'Non, non, je veux que M. Murray reçoive
une boîte à portrait: c'est lui qui a fait le plus pour
nous.' This I had from Orloff's own lips when he
gave me the box, which was surmounted by a very
good miniature of the Emperor set in diamonds.[1]

"I had a long conversation with Orloff, whose
character is in some respects as extraordinary as
his position—an illegitimate descendant (grandson)
of Catherine's favourite. He inherits the enormous
personal strength and stature for which the name
is so well known in Europe, and although he has
no recognised ministerial office in the Russian

---

[1] Forty years after this date, Murray added the following note to
this entry : "I have not noted here the several private conversations
that I held with the Emperor in his bedroom at Windsor. It was
my duty to attend him to his apartment every night after the Queen
and her attendants had retired. On three successive evenings he
invited me to follow him into his bedroom. In these *tête-à-tête* conversations he spoke to me upon a variety of subjects with what
seemed unrestrained openness, and frequently alluding to the difficulty of his own position in the world, being often obliged to do
things that he would fain have left undone, and repeatedly assuring
me that his only real happiness was in the bosom of his family. I
know not why he had selected me as the confidant of these *pensées
intimes*, but he frequently afterwards gave me proof of his continued
regard. Two or three years later, when I was Secretary of Legation
at Naples, the Czar paid a short visit to the King, and declined to
receive the Corps Diplomatique ; but he learned that I was there,
and ordered Orloff to invite me to his room at the palace, and
while I was there his Imperial Majesty came in and conversed
with me with his former friendly affability, but he received no other
of the Corps Diplomatique !"

Government, he is in fact the right hand and the mouthpiece of the man who unites in himself all the functions, legislative and executive, of the State. He is a soldier of bold, determined character, and resembles his master not a little in that frank, plain-spoken fearlessness which avows its object and goes straight forward towards it, without heed of difficulties, but not without a tolerably sagacious calculation of consequences.

" He seems much struck by the quiet, undemonstrative efficiency of our metropolitan police, respecting which he said to me, ' Whatever you do, beware of impairing that force : you are every year collecting together in your great towns innumerable multitudes and masses, amongst whom there must every now and then arise discontent and outbreaks. Collision with the military is very dangerous in England, even if you had soldiers enough, which you have *not;* but this police force, if well organised, will continue to be a permanent safeguard.' I left the Count with the impression that he is a very open, frank, straightforward, and withal a sagacious man, and a very useful servant of an autocratic lord. Certainly, so far as generous liberality can win golden opinions, no man ever better deserved popularity in one week than the Emperor during his stay in England, for besides the £500 per annum at Ascot (equal to a donation of £15,000), he ordered £1000 to be given to the Fund for Distressed Foreigners, £500 each to the National Monuments of Nelson and Wellington, and other acts of munificence upon a similar scale. Various are the rumours abroad as to the real

motives of his visit : the most obvious and natural
is probably nearest the truth—viz., a wish to cultivate a good understanding with England, and to
counteract the preponderating influence which the
trip to the Château d'Eu and other late occurrences
had tended to confer on France in respect to the
Court of St James's. Moreover, as we are ex-
pecting a visit from the King of the French this
autumn, the Emperor by his popular manners and
profuse generosity has rendered the game more
difficult for the former to play here with success.
The French press is very angry and bitter on this
subject, and those are not wanting who say that
the 'movement' party will not allow his Majesty to
return our Queen's visit. *Nous verrons.* . . .

"The Czar went through the ceremony of leave-
taking with the frank courtesy which is characteristic of his manners. After coming down the
staircase into the Marble Hall, he bowed over the
Queen's hand and kissed it; he kissed also the
hand of the Duchess of Buccleuch, and shook
hands with all the ladies-in-waiting, as well as
with the great officers of State, who were drawn
up to pay their devoirs at his departure. He
had almost reached the door when his quick eye
detected me, who had placed myself, as became
my rank, somewhat in the rear of the above-named
grandees : he returned immediately and gave me
his hand, saying in English, 'I thank you with
all my heart,' which acknowledgment of such slight
service as I had been able to render to himself
and his suite was very gratifying to me. It was
the first time during his stay that he had ad-

dressed me in English, as on all other occasions,
here or at Windsor, he spoke to me in French,
and once only in German. He stood up in the
carriage bowing to the Queen until it drove off,
and I read amiss the countenances of all the by-
standers if he did not leave behind him the impression that as a man, and one no longer in the
bloom of youth (48), they had rarely encountered
one of more high bearing and courteous chivalrous
deportment : as a monarch I have no space in this
day-book to discuss his qualities. . . .

"*June 24th.*—Heavy clouds are gathering in
the horizon, which threaten at no distant date
to break up the great Conservative party, and
with it Sir Robert Peel's Administration ; for
while on the one hand he is distrusted and disliked for his Liberal opinions by the old Tory
clique, the followers of the Buckingham and Newcastle school, he is equally out of favour with
that restless and unmanageable division of his
army who, under the name of 'Young England,'
daily inflicts its crude sophistries on the House
of Commons, with no other apparent principle in
common than a desire to find fault with everything, and to alter the poet's dictum into 'Whatever is, is wrong.' The fact is, that Sir Robert,
though a man of infinite skill and sagacity in
managing the House, has not the art of gaining
and retaining the confidence or attachment of its
individual members. He is conscious that his
opinions are in general much more 'liberal' than
those of the great body of his supporters, and
that they would desert his standard immediately

if they had any other leader under whose banner they could hope for success. This consciousness prevents him accordingly from consulting them much in the formation of his measures, and they of course complain that they are called upon suddenly to support his views, which have not been explained to them, and from which perhaps many of them dissent. Moreover, Sir Robert is well aware that the English are in the main so aristocratic a people that, in the tone of high and independent rule that he has assumed, they will not forgive his want of 'gentle blood,' and they will in his case exclaim loudly and rebel against a course of conduct which they would patiently have endured from a Howard, a Stanley, or a Plantagenet.

"*June* 28*th.*—The Government is no sooner out of the frying-pan than it is in the fire! For the last few days all London has been ringing with complaints against Sir J. Graham on account of his having caused to be opened at the post-office some letters belonging to one Mazzini, a leading emissary of the movement party in Austrian Italy, now hatching plots to revolutionise that country and throw off the Austrian yoke. At the request of the Government at Vienna the Home Secretary caused several letters to and from this individual to be opened, at which act of 'tyranny,' 'iniquity,' and 'espionage,' that many-headed monster the Liberal press is now declaiming throughout the land with virtuous indignation, which is loudly responded to by honest John Bull, the initial B of whose name ought certainly to have been a G.

" I do not blame the Liberal press, or Mr T.
Duncombe, or the Radical party in general, for
badgering Sir James on this occasion ; 'tis their
vocation to 'stablish a row and work upon it,
and a finer opportunity for ranting declamation
could not be found : but the impudent, hypo-
critical effrontery of the leaders of the present
Opposition in respect to this matter does, I confess, astonish me.   For Lord J. Russell, Lord Palmerston, &c., to get up in their places in Parliament and inveigh against the Home Secretary
in the bitterest terms for doing that which they
well know has been done by every one holding
office for the last century—this must indeed have
required the assurance of a practised lawyer or
a party leader.   I have good reason to believe
that Lord J. Russell has been compelled to resort
to this disagreeable but unavoidable measure more
frequently than any man living, and I have been
told by a person equally accurate and well-informed that, during one part of Lord John's Administration, he opened and read the greater portion of the letters written to and by his friend,
Daniel O'Connell, the great Liberator !

" Baron Stockmar told us an amusing anecdote
also at dinner yesterday, illustrative of the same
truth.   During the year 1830-31, when Lord Palmerston was at the Foreign Office, he (Baron
Stockmar), as confidential secretary to the King
of the Belgians, had occasion to transmit to the
king from time to time letters and despatches
upon secret and important matters connected with
the serious questions then in agitation on the

Continent.   His usual practice was to intrust
these to messengers, but upon one or two occasions, when no messenger was at hand and the
contents were not of vital consequence, he sent
them through the Foreign Office, although he
knew that tricks were sometimes played in
Downing Street as well as in Paris and Vienna.
On one occasion he happened to go into the
Bureau des Affaires Étrangères at Brussels, where
he saw a large parcel of his own despatches tied
together.   He had the curiosity to examine them,
and on close inspection discovered that those sent
through the Foreign Office had been opened and
resealed with a seal not very cleverly made
to imitate his own.   He took no notice of this
at the time, but on the next occasion of his sending a despatch through our Foreign Office sent
it open, and accompanied it with a polite note
to Lord Palmerston, stating that he did so to
save his Lordship the trouble of opening and re-
sealing it."

CHAPTER IX.

1844–1848.

LITERATURE AND DIPLOMACY.

COURT duties, though severe enough at times, were intermittent, and left Murray with uncertain leisure to dispose of. During his tenure of office as Master of the Household he kept up his literary acquaintances, and, besides preparing his volumes of travels, occupied his pen in various ways.

It is well known that the Queen's betrothal to Prince Albert of Saxe-Gotha did not command universal approbation when it was announced. He was suspected of being a Roman Catholic, or at least of belonging to a Roman Catholic family, and the position of that family among European courts was believed to be inferior to that which ought to be secured in the Queen's choice of a consort. To help to dispel these doubts, Murray wrote and published an anonymous pamphlet in

N

1840, addressed to his fellow-countrymen, showing
that not only was the house of Saxe-Coburg Protestant, but that their ancestors, the Princes of
the Ernestine line, were those who had, in fact,
done and suffered most in the cause of the Luth-
eran Reformation; that owing to their exertions
in that cause they had forfeited the Electorate,
and that their existing subordinate position in
comparison with other royal houses was the consequence of their fidelity to Protestantism.   To
this pamphlet was prefixed a pedigree showing
the descent of Prince Albert from Wittekind I. of
Saxony in A.D. 807; and it ends with a spirited
appeal to the people to turn a deaf ear to idle
reports, and to offer the Prince a fair opportunity
of developing the qualities of his character.

Besides this ephemeral, but useful, effort, Murray
was engaged during these years in the preparation
of a romance suggested by his American experience.   Fashion in fiction changes as lightly as in
any other product of civilisation; what holds the
imagination of one generation in thrall is often
flung aside by the next.   But the 'Prairie Bird,'
as already mentioned, has run through many
editions: it is still a favourite with our schoolboys,
and perhaps still more so with those of the United
States.   It is a romance of that kind which Feni-

more Cooper succeeded in making so popular,—
the stirring novel of adventure among Red Indians, which in the 'forties and 'fifties divided
every school playground into Mohicans and Delawares, Pawnees and Iroquois. It deals with the
fortunes of two English families emigrating to the
west, on the confines of the Paleface settlement,
and tells of the perpetual border warfare between
the rival races. The daughter of one of these
families is carried off in early childhood by the
Delawares, grows up in their lodges, and becomes
the adopted daughter of the great chief. The son
of the other house, Reginald Brandon, in whom it
is not difficult to trace some of the traits of the
author, many years afterwards goes on a hunting
expedition with an Indian party, sees this mysterious Prairie Bird, and straightway falls in love.
Through a series of thrilling adventures, involving
many delightful pictures of forest and prairie life,
and reflections of Indian habits and character, the
reader follows the young people to a felicitous conclusion and explanation of much misunderstanding.

The 'Prairie Bird' is not, perhaps, exactly the
kind of novel which is in most incessant vogue at
the present day: it is a story of action, of hairbreadth 'scapes by land and water, of bloody
encounters and scalp-raising, and of somewhat

melodramatic love-making. The "sex problem" does not come up in the remotest degree. Nevertheless, it is very good and exciting reading, even to those who are not in the secret of its composition. But it acquires an additional and romantic interest when it is understood that the novel was designed and executed as the sole expedient by which the author could communicate his feelings to the object of his affection. Forbidden by Mr Wadsworth to correspond with his daughter, no commands could prevent Murray from availing himself of literature as a channel of intercourse. Oolita—the Prairie Bird—was the name he had given his lady-love; none but she understood it—none but she could respond to the sentiments put by the author in the mouth of his hero—none but she interpret the significance of a story of true love overcoming apparently insuperable obstacles.

Apart from this hidden significance, not the least interesting part of the 'Prairie Bird' is contained in the notes, as is the case with some of the Waverley Novels. Probably few people are aware, for instance, that the term "Tammany," so familiar in connection with the municipal affairs of New York, is a corruption of Tamenund—the name of an ancient chief of the Delaware Indians, whose traditionary fame was so great that he became, as it were, their patron saint, and his name was conferred on any individual whom the tribe desired to honour in a special manner.

P. Fraser Tytler to Hon. Charles Murray.

"34 DEVONSHIRE PLACE, 1844.

"I finished 'Prairie Bird' yesterday, and not only I, but our house here (the ladies of which are probably better judges), have been deeply interested and much delighted with it. I will not enter into any enlarged criticism, although I have materials enough, for I read it slowly and marked many beautiful passages and situations, but I must say that the tale in its tendency, its descriptions, and its story is a very delightful one, and in the course of it I often felt happy and gratified that its author was a dear and old friend. I mean to *attempt* a little critique or review of it, but whether I shall succeed or accomplish anything bearable or *printable* is quite uncertain. The style to which I have been so long habituated is so very different from the light airy manner which pleases in periodical criticism. As to Gowrie—I was quite amused at your energy in thinking of instantly attacking a new subject, but much as I admired 'Prairie Bird,' the thought that arose oftenest to my mind was that its author was fitted for graver and greater things, and that there was a power of pure and accurate thought, of picturesque description, and of an easy unaffected style, which, if brought to bear on a high subject,

would bring out something destined to strike its
roots deep. It runs in my head that some eight
or ten years ago I read a novel founded on the
Gowrie Conspiracy, and written, I think, by the
Radical female editor of Tait's 'Edinburgh Magazine,' Mrs Johnston. It made some little noise at
the time, and was superior to the common run of
such works."

" Feb. 26th, 1844.

"I saw young Murray of Albemarle Street on
Saturday, and on sounding him about the Review[1]
of 'Prairie Bird,' he said he had heard it very
highly commended, and seemed disposed to do
everything possible or in his power, but referred
me to Lockhart as the sole manager of such a
matter. On speaking of the talents and energy
shown in the 'Travels' and of the power of writing in the novel, he said he wondered you did
not attack some greater theme, and on my explaining how little time you had for anything
like continuous study, he said, 'Why should not
Mr Murray occasionally write a review himself;
it would be a pleasant occupation.' I mention
this in case you should incline to think better
of the idea. I cannot speak from much personal
experience, but I know many eminent men who
have made review - writing a pretty profitable
business."

"April 15th, 1844.

"I have received a letter from my old friend

[1] For the 'Quarterly,' of which Lockhart was editor.

Alison[1] saying he will be delighted to write a
review of 'Prairie Bird' for Blackwood, if he will
consent to take it; but that he has found the
odium and jealousy subsisting between booksellers
so great that it is quite probable he (Blackwood)
may not choose to insert it. He mentions that he
had written some years ago a review of my History
for 'Blackwood's Magazine,' which Mr Ebony, as
he was nicknamed, did not choose to insert from
jealousy of his rival bookseller Mr Tait. This is
a bit of the secret history of literature which is
somewhat new and amusing."

Fraser Tytler, being an intimate friend of
Murray, may be suspected of partiality in his en-
thusiastic approval of the book, but here is a piece
of independent testimony from another and greater
historian, with whom Murray at that time does
not seem to have been acquainted :—

A. Alison to his Sister.

" We have all been reading with unmixed delight
the 'Prairie Bird,' which more than realised your
own eulogium. It has equally wiled me from
Dante and Freddy from 'Old Mortality,' and the
only annoying thing about reading the work is
that the volumes are in such request by the whole
household that there is always a difficulty in
getting the one you want. It is wonderful how
superior it is to Mr Murray's 'Travels in America';

[1] The historian.

this is his true vein. Many of his descriptions, both at land and sea, are fully equal to Cooper, and in the delineation of European elegance and refinement he is greatly his superior. But what strikes me most is the pure and upright feeling which pervades the work—a feeling very different from what is usually acquired in the precincts of Courts : perhaps it was the experience of that which drove him, like Rousseau, to the desert. I have seen no work for years which has taken such a hold of my imagination as it has done. Elizabeth says every morning at breakfast she feels as if she had parted with old friends, now that she is no longer with War Eagle and Wingemund. I hope he will continue to work the vein he has thus happily found out; for the food of the fashionable world in England is pretty nearly exhausted, and it will be a great thing to get a British Cooper to give us, instead of mawkish Commonplace, the fresh scenes and deep feelings of the Prairie."

Murray used to write at high speed, and often regretted that he could not follow his friend Rogers's example and spend more time in revising.[1]

---

[1] "During my whole life I have borne in mind the speech of a woman to Philip of Macedon : 'I appeal from Philip drunk to Philip sober.' After writing anything in the excitement of the moment and being greatly pleased with it, I have always put it by for a day or two ; and then, carefully considering it in every possible light, I have altered it to the best of my judgment, thus appealing from myself drunk to myself sober. I was engaged on the 'Pleasures of Memory' for nine years ; on 'Human Life' for the same space of time ; and 'Italy' was not completed in less than sixteen years."—(Rogers's 'Table-Talk,' p. 19.) This leisurely system is in curious con-

William Beckford ("Vathek") to Hon.
Charles Murray.

"LONDON, *2nd July* 1839.

"I will not lose a single moment, my dear sir, in thanking you for a delightful and *rare* present —two unvamped-up, unaffected volumes glowing with life and truth.—Believe me most faithfully yours,   W. BECKFORD."

Fraser Tytler, shortly before these letters were written, had brought his 'History of Scotland' to a conclusion, and had availed himself, as the following extracts show, of his younger friend's judgment in style :—

P. Fraser Tytler to the Hon. Charles Murray.

"*November* 13, 1843.

"I send along with this the 'Conclusion' of the History, which you so kindly promised to recast and alter."

"*Nov.* 20*th,* 1843.

"You have laid me under great obligations by your criticism and the kind pains you have taken with my two last pages. It is a great thing to have a *fresh* eye to look over one's manuscript, but still better and rarer to have a fresh eye guided by a pure and just taste ; and this, without

trast with that under which 'Peveril of the Peak,' 'Quentin Dur-
ward,' and 'St Ronan's Well' were given to the press within a single
year.

any flattery, but speaking in the 'beaten way of friendship,' I think you have. I have adopted all your alterations and the whole passage No. 2 as you have recast it, beginning 'and if now destined in the legitimate course of royal succession to lose,' &c. As to the 'sunshine,' I was for a moment a little doubtful, but I ended by feeling that you were right, and extinguished it."

"*Nov.* 21*st*.

"It is a singular coincidence that in speaking to my sister a few nights ago about the 'Prairie Bird,' I could not help saying that you had talents for far higher works ; and now, strange to say, scarce had the words escaped me when your letter comes with a sketch of your new History of Windsor Castle—a subject which, it strikes me, if treated as you would treat it, combining the *true* with the picturesque and the romantic—waving your historic wand and calling up Windsor with its Saxons, lords, and villeins—then Windsor under the Conqueror and his Normans—then peopling its halls with the mighty shades of the Henrys, and the Edwards, the Plantagenets, the Tudors, the Stuarts, and the Royal House of Hanover—in short, Windsor as you yourself describe it—with all its historical, architectural, and chivalrous associations clustering round the grey walls over which so many centuries have swept,—why, I do say (to bring this unmanageable sentence to a close) Windsor Castle, so treated, and its history thus written, would make one of the most attractive and interesting books that could possibly be conceived."

"34 DEVONSHIRE PLACE, 28 *Nov.* 1843.

"The news of your recovery gave me the sincerest pleasure : . . . but do not be too soon well or fly again at ox-fences or five-barred palisades till you are perfectly sound. Meanwhile our literary correspondence is getting so complicated that I scarcely know where to resume it—the History of Windsor—the Duplicates in the British Museum which we are plotting to remove to the Queen's library—the portraits of Bothwell (Mary's infamous husband), about which both Her M. and the Prince spoke to me—and the *best* mode of drawing up a catalogue and forming an interesting arrangement of the historical miniatures and portraits in the Royal Collection,—all these points have been more or less occupying my mind, and had it not been for the constant intrusion of those malapert imps, the printer's devils, with the sheets of vol. ix.,[1] would have been long ere this resumed. To-morrow I get the last sheet of the text of my volume, which you must allow me to send that you may give it one glance ; for you may already say to its closing strains—*quorum pars magna fui.* . . . As to the History of Windsor—I am afraid I must plead Johnson's candid apology— 'Sheer ignorance, sir !' and yet, such is the superficial nature of modern histories and historical antiquaries that one can scarcely argue that because Pote and Pine have found little or nothing —nothing is therefore to be found. As to the difficulty in the research for materials—that need

[1] Of his 'History of Scotland.'

not deter you; for I should gladly quarry, whilst you are polishing and breathing life into the marbles; and these pursuits have become so much a second nature to me that *labor ipse voluptas.* . . . Meanwhile, if these Royal progresses leave you a moment's leisure, think of other historical subjects. There is nothing pleasanter than these literary dreams. What would you say to a series of Lives of Eminent Men, chronologically arranged, written something after the manner of Plutarch— *i.e.,* more of biography in them than dry history, and written with a view to the education of that dear young Prince [1] to whom this country looks with such deep interest and affection, and on whose 'nurture and admonition' so much of its happiness may depend. I remember that, when writing the lives of Henry VIII. and Sir Walter Raleigh, it often struck me that a biographical series on a more compressed plan . . . would be . . . a very interesting and popular work. . . . On calling at Mr Seguier's the other day . . . I found that the curious picture of Lord and Lady Lennox at Darnley's tomb, which we rescued from its decaying condition at Hampton Court, had been cleaned and sent back to Windsor. The inscriptions, you may remember, had been mutilated —some intentionally, some by decay—and must be restored, which can be done, partly from a MS. copy of them which I took, partly from the old print which I had the honour of presenting to Her Majesty by your directions at the time, and which was engraved *before* the mutilation took place."

[1] H.R.H. the Prince of Wales.

The Same to the Same.

"4th Dec. 1843.

"Very far indeed am I from thinking you hypercritical. On the contrary, you do me the greatest service, and I draw upon your patience and acumen again by asking you to give a last look to my last sentence.[1] You will see that all your suggestions are adopted. I would fain hope it will *now* do, but one cannot perhaps be too fastidious in these last touches, though it is also a great matter to know when to stop. . . . It is in these things that a *true* friend is a treasure."

The projected History of Windsor Castle never went beyond the region of intention. There is no doubt that Murray possessed an enviable literary facility, and, had he been dependent on his own exertions for a living, might have realised a handsome one without much difficulty. His portfolios are full of scraps and unfinished drafts, both in prose and poetry; and the knowledge he acquired of various languages (he was able to read and converse in no fewer than fifteen) proves that he must have applied much of his leisure to hard study. During all his life he was keenly interested in past and present literature. Here

---

[1] The closing paragraph of the 'History of Scotland.'

is a funny little formal acknowledgment of his criticism, which a friend had passed on to the author of the subject thereof :—

" RYDAL MOUNT, 24 Nov. 1844.

" The praise is discriminating ; whether deserved or no is not for me to determine ; but I may be allowed to express my gratification in learning from Mr M.'s letter that poetry, certainly not composed with any view to please the higher ranks of society, has made so lively an impression upon the mind of one whose life appears to be passed mainly in the presence or precincts of a Court.—Believe me, truly yours obliged,

" WM. WORDSWORTH."

But the sphere of Murray's official duties was not favourable to the concentration of effort which alone leads to eminence in letters, and he was soon to be called to a more varied field of activity.

The following trifle in one of Murray's common-place-books bears the date 1844, and a note explains that the occasion of it was during a visit to the Archbishop of York at Nuneham, where the attentions paid by a certain sexagenarian bachelor, Mr Young, to a damsel of sixteen, Miss Elizabeth Johnstone, caused a good deal of merriment among the other guests. The lines were

supposed to have been found in Mr Young's room
after his departure :—

"ELIZABETH, or YOUNG'S NIGHT THOUGHTS.
(New Style.)

What's in a name?

"So Juliet said, but Juliet was a fool,
A childish miss, untaught in Cupid's school.
What other sound or word could e'er express
The charms suggested by the name of Bess?
Whether I lay a guinea or a tizzy
That none on earth is half so fair as Lizzy,
Or sing in Tuscan strains the *mille vezzi*
Of thy *leggiadra sembiante*—Betzy,
Or tell, in homelier phrase, the tears that wet
My cheek when thinking of my absent Bet,
Through all the changes of that magic name
Her form I see—her image still the same.
Sometimes I strive, with love-suspended breath,
To syllable thy name—Elizabeth :
Vain, vain attempt ! too soon there will arise a
Half-broken sigh, that cuts it to Eliza ;
Or, whispered low, like Zephyr through the trees,
Dies in the softened murmur of Elise.
In short—sweet name of Carthaginian Dido !
Æneas never loved thee half as well as I do."

In 1845 Murray resigned the Mastership of the
Queen's Household, which he had held for nearly
eight years, on being appointed Secretary to the
British Legation at Naples. He was also made
extra Groom-in-Waiting to the Queen, an appointment which he continued to hold to the end of his

life. Not a trace remains in his papers of record of his sojourn in Italy; but it was marked for him with peculiar melancholy by reason of the death of his mother, the Countess of Dunmore, on 24th May 1846.[1] Two characteristics distinguished this family—the parents and three sons—in a peculiar degree, namely, their deeply religious feeling, and their intense unclouded affection for each other. I have not thought it expedient to give many extracts from private letters in evidence of the first, though it runs constantly through all their correspondence, side by side with the affairs of every-day life. However, it is impossible to understand rightly a man's character without apprehending his feelings towards religion, and the degree in which his happiness depended on those nearest of kin, both of which may be illustrated by these passages from letters written after his mother's death by Charles's sailor brother Henry:—

Capt. the Hon. H. Murray, R.N., to
Hon. Charles Murray.

"*24th May* 1846.

"However much prepared for the worst, such a blow must come with a fearful power of desolation. Yet upon how few can it fall so lightly as upon

[1] The Earl of Dunmore died shortly after Charles Murray's return from America in 1836.

us! It is our blessed privilege to feel that every
emotion of sorrow, however natural and unavoidable, must be tainted with weakness and selfishness,
for we have the clearest ground for the assurance
that for her to die is gain. We mutually feel that
the grace of faith was most brightly developed in
her. We mutually feel that Christ was indeed
precious to her soul, and why? because we beheld
in her the good fruit of those goodly trees of
righteousness. There was no asceticism which
took a gloomy view of religion. The bright rays
of pure love pervaded everything, not only throwing a mantle of cheerfulness over all the innocent
endearments and amusements of social life, but
throwing the same mantle over all the duties of
spiritual life.

" ' God is love' was the bright motto inscribed
upon her heart, and in the eye of faith it was ever
raised before her as the sacred banner under which
every faculty was marshalled and pressed forward
continually in the glorious struggle of ' Holiness
unto the Lord.' "

" 12 PORTMAN SQUARE, *June* 1846.

" Here I am in the first step of my wanderings.
Last evening I gathered all our little household
together, and read them from the xi. Ezekiel, ' Thus
saith the Lord Almighty, Yet will I be to them
as a little sanctuary in the countries where they
shall come,' and ending ' they shall be my people,
and I will be their God.' I endeavoured to say a
few words to them upon the subject, and, by God's

grace, bring it home to them with comfort and profit. This morning at eleven we all read the 63rd Psalm together, and had our little prayer and parted—*such a parting*, all, all so saddened. And well they might be, for when will they again have the same happy experience in any other house? 'How blessed a thing it is for brethren to dwell together in unity!'

"I write all this to you, the *only one left* of the joyous five that once composed our unbroken family circle, because I know it will give you pleasure to feel that to the last I endeavoured to keep our mother's house what it ever had been, a house of prayer. Who can tell the rending of the heart-strings at leaving a home where the grace and goodness of God had been so long and so abundantly vouchsafed, where every new day brought a new blessing, and where I knew the effectual, fervent prayer of a righteous mother was so continually ascending?"

After nearly a year spent at Naples, Murray received in 1846 the appointment of Consul-General in Egypt. A remarkable man, Mohammed Ali, was then the Sultan's Viceroy in that country. Murray was deeply impressed by his powerful, if somewhat unscrupulous and tyrannical, character, and compiled an interesting memoir of him, which is too long for insertion in this place, but a few extracts may be given in order to show the sort of ruler with whom the British Consul-General had to do :—

"In the closing years of the eighteenth century a man, half trader, half soldier, began to distinguish himself in the wars of Egypt. His extraction was humble, but though indigent and meanly descended, though ignorant of everything beyond the rough life of a Turkish guard-house, and the chicaneries of a petty trade, the adventurer had no sooner been placed at the head of a body of troops than he showed himself born for conquest and command. Among the crowd of Osmanlis and Memlooks who were then struggling for the perilous inheritance of the Pharaohs, not one could compare with him in the qualities of the captain and the statesman. He became a general ; he became almost a sovereign. Out of the fragments of old provinces which had gone to pieces in the general wreck of Turkey, he formed for himself a compact and vigorous State. He created a power mightier than that which the arms and sympathies of Europe reared on the ruins of ancient Greece ; mightier than that to which Ypsilanti, with the aid of Russian arms, vainly aspired upon the Danube.

"The State he had rescued from anarchy, he ruled with the ability, severity, and vigilance of Abubekir or Hyder Ali. Rapacious and untaught, he had yet enlargement of mind enough to perceive how much the prosperity of subjects adds to the strength of Government ; and if sometimes mistaken in the method he adopted for attaining this object, he was always consistent in its pursuit. Out of a frightful confusion he educed at least an imperfect order. He was an oppressor, but he had the merits of protecting his people from all oppression but his own, and afforded them a security that they had not enjoyed for many ages. Such was Mohammed Ali, founder of the modern Vice-Royalty of Egypt, and one of the greatest Mussulman captains who has existed since Tarik gave his name to the heights of Calpe, and the stern retribution exacted for a lady's dishonour brought confusion to the banners of Roderick."

Mohammed Ali was born in a peasant's family at Cawala, a small town of Roumelia, in 1769, the same year that gave birth to the Duke of Wellington and Napoleon Bonaparte. His bright, intelligent nature brought him under the notice of a French merchant at Cawala, who took him into his household and taught him the principles of trading.

"The inhabitants of a village in the district of Cawala refused to pay a tax imposed upon them, alleging, probably with perfect truth, that it had already been levied. This tax was the hated *haratch*, an impost as detested as that which called forth the blow of Wat Tyler, or that which estranged the hearts of the Roman populace from Rienzi. It was a sort of poll-tax, paid only

by the Christian subjects of the Porte, and was a
perpetual source of difficulty. It was hated by
the Rayahs, partly from the humiliation attached
to it, and partly from its injustice. It was particularly obnoxious in Roumelia, where three-
fourths of the inhabitants were Christians. . . . It
is probable that in ordinary times the Governor
of Cawala would have ceased to press his claims,
whether just or otherwise. . . . But on this occasion his necessities were pressing, and he was
determined that the tax, whether due or not,
should be paid. While he still hesitated what
course to take, Mohammed Ali offered his services,
and with that boyish ardour which troubles itself
little with consequences, bluntly declared that
he would soon contrive to bring the refractory
villagers to reason. The Governor, half surprised
and half amused at the vaunt, but being at his
wits' end, placed a handful of troops under the
young man's orders, and gave him authority to
act as he pleased.

"His mode of proceeding was marked by all
that energy and decision which has usually
signalised the first exploits of successful military
adventurers. It was bold, artful, and characteristic. It illustrated vividly also the conduct of
the Turkish Government of Roumelia at the time.
It was a rule which had turned one of the most
smiling gardens of the ancient world into a wilderness for the fox and the jackal ; which had caused
the grass to grow in the streets of those beautiful
cities that were the delight of Hadrian, and where
Amurath I. and his successors had forgotten even

the palaces of the Bosphorus. It was a rule that had made the calling of an avenger and a robber the most popular that could be followed by the descendants of those Thracians whose valour had once been the boast of Rome, who had fought under Belisarius and Phocas for the fast-fading glories of the great empire, and who had rallied loyally round even the last impotent princes who swayed the sceptre of Constantine."

In short, Mohammed Ali combined strategy with force in the most approved manner, and the tax was wrung from the luckless villagers. This success secured Mohammed's appointment to the Governor's palace - guard, rapid promotion, and marriage with a relative of the Governor. In the war which broke out with the French in 1789 and ended in their expulsion from Egypt, Mohammed distinguished himself, and rose from post to post, till he attained that of Brigadier - General. He had acquired the full degree of popularity which an army usually accords to a successful general, which he did not scruple to turn to the purposes of his own ambition. He led his soldiers in revolt against Khosrow Pasha, the Sultan's lieutenant in Egypt, and in 1806, being then thirty-seven years of age, was appointed to the post from which he had driven Khosrow Pasha and his successor Khoorshid. To explain such a monstrous reward of rebellion, it is only necessary to mention that it was accomplished by the ordinary methods of Turkish administration—namely, a display of military force and a handsome bribe to the Sultan.

Nevertheless, this was the best thing that could happen to Egypt at this time. It gave the land a strong and sagacious ruler, able and willing to redeem it from the anarchy and poverty to which centuries of Turkish misrule had reduced it. But, having seized the power, a weaker man than Mohammed Ali might well have shrunk from the means necessary to keep it. One incident, which took place in 1811, may be told in Murray's own words :—

" While at Suez superintending the preparations for the Arabian expedition, the Viceroy received a letter from Mohammed Saz, his Kehia Bey, telling him that the Memlooks intended to waylay him on his return to Cairo. Instead, therefore, of remaining at Suez as long as he had intended, he left it that night on a swift dromedary, without letting any one know whither he was going, and reached Cairo with only four attendants by daybreak next morning. This intended treachery, and another plot revealed to him about the same time, determined Mohammed Ali to be beforehand with them. He was indeed thoroughly alarmed, and he laid his plans for the destruction of his enemies with all the craft and determination of his character. The Arabian expedition was ordered to be hastened by every possible means, and the investiture of Toosoon Pasha with the command of the army was assigned as the prelude to its immediate departure.

"An early day was fixed for this ceremony, and all the principal officers were commanded to attend at the Citadel to witness it. The Memlooks were also invited to be present. It was on the morning of the 1st of March 1811, the season when the hot south winds begin to blow, and the heat even in the early morning becomes intolerable to Europeans, that the Memlook Beys rode for the last time prancing and glittering along the streets of Cairo. There were still some fine fellows among them from an oriental point of view. There were men in that magnificent throng who would have galloped gaily up to certain death; who looked upon a battle as a sport; who possessed rude virtues, generosity, hospitality, even friendship; who protected those they loved, and whose affection was easily gained. There were in that brilliant crowd men of gallant soldier natures with open hands and frank tongues; men full of jests and racy humour; good mimics and lusty boon companions. The fatal days of Cholrakhyt and the Pyramids had decimated them. Their body was corrupted by the admission of three or four Frenchmen. But they still numbered four or five thousand horsemen, and, of these, 470 of their best men now rode in state to witness the investiture of the Viceroy's son.

"Chakyn Bey was the first who appeared at the head of his household; the other Beys followed, and the Viceroy received them with great pomp and courtesy in his great hall of audience. The coffee and conversation of the East beguiled the time during the ceremony. When it was over the signal for departure was given, and the Beys took horse to form part of a magnificent procession to the camp.

"A punctilious etiquette was enforced, and every one was compelled to take the place assigned to him by his rank. A corps of the famous Dehlis, whose reckless courage was the pride of Egypt, opened the march. They were commanded by Ouzoun Ali. Then came the Agha of the Janissaries, the Odjaquelys, the Yoldaches, and Saleh Kock with his Albanians in their white fustanellas. In the centre rode the Memlooks, led by Solyman Bey al Baout, renowned for his gigantic stature, and for the inimitable address with which he managed his horse and sabre. The main body of the infantry, the cavalry, and the civil authorities followed. So the column moved towards the gate of El Azab, opening upon the Square of Roumeleh.

"The road leading thither is now so changed that were a Memlook to return to life, he would not recognise the spot where he was trapped. But a credible witness, who was present on that dreadful day, relates that it was a winding and narrow pathway cut in the rock, and flanked by high houses and fortifications. Sharp turns and angles made it impossible for two horsemen to ride abreast; the ground was broken and rugged. No sooner had the Dehlis, Janissaries, and Albanians passed the gate of El Azab than Saleh Kock ordered it to be closed, and communicated to his men the Viceroy's orders for the massacre of the Memlooks. The Albanians immediately faced about, and their light active figures were seen ascending the rock with the agility of goats. The suspicion of treachery immediately flashed across the minds of the Beys, but escape or resistance were alike impossible. A volley of musketry from above revealed the horror of their position. On this preconcerted signal the troops in the rear, posting themselves in the neighbouring houses and behind walls, opened a murderous fire. Men and horses fell under a shower of balls. No courage could avail against an invisible enemy. In vain the Beys turned to fly, hoping at least to regain the Citadel and sell their lives dearly. They could neither advance nor retire; wherever they moved they were picked off by the sharp-sighted Albanians. Their horses, maddened by the shouts and firing, became unmanageable, slipping and falling at every plunge. Some of the Beys rolled themselves to the ground and endeavoured to disentangle themselves of the mass of clothes in which they were enveloped; but the unseen enemy shot them as they lay tumbling about on the ground. Chakyn Bey fell pierced with balls before the gates of Saladin's palace. His body was dragged through the streets with a cord round its neck. Solyman Bey el Baoub found his way, bleeding and half-naked, to the Viceroy's palace: there, gaining the harem, he implored the immemorial right of sanctuary in words dear to many generations of fugitives and captives—*Fy ard el Harem* ('under the protection of the women'). But he was dragged away by the prince's orders and beheaded with a ruthless ferocity, such as only fear could have inspired. Of all who had ridden up to the Citadel in the pride of health and strength, Emin Bey, who leapt his horse over a gap in the wall, was the only one who escaped.

"It is said that hardly had the *cortége* begun to defile when Mohammed Ali became unquiet. His uneasy movements betrayed his emotion. When he heard the first discharge of musketry his agitation increased to a degree quite uncontrollable. He grew pale and trembled. Perhaps he feared that his orders would be executed by faltering hands, and that a bloody struggle might end in his own ruin and murder. Perhaps he repented. The sight of wounded prisoners and trunkless heads soon dispelled all apprehension for his own safety, but could not restore composure to his face nor to his mind. At length the Genoese Mendrici, one of his physicians, entered the apartment where he sat, and approaching him said, with a gay air, such as only an Italian could have assumed under such circumstances,

'The affair is over; this is a happy day for your Highness.' The Viceroy replied nothing, but his silence was expressive, and opening his parched lips, he gasped out a call for water.

"The houses of the Memlooks were given up to plunder. They were stricken down, buying and selling, feasting and marrying. Immense spoils were found. Orders were given to exterminate all who could be found in the city. Punishment was denounced against any one known to harbour them or to facilitate their escape. For two whole days the pillage went on unchecked. Then the Viceroy, in his robes of ceremony, made a solemn procession through the city and put an end to the sack. Those who escaped the general massacre were permitted to retire where they pleased, and to remain unmolested. It is said that about four hundred and forty, with their chief Ibrahim Bey, were murdered in the Citadel. In the city and the country it is supposed that no less than twelve hundred more were sacrificed."

It may be asked how Murray could look with calmness, even with admiration, on the author of such a fearful enormity—a crime of which, when he went to Egypt, he heard from the lips of men who had witnessed it in all the hideous details. Murray could only say that the destruction of the Memlooks was a reform necessary to all other reforms: they frustrated all Mohammed Ali's plans; they had

twice attempted his assassination; he had to play
the game according to their rules or—lose it.

" It is clear that Mohammed Ali had been guilty
of a great crime. The offence cannot be vindicated.
Yet in order that the censure may be justly appor-
tioned to the transgression, the circumstances of
the criminal and of the time must be taken into
consideration. The destruction of the power of
the Memlooks was a reform necessary to all other
reforms. Their rule was tainted with all the vices
of oriental despotism, and with all the vices inseparable from the dominion of race over race.
The conflicting pretensions of the chiefs had produced a series of crimes and disasters such as can
hardly be found elsewhere in the history of the
world. A succession of dissolute Sangiacs, sunk
in indolence and debauchery, rioted away life, eat-
ing opium, fondling concubines, and listening to
buffoons, or they roused themselves only to indulge
in wholesale murders. The wealth of all Egypt
would not have purchased their allegiance to any
Government; no benefits could conciliate, no compact could bind them.

" Oriental politics are a fearful game. Mohammed
Ali was not only struggling for empire, but for life
and liberty. Fear is the most cruel of passions,
and he was beset by powerful, wily, and implacable
enemies. He had been for some time at peace
with them, when they had twice tried to murder
him, and had frustrated all his plans. He knew
that to temporise with them was useless, and to

punish them impossible. Where there is no law,
there will always be violence. There must be some
check on strong and reckless men. There was not
one among the Beys who, in a sound state of society,
might not have been tried and executed as a trait-
orous disturber of the public peace. They were
far worse than the Scottish chiefs who provoked
the massacre of Glencoe. They were more dangerous than the nobles of the League who dis-
tracted the Government of the last Valois. Their
horse, their clothes, their strength, their fine arms,
have invested them with the same kind of romance
which lingers around the splendid Cavaliers who
charged with Rupert at Edgehill, and the noble
gentlemen whose harness shone at Ivry round
Henry of Navarre. But they were in reality little
better than a horde of savage and illiterate men-
at-arms, who cared for nothing but booty, no
matter whence it came. It was dangerous for the
Viceroy to hold terms with them. It was still
more so that he should be known to have been
defied. The favour of the Porte always went to
the strongest : in an instant the Albanians, who
were ready to murder for him while prosperous,
might be hired to slay him, if good fortune deserted him for a single day. He could not eat
without the dread of being poisoned. Let those
who have never been compelled to make a choice
between innocence and greatness, crime and ruin,
pass judgment upon him ; while others are content
to remember how far from the path of right the
best natures have been hurried by the promptings

of fear and the lust of dominion. If judged wholly
by our notions, the massacre of the Beys was indeed an act of inhuman treachery. But it cannot
be looked upon with the same feelings of horror
that we attach to similar crimes which have been
perpetrated by Christian princes — the butchery
of the Swedish nobility by Christian II., and the
slaughter of the Templars by Philip the Fair : it
more nearly resembles the destruction of the
Janissaries, which was effected some years later
at Constantinople.

" If judged, then, by the public opinion of his
countrymen and co-religionists, the Viceroy would
be at once absolved. It is not saying too much to
assert that there was perhaps not a man in authority, from Bayazid to Candia, who would have
hesitated for a moment to act as he did. Moham-
medans are not educated on the same principle as
we are. They are accustomed from infancy to
bloodshed, and punishments such as make our
Christian nature shudder. They kill remorselessly
without passing among each other for ferocious or
cruel. A man who will order his servant to jump
into the sea to save a locust from drowning would
put out the eyes of a political rival, or maim and
torture him to death, without compunction. The
religion of Mohammed is of the sword and not of
peace. It has always consecrated the violence
and legalised the excesses of conquerors. The fall
of the Beys was an inestimable boon to Egypt :
the fall of Mohammed Ali would have rendered
her future hopeless."

Murray claimed for Mohammed Ali that he was a great ruler, not that he was a good man :—

"Not a single great ruler in history can be absolved by a judge who fixes his eye inexorably on one or two unjustifiable acts. With respect to the murder of the Memlooks, the charge against Mohammed Ali, when fairly considered, will amount to this, that he was neither better nor worse than other persons of his age and country; that the founder of a new dynasty in the East can hardly escape some cruel acts; and that he formed no exception to the common rule."

As to the internal administration founded by Mohammed Ali, Murray admits that in many respects it was faulty; but it was infinitely better than anything that had preceded it since the beginning of Turkish rule.

" Whoever seriously considers what it is to construct from the beginning, in a country which had been for centuries the scene of rapine, violence, and anarchy, the whole of a machine so vast and complicated as a Government, will allow that what Mohammed Ali effected deserves great praise. No Mussulman sovereign, since the brilliant domination of the Arabs in Spain, can be compared with him. His justice and toleration were fully equal to that of Saladin. His enlightenment surpassed that of the most famous of the Caliphs of Bagdad. Defective as was the police, heavy as were the public burthens, the oldest men in Egypt could not recollect a time of equal security and general prosperity. For the first time since the reign of Amasis the province was placed under a governor strong enough to prevent others from robbing, and not inclined to play the robber himself. The thanks of the traveller and the stranger are also surely due to him who has made Egypt almost as safe as Yorkshire, and far safer than some of the counties in Ireland."

Of Mohammed Ali's personal methods of administration many curious anecdotes are given. Here is one which he used to tell to Murray as reflecting creditably on his own sagacity as a ruler :—

"Stopping once upon his way from Alexandria to Cairo, and having determined upon making a canal, he sent for the chief engineer of the province. Having given him the length, breadth, and depth of the canal required, he asked the engineer in what space of time he would undertake to make it. The man took out his pencil and paper, and having made his calculations, answered that if the Pasha gave him an order on the governor of the district for the labour required, it might be finished in a year. The reply to this was a signal to the Pasha's servants to throw the engineer on his back and give him two hundred blows with a stick on the soles of his feet. This ceremony being concluded, 'Here,' said the Pasha, 'is an order for the

P

number of labourers you may require. I am going
to Upper Egypt; I shall come back in four months;
if the canal is not completed by the day of my return, you shall have three hundred more. The
work,' he would add, with much self-complacency,
' was punctually executed.'"

Undoubtedly, such a system was liable to intolerable abuse in the hands of subordinates. For
instance, on one occasion a quantity of plate was
stolen from Mohammed Ali's palace at Shoubrah;
the sheik of the Arabs and the *ghafirs*, or watch-
men, in the neighbourhood were thrown into prison
and severely flogged for supposed dereliction of
duty. The unhappy sheik declared that if he
were set at liberty he thought he might catch the
thieves, but that he could do nothing so long as
he was kept in chains. Accordingly, being set
free, he went straight to the slave-market and
bought a couple of negroes lately imported from
the interior, who could not speak a word of
Arabic. Next the sheik, having arranged convenient "testimony" with some of his comrades,
brought the negroes to the palace and accused
them of having stolen the plate. Mohammed Ali
ordered them to be bastinadoed till they confessed,
and if they would not confess, they were to be

hanged. The poor wretches, wholly ignorant of what was going on, thought they had been brought into the service of the palace, and were very well pleased, till they found themselves suddenly thrown down and cruelly beaten. Being unable to confess anything, half an hour later they were swinging from the trees at the back of the palace; the sheik and his comrades went free, and oriental justice was appeased.

In Egypt Murray renewed acquaintance with Harriet Martineau, whom he had met in America many years before, and he has left the following note about her visit :—

"Of all the women whom I have known or met in society, certainly Miss Martineau was one of the shrewdest in her observation and practical in her deductions. Her intellect is what we men are pleased to term 'masculine,' and her style remarkable for clearness and vigour."

Nevertheless, she was not infallible.

"One afternoon we met at the villa of my old friend S. W. Larking, on the banks of the Mahmoudieh Canal. In the course of our stroll through the garden we came to a small gate across one of the gravel walks, the pattern of which was new to Miss Martineau, who was walking in front. She

stopped, and, looking at the little gate in an attitude of intense admiration, exclaimed, 'How truly
oriental! what wonderful taste these Easterns have
in design!' She went on, and as Larking and I
followed through the gate, he whispered to me, 'I
got it out last week from Birmingham!'"

Bearing in mind Murray's early and consistent
hatred of slavery, it was a curious combination of
circumstances which rendered him the purchaser
of one slave, at least, for the British Government.
It came about in this way. A slave-girl, an Abys-
sinian Christian, having fallen into wretched health
and apparently dying, was thrust into the house
of an English resident at Cairo by a slave-dealer
who was just starting on a journey and despaired
of making any profit out of her. The English
family treated her well and restored her to health,
so that when the dealer returned from his journey
and found the girl in a thoroughly marketable
condition he promptly claimed his property.
Naturally the Englishman refused to surrender the
girl who had come under his roof by no culpable
act either of his or hers; but the Egyptian Government supported the dealer's claim, which was
according to law, and threatened to send a company of soldiers to enforce it. The English gentleman appealed to Murray, who could not interfere

directly, as he could not assume that the dealer would maltreat the girl. He therefore applied for instructions, and received the following characteristic reply from " Old Pam." :—

Viscount Palmerston to the Hon. C. A. Murray.

"FOREIGN OFFICE, *August* 5, 1848.

" I have in reply to state to you for your guidance, that if the slave-girl had been brought to the Consulate, we might have claimed a right to retain her, because the Consulate might have been alleged to be invested with the freedom-conferring qualities of British soil; but as she was left at the house of a British subject liable to the laws of the country, and as slave property is part of the Egyptian law, I fear it would be difficult to maintain that the slave-merchant is not by the law of Egypt entitled to have back his slave, or be paid for her.

" But it would be impossible to sanction the surrender of the slave; and therefore I hereby authorise you to pay to and charge in your accounts with this office a fair price for the girl, and then the British merchant may retain her in his service as a free servant, paying her the proper rate of wages.

" The price to be paid should be the value of the girl as she was when sent to the merchant's house, and it seems to me that £30 would be too much; £15 or £20 would be quite enough. But you may settle this as best you can.—I am, &c.,

" PALMERSTON."

The Hon. C. A. Murray to Viscount Palmerston.

"CAIRO, *November* 4, 1848.

"Agreeably to your Lordship's directions, I shall pay the amount requisite for the liberation of the said slave-girl—namely, £35 sterling—and charge the same in my account with the Foreign Office for the current year."

CHAPTER X.

1849–1857.

MARRIAGE AND LIFE IN THE EAST.

IT was during his residence in Egypt that the romance of Murray's early life was brought to a conclusion. It may be told in few words.

Mr Wadsworth, the wealthy owner of Geneseo, in the United States, died in 1849.[1] It is not clear whether Murray heard of this directly,

[1] Mr Wadsworth was a self-made man. Murray, in his volume of Travels, describes with enthusiasm the splendid estate he had won for himself in the fertile valley of the Geneseo: "Yet this scene, extraordinary and interesting as it was, possessed less interest to a contemplative mind than the venerable and excellent gentleman who had almost created it; for it was now forty-four years since Mr Wadsworth came as the first settler to this spot, with an axe on his shoulder, and slept the first night under a tree. After this he lodged in a log-house; subsequently in a cottage; and he is now (1834) the universally esteemed and respected possessor of a demesne which many of the proudest nobility of Europe might look upon with envy, where he exercises the rites of hospitality, in the midst of his amiable family, with a sincerity and kindness that I shall not easily forget."

but at all events there remains in his own handwriting an account of what happened thereafter.
When at Dresden in 1864 he received news that
James Wadsworth, the brother of his first love,
had fallen in one of the battles of the great Civil
War. That event brought vividly before him
the story of thirty years of his life, so vividly
that he told it frankly as follows to the love of
his later years :—

Hon. Charles Murray, C.B., to his Wife.

"EISENACH, 26*th May* 1864.

"After I sent off my letter to you by to-day's
post, I took a long walk in these beautiful hills
and woods. . . . Do you remember where we got
out of the carriage and went up a narrow winding
valley full of high beech-trees and steep over-
hanging cliffs? We only went up a small part
of it, for it was too far for you to walk, but I
followed it for miles—up to the very head, where
it opens out upon a wild elevated chase from
which one looks down upon the Castle of Wartz-
burg on this side, and over leagues of the Thur-
ingian Forest on the other. The beauty of that
walk is indescribable, and in the deep silence of
those enormous beech-groves I reviewed all the
events of my life connected with poor James
Wadsworth. I remembered how I had first seen
him in New York, when he was just starting for
a tour in Europe with his young wife: he was
about twenty-five and she about twenty, and

was, I think, the most perfect and faultless specimen of female beauty that ever I saw in my life.
I gave them letters to Lord Lansdowne and others
in London, and he gave me a letter for his venerable father at Geneseo. It was there that I met
his sister, and I believe that in less than a fortnight our fates were sealed. She was less beautiful, but more intellectual, more winning and
attractive (at all events to me), than his wife.
I visited them again before leaving America, and
our former ties were confirmed and riveted. Then
came a protracted correspondence of parents,—
mine would not hear of my abandoning my country and settling in America, and her father would
not hear of his only remaining daughter leaving
him to settle in England. Moreover, if *he* had
allowed it, I believe her sense of filial duty would
have prevented her from availing herself of the
permission. The letters on both sides became more
peremptory, and at last the whole engagement
was broken off, and all communication between
us positively forbidden. For fourteen years, during
which she refused several of the highest and best
offers in America, did she keep her pure steady
love in her heart unchanged by time and unsup-
ported by hope, and it was only after her father's
death, when we met accidentally in Scotland, that
I learnt that I could still claim her as my own.
. . . You know the rest of her short and sad
story. For a week after little C.[1] was born she
nursed him, oh with what joy and love ! . . . She
said to me suddenly, 'Charlie, is this death?' I

---

[1] Charles James Murray, Esq., M.P. for Coventry.

could not speak, for I knew there was little hope ;
then she desired that all others might leave the
room, and she made me come, and she kissed me
and comforted me, and told me that the one year
of unbroken happiness that we had spent together
was worth a lifetime, and that not one word of
unkindness or cloud of doubt had ever come between us. Then she took my hand in hers and
said to me solemnly, 'Promise me that when you
have recovered from this blow you will marry again.
I want you to be happy again in this world, and
you never can be so without a wife whom you
can love.' I need not tell you that my lips were
unable to utter any such promise; but I turned
her thoughts again to the *horizon céleste*, and I
read her the communion and other prayers, and
as her life-blood was ebbing away she repeated
faintly after me the Lord's Prayer as far as 'Thy
will be done,' when with a sweet smile upon her
face her spirit returned to her Father and her
God ! Why do I repeat all this to you, my sweet
darling ? Why, because you are part of myself,
and poor James Wadsworth's death has brought
it all home to me to-day in my solitary walk,
and all that is in my thoughts and heart should
be unburthened to you, blessed darling, whom
God has given to me to be my joy and comfort,
the future of all my sad memories as well as of
my present happiness; and if her beautiful spirit
can see what now passes on earth, she too will
bless you, Mavourneen, for realising her last
earthly wish concerning me, and for your sweet
tender affection for her child."

I have stated in a former chapter that, during these long years of waiting, Murray held no communication with Miss Wadsworth, save indirectly, through the channel of his published romance—the 'Prairie Bird.' There was a single exception to this silence. The following Indian poem was translated by him from the Delaware and sent to Miss Wadsworth, to whom the significance no doubt was perfectly clear :—

Song of Ah-to-menō or Wounded Eagle.

Ah-to-menō lies on the far Prairies; he puts his ear to the ground, he hears the tread of horses and the voices of the Chiefs, but he hears not the Song of Oolita.

Where is the soft-voiced Prairie-bird? Is she silent from sickness? Perhaps her heart is changed; perhaps she whispers to another warrior, and the wind brings not the sound to Ah-to-menō.

The wounded Eagle's wigwam is cold, an arrow has struck him deep, he has gone to smoke the pipe of peace among great chiefs of a far tribe, but he is a Delaware; his heart is strong; he can hear the mocassin of a creeping Sioux; he can see the squirrel if he stirs a twig on the highest hemlock—then let the Prairie-bird sing at the door of her lodge, Ah-to-menō's ears are open.

Oolita is still silent: is she sad, let her look up to the Manitto; he is good, he will pity Oolita and make her face bright.

Ah-to-menō dwells with the chiefs of the tribe; among their lodges he is welcome; their daughters have eyes like the antelope, and their tongues are like the mocking-bird, but the wounded Eagle remembers the soft voice of Oolito.

AH-TO-MENŌ NEVER FORGETS.

That is the whole touching tale—fifteen years of constancy almost destitute of hope, and without a syllable of direct intercourse, written or spoken; an unexpected meeting; a year of perfect happiness; a crushing blow; eleven years of solitary mourning, mitigated only by the duties of an incessantly active life and the care for his child; then—happiness once more; union with another, with whom, to the end of his days, Murray lived in perfect harmony and love.

Human relations of this nature are delicate matter for a stranger's hand. Discretion is prone to err in resolving what to reveal and what to withhold; yet the story of Murray's life would be incomplete without a reference, however brief, to the peace which he found in his second marriage. From a long series of letters to Lady Murray which are before me it will suffice to make a single other extract from one written the day before that quoted from above, which may serve to show the nature and extent of the confidence which existed between them and endured to the end. Murray had been reading a French book, 'Horizons Célestes,' which was a favourite of his wife.

Hon. Charles Murray to his Wife.

"EISENACH, 25*th May* 1864.

"I have been reading your 'Horizons Célestes,' my darling, for an hour. There are thoughts and expressions of almost unearthly beauty, and somehow I can scarcely imagine it written by a Frenchman! In some respects I feel with shame that the writer is too good for me, and that his spirit soars into regions where I would fain follow him, but cannot! Some of his reasonings which I can follow must be taken with a certain reserve; as, for instance, where he reproves, as human weakness and infidelity, feelings which are really a natural and necessary result of the circumstances in which God has placed us in this world. Speaking of our once loved but long since dead, he says, 'Si l'on venait vous dire, "Il est là!" vous vous trouverez plus embarrassé que ravi.' Very often this *would* happen; but, as I maintain, not from any untruthfulness or degradation in our nature. Suppose a son who is deeply and devotedly fond of his father, and that father, who is a prince or man of great possessions, dies when the youth is eighteen; say that after five years he married, has children, and suppose that five years again after that, when he has formed all these new ties and accustomed himself to the discharge of all the duties of his position, some one could enter and say to him, 'Your father is alive again, and is at the door,' would he not naturally be 'plus embarrassé que ravi'? Or take my own case. You will not doubt that I loved Charlie's mother; you know that I

loved her for fifteen years before we were married;
you have often let me speak to you of her endear-
ing qualities, and you know that I still love and
revere her memory as that of a saint in heaven ; and
how, when, after years and years of solitary existence, God has blessed me with the precious love of
Mavourneen, and that our daily thoughts, habits,
and affections are interwoven with each other,
could it be any reproach to me to say that, if some
supernatural influence were to come to me and
say, 'Elle est là!' I should be 'plus embarrassé
que ravi'? The truth is, . . . those authors
who depict and describe the feelings with such
eloquent analysis often forget, what God never
forgets, how they are necessarily coloured, modi-
fied, and controlled by the events and circumstances amidst which Providence has cast our lot.
M. de W., the Minister here, has just called and
kept me half an hour in conversation, thereby
bringing down my thoughts from 'les horizons
célestes' to a 'horizon prochain,' including of
course Schleswig-Holstein, anent which matter,
if to-day's telegrams are true, poor Denmark's
prospects from the Conference are darker than
ever !"

Returning now to the year 1850—Murray married Miss Elise Wadsworth, "the Prairie Bird,"
on 12th December : on 8th December 1851 she
died after giving birth to her son. Mrs Murray
had inherited a very large share of her father's
wealth, which she left by will to her husband.

Owing, however, to the nature of American law, which prohibited aliens inheriting property in the States unless they become naturalised citizens, Murray found himself debarred from any advantage under this will : his late wife's fortune passed to her brothers. These gentlemen, with singular generosity, exerted themselves successfully to obtain a special Act of Congress, waiving in the case of Charles Murray the obligation to become naturalised, and enabling him to enter upon possession of the whole property of his American wife.

Changes were already beginning to make the United States, as Murray knew them, hardly to be recognised.

J. Fenimore Cooper to the Hon. Charles Murray, C.B.

"COOPERSTOWN, *Oct.* 23*rd,* 1850.

"We are 'progressing,' as we Americans say, at a famous rate. New York must have doubled its population, nearly, since you saw it, and has quadrupled its show. Really good houses are built, such as would be so considered in any town in Europe. Mother Trinity has disappeared, and a substitute has been raised in her place which ranks with the new church edifices of England. It has a little too much of the partridge in the way of tail, having just so many feet, and no more, for its length.

"Taking all things together, I regard New York as the most remarkable town in the world. I can distinctly recollect it, a place of 50,000 souls, and now it has a suburb of more than 100,000! Trade is driving all before it, and has fairly invaded Broadway. The Globe, the Clarendon of your time, is turned into stores, and the City Hotel has been laid in the dust.

"Talking of the dust, which is so shortly to be my portion, one of the most painful of my recollections of my own travels is the great number of dead among the acquaintances I made. At one time it really seemed as if to know me was to die. Some remain, however, and among them is the noble-hearted Rogers. If you ever see him now, tell him that we all love him and often speak of him. I daresay my wife prays for him. . . .

"There is a good deal of trembling in our body politic, but I think nothing will come of it just now. The South has too much at stake to risk, and every day it loses, increases the disparity of the forces. . . . What we are to do with the blacks, God knows; but we shall never amalgamate. . . .

"Now I must tell you a little about the 'knockings.' In one word, they are the most extraordinary things I have ever met with. All attempts at explanation are failures. They are not confined to one family, or one place, but have been heard in fifty places. Bancroft stood on one side of a door and I on the other, each with a hand on the panels. To me he seemed to be knocking all over the door, and *vice versâ*. Both of us felt the

vibration of the door, which was one of our own
choosing, and where the 'ladies' were strangers.
I am inclined to think more exists than is dreamt
of in our philosophy. I am not cracked, but as
cool and clear-headed as I ever have been, but no
more believe that the 'ladies' produced the knockings I heard than I believe that you and I are
Turks. Depend upon it, it is the great mystery
of our time. . . . —Adieu. Very truly yours,
"J. FENIMORE COOPER."

During his administration in Egypt Murray
earned the complete confidence of the British
residents, which was testified by the presentation
in 1852 of an illuminated address to him in
"the triple capacity of Minister, Magistrate, and
Friend." The course of affairs in Egypt, even
before the existence of the Suez Canal had
rendered that country the highroad to India,
and letters from Lord Dalhousie, the Governor-
General, show how much he relied on Murray's
judgment and knowledge of oriental people :—

*The Earl of Dalhousie to Hon. Charles
Murray, C.B.*

"GOVERNMENT HOUSE, CALCUTTA,
April 18th, 1848.

"MY DEAR MURRAY,—The news brought by the
mail of February 24th, and confirmed and enlarged
by this one, are such as to suggest the keeping

Q

one's eyes as wide open as they will go. News
from your part of the world will be of especial
importance.   You will not think me needlessly
troublesome, therefore, if I ask you to do me the
favour of sending me privately, as you may see
occasion, a line or two, to let me know what facts
or what symptoms there are in and about the
Mediterranean. You will know very well what
sort of intelligence I want.   Let it be ever so short,
it will be acceptable and valuable."

" June 2nd, 1852.

"I rejoice that you have remained at your post.
Whatever the issue may be, people would have
said that it would have been better if you had
been there.   Indeed you truly say that 'we have
lippened[1] aye to Providence'; Lord Derby seems
as ready as his predecessors to add, like the old
song, 'and sae will we yet'!"

" April 3rd, 1853.

"The pleasure I had in learning that you were
again in Egypt was short - lived.   You have
thoroughly earned the promotion which you tell
me you are immediately to get; but I shall very
sincerely regret its effect in your removal from
Cairo and from your care of our interests there,
while everything for which your presence would be
valuable is still in so unsettled a state.   There is a
French frigate with a steamer and an admiral
going up the Red Sea now—what business can
they have there? and yet I have no right to ask

[1] Trusted.

the question. You will of course know what their professed object is and will divine their real one, and I should be glad to know if it is anything special."

"*August 3rd*, 1853.

" Naturally I feel a good deal of anxiety until this Russian business is settled, but I cannot think it possible that the Emperor can really go to war against such odds and with so bad a case. If he does, he is mad as Saul."

Perhaps the event by which the British public at home have most cause to remember Murray's Consul-Generalship is the important part he took in securing a hippopotamus for the Zoological Society — the first that had been in England since the tertiary age of geology, and the first in Europe since the early Roman empire. Murray persuaded the Viceroy, Abbas Pasha, to send a party of hunters in July 1849, specially organised for the purpose, to capture a calf on the White Nile. This they effected on the island of Obaysch : the baby hippopotamus travelled down many hundred miles, escorted by a company of infantry, to Cairo, where it was safely delivered to Murray in the month of November. By the friendly co-operation of the Peninsular and Oriental Company a chamber was constructed on their steamship Ripon, in which the hippopotamus was conveyed to England, and deposited in the Zoological Society's Gardens on 25th May 1850. Obaysch, for so he was named after the place of his capture, was supplied with a mate, Adhela, in 1853, and lived twenty-eight years in Regent's Park, dying in 1878. Mr Philip Lutley Sclater, the present secretary to the Society, remembers Murray frequently visiting his old pet, shouting to him in Arabic, when the enormous creature would come towards him, grunting loudly in recognition of one of his earliest friends. Murray makes allusion to this achievement in a journal kept during part of his time in Persia. His party had encountered lions on the journey from Bazrah to Bagdad.

"*March* 20, 1857.— . . . So there *are* lions here, despite my incredulity. So there are also in London, Paris, and everywhere else! I was one myself for a short time—*i.e.*, when I brought over to England the first hippopotamus that had been seen alive in Europe since the earlier days of the Roman empire, and I was called Hippopotamus Murray, a more noble *sobriquet* after all than 'Bear' Ellice, 'Poodle' Byng, and others that I have known to have their lion day in London—viz., 'Bull' Townshend, 'Bum' Gordon, 'Tiger' Bailey, &c., &c., with many others, not to mention lionesses and cubs. Egypt has many memories for me. I rendered at least three public services there—one to science, one to politics, and one to commerce. I brought the hippopotamus *out of it* alive to Europe ; I *kept* the cursed *tanzimat* [legalised anarchy] *out of it*, in spite of Sir Stratford Canning and the Sublime Porte ; and I brought the railway *into* it, in spite of French and Turkish intrigues."

In 1853 Murray finished his seventh year of office in Egypt, and was appointed to Berne as Minister to the Swiss Confederation. Being home on leave in August 1854, Lord Clarendon, the Foreign Secretary, sent for him and offered him the mission to Persia. Murray hesitated. He had been long away from England ; and if he went to Persia he must leave his motherless child behind him. He stated the grounds of his reluctance to Lord Clarendon, who seemed vexed, and observed that " as her Majesty's Government had paid him the compliment of appointing him because they thought him the fittest man to be sent on the occasion, he considered it his duty to accept it."

The impression on Murray's mind was, that if he intended to remain in the diplomatic service, to persist in his refusal would be fatal to his prospects. Therefore, after taking a day to consider it, he accepted the appointment, and leaving his boy in the good keeping of the Dowager-Duchess of Hamilton, he set off for his new sphere of labour as Envoy and Minister Plenipotentiary to the Court of Persia. Here was an admirable opportunity, duly appreciated by him, of increasing his knowledge of oriental languages and literature; but circumstances rendered Tehran anything but a bed of roses for the British Minister at that time.

England was at war with Russia, and although the chief stress of that war lay in the Black Sea, an advance might at any time be directed on the North - West frontier of India, which Russia, according to her traditional policy, had been steadily approaching for years. Hence it was the policy of the British Government to aim at maintaining the independence of Persia, in the event of its being threatened by Russia, and, on the other hand, to restrain Persia from renewing her former attacks upon Afghan territory.

The state of affairs, then, when Murray went to Tehran at the close of 1854, was this. Persia, which had occupied Herat in 1852, had entered into a treaty with Great Britain to evacuate that city, to refrain from exercising any rights of sovereignty in Afghan territory, and from sending troops to Herat, except when troops from without should attack that place. Persian foreign policy had assumed its normal character of a simultaneous flirtation with the Governments of Russia and Great Britain, Russia being for the moment the favoured swain.

The Shah, however, was a puppet in the hands of his ambitious Premier, the Sadr Azim, who, in order to maintain control of his royal master, encouraged him in debauchery and drunkenness, and meanwhile kept his eyes intently fixed on the coveted territory of Herat, awaiting the first opportunity which might present itself of seizing it.

Such an opportunity arose before Murray had been a year at Tehran. An insurrection took place in Herat; the reigning prince, Synd Mahommed, was killed, and Yuzoof Khan became ruler in his place. Under the circumstances the presence of a British Minister in Tehran became exceedingly irksome to the Shah and his Minister. At all hazards he must be got rid of, and oriental diplomacy was at no loss for means to bring about his disgrace. In June 1854, before Murray's appointment to Tehran, Mr Thomson, the Secretary to the Mission, had appointed one Meerza Hashem Khan to be First Persian Secretary to the Mission. This Meerza Hashem, who had been formerly in the Shah's service, and had married a lady of the royal family of Persia, had earned the displeasure of the Sadr Azim, and had sought privilege of sanctuary in the British Mission. Ten weeks after his appointment, the Persian Government intimated their disapproval of his employment in the Mission. Murray on his arrival, in order to please the Court of Tehran, removed Meerza Hashem from the secretaryship, and appointed him British agent at Shiraz. To this also the Shah's Government objected, refusing to recognise Meerza Hashem as British agent, and made his appointment the pretext for formulating odious charges against both Murray and Mr Thomson, whom they accused of having improper relations with Meerza's wife. This lady was seized and imprisoned, which was a violation of the rights enjoyed under treaty by the members and employees of the British Mission. Murray demanded her release, and an apology for the false charges made against him and Mr Thomson. The temper of the Persian Government may be understood from the following autograph of the Shah to his Prime Minister :—

The Shah to the Sadr Azim (autograph).

(Translation.)   *" December* 1855.

" Last night we read the paper written by the English Minister Plenipotentiary, and were much surprised at the rude, unmeaning, disgusting, and insolent tone and purport. The letter which he before wrote was also impertinent. We have also heard that in his own house he is constantly speaking disrespectfully of us and of you, but we never believed; now, however, he has introduced it in an official letter. We are therefore convinced that this man, Mister Murray, is stupid, ignorant, and insane, who has the audacity and impudence to insult even Kings! From the time of Shah Sultan Hossein (when Persia was in its most disorganised state, and during the last fourteen years of his life, when, by serious illness, he was incapacitated for business) up to the present time, no disrespect towards the Sovereign has been tolerated either from the Government or its agent. What has happened now that this foolish Minister Plenipotentiary acts with such temerity? It appears that our friendly Missions are not acquainted with the wording of that document; give it now to Meerza Abbas and Meerza Malcum, that they may take and duly explain it to the French Minister and Hyder Effendi, that they may see how improperly he has written. Since last night till now our time has been passed in vexation. We now command you, in order that you may yourself know, and also acquaint the Missions, that until the Queen[1] of England her-self makes us a suitable apology for the insolence of her Envoy, we will never receive back this her foolish Minister, who is a simpleton, nor accept from her Government any other Minister."

[1] The exceedingly objectionable term "Malikeh" is used in the original.

Shortly before the time that this firework was discharged, Dost Mahommed, ruler of Cabul, advanced against Candahar, which afforded a pretext for the Persian Government to disregard the treaty of 1853 and to lay siege to Herat.

Meanwhile Murray's request for the release of Meerza Hashem's wife having been refused, and the offensive insinuations regarding her relations with the British Minister and Secretary having been publicly repeated, Murray determined to strike his flag and retire from Tehran. This extreme step received the approval of Lord Clarendon, then Secretary of State for Foreign Affairs. Murray therefore withdrew with the British Mission to Tabreez, in Turkish territory, leaving Mr Stevens as Consul to act in his absence. But this also displeased the Shah, who wrote as follows to his Prime Minister:—

The Shah to the Sadr Azim (autograph).

(Extract translated.)

"Minister for Foreign Affairs.   *November* 22, 1855.

"I have seen the British Minister's letter, and I am aware of his intention to leave, and of his request for a Mehmandar. Indeed, if the advantages which are to accrue to us from the residence of a British Minister here are those which we see, it is for the benefit of both Governments that he should quarrel and depart. Whenever I contrast my own sincerity to the British Government, and the expectations which I entertain at heart from their friendship with the conduct of the Mission, I am drowned in a sea of amazement. . . . With regard to what he has written, that he will leave a Consul here, if by Consul he means Mr Stevens, whose proceedings and mischief-making, while living in Tabreez, would fill ten books, and whose proceedings here are just what you now see—when Mr Murray, as Minister Plenipotentiary, has become the cause of coolness and misunderstanding in this way between the two Governments, what are we to expect, and what confidence can we have in a person like Mr Stevens, notorious for his mischief-making? If the British Minister goes, let him take with him Mr Stevens; let him place some one else in his place. Send a copy of this autograph in answer to the Minister's letter, and prepare the details of his conduct for the information of the British Ministers, together with the real truth of the question. If the British Minister desires the humiliation of this Government, of course we, so long as we have the power, will not submit to any indignity."

It is obvious that the policy and intentions of the Persian Government at this time rendered the presence of any British representatives whatsoever at Tehran exceedingly inconvenient. Consul Stevens, however, remained, and continued to send reports on the course of events to the

British Foreign Office, Lord Clarendon having instructed him (May 15, 1856) to "abstain from all communication, direct or indirect, with the Persian Government."

On the same day Lord Clarendon replied through Lord Stratford de Redcliffe, Minister at Constantinople, to overtures on the part of the Persian Government for the return of the British Mission to Tehran, provided Mr Murray were recalled and another Minister sent in his place.

The Earl of Clarendon to Lord Sratford de Redcliffe.

"FOREIGN OFFICE, *May* 15, 1856.

"Her Majesty's Government have no wish to prolong, unnecessarily, an estrangement which was created by the acts of the Persian Government; but they cannot consent to accept an inadequate reparation from that Government. They require that it should be made by the Persian Minister, who was the author of the wrong; that it should be ample in its character, and brought publicly to the knowledge of the inhabitants of the capital.

"In the next place, although, if any well-founded objections of the Persian Government to the employment of Meerza Hashem as Agent, at Shiraz, of the British Mission, had been duly brought before them by that Government, her Majesty's Government might have refrained from sanctioning his appointment; yet as no sufficient explanation has been given of the reasons on account of which the Persian Government made their objection, and as the Persian Prime Minister has thought fit to impugn the motives of her Majesty's Minister for insisting upon the employment of the Meerza at Shiraz, her Majesty's Government must now require that Meerza Hashem should proceed to Shiraz as Agent of the British Mission, his wife being at once restored to him.

"If the course which the Persian Government may determine to take on this matter should admit of the return of her Majesty's Minister to Tehran, her Majesty's Government will consent that the whole of the correspondence between her Majesty's Mission and the Persian Government, in regard to the appointment of Meerza Hashem, should be mutually withdrawn and be cancelled ; but her Majesty's Government will expect and require that when the British flag is again hoisted over the residence of the British Mission, the reconciliation which will have been effected between the two Governments shall be made known to the inhabitants of Tehran by a salute of twenty-one guns, to be fired in honour of the British flag. The Sadr Azim must also immediately afterwards pay a visit of ceremony to her Majesty's Minister, who would return that visit the next day.

"Your Excellency will communicate to the Persian *Chargé d'Affaires,* for the information of his Government, the observations contained in this despatch."

It will be observed that Murray himself had not

been responsible for that which had been made the chief subject of complaint against him,—the appointment of Meerza Hashem as first Persian Secretary to the Mission,—seeing that Hashem's appointment had been made before Murray's arrival in Tehran.

On the same day, May 15, instructions were sent by Lord Clarendon to Murray to proceed with his Mission to Bagdad. By this time the Persian troops had invested Herat.

On June 23rd Lord Stratford de Redcliffe prepared an ultimatum to be presented to the Shah, of which the first article stipulated that the Sadr Azim was " to write in the Shah's name a letter to Mr Murray, expressing his regret at having uttered and given currency to the offensive imputations upon the honour of her Majesty's Minister"; that Mr Murray should be received on his return to Tehran by persons of high rank, who should escort him to his residence; and that the British flag should then be hoisted with a salute of twenty-one guns. The remaining articles provided for the withdrawal of Persian troops from Herat, and that the question of Meerza Hashem and his wife should subsequently be submitted to a convention.

No notice having been taken of this ultimatum,

instructions were sent from the Foreign Office to
the India Board [1] directing the despatch of an
expedition to the Persian Gulf. On November
1st, 1856, proclamation of war between Great
Britain and Persia was made. The British fleet
bombarded Bushire in the Persian Gulf on December 17th, and the land forces under General
Stalker came up in time to receive the surrender
of the garrison. On January 15th, 1857, General
Outram left Bombay with a strong force and
landed at Bushire on the 27th. He encountered
the Persian army under Soojah-ool-Moolk near
Kooshab on 8th February, and completely defeated them, and again at Mohammerah on 24th
March. Meanwhile a treaty of peace had been
signed at Paris between the Queen of Great
Britain and the Shah of Persia, which was afterwards ratified at Bagdad on 2nd May. In this
treaty reference was made to a separate note,
which provided that full reparation should be
made to Mr Murray for the personal affronts
offered to him, that the Shah's apology should
be transmitted through the Sadr Azim to Mr
Murray, that all imputations against Mr Murray should be withdrawn, and that he should be

[1] It will be remembered that the Government of India was still in
the hands of the East India Company, under the Governor-General
in Council.

invited by the Shah to return with the Mission to Tehran.

Now this dispute has been reviewed at somewhat greater length than it may seem to deserve, considering the lapse of years since it was settled; but Murray's conduct at the time was sharply criticised in the British press and in Parliament, and the ugly stories circulated by the Sadr Azim and his agents received some degree of credence in this country.[1]

Hon. Charles Murray to Capt. Hon. Henry Murray, R.N.

"OOROOMIAH, 5th April 1856.

" By the last papers that reached me at Tabriz, I learnt that some of the London journals had begun to abuse me; among others, the 'Times,' saying that I had broken off the good understanding between two allied countries on account of a foolish dispute about a woman. These wise men writing in their garrets in the City or the Strand, scatter their thunders over the earth, and condemn, without the slightest knowledge of causes or events, those who are at a distance conscien-

[1] While preparing this memoir I received an illustration of how easily dirt sticks if enough of it is thrown. Speaking to a gentleman who had known Mr Murray slightly in his later years, I asked if he could tell me anything about the origin of the Persian quarrel. "Oh yes," he replied; "let me see ! Murray got mixed up with some woman there, didn't he ? I don't remember much about it, but I am pretty sure there was a woman at the bottom of the trouble."

tiously endeavouring to uphold the honour and interest of England, and the placid citizen seated at his cosy breakfast-table cries 'Amen!' to their unjust sentence.   They know as much of Persia as I know of the moon; they write as if laws, usages, and conventional modes recognised in Europe were current here, and as if a Mirza appointed by the British Mission were like an attorney or scribe engaged by a Foreign Mission in London.   The doctrine of protection and sanctuary as accorded to the British and Russian Missions here for fifty years past, which (whether founded in right or in error) has been held inviolate and has saved the lives of hundreds of Persians, among others that of the present Sadr Azem himself, is to these sarcastic gentlemen a rock of offence, and *I* ought to have been the first to give up to insolent and arrogant demand a privilege enjoyed by all my predecessors and my present colleagues.   They are ignorant of facts which must come out if the correspondence is laid open by Parliamentary inquiry; such, for instance, as that for weeks and months the Persian Government had refused me redress for the injuries complained of by our subjects, and for direct affronts offered to the Mission in the maltreatment of my servants; that the Sadr Azem, secretly on an understanding with the Russian *Chargé d'affaires*, had insulted the English and the French Governments by a pretended proposal of active alliance *against* Russia, the draft of which proposed treaty was in the hands of the Russian as soon as, if not before, it reached us; nay—it was translated to M. Bourée by the *Sadr's*

R

*confidential secretary, the son of the first interpreter
to the Russian mission :* it was on discovering this
fact, and on ascertaining that in spite of my re-
monstrances this individual continued to be the
confidential go-between of the Sadr and M. Bourée
in all their communications, that I felt convinced
that the *first* was playing us false, and the *second*
either infatuated or false to English alliance, I
could not tell which. Motives are not within
the sphere of man's cognisance ; it was enough
for me to know that from that time I could neither
trust the Sadr nor my colleague."

"BAGDAD, *May 8th,* 1856.

" Here I am once more, dear Hal, in the city of
the Caliphs, having plunged at once from the snows
of Kurdistan into this burning plain, with a ther-
mometer already at 98° in our coolest room, and
knowing that it must soon rise to 120°. I am
thankful, however, to be able to add that none of
my party have suffered in health, and that flies
and perspiration are our worst grievances. Since
I last wrote to you several posts have arrived from
England, but *not one word* from the Foreign Office
about the rupture with Persia, nor any intimation
of the views or intentions of her Majesty's Government. You may well believe that this protracted apathy on their part has caused me the
greatest mortification, as it will assuredly be pro-
ductive of most disastrous consequences to the
interests of Great Britain in Asia. Had her
Majesty's Government, *immediately* after approv-
ing my conduct in withdrawing the Mission from

Tehran, sent out an energetic despatch, peremptorily demanding reparation for the repeated insults offered by the Persian Government to the British flag, with a distinct intimation that if refused coercive measures would be adopted, I *know it as certainly* as that two and two are four, the Persian Government was prepared to concede all our demands at once. I should have gone back to Tehran with increased strength and influence, and not a Persian soldier would have marched in the direction of Herat. Now, by wasting four months in silence and inaction, our Government has given currency to the falsehoods and slanders circulated by the Sadr Azem against myself and the Mission, one of which was that the rupture which had taken place was a paltry personal quarrel with myself, and no way affecting the relations of the two countries. Has not the conduct of our Government been such as virtually to corroborate this statement ? Is not the British public, indeed the whole world, justified in inferring that if the British Government really felt itself injured and insulted by that of Persia, they would within four months express *some* dissatisfaction, and demand some reparation ? Is it not quite natural that the Press, the gossips in private circles, and the talking busybodies in Parliament, should all fall upon *me* as an indiscreet embroiler of our friendly relations with a foreign Power ? The general grievance-hunter and calumniator of the absent, whom the public in England look upon as an oracle in all political questions in Asia, because he was an energetic excavator of antiquities

at Nineveh, gets up in his place in Parliament
and pronounces me ignorant of the customs and
language of Persia, makes a fine tirade upon the
insignificance of the Mirza Hashem dispute, and
throws mud at me in order to dirty the Government. Lord Palmerston answered him, it is true,
but gave none of the details necessary to contradict his statements and to remove the impression
made by his speech on the public mind. The
newspaper critics of course follow in the same
strain, although in truth Mr Oracle Layard knows
no more of Persian affairs than I do of those of
Brazil. He once made a rapid march through
the country, I believe, on his way from India to
Constantinople, but he never resided in it, and
knows absolutely nothing of its politics, laws, or
institutions. He gravely tells his hearers that we
have no right to appoint *any* agent at Shiraz, not
knowing that we *have had* one there for a score of
years, whose functions (such as they are) have been
a score of times admitted and recognised by the
Persian Government, and in appointing Mirza
Hashem to that post we merely changed him for
another Mirza, also a Persian Government. Mr
Layard also told his hearers that the Shah had by
Moslem law a perfect right to take Mirza Hashem's
wife from him and seclude her elsewhere, whereas
if Mr Oracle had known the first rudiments of
Moslem law, he would have known that, according
to it, no earthly prince or potentate can separate
a wife from her husband without the consent of
the latter : a married woman might indeed be
imprisoned by a decree of the Moshtehids—*i.e.,*

chiefs of religion — if adultery can be proved against her, but that must be the result of a regular trial, and must be substantiated by the positive evidence of *delictum flagrans*, given by three witnesses. It is needless to add that in this case, although the poor woman was belied, calumniated, and imprisoned by the Sadr Azem, there was no proof of adultery adduced, or even attempted. The latter fact has caused me no little surprise, considering the unscrupulous nature of the Sadr's character and conduct; for just as he compelled some of the Ulema to seal and subscribe his lies against me, he could in Tehran have easily obtained a dozen witnesses to swear that they had seen Mrs Mirza Hashem in my bed or in that of my groom. Naturally enough, the uncontradicted dicta of the Nineveh oracle are received as gospel by the newspaper writers, and the consequence is that I have already seen in the 'Times,' the 'Home News,' the Indian papers, &c., that I know nothing of Persia or the Persian language, and that in this foolish quarrel the Mission is all wrong and the Persian Government all right. Strange world; for the fact is, that one of the reasons which made the Sadr dislike me and try to get rid of me was because I had begun to hold *tête-à-tête* interviews with the Shah, at which neither he nor any of his spies were present. It is of comparatively little importance that my conduct and qualifications should be for a time misrepresented, because some day or other the truth must come out, and my skin is not so thin but that I can eat heartily and sleep soundly under the 'slashing' articles and speeches, whether uttered by oracular newspapers or senators; but the injury already done to the public service by the silence and inaction of our Foreign Office is very great, and is daily increasing."

"BAGDAD, *April 5th*, 1857.

" I was truly glad to find here, on my return from the Gulf, your letter written from the dear old shop[1] on the 10th, and could not help thinking of the merry hours we have often spent on that day enlivened by Rob of Carnock's fiddle—the reel—the country dance—the whisky-toddie, and Bab at the Bowster as the grand finale ! and now your pow's as frosty as was that of the " dear old white head "[2] in those days, and I am a fusty old diplomat—baited by the Sadr Azem, the 'Times,' and the devil. Well, well, the past cannot be recalled : if it could, I should try to recall *many* acts of folly that I have committed, and among them all perhaps the greatest, the having allowed myself to be persuaded to come out to this nest of intrigue, falsehood, and villany comprehended in the word Persia. It is really monstrous that England, France, Russia, and other civilised Powers should talk of the 'honour' of the Shah, and treat with him as if he were a Prince within the pale of civilisation."

It is true that Lord Palmerston vigorously defended in Parliament the attacks made on the British Minister at Tehran, on whom was laid the whole blame of the Persian war. But Murray complained, not without reason, that the discredit-

---

[1] Dunmore.   [2] His father.

able rumours which had been set afloat about him might have been disposed of at once by publishing the whole correspendence.[1]

Hon. Charles Murray, C.B., to Earl Cowley.

"BAGDAD, *April 23rd*, 1857.

" I can honestly congratulate you on your treaty, which seems to me satisfactory and comprehensive. The general feeling in England against the war with Persia seems to be owing to the (to me inexpressible) conduct of our Government, in withholding from the House of Commons and the country all information as to the course and events which compelled me to withdraw the Mission from Tehran. A gossiping press and a gossiping public have spread far and wide the story of Mrs Hashem, and the country knows nothing further on the subject ! What wonder, then, that all classes should be 'dead against' a quarrel said to have originated about so trifling a question ? John Bull, it is true, hates war and war taxes ; but he does not like to have his representatives and his flag abroad treated with insult and contempt : and if the Government had laid the correspondence before Parliament at or before the opening of the session, and the country had been made aware that for months I had been made the object of unprovoked and oft - repeated insults by the Persian Government ; that British subjects had

---

[1] This was done after the conclusion of peace, and the above condensed narrative of events is drawn from the Foreign Office bluebook containing the correspondence, "Affairs of Persia, 1857."

been injured in their persons and property; that
one of my servants had been beaten by some of
the Shah's attendants; that another's house had
been broken into, himself beaten, and his property
stolen; that the Mission had been, for the first
time during a series of years, excluded from its
accustomed seat at two national solemnities; that
the Queen's name had been mentioned by a
prince of the blood at a public dinner in terms
too filthy to be repeated; and that for each and
every one of these indignities all redress and indemnity was obstinately refused,—if the public
had been aware of all these facts, they would
then have known that the seizure and imprison-
ment of our Mirza's wife, and the gross and
offensive calumnies with which they accompanied
that outrage, were only the last drops poured
into a cup already overflowing, and that if I did
not wish to be *kicked* out of Tehran, I had no
choice but to withdraw from it.

"The fact is, the Sadr wished to organise his
expedition against Herat; my presence at Tehran
was an obstacle thereto; so I was to be worried,
insulted, and calumniated until I should be compelled to go. If all these *facts* had been before
the public, do you think there would have been
the same indifference to the origin of the quarrel,
and the same disposition to treat it with the
ridicule that now exists? That our Government
have damaged themselves by this silence seems
to me clear; that they have damaged *me* by it is
beyond a doubt; for the public, both in and out of
England, have been taught to look upon me as a

sort of hasty, petulant *brouillon*, who jeopardised the gravest interests from personal pique."

Lord Clarendon defended his envoy as loyally in the House of Lords as Lord Palmerston had done in the Commons, and Murray was duly grateful, although tickled by some of the arguments put forward in his defence.

Hon. Charles Murray to the Earl of Clarendon.

" I was much amused at the debate in the House of Lords in which Lord Ellenborough attacked, and you defended, my humble self; and I think you will laugh too when I tell you what caused my mirth. . . . You took up the cudgels manfully in defence of my appointment, and stated (as your speech was reported in the paper which I read) that I had been selected because I had 'resided six years in India and spoke the Arabic language.' Now as I happen never to have been in India, and as Arabic would be about as useful a language to possess at Tehran as German at Madrid, I thought it probable that some noble lord would get up and give you a broadside. However, they seem to have been perfectly satisfied, and held their peace ! If any noble or learned lord in future should impugn my polyglot character in your presence, pray remember that I can read and converse tolerably in Persian and Turkish, the two languages current at Tehran."

Murray resumed his duties at Tehran, and was

soon on the best of terms with both the Shah and the Sadr. But he had suffered so severely from dysentery at Bagdad that he was reluctantly compelled to write home for a year's leave of absence:—

"I say most reluctantly, because the Shah, having become convinced of all the Sadr's peculations, extortions, and other delinquencies, had dismissed and disgraced the all-powerful Minister. His Majesty then sent for me, and conversed with me frequently, confidentially, and *tête-à-tête*, on the best means of carrying on the affairs of his Government."

It might be difficult to calculate how much of this improvement in Murray's relations with the Shah was owing to the removal of a serious disability which the British Foreign Office had, for the first time, imposed on the Queen's representative at an oriental Court. It had been the immemorial custom for embassies and missions to present themselves before the monarch and his chief Ministers with their hands full of gifts. The Eastern mind was, and perhaps still is, incapable of realising diplomatic relations without the interchange of presents, and Murray knew enough of the customs of Asiatics to cause him to remonstrate vigorously when it was announced to him on his appointment that in future no provision would be made to comply in this respect with these customs. Perhaps it was pressure by the Treasury—perhaps the irksome task of defending in the House of Commons, session after session, the vote for Secret Service money—perhaps it was an attempt to import a loftier spirit into negotiations with foreign Powers,—whatever was the cause, the Foreign Office turned a deaf ear to Murray's representations, and he had to present himself empty-handed before the Shah and the Sadr, which had a shabby appearance compared with the profusion of gifts brought by the representatives of France and Russia. But before he left Tehran this humiliating condition was removed, which contributed, no doubt, to the reestablishment of good understanding.

In addition to this apparently childish consideration, Murray was convinced that, in dealing with oriental Governments, nothing is gained and many risks incurred by beating about the bush. The Eastern mind is exceedingly credulous; Ministers and masses alike are easily persuaded that patience shown out of courtesy by a European Power to the interminable prolixy of oriental diplomacy arises from fear. To the huge mass of papers referring to these events in Tehran is affixed a note in Murray's handwriting to the following effect:—

"It is curious to remark that the Whig Government in 1857 committed precisely the same blunder in Persia that the present Government in 1883 have committed in Egypt. They both lost a golden opportunity by unjustifiable hesitation and delay. After spending upwards of three million pounds and a number of human lives in war, they obtained from Persia exactly the same apologies and indemnities that I had asked for before I left, and which I could have obtained without the loss of a guinea or a man, if they had sent one single firm and decided despatch. The blunders of the Gladstone Cabinet in Egypt of a similar kind are too recent and well known to require recapitulation."

Before concluding this notice of Murray's service in Persia, a few extracts may be given from his journals. Owing, probably, to the unwelcome leisure thrust upon him during his enforced exile from the Persian Court, these journals were more regularly kept than it was the custom of the writer to do, and they contain many vivid and amusing passages of sport and travel, as well as commentary on those books which Murray, at all times an avid reader, carried with him.

"I was accompanied on this trip by my *attaché*, Lord S. Kerr,[1] and by Timoui Mirza, the youngest of the Persian princes who visited England about the year 1835. He was then, and still is, a hunter second only to Nimrod himself.

[1] The present Marquis of Lothian.

"On this occasion he brought with him his hawks and his greyhounds, and I had an opportunity of seeing for the first time the interesting sport of hawking the antelope. The chief interest of the sport consists in training the hawks and the greyhounds together, so that they should know each other and work together, so that whatever may be the number of the herd both should always single out the same antelope. These animals are of a different species from those in the Arabian desert, being much larger and more fleet, so that no unassisted greyhound can take them. The males have long straight horns, and the females none at all, so that the hawk always singles out the latter, being taught by experience the danger of striking the head of a male when going at full speed. The method of hunting is as follows: the hunter holds one or two greyhounds in a slip, generally tied to the pommel of his saddle—the hawk, hooded, is on his wrist: as soon as he sees the antelope, he approaches them sidelong at a slow pace, and if he can succeed in gaining the windward of them at a distance of three or four hundred yards, he rides at full speed towards them, hallooing to his dogs. As soon as he is sure that they are the game, he slips them, and as the antelopes scarcely ever go off at their fullest speed before the dogs are tolerably near them, the hunter gallops onward and unhoods the hawk, which no sooner descries the antelopes than he pursues them, and wheeling for some time around and over them, he stoops on a female and strikes her on the head, beating her about the eyes with his

wings : meanwhile the well-trained greyhound, as
soon as the hawk has passed him and is in pursuit
of the quarry, has no more eyes for the antelope ;
he looks only at his feathered ally in the air, follows him in all his turns, and at last arrives in
time to seize the luckless doe, which, being tormented by the hawk's talons and wings, falls an
easy prey.   If the wind is high, the antelope,
always running against it, can generally escape
the hawk ; but if the day be still, and both hound
and hawk good, she can rarely escape.   The training of the hawk is as various as their size and
species : some are trained to take the hare and the
bustard, others the heron and crane, others the
partridge and black pheasant ; while the smallest,
swiftest, and boldest of the falcon tribe, the *shahyn*
in Persia, will sometimes strike in mid-air the
kerajorsh or black eagle, the deadly enemy of his
race, and fall headlong with his gigantic adversary.   Most of the other hawks have such a dread
of the *kerajorsh* that if one is visible, at whatever
distance in the sky, they will not fly even at their
favourite game.

"*March 6th*, 1857.— . . . Heavens! what a
place is this Makel, the very paradise of fleas! not
like the ignoble vermin sung by Burns 'who creep
and sprawl and sprattle,' but joyously jumping and
swarming like locusts ; on the bed, in the bed, on
the floor, and on the table ; in every article of
clothing they find a haunt and a playground."

He was travelling along the Euphrates with a
strong Turkish escort, which failed to give him

much sense of security against marauding bands
of Arabs :—

"*March* 12*th*.— . . . As a specimen of the re-
spect paid by the Arabs to the Turkish authority,
I may note that yesterday a boat arrived at Basrah
from Bagdad, and as it was laden with wood for
the service of our Government steamer, the Consul-
General had obtained a firman addressed to all the
Arab sheiks on the banks of the Tigris, by the
Pasha of Bagdad, setting forth that the said boat
was to be exempt from all tolls, duties, charges, &c.
Be it remembered, too, that the aforementioned
Pasha is his Highness the Governor-General of all
Mesopotamia, and heaven knows how many dis-
tricts beside, with a salary exceeding that of the
Governor-General of India. When the boat, de-
scending the Tigris, reached the place where the
above Mohammed resides, one of their sheiks came
out to demand the customary toll. The captain
exhibited his Highness's firman of exemption ; the
Arab spat on the document, saying in a stern voice,
'There is my answer to your firman—now pay.'
Such is Turkish Government in 1857 ; such is the
result of the *tanzimât* which were to regenerate
Turkey and reinvigorate 'the Sick Man' ; and such
the state of the Arabs who are duly mentioned in
his Highness's annual reports to Stamboul as being
perfectly quiet and obedient to the orders of the
Sublime Porte ! Sublime Farce ! Sublime Humbug !

"*March* 13*th*.— . . . I finished to-day the
second reading of Bulwer's 'Ernest Maltravers,'
and its continuation, 'Alice, or the Mysteries.'

Although this work is written in many places with Bulwer's usual force and eloquence, and though the author tells us in the preface to the later editions that he considers it the most complete and carefully written of his works of fiction, there are many points in it that I do not like. That a disgusting brute, a burglar and murderer such as Luke Darvil, should have a daughter, pure, innocent, and showing every mark of highbreeding in mind, character, and form, such as Alice was, may be pronounced, if not impossible, certainly too improbable, for a tale of fiction. It would have been easy and more natural had the brute stolen her in early childhood from some more respectable parents. The metaphysical and political discussions in the book are too frequent and too tedious. Lord Doltimore's character and relations with his wife are a broad caricature of a certain peer living at the time that the work was published, and whose *name* the author has taken with the change of one single letter in it. . . . If this be nature, it is not the nature that Scott and Shakespeare have studied and painted! nor is it less offensive in my eyes to see a low intriguing scoundrel and swindler and forger like Lord Vargrave introduced on the stage as a British Peer—a leader of a political party and a British Cabinet Minister in the nineteenth century. If a Chartist were to write a novel purposely to degrade the aristocracy, and were to draw such a portrait regardless of all probability or truth, it would not be surprising; but one does not expect it from an M.P. and a gentleman who traces his ancestry to the Conquest.

"*March* 16*th*.— . . . Just at the bend of the
river where the Hy enters it from the Tigris is
a small date-grove, which was once a garden,—
perhaps they may call it so still, for here and
there are a few peach and pomegranate trees and
a few old vines, untrained, spreading their long
arms in all directions as if supplicating for nurture
and support. Thither I bent my steps, for the
little grove was tempting at this season of early
spring ; the trees were just throwing out new buds,
blossoms, and leaves, and half-a-dozen merry wood-
peckers were rapping their sharp beaks against the
bark, and showing their bright plumage as they
hovered over the stream or flew from branch to
branch of the palms. One solitary little flower
caught my eye, the first-born of spring ; anywhere
else I should have welcomed it as a friend, but
here I looked angrily on it as the forerunner of
burning heat and scorching sun. Suddenly my
ear was arrested by the sound of a boy's voice
carolling an Arab ditty at the utmost stretch of
his youthful lungs to the accompaniment of a
creaking water-wheel, which two yearling cows
were turning under the songster's direction for
the purposes of irrigation. I drew near unper-
ceived and watched him : how merrily the urchin
sang as he stood on a little mound of clay, while
his two patient companions came and went over
a space not more than eight or nine feet in length.
Instinctively, or rather habitually, they stopped
a few seconds at each turn, first to let the leather
buckets receive the water and then discharge, a
palm - stick in the boy's hand occasionally quick-

ening the apprehension of their duty. Oh ye
Sybarites, of whatever age or sex, who live in
the luxuries of city life and yawn with satiety
and ennui, when the bounty of heaven has placed
within your reach such abundant variety of occupation and enjoyment, come hither and take a
lesson from this Arab boy! From morn till eve
his buckets fill and are emptied; his mute companions pass and repass in that circle of three
yards, which circumscribes all his day's occupation
and enjoyment! Look at his ruddy brown cheek,
his bright sparkling eye, listen to his merry carol,
and blush for your insensibility and ingratitude!

"*March* 21st.— . . . Another strange feature
in this extraordinary genius [Lord Byron] was his
total incapacity to form an opinion on the merit
of his own productions. Not to dwell upon the
well-known instance in his early days when he
sent to his literary friends for publication a dull
paraphrase on Horace's Art of Poetry, that would
have been itself assuredly damned, and have
dragged him down with it, if anything could
have done so; and forwarded to them at the same
time a wild broken fragment in the Spenserian
stanza, which they were instructed to read and
then burn, as being good for nothing! The former
fortunately fell into the river Lethe, and was
drowned; the latter fell into the hands of Mr
Dallas, and was saved—it was 'Childe Harold'!
This may not be so incredible at twenty-three,
but what shall we say to the poet who, after he
had completed 'Childe Harold,' 'The Corsair,'
'Bride of Abydos,' 'Manfred,' 'Don Juan,' and

all the other immortal productions of his pen, repeatedly named his translation of Pulci's 'Morgante' as his 'greatest work,' the 'best thing he had ever done,' and only one year before his death designated it as 'the best translation that ever was or will be made.' If a man of such splendid genius, joined to a sagacious observation of the world and mankind, could be thus blind to the merits of his own productions, what wonder is it if 'we petty men' are blind to our own faults and failings?

"*26th March.*—Read this morning for the second time Macaulay's remarkable review on Basil Montague's edition of Bacon, and it set me a-thinking on the inconsistency of human nature and the fallacy of human judgment. With what a merciless hand does the critic contrast the enlarged views, the all-grasping knowledge, and the profound sagacity of the philosopher with the time-serving pliancy of the courtier, the corruption of the judge, and the selfish ingratitude of the man! with what an acute and unsparing pen does he show up the blind partiality of the editor and biographer in slurring over and palliating the acts of meanness and servility of which his hero had been guilty. With what admirable truth and eloquence does he portray the effects which prejudice and partiality produce in warping human judgment, and what dangerous snares they are in the path of the biographer or historian! and yet this same accomplished critic, while 'pulling the mote out of his brother's eye,' writes his own 'History of England' in a spirit of partiality, or rather partisanship, so transparent that with all its merits of style, descriptions, and illustration, it deserves rather to be called a ' Defence of the Whigs ' than a ' History of England.' A popular book it is and always must be, in common with everything written by the same gifted pen, but it never will be a guide to the future historian or to the candid student of our political history. . . . It would appear that minds of the most opposite character are equally liable to fall into this snare—at least it has perverted the judgment of the pompous, prosy, and ponderous Alison as much as it has that of the excursive, eloquent, and brilliant Macaulay. Of these later times, the only historian I know *totally* free from this charge is P. F. Tytler in his ' History of Scotland '—a heavy book, I grant, and written in a dry style ; but his only object was *truth*, and to the ascertainment and portrayal of that he sacrificed every other consideration."

Whatever merit may be attached to these meditations in the wilderness, they must be credited at least with impartiality, for Murray was personally acquainted with all these historians—Macaulay, Alison, and Fraser Tytler—and was an intimate friend of the last. Perhaps the key to his tone may be supplied in a note attached to the previous day's entry—" Never write or do anything else when you are bilious."

" 28*th* *March*.—This morning read before breakfast Macaulay's review of Gladstone's 'Church and State.' How strange that a mind so exercised in reasoning and disquisition as Gladstone's should have failed to see the glaring fallacies into which his High Church doctrines have led him! Strange also that Macaulay, in combating with varied argument and illustration the proposition that the ruling power in a State is bound to inculcate and enforce on his subjects the form of religion that he conscientiously believes to be the best, should have omitted to instance Saxony, a Protestant country, indeed the cradle of Protestantism, which is now governed by a king who (with all his family) is a Roman Catholic, and Belgium, a Roman Catholic country, which is now governed by a Protestant king. Is it not obvious that if either or both of these princes were to adopt Gladstone's tenets, he or they would be very shortly deposed, and their kingdoms become a prey to civil war and anarchy?"

This journal, with its vivid reflections of oriental strategy, diplomacy, and social life, repeating themselves from age to age, interspersed with reflections on men and books, is perhaps the best, though not the only, literary work with which Murray kept ennui at bay during months of forced inactivity. His Egyptian experience, still fresh in his memory, was the source whence he drew a novel written at this time—'Hassan, or the Child of the Pyramid.' The means of

familiarity which so many English readers enjoy
with Egyptian life and scenery did not exist in
those days : the Nile is as accessible now to
pleasure-seekers as the Rhine was then, and this
may have shorn 'Hassan' of much of the popularity with which it was received nearly forty
years ago. The most permanent feature of interest in the book is the description of Mohammed
Ali, drawn from life.

In a memorandum prepared by Murray of his
service in Persia, there is an amusing account of
his final relations with the wily Sadr Azem.

"It is not my intention to record here all the
events that occurred during my residence in Persia,
nor even all the successive injuries or insults to
myself or to the British flag, which led to the
rupture between the two countries ; but any sketch,
however slight, would be incomplete without some
notice of the character and proceedings of the
man who represented in his own person all the
departments, deliberative and executive, of the
Government with which I had to deal. The
Sadrazem Mirza Aga Khan was at this time
between forty - five and fifty years of age ; but
his long face, with a long Persian cap above it
and a long flowing beard below it, gave him the
appearance of being older than he really was. He
was an admirable specimen of the modern Persian
of the upper class : grave and dignified in appear-

ance when in company, yet his manner and conversation were both easy and agreeable in *tête-à-tête*.
He had a great deal of drollery and wit, though
the latter tended towards obscenity when not
checked by the presence of some one before whom
he was obliged to act his part. I know not which
was most constantly between his lips, falsehood
or his *kaliän*, for he smoked from early morning
till late at night without ceasing. He was an
adept in every form and species of lie—the figur-
ative, the implied, the circumstantial, and the
direct : all these he told with a readiness, fluency,
and *bonhomie* that were really charming, and
he took care that this talent should not rust for
want of practice. Let one illustration of this
suffice, selected out of a hundred I might record.
Not many weeks after my arrival, I had gone to
pay him a visit and to talk over with him some
affair of little moment. While smoking our *kaliäns*
tête-à-tête, he took occasion to offer me some friendly
counsel and warning in the following language :
' As you have not been very long in our country,
let me give you this friendly information—that
all Persians are naturally and habitually liars.'
(As a Kajar, perhaps his Highness considered himself to be, properly speaking, a Turk.) ' You
must not believe a word of what they may tell
you. Whilst you remain here, if ever you want
accurate information on any subject whatever,
always come to me ; I will never tell you anything but what is strictly true.' And as I expressed myself duly grateful for his kindness, he
added an asseveration the weight and solemnity

of which no man who has not been in the East
can appreciate. Passing his hand caressingly down
his flowing jet-black beard, he said, 'Remember
that for every falsehood that I tell you while
you reside in Persia, I will give you leave to
pluck a hair out of this beard.'

"It was about a year after this conversation
that the following incident occurred : An Indian
British subject residing at Kirmanshah had sold
to the Governor, or some of the principal authorities in that town, a certain number of valuable
Cashmere shawls, for which, notwithstanding repeated applications, he had been unable to obtain
payment. His patience being exhausted, he applied to me to obtain an order from headquarters
for the settlement of his claim. As his memorial
was accompanied by all the requisite *pièces justifi-
catives*—including even a note bearing the Prince-
Governor's seal, and acknowledging the debt
eighteen months back and promising early payment—the case was as simple a one as could well
be presented. I took the papers with me to the
Sadrazem and submitted them to his personal inspection. As he could not dispute their genuine-
ness, he told me that he would write to the
Prince-Governor and order the money to be paid
immediately. Two or three months elapsed when
I received another letter from the merchant, informing me that he had not received a farthing,
and in answer to his applications could obtain
nothing but a repetition of vague promises. Armed
with this letter, I went again to the Sadr and
expressed my regret and displeasure at the non-

fulfilment of the promise made to me respecting this case. The Sadr, with well-feigned symptoms of surprise and anger, broke out into violent abuse of the Governor of Kirmanshah—calling him the son of a burnt father and other injurious epithets, vowing at the same time that he had given the strictest orders months before for the immediate settlement of this claim. He then turned to me, and, with an air of perfect courtesy and candour, expressed his regret at what had taken place, adding, 'At all events, there shall be no further mistake now.' He then called for one of his secretaries, and dictated to him in my presence a letter to the Governor, ordering to settle this claim without an hour's delay ; and, having affixed his seal, he handed me the note, saying, 'Mashallah, you can read Persian. Is this clear enough ? Are you satisfied now ? '

" On my answering in the affirmative, he delivered the letter in my presence to the Secretary, saying, ' You will order a *khupper* [mounted courier] to go off immediately with this letter to the Governor of Kirmanshah.' His Highness then turned to discuss some other matters with me over a *kaliän*.

" A few weeks had elapsed since this conversa tion, when a rough - looking Kurdish horseman, whose appearance denoted that he had made a long and hard journey, presented himself at the Mission gate, and expressed a wish to see me. I ordered him to be introduced, and summoned my Persian Mirza to be present at the interview. The purport of his tale was that he belonged

to a tribe that had long been in revolt against
the Persian Government, the chief of which had,
on a previous occasion, some years previous to
my arrival, been indebted to the good offices of
the British Mission.   This chief, having been
lately on a marauding expedition near Kerman-
shah, had intercepted a courier of the Sadrazem's, riding in all haste to that city.   The
Kurds, who had hoped that he was a bearer of
some treasure, were disappointed at finding on
him nothing but two or three letters addressed
to the Prince - Governor ; these they had seized,
and dismissed the man uninjured.   On examining one of the letters, they discovered (although
their skill in handwriting was but small) that
the words *Eltchy Anglyz*, 'English Minister,'
occurred more than once ; so the chief, anxious
to requite the former kindness of the Mission,
and thinking that the letter might have some
interest for me, sent off a horseman with orders
to deliver it into my hands.   Having ordered
the man some refreshment and made him a small
present, I dismissed him with a note of acknow-
ledgment to his chief, and proceeded, with my
Mirza, to examine the letter.   It proved to be
a note in the Sadrazem's own hand, and sealed
with his private seal, to the Prince-Governor, informing His Highness that on a late occasion he
had been obliged by the importunities of the
British Minister to send him official instructions
to settle the claims due to a troublesome fellow,
an English merchant, but that this had only

been done to stop the mouth of the British
Minister, and that His Highness was at liberty
to pay the money or not to pay it—in short,
to put off his creditor with any excuse that he
might find convenient.

"A few days later, with this precious note in
my pocket, I went to call on the Sadr, and asked
for an interview. As soon as *kaliän* and coffee
had been presented, and we were left *tête-à-tête*,
I said to him—

"'Does your Highness remember telling me
soon after my arrival that I might always rely
upon your truthfulness, and that you would
permit me to pluck out from your beard one
hair for every falsehood that you might tell me
during my stay in Persia?'

"'Yes, I remember it well,' said he; 'and what
then?'

"'Only,' I replied, 'that if I had availed myself of your permission, your Highness would not
now have one hair left in your beard!'

"He laughed at this sally, but declared, with
renewed asseverations, by the head of the Shah,
by the life of his son, and others equally sacred
in the eyes of Persians, that he had always told
me the truth and had never deceived me.

"'Does your Highness know this handwriting
and this seal?' said I, drawing the note out of
my pocket. I watched his face while he looked
at it,—denial was impossible : without the slightest appearance of shame or confusion, he looked
up at me with a good-humoured smile and said,

'Well, you *are* a clever fellow! How on earth did you get possession of this?'

"It was almost impossible to be angry with such imperturbable and good-humoured effrontery; nevertheless, it was almost equally impossible to transact business of any importance with such a man."

CHAPTER XI.

1859-1867.

DRESDEN AND COPENHAGEN.

In March 1859, the transfer of the Persian Mission from the Foreign Office to the Indian Department having been effected, Charles Murray placed his resignation in the hands of Lord Malmesbury, and was appointed Minister at the Court of Saxony. Shortly after he had taken up his duties there, Lord John Russell, who had become Foreign Secretary on the fall of Lord Derby's Administration, wrote as follows :—

"PEMBROKE LODGE, *October 26th*, 1859.

"DEAR CHARLES MURRAY,— Should you like to accept the appointment to Stockholm, which will be vacant next month ? Your present Court is a very small one, and although there is a Charles XIII. instead of XII., still *Charleses* count for something in the world. However, let me know your wishes. . . . —Yours truly,

"J. RUSSELL."

Murray, however, did not avail himself of this invitation. He continued at Dresden, though he returned to London in 1862 on the occasion of the visit to Great Britain of the Viceroy of Egypt, whom he was specially appointed to attend.

Right Hon. W. E. Gladstone, M.P.,[1] *to Hon. Charles Murray.*

"11 CARLTON HOUSE TERRACE, *June* 1862.

"MY DEAR MURRAY,—I do not feel quite sure whether it would be an act of courtesy or presumption were I to ask the Viceroy of Egypt to honour my wife and me with his company to dinner; but as, on the whole, the fault of being officious may be slighter than that of neglect, I venture to ask you, as I believe you have taken some charge in connection with his movements, whether you think I might with propriety and agreeably to his convenience forward such an invitation. . . . If you can answer me in the affirmative, you will, I daresay, have the kindness to mention what suite of Easterns he has in attendance. Pray forgive this trouble, and believe me sincerely yours,   W. E. GLADSTONE."

Murray's decision to remain at Dresden proved to be a momentous one. The intimacy which had long existed between him and the family of Lord and Lady Castletown bore fruit which can

[1] At that time Chancellor of the Exchequer.

The Hon Charles Augustus Murray
at the age of 30
from a photograph Davion

From a photograph, Dresden.

The Hon. Edythe Murray.

Swan Electric Engraving Co.

have been little foreseen by any of them. His solitary, desolated life was restored to him, bright once more and full of tender anticipations, by the fate which won for him the affections of the Hon. Edythe Fitz-Patrick. This event, the marriage which followed on November 1st, 1862, and the years of tranquil happiness which ensued, combine to throw a formidable obstacle in the way of Murray's biographer. There is an end to the journals which he used to resume from time to time as a relief from loneliness. Letters there are, to be sure. But the letters of a man to his betrothed, still less, perhaps, those to a young wife, are not those which he would choose to lay open to the public, or that the public would most care to peruse.

It is true that among these letters are many reflections of the mind of the writer, cultivated, experienced in the world, yet deeply religious, yet again critically dissatisfied with much that is taught by religious people. The letters to his betrothed are the outpouring of such a mind, long pent up and feeding on its own thoughts, rejoicing now in the solace of communion with a fellow-spirit, with whom Murray was not ashamed to discuss the profoundest spiritual problems, to whom he delighted to impart shrewd criticism.

Hon. Charles Murray, C.B., to Hon. Edythe
Fitz-Patrick.

"*21st September* 1862.

"I have just returned from St George's, where I heard one of the stupidest sermons ever preached. It was on the ten lepers referred to in the gospel of the day, and such a mess as the poor man made of it I never heard. He spoke of leprosy as a disease peculiar to the Jews before the Christian era, and evidently did not know that it exists to this day in Asia in all its horror. I have a very kind note from old Lord Lansdowne, to whom I notified our engagement, and he wishes to know when and where the marriage is to take place. I wish I could tell him the day, Mavourneen, I do so long to have it fixed!"

"29*th September.*

"It is true that, owing to the early teaching of the best of mothers, and an excellent education, and an inquiring mind not always averse to study even in youth, I have acquired no small knowledge on most of the subjects connected with our religious belief. Few have known better than I the path of duty on the grounds of Faith ; but, oh Edythe, my life and my conduct have fallen so far short of my knowledge, that while you in your fondness are clothing me with the attributes of a saint, conscience tells me but too plainly that I have been one of those whom the Scripture describes as 'deserving to be beaten with many stripes.'"

" CLARIDGE'S, 16*th October*.

" Mavourneen, a curious thing I have found out is that Love, which sweetens everything else in life, turns claret sour; but this is an enigma that I can only explain to you when we meet !"

Of the course and nature of his official duties at Dresden few traces remain among Murray's papers.   The dispute about Schleswig-Holstein, whereby gallant Denmark, misled by reliance on the implied support of Great Britain, was plunged into an unequal combat with Prussia and Austria, distressed him very much, in common with most well-informed Englishmen, who saw the honour of their country jeopardised by the abandonment of the Danish cause.   Yet he acknowledged how impracticable was the claim of Denmark.

" The union of the Duchies," wrote Murray to his wife in 1864, " under the nominal sovereignty of the King of Denmark, but with a German population, laws, and institutions, and under the immediate protection of the Confederation, is an absurdity, and if it were now established would not last three years."

References, however, to politics are rare in the letters written to his wife during her brief absence from Dresden.   Rather he seemed disposed to discuss with her books that he had been

T

reading and problems suggested by them.   Here
are his comments on a French writer's speculations
about a future state of happiness :—

"He is doubtless successful in disparaging, almost ridiculing, the notions hitherto entertained
of our future heaven by many of the wisest and
best men, heathen and Christian; but I cannot
say that I think his own notions more happy
in their conception, excepting as regards himself
individually. He (or perhaps she) is evidently of
a pious, contemplative, poetical turn of mind, one
who has lived a pure and good life (humanly
speaking), one who has had one object of his deep,
abiding, and absorbing affection and had lost it.
Thus his heaven is imagined as a beautiful repetition of this life, with its recollections all vivid,
its memories all preserved, and its one great love
renewed in everlasting youth and purity, and in
the brightness of the Eternal Presence.   This is
truly a grand and inspiring vision; but to how
many of the millions on earth is it applicable?
Take the case of S. B., the daughter of a worthless profligate father and a drunken ill-tempered
mother : she is neglected, ill-used, perhaps beaten
by both; but by means of a school, a relative,
a friend, Providence has endued her with a pure
and patient spirit and a mind partially cultivated.
She is then perhaps married to a man who proves
as worthless and profligate as her parents, and
she passes a life of constant suffering and misery
till God in His mercy removes her from it.   What

is her heaven to be ?   Where for her are the sweet recollections, the tender memories, the loves and endearments of her earthly life to be renewed above ?

"But without taking such an extreme picture, take the honest, ignorant boor who has passed his whole life at the side of the cart or the tail of the plough, who can neither read nor write, and who can scarcely understand half the parson's sermon, though he follows its precepts to the best of his ability.   Where for him are the earthly associations or memories that can be expanded into an eternity of happiness for an immortal soul ?   In this, and in scores of other instances of men, women, and children, I find our author's notions on this subject quite as wide of any satisfactory conclusion as those of any of his predecessors. Indeed, how could we expect that any uninspired mortal could succeed in a task in which the most beloved and most loving of the apostles has (with reverence be it spoken) so signally failed ? for no human spirit can imagine eternal happiness to consist in the endless unvarying repetition of the scene portrayed in the fourth chapter of the Revelation.   Our best course is to content ourselves with the assurance that Omnipotence *can* make us perfectly and eternally happy, and Almighty Mercy has promised that He *will* do so.   May we not leave the *how* in His hands ?"

One cannot but smile at the reluctance of this energetic, active, enterprising mortal to accept the

prospect of heaven as a never-ending rehearsal of
the ceremonies described in the fourth chapter
of the Apocalypse.

Though profoundly reverent towards spiritual
things, Murray could not bring himself to inquire,
with any degree of patience, into what is commonly called spiritualism :—

"I need not tell you, darling, that I abominate
all the spirit-rapping race : I have never heard of
any good or scientific truth coming from it, and I
have heard of a great deal of moral and mental
evil resulting from it. God's world, as He has
made it appreciable by our senses and by our un-
derstandings, is vast enough and wonderful and
lovely enough to occupy all our best and highest
faculties during the longest life granted to man.
If we wish and endeavour to extend the flight of
our thoughts beyond its boundaries, our strivings
should be upward toward Him and his Holiness,
and not to plunge into the dangerous unrealities
of demonology."

The following, written in 1865, illustrates Murray's old-fashioned observance of the Lord's Day,
and at the same time reveals the quaint notions
which prevail in certain European quarters regarding the principles governing the British newspaper
press :—

"Last night, after dinner, they all went to the

Opera, while (as it was Sunday evening) I declined : so I went into the garden, and spent my evening till dark with you and my cigar under the great leafy horse-chestnuts. Then I read a little, and went to bed early, having to be called at 5. Is it not strange that the Duke,[1] who knows me so well, and knows that I never go to any play on Sunday, should just have selected the 29th as the only day that he could see me ! H.R.H. told me some queer things, if *true* (and . . . his information is generally very good)—viz., that at the commencement of this Schleswig - Holstein war the Danish Government had been advised to put a gold muzzle on the English press, and had expended £100,000 thereon ! He named all the papers bought, and the share of the 'Times' was £16,000 ; *he* had advised the Prince of Augustenborg to secure it by giving £20,000, but he had declined."

King John of Saxony, who reigned 1854-73, was a distinguished man of letters. Murray records how an Italian *littérateur*, on being presented to the Saxon Minister at Naples, exclaimed enthusiastically : " Ah, monsieur ! je suis charmé de trouver occasion de vous exprimer le profond respect que je ressens pour Sa Majesté votre souverain." (A low bow from the Minister.) " Je l'ai toujours considéré comme le premier *dentiste* de l'Europe." Consternation on the part of the

---

[1] Ernest II., Duke of Saxe-Coburg and Gotha.

Minister—till it flashed upon him that a compliment was intended to his royal master's accom-
plishment as a translator and annotator of Dante,
and that the literary gentleman had been bearing
tribute to his rank as a *Dantiste.*

The tremendous strain of the great Civil War
in America caused much anxiety to the holders
of American securities. The bulk of Murray's
property being of that nature, he took counsel
with Mr Motley, the historian, who was then
United States Minister at Vienna. His reply is
exceedingly long and detailed, but part of it may
be quoted, circumstances having amply justified
the confidence which Motley entertained as to the
resources of his country, though it is possible to
see that he underestimated the rate at which the
wealth of Great Britain was to accumulate :—

John Lothrop Motley to Hon. Sir Charles Murray.

"AMERICAN LEGATION, VIENNA,
16*th May* 1864.

" DEAR MURRAY,—You ask me as to the solvency of the United States, whatever may be the
amount of their debt at the conclusion of the
war. Of course I shall only speak of the country
as a whole. My own faith as to that point has
been perfect ever since the war fairly began. The
overthrow of the Union is to my mind an impos-
sibility ; the suppression of the mutiny and the

annihilation of its sole cause — negro slavery — I
consider certainties : I don't argue this. It is
nothing to me at this moment how many or how
few people at home or abroad share this conviction.
I can conceive of no other result, and I simply
take it as a postulate in answering your questions,
because any speculations as to the condition of the
country, supposing it to be ultimately broken up
into two or three dozen States or groups of States,
are to me entirely without interest—as much so
as disquisitions as to the future of Mexico or Lap-
land.   The solvency of the American Republic depends, of course, upon its stability and its will to
pay its debts.   As to its ability.   The united
commonwealth is the richest country that ever
existed ; in the three elements of production—
labour, capital, land—of which the wealth of all
nations consists, nothing like the expansiveness
seen in the United States was ever heard of.

" 1. *Labour.*—The population, with the exception of a few scattered individuals, belongs entirely
to the producing classes, and doubles itself every
twenty-two years.   In Europe, especially in the
two leading nations, France and Great Britain,
population increases in a steadily diminishing ratio ;
every decade shows a less proportionate increase.
Thus, in round numbers, in the first year of this
century the population of Great Britain and Ireland was sixteen millions ; it is now about thirty
millions, not having quite doubled since the year
1800.   At the same epoch the United States had
about five millions ; they have now about thirty-
five millions, having increased sevenfold.

" 2. This increase of labour would, of course, be a danger instead of a source of strength if the other elements of wealth did not expand proportionately; but Capital increases with still more astonishing rapidity.   In ten years, between 1850 and 1860, the capital of the United States increased about 129 per cent; in the same period the wealth of Great Britain and Ireland increased about 35 per cent.

" The actual valuation of the two countries shows (in round numbers) in Great Britain and Ireland at the present moment considerably more than double the capital of the *loyal* States, but the annual production of the loyal States is greater than that of Great Britain and Ireland.   The figures are—

Value of real and personal property in the year 1863 in Great Britain and Ireland . . 33,403 million dollars.		
Value of same in the loyal States . 14,000 ,, ,,		
Product of the year 1863 in G. B. and Ireland 3,340 ,, ,,		
,, ,, ,, Loyal States 3,719 ,, ,,		

Great Britain is probably the richest country in the world at this moment, but it is easy to calculate from these data in how very few years the United States will be a far richer one.

" 3. But this unexampled increase of labour and of capital might be appalling, were the future of the country cramped for want of those natural agents without which no wealth could exist, and which are massed under the general term *land*, as the third factor of national prosperity.   The territory of the United States is about as large as that of all Europe, and is even richer than that in

mineral resources, fertility of soil, internal navigation, and in many artificial improvements, such as
canals, railways, and labour-saving machines.   Our
system of inter-colonisation, by which the population distributes itself when necessary over a wide
surface without expatriation and without losing
the power of concentrating itself when desirable, is
a phenomenon altogether new in history.   Thus
we have land enough for a population of 400
millions without crowding more than people are
now crowded in England: when that limit is
reached other problems may arise, and may be
solved by those who come after us.   We have
enough for a century or two.

"So much for the wealth of the United States
Commonwealth ; so much for its ability to pay its
debts—my tailor might as well doubt my ability
to pay his very modest bill at the end of this
year. . . .

" Whenever I have anything to invest I always
buy United States bonds : the interest being paid
in gold makes it about a ten per cent investment.
As I don't expect a higher rate than that, and
know no better security than the promise of the
United States Government, I am content.   Others
may prefer the stocks of the new Mexican empire
or of Jeff Davis's Confederacy—I am quite willing.
Ten per cent a-year is a high interest for a strong
Government to pay, but not extravagantly so when
it has such a tremendous insurrection to deal with.
—Yours truly, J. L. MOTLEY."

In 1866 Murray, having completed seven years

at the Court of Saxony, was appointed Minister at that of Copenhagen, receiving, in recognition of his past services, promotion to the rank of Knight Commander of the Bath (he had been C.B. since 1848). Among the private letters of this period some are from well-known people. With characteristic energy Sir Charles, now in his sixtieth year, set himself to learn the Danish language. "I admire," writes Lord Stanley, Foreign Secretary in 1867, "your energy in learning Danish. It ought to be easy to one who knows German and the older forms of English; but the literature is not extensive."

Of course Sir Charles and Lady Murray made the acquaintance of Hans Christian Andersen, then at the height of his popularity. He used often to visit the British Legation and read to them his stories in Danish.

Hans Christian Andersen to the Hon.
Lady Murray.

"Copenhagen, *November* 1867.

"I knew and loved these countries [England and Scotland] before my feet trod them. With Marryat's 'Jacob Faithful' I had long before sailed up the Thames; by Dickens I was led into London's narrow lanes, and I listened to the throbbing hearts there; and in 'Night and

Morning' Bulwer opened to my gaze the rich landscape, with its towns, its churches, and its villages.

"I was at home on Scotland's mountains, and familiar with its deep lakes, lonely paths, and ancient castles: Walter Scott's genius had wafted me thither; Walter Scott's beneficent house had extended to me the spiritual bread and wine, so that I forgot the earthly.

"I was intimate with Shakespeare's land and Burns's mountain before my corporeal eye beheld them, and when at length I visited them I was not received as a stranger. Kind eyes regarded me, friends extended the hand to me. Elevated and humbled at the same time by so much happiness, my heart swelled with gratitude to God."

Mr Stirling of Keir, better known in later years as Sir William Stirling - Maxwell, had recently succeeded to his uncle's baronetcy.

Sir William Stirling-Maxwell, M.P., to the Hon. Sir Charles Murray.

"HOUSE OF COMMONS, *March* 20, 1866.

"Thanks for your kind note of congratulations. I did not take my uncle's baronetcy at once, because of the rarity of female descents of baronetcies, and because, although he was advised that his went in the female line, I thought it safer to lay the case before the Lord Advocate and other counsel, who gave their opinions to the same effect

as the former advice, only two months ago. My
mother's family,[1] now come to an end in the male
line, was a good old stock, of which any relic is
interesting and valuable to those sprung from it.

"The Reform Bill is, as you may suppose, the
general topic of talk and speculation. . . . John
Bright, having seen his error in being wheedled
into opposing the Derby Bill, was, or affected
to be, in the secrets of the Government, and
announced that he warmly approved. 'Warm
approbation' from Bright was enough to ensure
the Bill a cold reception from both Whigs and
Tories. . . . So far Gladstone has led the House
with great good-temper, prosperity, and success,
but his rank and file, and some of his colleagues,
seem to like him none the better on that account.
Lord Russell looks rather shaky, as if he 'couldn't
be thankful'! If he could but have consented to
do so on the front red bench of the Lords, he
might, in the dearth of popular idols, have ripened
into a Palmerston."

*Colonel George Grey to the Hon. Sir Charles
Murray, K.C.B.*

"OSBORNE, *Aug.* 7, 1867.

"I yesterday sent to the Foreign Office by the
Queen's command a copy of the Prince's 'Early
Years,' to be forwarded to you by the first opportunity. You will find it recorded in the first
page as a gift from H.M. to you, in her own
handwriting. It is having a great sale, though

---

[1] Maxwell of Pollok.

there are some few, like Higgins, Reeve, & Co., who sneer, and say there is something unbecoming in a woman laying bare the inmost recesses of her heart in this manner. It has been well received by the immense majority, and has gone far, as all admit, to restore the popularity, of which, by her long seclusion, the Queen had lost a good deal. If the volume is calculated to do good by the example of such a character as the Prince's, why is the advantage of being able to study it to be reserved for our posterity?"

Agreeable as Danish society must always be to educated Britons, and varied though the interests were which the Murrays found in Copenhagen, the experience of a single winter was enough to convince Sir Charles that the climate was too severe as well for his wife's constitution as for his own, long accustomed to sub-tropical skies. Accordingly, on a redistribution of posts taking place, and a vacancy occurring in the British Legation at Lisbon, he applied to Lord Stanley and obtained that appointment, although it could not be considered in the light of professional promotion from Copenhagen.

CHAPTER XII.

1867–1882.

LISBON AND RELEASE FROM SERVICE.

THE affairs of Portugal during Sir Charles Murray's term of office at Lisbon were not of such a stirring nature as to merit record in these pages. But the neighbouring kingdom of Spain was in such a critical condition as to attract the attention of all the great Powers at this time, and Sir Charles was employed by the British Government to undertake delicate negotiations with a view to bringing about a succession to the Spanish Crown which might conduce to the general peace of Europe.

It is well known that these, as well as other negotiations, fell through, and that the Spanish succession, as ultimately decided, formed the pretext for France going to war with Germany in 1870. It would therefore serve no good or interesting purpose to retrace the various steps in this diplomatic labyrinth. It is sufficient to say that Great Britain had no special or general interest in any dynasty : the only concern of her Ministers was to further such developments as might keep the other Great Powers in good-humour. " The pressing want of Spain at this moment," wrote Lord Clarendon to Sir Charles at the beginning of 1869, " is a king : if the throne were occupied by a sovereign who commanded the confidence and respect of the nation, rivalries and angry passions would subside, and order would be soon restored."

The difficulty was to find such a sovereign, and Sir Charles was directed to sound Dom Fernando, the father of the King of Portugal, to ascertain if he would reconsider his decision to decline to become a candidate for the Spanish throne.

" The Emperor Napoleon III.," continued Lord Clarendon, " maintains the strictest neutrality, and has not to any one expressed even a wish respecting the form of Government that is to be established in Spain ; but as he cannot desire a Republic or the Duke de Montpensier on his frontier, it is fair to infer that he would be glad to see Dom Fernando on the throne. No Italian Prince would find favour either in Spain or in France."

Sir Charles reported at considerable length his interview with Dom Fernando, with whom he was on very friendly terms, and concluded with a sketch of that Prince's appearance and manner :—

"The manner of Dom Ferdinand during this interview reminded me forcibly of that of his uncle King Leopold, when I held with him, nearly thirty years ago, a conversation on a matter similarly delicate. There was the same slow, careful enunciation, and an air of *bonhomie* mingled with a certain grave slyness in the expression of the countenance which left you with the impression that there was *something* in reserve beyond what he thought fit to tell you. That 'something' in the present instance I take to be that beneath the unimpassioned coolness, not to say indifference, which he exhibits, ambition within him is dormant, not dead; and that, despite the struggle that it would cost him to give up his present life of agreeable, artistic leisure and enjoyment, if he were really invited to that throne by a decided majority of the Spanish nation his present *nolo episcopari* would not be found irrevocable."

Earl of Clarendon to Hon. Sir Charles Murray, K.C.B.

"FOREIGN OFFICE, *February 8th*, 1869.

"MY DEAR MURRAY,—You executed my commission very promptly and well, and I am sorry you did not have the success you deserved.

"I can't wonder at the ex-king's determination

not to jump into such a hornet's nest as Spain, but he would do a real service to this unfortunate country if he would reconsider his decision, and Europe would be much obliged to him. If he was invited by the Spanish Cortes in a manner to make him feel that he might reckon upon the confidence and support of the country, he might accept experimentally. He would retain his palace at Cintra and suspend his enjoyments and occupations there until he saw whether the neighbouring throne would suit him. He would be in much the same position as King Leopold, who always told the Belgians that he didn't want them and that they didn't want him, so they had only to say the word and he would immediately start for Claremont. King Ferdinand might in the like way announce this if he and the Spaniards didn't like each other. They have only to make it known by a vote of the Cortes, and he would bow to it directly without any one having a fear of civil war on his account. There would be something new, which would not, I think, be unpopular, in a sovereign entering on his duties upon such terms with his subjects. The acceptance by King Ferdinand would place the Emperor Napoleon under just obligation, and he might rely on all the support that France could afford. If you think it absolutely useless, do not trouble him any more, but if there is a loophole, pray intrust the above considerations to him.

"I have been detained so long at the Cabinet that I can write no more.—Yours very truly,

"CLARENDON."

U

Lord Howden to Hon. Sir Charles Murray.

"BAYONNE, 23rd May 1869.

"This is the day of the elections in France, and nobody has any idea of how they will turn out. I think there is little doubt that Government will have a considerable numerical majority, but the minority will be very violent and very inconvenient, deriving daring and strength from a discontent (or disgust if you prefer the word) which exists in the country, and from a general excitement very different from the complete apathy which characterised the elections of 1863. The Emperor has lately entertained ideas of dynastic danger which never tormented him before. He has been much acted on by Marshals Niel and Bazaine, and they say even Macmahon, and I am not without fear that an unruly Chamber might produce a wish for war as a derivative.

"H."

Hon. Sir Charles Murray to the Earl Granville.

"CINTRA, *July* 10th, 1870.

"I happened to be calling on his Majesty some time ago, I forget the precise date, but it was just after General Prim had distinctly stated in answer to an interpellation in the Cortes, 'The Government had given up all idea of King Ferdinand as a candidate, and that no communication had been held with him in that sense since last year.' 'What a liar that fellow is!' said his Majesty to me; 'why, I have now in that bureau a letter

from him lately received, in which he urges me to
reconsider the refusal which I have been obliged
to repeat more than once : by making it public I
could expose him to all Europe, but it is not worth
while.'

" Now follows a circumstance more extraordinary.
Yesterday evening at the Palace of the Ajuda,
while the Council was being held, the Duke of
Saldanha took King Ferdinand aside, and pressed
him most urgently to proclaim himself a candidate
for the Spanish crown, assuring him that success
was certain, and that it would be the means and
the only means of avoiding the risk of civil or
European war. 'Why, Duke,' said the King in
astonishment, 'not only have I on former occasions given you my reasons for declining this
honour when my name seemed to carry with it
greater probabilities of success than that of any
other candidate, but assuredly you would not have
me to appear *now* in the field in opposition to my
own son-in-law, who has just received and accepted
General Prim's offer, and in regard to whom you
have published the General's telegram informing
you that if his success is prevented, he will proclaim a republic.' 'Oh,' replied the Duke, 'if
your Majesty will only authorise me to say that
you accept, *I will easily arrange all that with
Prim.*'

" I do not know how it strikes you, my dear
Lord, but there is to me something inexpressibly
offensive, not to say disgusting, in seeing these
two plotters, the one a selfish military adventurer,
the other (as Lear says of himself) ' a very foolish

fond old man,' self - constituted premier by a
treasonable *coup-de-main*, setting at nought the
opinions of the people's representatives in two
countries, professing to be under constitutional
government, and bargaining and jobbing and
chaffering about the crown of Spain as if it were
a bauble, the only use of which was to swell their
own self-importance. Last year I had, by Lord
Clarendon's private instructions, several confidential interviews with King Ferdinand on this subject, the result of which I periodically reported
to Lord Clarendon; but though his Majesty's
language was always firm and consistent in the
negative, I never left him without an impression
(and it is one that I still entertain) that his
refusal was owing to the quarter from which the
offer came : he would not accept the Crown from
the hands of Prim and his associates, even although they might have been able to back their
offer by obtaining a majority for it in the Cortes ;
but if he had been called for by the unmistakable
voice of the nation, plainly expressed in the
Chambers and elsewhere, I am of opinion that
notwithstanding all the weighty reasons that
were in the opposite balance, he would not have
refused to obey the call. Nothing that his Majesty ever said to me in words authorised me
to draw this inference, and yet I am sure it is
a correct one. . . .

"From a despatch, of which Lord Clarendon
sent me a copy some weeks ago, addressed by Mr
Layard to the Foreign Office, I regret to find
that I have formed so different an estimation of

General Prim's character from that which is held by Mr L., who speaks of the General as a man on whose candour and frankness he is able and disposed to rely. As Mr L. has much better opportunities of judging from personal intercourse and observation, and as it is of much more consequence to *you* that his opinion on that point should be correct, I hope it may prove so. I have given you some of the grounds on which mine has been formed."

The Hon. Sir Charles Murray to Earl Granville.

"LISBON, 9*th August* 1869.

"On most political subjects the Portuguese as a nation are extremely indifferent, but on this one they are, at least for the present, firmly and determinedly in earnest. They believe that to them annexation to Spain would be absorption, and the loss of their independence and of their place among the nations. Such being the state of feeling in Portugal, it is easy to imagine how difficult it must be for King Ferdinand, who has much regard for and is respected by the land of his adoption, to take a step which would not only be a break-up of all his domestic ties and habits of life, but which he must well know to be intended by those who urge him to it, to be a step towards that Iberian union which is now so obnoxious to Portugal. Another obstacle scarcely less grave seems to me the fact that (so far as I am able to learn here) the Spanish nation has not recently, either through its Government or its Cortes, expressed openly any wish to offer the crown to King Ferdinand. I am not aware whether General Prim carries in his pocket such a majority in the Cortes as to enable him to say to King Ferdinand, 'Say yes, and I will place the crown on your head': if he does not, it would seem scarcely consistent with King Ferdinand's character, position, and rank to enter the lists as a competitor with the Alphonsists, the Republicans, the Montpensierists, and other parties, for a crown which he has repeatedly declared that he does not covet."

Hon. Sir Charles Murray to Earl Granville.

"CINTRA, *August* 11*th*, 1870.

" M. de Los Rios, the Spanish Minister at this Court, was instructed by General Prim to renew formally to King Ferdinand the offer made to him last year, with an assurance that every reasonable condition he might wish to make would be complied with, and that it was the only remaining chance of saving the peninsula from civil war and long years of trouble and disorder. King Ferdinand, though still unwilling to leave his home and the land of his adoption for so uncertain and dangerous a position, replied that he would reconsider his former decision, provided that certain preliminary conditions, personal and political, were complied with. The personal conditions, the necessity for one of which has arisen in the course of the last twelve months, were the position to be accorded to his wife, Countess Edla; and the

other that (while leaving the amount of his civil
list to the liberality of the Spanish Cortes) he
should be assured, in the event of circumstances
compelling him to abdicate, of an appanage or life
income equal in amount to what he enjoys here,
and which he must resign if he goes to Spain.
I do not think that any serious difficulty occurred
as to the acceptance of either of these conditions,
though it is obvious that at best they offered
King Ferdinand but very imperfect security; for
although it might be stipulated that the Countess
should enjoy her proper social rank, but without
any political position, no stipulation of the kind
could compel the proud Duchesses and Marquesses
or Condessas of Spain to frequent her salons or
invite her to theirs; and with respect to the life
income, it cannot be supposed that if the King
Ferdinand were obliged to abdicate, either by the
success of a competitor or by the proclamation of a
republic, he would ever receive a dollar of this
stipulated appanage.   The political conditions
which the King wished to establish were that he
should be invited by two-thirds of the Cortes, that
the absolute independence of Portugal should be
guaranteed, and the insertion of a clause in the
Act of his own election to the sovereignty to the
effect that the crowns of Portugal and Spain should
not be worn by the same king.   The first of these
General Prim declared to be impossible in the
present divided state of the Cortes and of the
country, so it was laid aside; the independence
of Portugal willingly guaranteed—in words; but
the third and last was declared to be unconsti-

tutional and impossible to accept. So for the present the negotiations are interrupted. The truth is, that on these two last points the desires and wishes of the two respective parties to the negotiation are opposite. King Ferdinand knows that in all human probability the Iberian Union is only a question of time, and will sooner or later be effected; but he also knows that it is a prospect deprecated by and hateful to nineteen-twentieths of the population of Portugal, the only political question on which they feel strongly and almost unanimously. . . . The King was very anxious to learn from me the views of the Queen and of her Majesty's Government on the subject of his accept-ance of the Crown of Spain and on that of the Iberian Union; but as you have not written to me, either privately or officially, a single line on either of these topics, I was obliged to be very guarded, and I fear unsatisfactory, in my replies."

King Ferdinand's decision proved irrevocable; at least the necessary preponderance of Spanish public opinion was not forthcoming. The crown was offered to Prince Leopold of Hohenzollern-Sigmaringen, with the result of a European war, which it had been the earnest desire successively of Lord Clarendon and Lord Granville to avert.

Nobody ever anticipated the requirements of a biographer in a less degree than Sir Charles Murray. It seems never to have entered his head that he should form the subject of a

memoir; hence little help can be had now from
his correspondence, of which only those fragments
have been preserved which referred to negotiations, and literary or artistic questions, of which he
wished to keep memoranda. Nevertheless, among
the few letters which remain there are some which
are still of interest, either by reason of the writers
thereof or from reference to passing events.

*The Hon. R. Lytton (afterwards first Earl of
Lytton[1]) to the Hon. Charles Murray.*

"MADRID, *June 6th*, 1868.

"You must indeed have been thinking me dead,
if not in the flesh, at least in the spirit of gratitude, all this while; but I yet hope that you will
pardon my many previous sins of omission in consideration of the great anxiety and fatigue which
are my excuse for them, when I tell you that the
whole of our household, my wife, self, the two
children, the two nurses, have been a *tour de rôle*
on the sick-list ever since our arrival here. . . .

"First about 'Gil Blas.' I find that there is no
edition of this book to which *literati* here attach
more value than to any other. They regard the
book as the translation of a French translation
from a last Spanish original. I had therefore
commissioned a bookseller to get an edition of
the book, having regard only to the excellence
of type and paper, since the text of all editions

___

[1] Known in literature under the pseudonym of "Owen Meredith."

is said to be the same. But on the morning after I had done so, Lady Murray's letter to my wife arrived, and I at once countermanded the order.

"As regards the Spanish Academy Dictionary, I have ascertained from members of the Academy here that they are at this moment engaged on a new edition of this dictionary which they hope to have finished in about six months. . . .

"By the way, I must tell you an anecdote which I mean to send to M. Arnold, as he is the great advocate for the establishment of an Academy in England. Salamanca had built a new sort of boulevard here which was to have been called Ronda del something or other; but wishing to pay a compliment to Narvaes, he altered his mind and called it Boulevard de Narvaes : whereupon the Academy writes officially to the Municipality pointing out that the word *boulevard* is not Spanish, but an authorised Gallicism, and instructing the Municipality to efface the word from the sheet and replace it by Ronda. The Municipality replies that it cannot make the required change without higher authority. The discussion is referred to the Government, and at present a sharp correspondence is still going on between the Ministry of Public Works, the Minister for Education, the Academy, and the Town Council, on the subject of the word 'boulevard.'

"We are tolerably comfortable here, and have the advantage of being close to the Museum, where I intend to pass all my mornings by-and-by. As yet, however, I have had no time to do anything I like doing, though we have indeed been

going the round of a vicious circle of dinners and
evening parties, which have brought me entirely
to the conclusion of the philosopher who said that
life would be a tolerably pleasant thing if it were
not for its amusements. I find Madrid much more
sociable than Lisbon. The town itself, too, is
handsomer and more civilised. Though horribly
dear in the price of all things, yet by paying for
it you can get nearly all you want, which is not
the case at Lisbon. There is less dearth of
verdure here, too, than I expected to find. Besides the Retiro, which is really a fine public
garden in the heart of the town, the Casa de
Campo and the Florida just outside the gates
Galera are full of charming walks and drives.
Altogether, I think Madrid has been underrated
by those, at least, from whom I derived my first
impressions about it. The Gallery is glorious, and
half of what Ford in his handbook says of its
contents is singularly untrue. Many of the pictures which he describes as ruined by cleaning and
restoring have obviously never been touched, and
are in perfect condition. One Titian in especial
which he says has been scraped to pieces is in a
deliciously pure state, with every trace of the
master's brush as fresh as can be. The Raphaels
doubtless are the worse for the restorers, but I
doubt if they were ever worthy of their reputation.
Like many others of Raphael's most celebrated
pictures, they are hard, flat, bricky things, and I
can't believe that the colouring of them could at
any time have been much less unpleasant than it
is now. The king of this Gallery is certainly

Velasquez. By Jove! what a marvellous fellow
he is! There is scarcely any paint on his canvas,
yet the effect is nature itself, and the facility
equal in all ways to that of Rubens. No man
could have painted the 'Weaving Women' who
had not painted immensely before. Yet how few
pictures of Velasquez are there even here. I
wonder what has become of the rest? hundreds
of them must have been destroyed. I see English
people sometimes in this Gallery, women especially, hurrying past Velasquez, turning their faces
contemptuously from Rubens, looking timidly at
Titian, and standing in sham ecstasies before a
prim, ill-drawn Fra Angelico in distemper, for
hours. It almost makes me wish that Ruskin
had never been born.

"There is a fair Italian theatre here just now:
I have only been to it once to see a badly written
drama by some Neapolitan author unknown to me,
though not to fame I suppose. Rossi the actor,
however, appears to me to have some excellent
qualities about him, spoilt like all Italian acting
by exaggeration, too much declamation, and too
little by-play. But I am told he is very good in
'Othello,' which I hope to see him in. Do you
know anything of him? The Opera here appears
to be excellent. The theatre itself one of the
finest I ever saw. The season is over now, however, and I only visited it once before the opera
season closed, and once after on a gala night given
by the Queen in honour of her daughter's marriage, to see a play of Lope de Vega, which I
found intolerably dull—doubtless because I could

scarcely understand a word of it. . . . Your conversation with Avila about Mr L.'s case amuses me very much. *J'y reconnais mon homme,* though Avila is far less dilatory and evasive than any other Portuguese Minister I ever had to deal with. But the policy of all of them is 'cunctando non restituere rem.' If you settle the L. case with Avila (as I hope you will), you will certainly be able to congratulate yourself on having settled a case which is at least twenty-five years old, and which all our previous members have failed to move a step forward.

"Oh! I must tell you that during two days of cold and cough which sent me to and kept me in bed, I re-read with immense pleasure the 'Prairie Bird.' I had not seen it since I was a schoolboy, and it was almost a new book to me. It is full of 'go,' and the true *vivida vis* of narrative interest —carries one on with it at a hand-gallop. How very few of our first-class writers since Scott (who certainly had it supereminently) either have or use the gift which you evidently possess in a high degree of 'telling a story'! The story of Dickens's novels is always badly put together; his effects, wonderful in themselves, come one after the other, but rarely one *out* of the other. Thackeray has scarce any story at all, and such story as he has he talks of—he doesn't tell it. I wish you would do for the savages of London, Paris, and the fashionable watering-places what you have done for the savages of North America. Would a modern 'Gil Blas' be impossible, if there were but a modern Le Sage?

"I am afraid that this scrawl will be quite illegible. It has been interrupted, broken off, and recommenced a dozen times since I began it, and meanwhile I have received your telegram about ' Don Quixote.' Unlike 'Gil Blas,' I find an *embarras de choix* about the editions of this book, of which there appear to be multitudes, each hotly extolled or decried by the bibliophili. Your telegram only reached me yesterday afternoon, and already I have a long list of them. There is no lack of small editions, of which I will forward you the best I can get in a day or two. The Dictionary and the Comedies are already on their way to you.

"Yes, indeed! Labouchere [1] as a reformer of abuses is a wonderful spectacle, but nowadays men seem to be valued less for what they are than for what they call themselves. It reminds me of the story of an Englishman who advertised for a French governess for his daughter. A ballet-dancer presented herself. 'I speak the purest Parisian, am lively and intelligent, just the person for the place.' 'Yes, but a *danseuse*—impossible!' 'Mais qu'est ce que ça fait, monsieur; je changerais le nom!' . . .

"The other night I met here one of those very old chamberlains of your very old Infanta Isabel: I believe he has come here with a letter from the Infanta to the Queen of Spain about her daughter's marriage, but he lost his overcoat with the letter at the station or in the train. The coat was eventually found, but not the letter, I am told."

[1] H. Labouchere, Esq., M.P., formerly in the diplomatic service.

The Same to the Same.

"VIENNA, 24th April 1872.

"*We* thank you, dear Sir Charles, very sincerely for your kind and welcome letter. Our 'young Astyanax, the hope of Troy,' and his dear mother are both of them going on well. Judging of the physiognomy of this remarkable baby [1] (of course we think him remarkable), I should say he must be about seventy-six years of age, and naturally very tired of life, but resigned to the boredom of it, which he supports with a sort of clerical dignity and a look which seems to say to all visitors : ' I am sorry to receive you in this fashion, but you will understand that I am obliged to try and look like a baby, as it would not be *convenable* for Mrs Lytton to be supposed to have given birth to a ready-made bishop.'

"I rejoice to think that there may be really a chance of our meeting somewhere this year. My own plans are rather complicated, and subject of course to higher powers. But an attack of pleurisy which I had this winter has left me rather shaky, and the doctors tell me it is absolutely necessary I should pass next winter in a warmer climate. That is easier said than done. I had intended to take no leave this summer, in order to secure a long one for the winter ; but I think that in July I shall be obliged to go to England for a month to see my father, and, as Edith is not in a locomotive condition just now, I shall leave her with the children at a house we have taken in the country near

[1] Henry Meredith Edward, died 1st March 1874.

here for the summer. The whole of the month of June, however, I expect to pass (also alone) at Carlsbad, being in much want of the waters there. What German bath do you think of going to? is there any chance of our meeting there? For gout, liver, and stomach, &c., Carlsbad is sometimes most efficacious, but I hope you suffer from none of these plagues. I have a liver which I should be very glad to exchange with some one else's. Perhaps I may have a glimpse of you in England later? I wish the diplomatic fates had left us longer with you at Lisbon.[1] I should be much tempted to re-visit those glimpses of the moon next winter if they were not so difficult to get at, and my house-hold gods so difficult to move. As it is, if we can get away from Vienna when the terrible Vienna winter begins, I think we shall probably hibernate in Italy somewhere. I suppose the Vienna Exhibi-tion for '73 will hardly tempt you here? The sentiment with which the prospect of it inspires me is a strong desire to get away from this place before it begins. . . . You would hardly know Vienna again, if you have not seen it lately. It is much increased in size, and now one of the hand-somest and certainly quite the dearest capital in Europe."

Sir William Stirling-Maxwell to Hon. Sir Charles Murray.

"R.Y.S. ITA, OFF PORTSMOUTH, *May* 27, 1872.

" I should like very much to see your pictures

---

[1] Mr Lytton had been First Secretary of Legation at Lisbon under Sir Charles.

by Henri Blès. . . . Your story about the added figures is very curious, and I daresay quite true. We should hardly nowadays take such liberties with good pictures 100 years old, but such things have been done.

" We spent Easter at Castlehill (Lord Fortescue's), and there F. showed me a good portrait by Lely of the Duchess of Portsmouth, to which the following history attached. In his boyhood and youth the lady in question was known as the wife of Lord Clinton, who rebuilt Castlehill about 1740 or so. Some twenty or thirty years ago his father, the late Lord F., had a painter there to look at the pictures and do some restoration. Lady Clinton wanted cleaning, and in the course of the operation the artist said he believed there was another face underneath. Lady C. was very ugly, and there was another portrait of her in the house. So the cleaning was continued, and her ladyship vanished, leaving the fair La Querouaille in her place ! It is supposed to have been a piece of economy on her lord's part to use up an old Lely in this way instead of having a new portrait painted."

The Same to the Same.

" KEIR, DUNBLANE, *December* 16*th*, 1872.

" Nothing stirring here except the Kincardine-shire and Forfarshire elections, by which it would appear that to be a landed proprietor in Scotland is in itself a disqualification, in the eyes of farmers, for a Scotch seat. I should be very grateful to any one who can tell me the cause of this obvious feeling of clan disaffection, not to say hatred. The causes commonly alleged are Game and Hypothec. The first may here and there have some effect where there is game, but as the rule is that there is no game, it cannot be a general cause. In the second I do not myself believe at all, except in the case of some capitalist farmers who see in the abolition of the law an opportunity somewhat better than they have at present of getting farms cheaper, and (in the case of the very large ones) even at their own price. But that it is not generally hateful I think my own experience as a candidate is worth something. I proposed myself in favour of trying the amended law for hypothec, and repealing it if found unsatisfactory, and the result was that I was never asked a question on the subject either by friend or foe. If the alleged causes cannot be the real ones, it is only the more certain that some other cause, and that a very real one, is at work. He would do good service who should discover and show how it is to be removed.

"I am amused in Thiers' evidence about the affairs of 1870—at the shrewd dig in the ribs the little man in his dire distress and extremity continued to administer to Granville and Gladstone. They offered to forward a proposal to Bismarck for an armistice, if it was to be understood they were not to recommend it. 'Are the position and functions of England that of a post office?' It is not only a post office in foreign affairs, I fear, but an office at which a stick thrown at the window will bring handsome payment of the toll!"

Lord Lytton[1] *to Hon. Sir Charles Murray.*

"KNEBWORTH, 29*th May* 1873.

"My delay in thanking you for the great pleasure I owe to your delightful and most kind letter
is an indirect answer to one of its friendly queries,
being a proof that instead of increased leisure,
increased business and trouble of all kinds has
fallen to my lot; for within the last three months,
by heaven, I have nearly worked the head off my
shoulders and the legs off my hips! A thousand
reasons, all excellent (at least I think so, since I
have adopted them), but too complicated for explanation or even recital in this shabby scrap of
a note, decided me not to relinquish immediately
the old trade to which I have been for upwards of
twenty years apprentice, and of which I am now—
the gods be thanked—sufficiently independent in
a pecuniary sense to be able to decline many posts
which a year ago I should have felt bound to
accept. Lord Granville had considerately given
me unlimited time to set my private affairs in
order before joining my present posts at Paris;
but as Lyons wanted to come to England, and
was afraid of rousing the wrath of the barbarous
gods of the British Press if we were both of us
absent at the same time, and anything were in the
meanwhile to happen at Paris, I had to hurry over
there to relieve guard, and whilst there, what with
my own business and that of the Embassy, I was
as restless as Noah's dove, though, unlike the
dove, I had left my olive branches behind me. It

[1] Lord Lytton succeeded his father in January 1873.

was there, in a perfect Sahara of official routine, that your letter, ' breathing of Flora and the country green,' reached me like a whiff of sweet air musical with the harp notes of Apollo, and fresh from the pines of Mount Ida.   You see how impossible it is for a diplomatist in these dry days to unloose from himself the ligatures of red tape, even though he bring back to the halls of Vathek a culture as long as, and a heart far longer than, Beckford's.   You thought to send me a packet of Cintra flowers, and your packet contained—guess what — a huge quantity of india-rubber bands, enough to keep within bounds the official correspondence of half-a-dozen embassies!   The unintended gift was perhaps more appropriate than the intended one. . . . It has cost me a heroic wrench to resist the almost overpowering temptation to settle down for the rest of my days in this dear old home of my boyhood, which I never quit without a pang, nor return to without an ineffable sense of refuge and repose.   The life I should naturally lead here—half student, half country gentleman—is certainly the life most congenial to me ; but could my dear father have foreseen the premature and terrible bereavement which has given me the option of leading such a life, I believe he would have cancelled the decision I have forced upon myself, against all my natural inclinations, to continue in my profession for the present.   He has, however, left me voluminous materials for his biography.   To write that biography I now regard as the chief duty of my future life, and if I find professional duties incompatible with the fulfilment of this one I shall resign—not, however, till I have made the trial.

"I have a book of my own (two new volumes of verse) in the press, and nearly ready for publication. I should like to send it you whenever it comes out. But its progress is at present somewhat impeded by an obligation I have undertaken to complete this year a collected edition of my father's speeches, with a short prefatory sketch of his political life.

"I could not resist the temptation to show your letter to Forster, who is, as I knew he would be, delighted by all you say of his book about Dickens. There is just now a direful controversy being waged between Hayward, Mr Crosbie (the ex-diplomatised), and Stopford Brooke (the popular preacher) over the dead body of poor Mill. . . .

"What a *gâchis* in France! The only thing upon which one can congratulate the French is the ease and rapidity with which they are clearing off their heavy war indemnity. But even this is rather like congratulating a man with diabetes on the quantity of sugar he produces."

Hon. Sir Charles Murray to his Wife.

"OEZNHAUSEN, 4th September 1873.

"What a pretty note you sent me from Mme. de R.! I think in the way of *style* there is nothing so perfect as a letter written by a cultivated Frenchwoman! They have a trick or knack of expression that 'gives to airy nothing' not only a semblance but a substance of beauty! We English can write,

according to the feeling of the moment, a thoughtful, a droll, an earnest, a tender, or a loving letter—
these form indeed the substantial food of correspondence ; but we cannot make the light impal-
pable *soufflée* that is the glory of the Frenchwoman's *cuisine!*"

Lord Lytton to Hon. Sir Charles Murray.

"KNEBWORTH, *July 27th*, 1874.

" Your very kind letter adds to the temptations
of life, and could I increase its capacities in like
measure, the result would be an additional pleasure to myself. But to a stone nymph who, fixed
to a garden fountain, can only spout so many
gallons of water per diem, what avail is an invitation from the neighbouring mountain to come
and drink her fill at the head-spring? For the
rest of my short and uncertain stay in England, I
fear I am tied and tethered to Knebworth. I came
home this year to settle, if possible, a mass of
personal business still unsettled and claiming daily
attention. I am living too in daily fear of a
summons from Lyons to relieve guard at Paris,
now that the political madhouse at Versailles is
dispersed, and yet I am engaged to receive a succession of kinsfolk at Knebworth up to the 15th
of August. If my stay in England survives that
date, and if you are then still in town, I will most
gladly avail myself of your kindly offered hospitality ; but I cannot before then extricate myself
from the web I have woven around me here, and
you talk of soon flitting to rejoin the seagulls.

What seagulls? Iberian or Britannic?   I wish I
could get to the sea myself, for I much feel the
want of sea-air and sea-bathing, but I cannot stir.
Shall you be passing through Paris this winter? if
so, I shall hope to see you there.   But in any case
my present home-sickness is so strong that I cannot face the prospect of any long continuation of
official exile, and as I presume that neither do you
intend, *pro bono publico*, to leave your English
home permanently uninhabited, I shall look forward to other opportunities of meeting on British
soil, and seeing all the treasures you have collected
at Oaklands, when I have cast my diplomatic skin."

Lord Lytton's intention to abandon diplomacy
in favour of residence at Knebworth was never
carried out.   He died in 1891 as British Ambas-
sador in Paris, after discharging the office of
Governor - General of India from 1876 to 1880.
His first appointment as chief of a Legation was
to the Court of Lisbon, vacated by the retirement of his friend, Sir Charles Murray, from the
service.

This took place in the autumn of 1874.

The Earl of Derby to Hon. Sir Charles Murray.

"FOREIGN OFFICE, *October* 14*th*, 1874.

"I need hardly say that I have received with
sincere regret the expression of your determination to retire from our service, but I cannot con-

tend against the valid reasons which you put
forward for preferring a private life.   You will
carry with you into retirement the consciousness of duty efficiently discharged during a long
series of years, and we shall console ourselves
with the hope of seeing more of you when your
residence is fixed in England.

" I can well understand that the Peninsula
should not be a pleasant residence just now, and
I see not the slightest prospect of early improvement.   I shall not make your intention public
until I hear from you officially. — Believe me,
very sincerely yours,   DERBY."

Sir Charles at the time of his retirement had
completed his sixty-eighth year, and though still
vigorous, it was not unnatural, nor did it arise
from indolence, that he should incline to spend
his remaining years in the retirement of a home
which he was so capable of enjoying.   His diplomatic career, through the vicissitudes of promotion, had scarcely fulfilled to him the promise
of its outset.   Sir Charles referred to this disappointment in a letter to Lord Stanley in 1867,
when he was asking for an exchange that should
spare him another winter at Copenhagen, which
he dreaded :—

" I had indulged a hope that as the transfer of
the Persian Mission to the Indian Department,
when you presided over it in 1859, had been the

cause of my being tumbled down to the bottom of the diplomatic ladder when I had climbed half-way up it, you would now have been glad to fulfil the expectations which the frank and friendly answers to my letters had led me to entertain, and that even if you had felt yourself called upon, for reasons into which I have no right to inquire, to give the posts at Constantinople and in Italy to two of my colleagues who are both my juniors by five years as Ministers, you would not, after I had asked urgently for a removal, have sent another of my juniors to Lisbon without giving me the offer of it." [1]

This is the only passage 'in the whole of the papers examined by me which betrays the slightest feeling of disappointment. Murray's nature was far too sunny and versatile to allow any such feeling to rankle, and he retired in 1874 to live on his own means, supplemented by a thoroughly well - earned pension, to devote himself to the society of his wife and boys, and to indulge his literary tastes with greater freedom than he had ever enjoyed before. He purchased Oaklands Hall, near Kilburn, and set to work to enlarge the house and store in it his books and pictures. There are few papers remaining after this period to illustrate his daily life and habits, except letters

---

[1] The offer of Lisbon was subsequently made to and accepted by Murray.

to his wife, when he was absent from her on visits to Continental baths and other health - resorts, and occasional letters from friends, generally on literary subjects.

The following letters, undated, must have been written by Mrs Norton a few weeks before the death of her husband in February 1875, when the Murrays were touring in the Mediterranean :—

The Hon. Mrs Norton to Sir Charles Murray.

"NAPLES, *January* 1875.

" I thank you so for your kind note. You do not know that *the sole survivor*[1] of my three beautiful sons lives in the island of Capri, and has lived there these twenty years, off and on. Sometimes I come to see *him*, sometimes he comes to see *me*, but his only adopted *home* is this little island—which appears and disappears fitfully to our view, at present, like Gwendolen's castle in Walter Scott's (little. read, but lovely) ' Triermain.'

" My eldest son[2] was here as first *attaché* to kind old Sir William Temple. The younger[1] went and inamorated himself of a Capriote, and married her, to the extreme fury of his father's family. At first they would not permit him to return to England, or help him to enter any profession (with the usual wisdom of angry people). Now that he stands in direct succession to the peerage, they

[1] Thomas Brindsley Norton, afterwards fourth Lord Grantley.
[2] Died in Paris in 1859.

have tried once or twice to wean him from Capri; but he is in wretched nervous health, and always glides back again into his sunny lair.

"*There* is my tie to Naples. The weather has been bad, and I have not yet crossed to Capri; but in this same hotel are poor Lady Anna Maxwell's[1] sisters, her husband, and John Hamilton[2] (who married the youngest), for friends and companions. You were almost the last visitors at Keir, I think, with your beautiful child,[3] of whom she wrote me a long description, before the time of the dreadful tragedy of her death. Her good constitution bore the torture of burns and the amputation of three fingers of the left hand for a whole fortnight, with good promise of recovery, before she suddenly sank and died.

"Sir William is much broken and out of health himself.[4] He goes away, I believe, in a couple of days on his way by Florence to England.

"I go to Capri for a week as soon as the boatmen believe in their Neapolitan weather. I scribble all this in case you call after we are gone out. . . .

"As to growing old, I don't believe in it. I agree with Marie Kalerzi, who said, 'On n'en saurait rien, si ce n'était pour les autres: les autres vieillissent.' But it is respectable and

---

[1] Wife of Sir William Stirling - Maxwell. She died, after an accident from fire, in December 1874.

[2] Created Lord Hamilton of Dalziel in 1886.

[3] Cecil Murray, died in 1896.

[4] Sir William Stirling-Maxwell married Mrs Norton in March 1877, and she died in June following.

proper to have a little gout, that one may not seem to flout the old age of 'les autres.'—Yours always most truly, CAROLINE NORTON."

The Same to the Same.

"HOTEL SIRENE, SORRENTO, *Sunday* [1875].

"My grandson [1] is too young for '*tochers*,' but not for introductions. He is sprouting a little absurd moustache (which I believe he shaves), and is a courteous and music-loving youth. He already nestles in the arms of Grüner,[2] whose kindly notice I petitioned for on the strength of friendship with some of my friends long ago. His name is Richard Brinsley Norton, and his address is at Herr Baron Fuickenstein's (which sounds like a chamberlain in one of Offenbach's *opera-bouffes*), at 12 Winckelmann Strasse, in Dresden. I send you this note in the most roundabout way, fearing if I direct (as any simple Christian might) to your residence at Rocca Bella, and you should have left that pirate nest by the sea, it would never be forwarded. . . . I cannot help thinking all the drainage and alterations going on at Naples make it unhealthy. It reminds me of Edmond About's remarks on the superfluity of repairs of churches, houses, roads, and bridges *everywhere*. 'Partout on voit la rage du mieux,' says that delightful writer; and I wish the 'mieux' (of which Naples stood in great need) were not in such a state of transition."

[1] The present Lord Grantley. He had just been appointed *attaché* at Dresden.

[2] Professor Grüner, Librarian of the Royal Library at Dresden.

Hon. Sir Charles Murray to his Wife.

"TOUGH-MEAT AND SKIM-MILK HOTEL,
EASTBOURNE, 1875.

"I have been reading the 'Standard' of yesterday during breakfast, and saw there a notice of
a book by a Mr Drummond (brother of Lord
Strathallan), describing his sporting tour *of five
years* in S. Africa; and the number of lions,
elephants, rhinoceros, and other wild animals, as
well as buffaloes, antelopes, &c., &c., which, during
that time, by his own account, he has slaughtered
by hundreds if not by thousands, seems almost
incredible! The newspaper critic thus finishes his
article : 'A score or two of hunters as unsparing
and indefatigable as Mr D. would soon annihilate
the game of a whole continent.' . . . This tallies
with what I saw and read forty years ago in the
Far-West prairies, amid those vast herds of buffalo which pasture there. The Indians (savages!)
kill exactly what they require for their food,
dress, and tents, while the white men (*Christian*
sportsmen and *civilised* traders) slaughter them
by thousands to take the buffalo tongues and
hides, leaving the carcasses to be devoured by
wolves and vultures." [1]

[1] Such was Murray's impression, derived from his experience with
the sportsmanlike Pawnees ; but the general run of Indians were no
whit less bloodthirsty than the white men. Catlin ('North American
Indians,' vol. i. p. 256) describes scenes of almost incredible butchery,
and foretells, so far back as 1840, the ultimate extinction of the bison.
He relates how, when he was on the Upper Missouri, six hundred
mounted Dakotas started after a huge herd at noon, returning at

The Same to the Same.

"AIX-LES-BAINS, *September 25th*, 1875.

" Yesterday evening I tried to console myself for your absence from my dinner-table by inviting two very agreeable elderly persons to share my meal. They made themselves so agreeable that I did not require to utter a word ; I had only to listen to their lively and witty sallies. The lady was much the older of the two, and both in the earlier and middle portions of her life had been rather too celebrated for her gallantries ; but now that her advanced age had reduced those to matters of memory, and she was living perforce a respectable life, I naturally expected that, if she alluded at all to those discreditable bygone days, it would be with some expression of satisfaction at the change that time had wrought in her way of life. You may imagine, then, my surprise at hearing her say in regard to those old days, ' Qui m'aurait proposé une telle vie (comme celle que je mène à present) je me serais pendue ' ! Now I know you are dying to learn the names of this old couple, so I will satisfy your curiosity—St Evrémond and Ninon de l'Enclos. If you get this before you leave, bring my cigars with you. Remember, when you come to the frontier and the *visite des bagages*, to curb that little spirit of impatience which is apt to break forth in you at

sundown with no fewer than fourteen hundred fresh buffalo tongues, which they sold to the Hudson Bay traders for a few gallons of whisky. The carcasses were left where they fell, to be devoured by wolves.

sight of a French official. Don't forget that the more you irritate them the deeper will their paws go into your box; and if they find the box of baccy, you must prepare a *petite scène de comédie* with Marcelline—turn suddenly upon her, and ask her how she dared to bring cigars for her husband in your box, and thus, on paying the duty, you may save them."

Perhaps there never was a less legible hand than that of the writer of the following, which must therefore be taken "errors excepted":—

Dean Stanley to Hon. Sir Charles Murray.

"DEANERY, WESTMINSTER, *Good Friday*, 1878.

"It so happens that Farrar (who is now my neighbour and colleague as Canon of Westminster) has written an essay on this very subject of Matt. xix. 24, which contains all the information which you desire. . . . It there appears (1) that the proposal to turn *camelus* into a cable is quite unwarrantable; (2) that the use of 'needle's eye' to express an impossible passage for a huge creature is proverbial amongst the Rabbinical writers for chimerical projects, usually not in connection with a camel, but an elephant. Therefore no further illustration is needed.

"But (3) the illustration which you mention of the wicket-gate of a town is given in Lord Nugent's. . . . This I imagine is the book in which you saw it, and to which the 'Family

Herald' alludes.   The town where he reports himself to have seen a gate so called is not Jericho
(which in its modern state of sporadic ruin has
no gates), but Hebron.   Farrar also refers to Sir
J. Ch——'s —— '—— in Rome.'   But the most
precise and interesting account is from a nameless
traveller whose letter he quotes, who in 1835 saw
a camel trying to push through a gate, so called,
in the house of a Jew in Morocco.

"Old David Morier, who died this year, had a
Bible annotated with oriental references to customs
in Persia and elsewhere, by his brother Hadji
Baba.   If you would like me to look at this or
—— I will do so.   I think that the name of
the gate probably sprang from the same run of
thoughts that produced the proverb.   I never fill
[? fall or fell] in with anything of the kind myself.
—Yours sincerely,   A. P. STANLEY."

CHAPTER XIII.

1882–1892.

HOME LIFE.

IN 1882 the Murrays abandoned the home at Oaklands Hall, which they had occupied for eight years, and went to the Grange, a beautiful house near Old Windsor, which they had built for their son Cecil.

There is a letter early in that year from a famous old sportsman, Horatio Ross, then in his eighty-first year, enclosing a card target showing his practice at fifty yards with a rook-rifle. He exults with the glee of second boyhood over the steadiness of his octogenarian eye and hand, and advises Sir Charles to take to rifle-shooting as an agreeable pastime for old age.

During the autumn of 1882, and occasionally in subsequent years, Lady Murray's health prevented

Y

her accompanying Sir Charles to Baden-Baden and
other baths recommended for his increasing infirmity; but always when separated from her, his

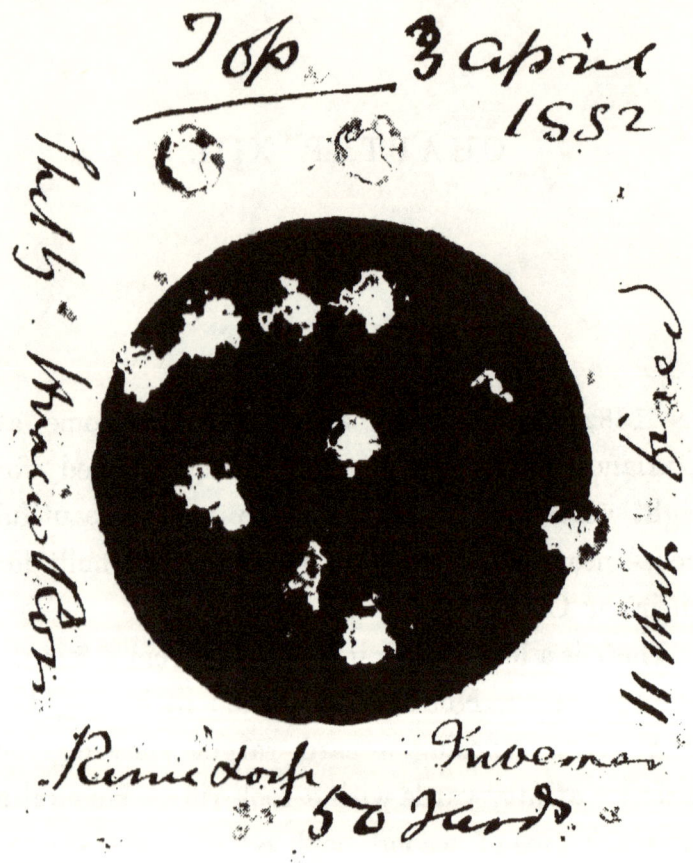

Horatio Ross's Card Target.

letters were almost daily. The sudden death of
Lady Murray's aunt suggests some serious reflections on the uncertainty of life :—

Hon. Sir Charles Murray to his Wife.

"BADEN-BADEN, 28*th Sept.* 1882.

"There is a curious Persian allegory on this subject by my friend Sâdi, in which he is presenting human life under the familiar image of a caravan-journey, the conductor of which is the Angel of Life and Death. After a halt or rest, he suddenly orders the tents to be struck, and the trumpets to sound and drums to beat, for the onward march. The foolish and careless traveller in the company says, 'I cannot find my boots; I have not packed up my travelling-bag; I have not passed my girdle round my loins; I am not ready to start.' But the relentless angel passes on with the caravan, leaving behind the thoughtless traveller, whose fate will probably be to perish in the desert for want of guide, water, and friendly aid. 'Wherefore,' adds Sâdi, 'O man! keep your travelling-bag always packed and your loins always girded.' A greater than Sâdi has given the warning almost in the same words."

"BADEN-BADEN, 4*th October* 1882.

"CARISSIMA,—We had some happy days at Oaklands together, for which we ought to be thankful, and I am glad to think that if we are spared we shall still have at the Grange. . . .

"The dinner yesterday at the Emperor's[1] was rather a slow affair in respect to liveliness, but its brevity in respect to time would have satisfied even you. We sat down at 5 and rose from table at 6! fancy losing the best hours of the

[1] Of Germany.

afternoon in a stuffy dining-room; and as there was no theatre open and no soirée anywhere, *how* were the diners in evening dress expected to kill time from 6 to 11 ? Those are occasions on which the smoker of a big cigar has some advantage over his fellow-creatures, but to fill up the space of time, or even the half of it, one would require to have a cigar as big as a trumpet, and to be a smoker like the P. of W."

Sir Charles's son, Cecil, was now seventeen His education had been the object of his father's tender solicitude, and already Sir Charles was enjoying the reward of recognising in the lad a love of learning and literature not less intense than his own. Graceful little passages of classical correspondence passed between them; here is a "bulletin for Cecil" about his father's health :—

" BADEN-BADEN, *May* 31*st*, 1883.

" Grata oculis avidis advenit epistola Mammæ,
 Supremum ut tetigit Maia venusta diem.
Paulatim exosum domuit Lavillia morbum,
 Debilis et calamum dextra tenere valet;
Surrectusque toro calidâ de fonte salubres
 Haurire incipiam cras redivivus aquas.
Mille mei labris dulci des oscula matri,
 Sisque memor nostri Cæcile care.—Vale !"[1]

---

[1] Welcome to my hungry eyes came your mother's letter, just as lovely May reached its last day. Laville [gout medicine] has gradually overcome my odious ailment; and, having risen from [sick-] bed, I shall presently drink as a convalescent the wholesome waters of the hot spring. Give a thousand kisses from my lips to your mother, and ever remember me, dear Cecil.—Farewell.

It was not only with the literary part of his son's education that Sir Charles occupied himself incessantly :—

Hon. Sir Charles Murray to Mr Reginald Smith.[1]

"VILLA VICTORIA, CANNES, *May 3rd*, 1883.

" I forget whether I ever showed you a commentary on the Psalms that I wrote a year or two ago for my wife and Cecil, with a view to explain to them the general *construction* of what is called the Book of Psalms, and also some of the more obscure passages, in some instances rendered so by defective translation. I worked through the whole book in Hebrew, and of course in my commentary took a great many hints from Perowne's excellent work. . . . I was first led to make this commentary by a feeling of dissatisfaction that came over me when I found how often, in repeating the Psalms in church, I did so rather like a parrot than a reasonable being, and that many of the verses conveyed no intelligible meaning to my mind. I believe there are hundreds of educated persons who, if they would examine their consciousness in this matter, would find themselves in the same predicament."

Lord Lytton to Hon. Sir Charles Murray.

"KNEBWORTH, 19 *April* 1883.

" Of course I entirely agree in all you say about India and the *Ewigblinde* at home. I believe that Ripon's ambition is to be remembered as

[1] Of Messrs Smith, Elder, & Co.

the Gladstone of Hindustan.   The Natives call
him the God-man, and the wind of their hurrahs
seems to have got into his head—never, I think,
a very strong one.

"I will re-read my little fable by the light of
your friendly criticism; but don't you think
'slop*ing* tugged by swell*ing*, &c.,' has unpleasant
sound?"

The Same to the Same.

"25 *April* 1883.

"I am afraid I am impenitent and impenetrable,
but the description of a ship *urged* by her sails
seems to me untrue.   With the verb 'to urge' I
can only associate the idea of impulsion, which is
inapplicable to the action of a ship's sails.   You
'urge the flying ball' when you throw it or hit it
with a bat.   You urge the pace of a horse when
you whip or spur him; and you urge a cause or an
argument when by word or deed you push it forward.   But the horse does not *urge* the coach to
which he is harnessed; he pulls it.   The locomotive does not urge the train; it draws it.   The
wind urges the sails of a ship, but they do not
urge the ship, they *pull* it.   The ship is not
pushed forward by them; it is *pulled* forward.   I
employed the word 'tug' as rather stronger than
'pull,' to imply the straining of the sails upon the
cordage, the masts and the spars to which they
are attached, under the pressure of a stiff breeze."

In the autumn of 1883 Sir Charles, in order
to transact some business connected with his

American property, revisited the United States, after forty-six years' absence. Naturally he was as much amazed as interested by the great changes which had come over once familiar scenes. Returning to Europe, he resumed correspondence, chiefly on philological matters, with various learned men. Most of this is too technical to be of general interest, but occasionally amusing passages and allusions occur.

Professor Max Müller to the Same.

"MALVERN, 23rd Dec. 1883.

"In German *iren* is a denominative termination, not borrowed from the French, but used too freely to make foreign verbs conjugable. The termination *able* is a case in point. It is of course applicable to Romance words only, but we now talk of 'understandable,' 'knowable,' &c. We get into habits, and when we are taken to task, we say what a bootmaker in a Swiss village once said to me, when he had made me a pair of boots on the one last which he possessed, 'Cela vous va rudement bien'!"

Lord Acton to the Same.

"CANNES, *April* 1885.

"Of the two most extraordinary coincidences I ever knew, one happened to myself. I was at Lucerne with my son, having left Lady Acton here. We were driven away by bad weather, and resolved to sleep at Lausanne. There, at the Hotel Richemont, I found a telegram from Lady Acton, who had not heard of our plan, but read Lausanne for Lucerne on my despatch from the latter place.

"The other is 200 years old, but has escaped notice. Sir Edmundsberry Godfrey was found lying dead under Primrose Hill, which was [then] called Greenberry Hill. Three men were hanged for it, and their names were Green, Berry, and Hill."

Hon. Charles Murray to his Wife.

"BATH, 1885.

"CARISSIMA, — My first whole day of solitude is drawing to a close, and ennui, that terror of fine ladies and gentlemen, has not yet invaded me! . . . I have invited Keats to pass an hour with me. He is not, in my opinion, to be classed in the first rank of poets; still, with the exception of some of Wordsworth's and Milton's, his sonnets are perhaps the best in our language. I suppose it is heresy to say so, but I never could bring myself to consider Shakespeare's Sonnets as worthy of his great dramatic reputation! Some day I must read them again and see whether I condemn this opinion as erroneous."

In the following year Sir Charles revisited his old home at Dunmore.

The Same to the Same.

" POLMAISE CASTLE, STIRLING,
Oct. 3rd, 1886.

" Yesterday the weather was lovely, and Mrs
M.[1] drove me to Dunmore with Mrs A. The old
housekeeper knew me, not from *old* times, but from
our last visit, and we went all over the house,
which, although of course wearing a cold, deserted
look from being so long uninhabited, was very
clean and tidy, and might be made again *comfy* in
a very few days. You may imagine what old recollections the visit evoked, especially the library,
where the old books repose on their old shelves,
uncovered by glass or paper, and many of them
exactly in their old places ; so that I could see the
book which my father took down and read by the
fireside. My mother's boudoir, which had been so
pretty and cosy, was quite *méconnaissable* from the
changes made in it during successive occupations ;
but I went on to the room beyond, which my
parents occupied during the latter years of my
father's life, and where he breathed his last exactly
fifty years ago (1836). Thence we went through
the wood, which looked as beautiful as ever, and the
garden, and to the dear old tower and church. I
found a few faded flowers and chaplets on my elder
brother's tomb : who placed them there I know
not, but the whole scene and its associations moved
me exceedingly, and called up feelings and recollections which you can more easily imagine than I
describe ! Mrs M. was very kind, and showed

---

[1] Mrs Murray of Polmaise.

great tact in leaving me, both in the house and
at the church, for several minutes alone."

"CARISSIMA,—I sit down this Sunday evening
to have a little after-dinner chat with you, having
enjoyed a most delightful afternoon drive round
the borders of the lake. You can hardly imagine
the pleasure I derived from the soft fresh air and
the lovely scenery : besides this, I had the comfort of a most cheering companion—guess who?
male or female, young or old? None other than
my old friend Gray, the author of the 'Elegy,'
whom I had evoked from the recesses of my old
cobwebbed memory, to express and share my
feelings. Do you remember his fragment of an
'Ode to Vicissitude, an invalid's first outing on a
fine spring day'?—

> ' Now the rosy morn aloft
>   Waves her dew-bespangled wing,' &c.

. . . I think the last four lines on the skylark
are beautiful, and quite worthy of being placed
beside Shelley's masterpiece on the same subject.
It is the fashion in the present days of *advanced*
criticism to decry Gray as a poet, but his 'Elegy'
will last as long as the English language, and will
be remembered when Swinburne will be forgotten
before twenty years shall have passed over his
grave. If to be unintelligible to ordinary minds
is the great aim and merit of poetry, then R.
Browning *is* a great poet, and Homer, Virgil,
Shakespeare, Burns, &c., &c., are *not*."

" You must not think that I am dull for want of *society*: the *curé*, your letters, and a few old friends like Gray, Sâdi, &c., together with lots of *novels* while I am lying down, fill up my time completely and pleasantly. I think I must have swallowed nearly a dozen volumes of Tauchnitz since you left, some few of them amusing from their plot and descriptive merit, the greater part amusing (though not so agreeable) from the wonder thereby excited that any one should have dared to publish such rubbish, and that Tauchnitz had accepted it! The grossest as well as the commonest blunder of these second- and third-rate novelists is their persistent introduction of dialogue among their *dram. pers.*   They begin by describing Mr A. as a man of brilliant wit in conversation, Lord B. as a poetical genius, Mr C. as a profound scholar and critic, and when in the second volume these persons appear on the stage—to exhibit their announced qualifications — their conversation is nothing but the dullest commonplace trash."

In his later years Sir Charles Murray was easily induced to talk of his early days, and much younger men than he enjoyed his reminiscences, which formed a link with a far-off past. Mr Reginald Lucas, a friend and contemporary of young Cecil Murray, used to get him to talk of Rogers's breakfast - parties.   Sir Charles observed that proceedings there generally depended

on whether Macaulay or Sydney Smith got the
start. One or other always took the lead—and
kept it. On one occasion Murray was sitting
next Sydney Smith when Macaulay began, and
went off at score. After controlling himself for a
considerable time, Smith threw himself back in his
chair, exclaiming, "If only the man would *sneeze*,
I might have a chance."[1] Sir Charles told Mr
Reginald Smith, who, as a young man, knew him
well in his last years, that the secret of Sydney
Smith's jokes lay in his inimitable facial expression.

The same could not be said of another illustrious character in that circle. Walking with
Mr Reginald Smith one day down Pall Mall, Sir
Charles said as they passed the "Rag": "I recollect
dining at a large party there long ago. Somebody
sitting next me asked, 'Who is that man opposite
with an extraordinarily stupid face?' 'That,' I
replied, 'happens to be Sir Walter Scott!'"

About Rogers there is the following in one of
Sir Charles's note-books :—

"It has often been asserted verbally and in

---

[1] There are many allusions in T. Moore's journals to these gatherings and similar parties in other houses. Thus—"Dined at Lord
Lansdowne's: company—Lord Auckland, Macaulay, Rogers, Schlegel,
Charles Murray, &c. Rogers seated next Schlegel, and suffering
manifest agony from the German's loud voice and unnecessary use
of it."

print that Rogers was in the habit of making puns and *jeux de mots*, and nothing can be further from the truth. But one or two of the *bons mots* are, I believe, justly attributed to him, as, for instance, the epigram on the well-known Ward —Lord Dudley—which was the distich :—

> ' Ward has no heart, they say—
> But I deny it ;
> He *has* a heart—and gets his speeches by it ! ' "

This was written in revenge for Ward's severe handling of the " Pleasures of Memory " in the ' Quarterly.' And another incident :—

" Rogers was going to Cambridge by the coach, and he was sitting on the box by the driver, and was annoyed at seeing that their progress was slow, and that other coaches passed them. He asked the driver, ' What's the name of this coach that you're driving ? '

" The man answered, ' It's called the " Regulator." '

" ' Ah, I see,' said Rogers, ' it's very well named —for all the other coaches go *by* it.' "

Mr John Murray (the publisher) to
Hon. Sir Charles Murray.

" 50 ALBEMARLE ST., *Nov. 2nd*, 1888.

" I am very glad you happen to have been so attracted by the article in last ' Quarterly ' on Sam Rogers ; among other reasons, because it has drawn from you so long and pleasant a letter to me. We do not often tell the names of writers in the 'Q. R.,' but in this case I am happy to be able to make an exception, and to inform you that the writer of the paper is my old friend, and I daresay yours also, Lady Eastlake. To my mind the character she gives of Sam is a little *couleur de rose*. She has sunk all his ill-natured sayings and doings, of which I know something. I have in my possession Byron's savage verses about him— a retort for certain sayings and doings against Byron which excited the poet's ire in no moderate degree."

It was inevitable that, retaining as he did all his faculties and love of cultivating society to the end of his long life, Sir Charles should have been urged very frequently, especially by those who possessed the publisher's instinct, to compile his reminiscences.

Hon. Sir Charles Murray to Mr Reginald Smith.

" VILLA VICTORIA, CANNES, *Jan.* 24*th*, 1889.

" DEAR REGINALD,—It is rather curious that your suggestion of my trying to cook up my reminiscences should have reached me only a few days after I had received a similar one from my wife and Cecil, urging me to write something in the shape of an autobiography. I feel, however, that my memory is not equal to the task,—it is wofully defective now ; and though I have known many interesting persons, and have been witness to many interesting events, in my long life, I have played such a secondary part in the drama that I do not think my record could have any interest to the public in general. . . . I could only attempt an introductory chapter giving my boyhood and college life ; then I would hand over all my MSS., diaries, and memorandum-books at my death to my wife, Cecil, and you, and any others you might select, with full authority to burn, destroy, or publish, as you might think fit."

He told Mr Lucas he had always been far too lazy to keep a regular journal, but to the last his pen was active in correspondence either with those he loved, or with those with whom he loved to discuss intellectual subjects. He often expressed distress, as an old Whig, because of the ways into which the Liberal party had been led. Writing in 1889 from the Travellers' Club to Mr Reginald Smith, he tells him that he had spent " three days with an old friend, Mr Duncan, who beats me in antiquity by three years ; but he is as deaf as a post, or as a Home Ruler is to argument."

Here is an echo of early days :—

Cardinal Manning to Hon. Sir Charles Murray.

"ARCHBISHOP'S HOUSE, WESTMINSTER,
Dec. 28, 1889.

"If I am not mistaken, I remember you, and your countenance, as clearly as if I had seen you yesterday.　The last time, I think, I saw you playing tennis at Oxford.　There are few of our day surviving.　A day ago I heard from Gladstone, whose health and vigour are wonderful. . . . Not many men can play with 65's and 70's as we can, and I hope that you are as strong as your handwriting implies."

Hon. Sir Charles Murray to his Wife.

"VILLA VICTORIA, CANNES, 1890.

"I showed Sir Joseph Crowe the sketches in your portfolio to-day. . . . I fear we have not got his Life of Raphael.　He tells me that it cost him more than four times the labour and time that the Life of Titian did.　It is a curious, I might say a sad thing, to see a mind so gifted to develop, appreciate, and describe all these works of the highest art, obliged now to devote itself entirely to the details of national commerce and trade."

The Same to the Same.

"PARIS, 28*th* Nov. 1891.

"I have read Mrs Oliphant's Life of her cousin Laurence Oliphant, one of the most extraordinary creatures that ever lived, combining in himself energy, wit, fun, satire, love of adventure, with a depth of religious mysticism bordering on insanity, yet always accompanied by a heroic *motive* of self-sacrifice."

Cecil Murray having made excursions into literature, his father writes hoping that he might see a French story he had just published :—

Hon. Sir Charles Murray to his Son Cecil.[1]

"MACKELLAR'S HOTEL, LONDON,
July 1892.

"I wish to suggest to you the *motif* for another that has occurred to me, which I think you might extend into something—at all events *new*. I would call it ' La Complainte d'une Oie.' Of course I only pretend to give you the *heads* and the suggestions: the ancient ancestry of the goose—visiting Egypt from the northern climes of Scythia—her superiority over man—the ' animal impulse ' of Pythagoras —then the saviour of the Roman Capitol from the Gauls, with the cruel rites which followed. Then in later times the quills from their wing which transmitted for certain the words and thoughts of poetry, historians, &c., &c.—then the *petites oies* of Louis XIV.'s time as recognised love-tokens ; while in compliment to their wing all writers have been designated as *hommes de plume*, whilst in these later days their higher vocation has been degraded into— . . . Gillott's *steel* pens ! If you cannot make out a ' Complainte de l'oie,' your imagination must be asleep or paralysed by Schwalbach water."

[1] Mr Cecil Murray died at sea, under most painful circumstances, on June 3rd, 1896, the first anniversary of his father's death.

z

CHAPTER XIV.

1892–1895.

LAST YEARS.

THE sands were running low.

To many who wintered at Cannes a few years ago must the remembrance be fresh of the handsome white-haired old gentleman, with his kindly greeting ever ready to welcome an acquaintance, and his old-fashioned courtliness of manner. Ambition—so much of that as he had ever cherished —was long since dead; memory was still quick, stretching back into a world which few men living could have recognised. Still Sir Charles read much and studied, wrote much to his friends at a distance —a fast dwindling band—and enjoyed the presence of those who chanced to be at hand.

But bodily infirmity was creeping on.

Of his sons, the elder had long ago made a career

Ch. A. Murray

for himself—first in diplomacy, then in Parliament —and had been married for twenty years :[1] the younger had given bright promise of distinction, and for him Sir Charles's hopes were high. Lady Murray's health was the occasion of constant concern to him, yet she was almost always able to be with him, and he never ceased to express his gratitude for the companion which he had found after so many years of solitude. On his last birthday they happened to be separated, and these are perhaps the last words he ever penned to her :—

"VILLA VICTORIA, CANNES, 23rd *Nov.* 1894.

" CARISSIMA,—Dupuy sent me in some beautiful flowers ; so my table, rooms, &c., were all bright, with a brilliant sun, and nothing was wanted to enlighten my 89th birthday but the presence of the dear faces at Florence, and that was compensated for by the receipt of your dear letter.—Ever your own, C. A. M."

They spent the winter of 1894-95 together at Cannes as usual, and started on the homeward journey in the last week in May. During what was intended to be a short halt in Paris, Sir Charles became affected with a drowsiness very unusual in him. The doctor who was called in saw

[1] Mr C. J. Murray, M.P., married in 1875 Lady Anne Finch, only daughter of the Earl of Aylesford.

nothing to cause anxiety, save that any sign of weakness in a man of fourscore and eight years was to be dealt with very carefully. For a week he remained subject to this occasional drowsiness, but on Saturday, June 1st, he told his valet to pack his things, as he was resolved to start for England on Monday.

When that day arrived Mr Charles Murray had come, summoned by telegram. He and Lady Murray were with Sir Charles at noon on Monday, 3rd June 1895. None other was in the room, the younger son, Cecil, having left with a message to the doctor, when quietly—peacefully—the frail bond was severed and Sir Charles Murray was no more.

In the course of this narrative I have refrained (lest the left hand should learn what the right had been doing) from quoting any of the numerous allusions in Sir Charles's letters to various bene-volent schemes in which Lady Murray was con-stantly occupied. It may be permitted, however, to mention in this place that, in memory of her husband and only child, she has this year (1898) founded and endowed at Antibes a Rest Home for brain-workers—artists, writers, musicians—where, for a very moderate payment, they may enjoy the boon of repose and retirement under a Southern sky.

In preparing a narrative, however severely condensed, of the life of one lately departed, it is an important, and not the least arduous, part of the work to decipher masses of correspondence and other manuscript. In the present instance, as has been mentioned elsewhere, very little of Sir Charles Murray's side of the correspondence has been preserved; at least, very little has been at the disposal of his biographer, for the reason that, except his wife, nearly every one of his intimate correspondents had preceded him to the grave. Nevertheless, the man's character is reflected almost as faithfully in the general tone of letters addressed *to* him as in those written *by* him. It came, therefore, as a puzzling surprise to find in a bundle of letters in the hand of a certain distinguished traveller, now no more, raillery, quotations, and allusions of a kind totally different from anything that had transpired elsewhere. It is not implied that they were in themselves objectionable or malicious, but they were such as it was impossible to reconcile with the lofty and large-minded nature revealed in the rest of the correspondence. There was nothing to indicate to whom these letters were addressed, save that they were marked on the outside "—— to C. A. M."

This discovery caused the compiler of these

pages no little perplexity—even some dismay; for it became obvious that, if Murray had numbered the writer of these letters among his familiar correspondents, the estimate of his character which had been shaping itself must undergo very extensive review. Was it possible that certain parts of Sir Charles's correspondence had been intentionally destroyed, and only those parts preserved which would best bear the scrutiny of a stranger?

Presently the mystery was solved.

A closer examination of the papers, after an interval of some days, revealed beyond any doubt that they had *not* been addressed to Sir Charles Murray, but to another individual altogether, by whom they had been forwarded to Sir Charles, on account of a quantity of interesting oriental lore which they contained.

Although, as he confessed himself, unsuccessful in many attempts to keep a consecutive journal, and careless, perhaps intentionally so, in preserving letters, Sir Charles Murray left a considerable number of interesting memoranda and drafts of study. There are several commonplace - books, each of which was originally intended for a separate subject, such as comparative philology, commentary and criticism on Scripture, Persian or

Arabic proverbs, poetry, original and otherwise, &c. These were generally written only on one side of the page, the *verso* being left blank. On these blank sides have been jotted down a number of anecdotes and quotations, sometimes illustrating the matter on the opposite page, at others strangely in contrast with it. The following, for instance, occurs with the date 1888 attached, in a volume of manuscript notes and studies in Persian literature compiled many years previously :—

"I had a curious conversation lately with Lord Ashburnham, the sale of whose collection of MSS. caused so much discussion in the press in 1886-87. He offered one large group to the British Government for £7000, who refused to purchase at that price. He sold them to a foreign purchaser for £8000; then he got them back again in exchange, and afterwards sold the same group to the British Government for £45,000 !

"Still more curious is the history of a splendid suit of armour in the finest Milan steel, inlaid with gold, said to have belonged to François I$^{er.}$ It was in the house of one of the Rothschilds at Paris, and Madame de Rothschild said that it annoyed and startled her in the place where it stood, so the Baron sold it to the late Lord Ashburnham for 1000 guineas. A great Jew dealer in antiquities often came to Lord Ashburnham with a view to purchase it, and Lord Ashburnham, to get rid of his importunity, told him he should not have it for less than 4000 guineas. To his surprise the dealer closed with the offer, carried it off, and within forty-eight hours sold it to Sir R. Wallace for £12,000. Afterwards it was deposited at the Pantechnicon while Sir Richard's house was being rebuilt; and in the great fire which took place at that establishment, it was so mauled, blackened, and broken, that among the ruins it was sold for £12. The crafty fellow who bought it spent much labour in mending, burnishing, and setting it up again, and Lord Ashburnham told me that the man had sold it again in Paris for several thousand pounds.

"*N.B.*—Lord Ashburnham told me that he had already sold MSS. to the extent of £93,000, and that he had a considerable quantity left; so his father must have been a most industrious and successful collector."

Here is another jotting from the same book, owing, apparently, to Murray having made the acquaintance of one of the characters referred to during his service in Egypt:—

"Emile de Girardin was the natural son of the Marquis de Girardin, by whom he was not recognised until he had begun to make himself a name in literature.

"His first attempts at making a living by his pen were not successful, but he had been fortunate in making the acquaintance, and afterwards securing the intimacy and friendship, of Latour-

Mezerai, the prince of Parisian *viveurs* and dandies, who occupied a place in the society of the French capital similar to that filled about the same time by Count d'Orsay in London. In his early days de Girardin, in a mood of melancholy brought on by poverty and disappointment, wrote, in imitation of the style of Rousseau, his first work called 'Emile.' It fell quite flat, and brought the author neither money nor fame; so in despair he was trudging off to the banks of the Seine, when he met Latour-Mezerai.

"'Où allez vous?' asked Mezerai.

"'Me noyer,' replied Emile.

"'Sérieusement?'

"'Oui; très sérieusement.'

"Mezerai, having ascertained the cause of his young friend's depression, comforted him as best he could, and cheered him with a hopeful assurance of the future; but, not having any pecuniary resources wherewith to start his encouraging projects, he suddenly exclaimed—

"'Tiens! nous allons fonder un journal.'

"'Avec quoi?' asked Girardin.

"'Avec rien.'

"'Sans le sou?'

"'Oui; sans le sou.'

"'Qui l'écrira?'

"'Personne et tout le monde.'

"'Et comment s'appelera t-il?'

."'*Le Voleur*'!

"And thus, with sharp wits and scissors, did this audacious couple hunt up and cut out extracts from recent publications of every kind, and republish them in a cheap journal bearing the above name. It became a great success, and de Girardin soon followed it by others of a better stamp, till he became the greatest journalist in France. Latour-Mezerai, after being for a long time the lion of Parisian *salons*, died at last as Prefect of Algiers."

It is possible that an amusing story about Mr A. Solomon, R.A., may have found its way into print elsewhere : even if so, it seems worth repeating. His picture, "Waiting for the Verdict," attracted much admiration when it appeared in the Academy Exhibition ; but as Solomon had not yet been admitted an Associate, he had not the privilege of being hung on the line, and his work was "skyed." Thomas Landseer was gazing in delight on the picture when a bystander remarked to him, "There is Solomon in all his glory."

"Yes, indeed," replied Landseer ; " but " (pointing along the line of privileged pictures), " not R.A.'d like one of these."

The above stories certainly have no reference to the analysis of Sâdi's poetry and texts of the Koran, among which they find a place. But sometimes the connection is clear, as in the following instance, which occurs among some pages devoted to the study of the metaphorical use of terms among different races.

In the midst of a discussion of the various meanings of the word " bar " in English, Murray pauses to tell about something which happened to an acquaintance whom he made in New York in 1834. This gentleman, Mr B., when he first came to New York many years before, had gone two or three times into the bar of the City Hotel, where he was served by the barman among the customers.

One fine afternoon, after a rainy morning, Mr B. strolled into the bar, and, after taking his glass, handed his umbrella to the barman, asking him to take care of it for a few hours. In the course of the afternoon Mr B. received the offer of a lucrative appointment in Cuba, which he accepted. The vessel was on the point of sailing, and Mr B. had to start at once. It was twelve years before he returned to New York, when, strolling into the City bar one morning, the barman, after looking steadily at him for a minute, said, " How do you do, Mr B. ? here's your umbrella ! " and handed it to him across the counter.

Scripture was the subject of Sir Charles's life-long and daily study, but he was hardly less constant and regular in his devotion to Homer, the Persian Sâdi, and Shakespeare. Hardly an event of moment could pass without finding its reflection for this faithful student in the works of one of these poets.

During the disturbance in Parliament about Mr Bradlaugh taking or not taking the oath, Murray jots down that this is how the question was viewed by Shakespeare (*if* Shakespeare wrote ' Pericles ')—

> " I'll take thy word for faith, not ask thine oath ;
> Who shuns not to break one, will sure crack both."

And here is a translation of one of Sâdi's moral lessons :—

THE DROP OF RAIN.

> " Fall'n from a passing cloud, a drop of rain
> With humble awe beheld the ocean plain.
> ' What place ? what sea is this ? and what am I ?
> If this is Being, I'm Nonentity ! '
> The modest drop, thus murmuring, self-abased,
> Was by an oyster's venturing shell embraced :
> Cherished by Fate, soon shone the watery gem,
> A pearl upon a regal diadem.
> Thus was Humility with glory crowned—
> It sought a hovel, and a palace found."

A thorough acquaintance with oriental languages, and his familiarity with their idioms, enabled Sir Charles to appreciate and enjoy many expressions of which one who had to rely on the services of an interpreter would have missed the point. Thus one day when riding with Sir Charles Napier, then on his way back to England through Egypt, Murray received a summons by a mounted *cawass* to attend the Viceroy immediately. He asked the General to ride slowly on towards Alexandria, where they intended to inspect the French fortifications, and went off to his interview. When it was over he galloped after the General, but on coming to a projecting bastion where the road divided he was uncertain which to follow. Murray asked an Arab sentry if he had seen a Frank horseman pass, and which road he had taken. The man reflected a moment and replied, "Yes, I saw one *abou mouquâr*, and he took *that* road." Now *abou mouquâr* means "father of beaks," and might be applied either to an eagle or to a man who, like Sir Charles Napier, was remarkable for his aquiline nose.

On another occasion, in 1852, he witnessed a strange instance of superstition at Cairo. A certain sheik, in high repute as an astrologer, was invited to discover a treasure supposed to be buried at a place called the Seven Girls, about two miles south of the city. Having inspected the spot, he declared that there was no treasure there, but that the soil was of such peculiar virtue that anybody who rolled in the sand would be cured of any disease he might have.

"The report spread like wildfire, and soon crowds were seen hurrying to the spot to *roll* off their infirmities,—thousands of all ages and of both sexes: the road from the city to the Seven Girls was as densely thronged from sunrise till the afternoon as the Epsom road on the Derby day. Among others a fat Turkish Bey went out there in his carriage, and rolled about in the dust till he vomited: naturally he felt relieved, and loudly proclaimed the efficacy of the cure. I was much amused at seeing dozens of fellahs, with real or imaginary diseases, rolling about in all directions until they grew giddy and stupefied, sensations which they attributed to the magic power of the earth beneath them."

Murray's love of language led him to a close study of the original of the Scriptures, and his knowledge in Hebrew and familiarity with Greek caused him to scrutinise closely some of the best known passages in the Bible. Among other things he pointed out the confusion which has arisen in both languages between words signifying "spirit" and "wind." For instance, in Psalm civ. 4, he held the splendid verse, "Who maketh His angels spirits; His ministers a flaming fire," to be a faulty rendering :—

"As all the context is laudatory description of the wonders of creation, it would seem a more apposite and faithful version to read, 'Who maketh the winds His messengers, and the flaming-fire [lightning] His ministers.' Our Biblical version follows the Septuagint; but I think Gesenius right in preferring the latter rendering, which is certainly nearer to the simple meaning of the Hebrew text, especially in respect to the word 'winds,' which our translation renders by 'spirits.'"

Of greater importance, because more seriously disguising the sense of the original, seemed to Murray the liberty which English translators have taken with one of the grandest verses in the New Testament—" The wind bloweth where it listeth," &c. (John iii. 8) :—

"This translation, although the authors of the Revised Version have retained it in the text, and although it is supported by the authority of Luther, I hold to be decidedly erroneous, on the ground that it renders the Greek word πνεῦμα in the beginning of the verse by the word 'wind,' and in the latter part of the same verse by the word 'spirit,' a liberty which I do not think any translator is justified in taking. . . . It is to be observed that there is not another instance in any of the writings of St John, nor indeed in the whole New Testament, in which πνεῦμα is, or can be, rendered as 'wind.' This, in my mind, is decisive of the question.

"The Roman Catholic Testament, following the Latin Vulgate, translates literally, and I believe correctly, 'The Spirit breatheth where He listeth, and thou hearest His *voice.*' Φωνὴ signifies properly and etymologically ' the voice,' and not the sound of wind."

Sir Charles acknowledged that, in many respects, the Revised Version was a valuable improvement on the Authorised Version; but in some passages he regarded it as the reverse. One of these he considered to be Mark v. 36 : "As soon as Jesus heard the word that was spoken," which is an exact rendering of the original Greek. This is altered in the Revised Version into : "Jesus *not heeding* the word spoken," with the marginal alternative of "overhearing"; both of which, in Murray's judgment, were incorrect.

The following passages from a criticism on Professor Drummond's 'Natural Law in the Spiritual World' illustrate the deep and constant thought which Sir Charles devoted to the problems of religion.

Hon. Sir Charles Murray to the Dowager
Lady Castletown.

"VILLA VICTORIA, CANNES, *Feb.* 24, 1884.

". . . In spite of the many disputable tenets that it maintains, and the doubtful analogies by which it illustrates them, I think it is a book that you may read both with interest and improvement. . . . The object of the work is undeniably good;

. . . the author's knowledge of science is apparently extensive, as is also his acquaintance with the writings of Darwin, Herbert Spencer, Harrison, and all the modern school of evolution, biology, and the other 'ologies,' treated by writers who are termed the 'advanced thinkers' of the day.   I must own that I neither study them much nor respect their opinions, which seem to me to tend *generally* to scepticism, and such *thinkers* as Bacon, Barrow, Milton, Pascal, Newton, &c., &c., are quite 'advanced' enough for me ; but the author's studies and reflections, instead of leading him to scepticism, have led him to a Christian creed so high that it is difficult to follow him. . . . It seems to me that in his illustrations in the field of natural history some of the author's statements are inaccurate. . . . While stating that life cannot be given from without, but is permanently fixed and rooted in the organism of every living thing, he says 'the life is *in* every plant and tree, inside its own tissue,' but he forgets that without the oxygen of the air that feeds the leaves, and the earth-moisture that nourishes the roots, the plant could have no life at all.   Numerous errors of this kind are to be found in the volume : it is better to pass them by and consider some of the more important parts of his general argument. . . . The author works out this distinction between the moral man as dead, and the spiritual man as alive, at considerable length. . . . If we are to admit, as this author maintains, that there is the same *organic* and essential difference between a spiritual and a moral man that there is between a man and a stone—the

2 A

one being alive and the other dead—we should shut out from the doors of Heaven probably 90 out of 100 struggling, praying, striving, falling, again rising, sincere but frail Christians, who, according to this hard-and-fast line of distinction, have been dead and alive again several times. Again, if there can be no eternal life for any man except for him 'who lives in Christ and Christ in him'—what are we to say of the lot ordained for the thousands of millions who have lived, now live, and yet will live on this earth, who have never even heard of the name of Christ? . . . No man's creed would seem to me either reasonable or Scriptural which should exclude for ever from the Golden Gates of the Eternal Life hereafter such men as Homer, Socrates, Aristides, Plato, &c., &c."

Devout though he was and profoundly reverent, Murray, although ready to accept articles of faith which were *beyond* his understanding, would never yield assent to those that were *contrary* to it.

" Belief is an act of the understanding, not of the will, and whatever amount of argument or apparent evidence might be presented to me to prove that God was unjust, or that two and two made five, I *could* not believe it by any effort of will. It is therefore useless for any human law-giver or Church to endeavour to enforce a dogma upon any one whose conscience and understanding repudiate it. I think it has been an act of repre-

hensible unwisdom on the part of the Church of
England to *oblige* its ministers to read the so-
called Athanasian Creed on stated days in church,
seeing that it is a well-known fact that ninety-nine
out of every hundred of the laity cannot understand it; and that nine out of ten of the better
educated, who have examined and studied it, hold
it in aversion. These last regard it as a creed
composed by some unknown author three or four
hundred years after the Christian era, in which,
after a laboured and wordy attempt to fathom the
unsearchable and define the incomprehensible,
more than half the Christian world is consigned
to perdition by the declaration, that whosoever
does not faithfully believe it, cannot be saved."

To how many earnest worshippers must the
same difficulty have occurred; but how few have
the moral courage to face it !

It is impossible that any honest religious thinker
in these times can refuse to examine the authority
for the doctrine of everlasting punishment, which
becomes the more repugnant to human ideas of
justice in proportion as those ideas are based on
the doctrines of Christ and permeated by the
spirit of His teaching. One turns over the pages
of these note - books, therefore, confident that
Murray will have something to say about it, and
curious to know how it presented itself to his frank
and simple nature. He faces the problem boldly

enough : he admits that we have exactly the same authority for believing in the eternity of punishment as in the eternity of bliss; he brushes aside all significance in the apparent distinction indicated in Christ's own words, " These shall go away into *everlasting* punishment, but the righteous into life *eternal*" (Matt. xxv. 46), by showing that it is an arbitrary one created by the translators, the word in the original Greek—*aἰώνιον*—being the same both for "everlasting" and "eternal"; and he discusses various authorities on both sides at considerable length.

The Hon. Sir Charles Murray to the Dowager Lady Castletown.

"THE GRANGE, OLD WINDSOR, *Nov.* 1, 1885.

" For myself, I shun all *dogmatic* utterances about a future state, even when they pretend to be founded on the book of Revelation, or other isolated texts of Scripture, as I think they come under the denomination of those curious questions which St Paul taught us to avoid. The holding of doctrines and dogmas has been the *curse* of Christianity since its foundation. . . . Two-thirds of the heresies that divided the primitive Church were founded on the contested acceptation of single texts. Not to mention scores of minor heresies (so - called), the two great Churches of the East and of the West, with many millions of followers attached to them, were separated, and have remained ever since irreconcilably separated, upon the question whether the Holy Spirit proceeded from God alone, or from God and Jesus Christ. Surely angels might weep to see Christians — nominally the followers of the holy and sinless Jesus—not only wasting their time for centuries, but shedding each other's blood, in disputing over verbal differences such as this ! . . . I am a member of the Church of England, having been baptised in it, and I hold to it in preference to any other Church, . . . although there are several things in its Liturgy which seem to me serious errors ; among others—compelling its clergy to read in church the so-called Athanasian Creed on stated occasions. I have no objection to any man, lay or clerical, who approves it and thinks he understands it, reciting it for himself; but I do not think that any Church, calling itself a Reformed Church, has a right to order its clergy to read as a creed *necessary* to salvation, a document written by some French or Spanish bishop five or six hundred years after the Christian era, dubbing it by the name of St Athanasius, and ending by the monstrous declaration that whoever does not believe it faithfully cannot be saved—words that exclude from salvation three-fourths at least of the Christian community on earth."

Sir Charles Murray, than whom no man ever gave more earnest thought to problems of which the solution lies beyond the grave, declined to

pronounce a definite opinion on them. Nevertheless, the tendency of his judgment is revealed in
the following sentences from one of his note-
books :—

"It is remarkable that Bishop Thirlwall, the
profoundest English thinker and theologian of this
age, never made this question the subject of one of
his sermons or charges to his clergy. But there is
a short letter of his extant to Professor Plumptre,
in which he thanks him for his admirable sermon
on the 'Spirits in Prison,' and terms it 'one of
the most valuable gifts the Church has received in
this generation.'[1] Now that sermon of Plumptre's
was directed forcibly and specially against the
doctrine of eternal punishment. If Thirlwall be
mistaken—*mallem cum Platone errare !*"

[1] Thirlwall's Letters, p. 334.

INDEX.

Abercairney, the house of, 3.

Absolomina, verses to, 87.

Acton, Lord, letter to Murray from, 343.

Adventures among the Pawnees, 96 *et seq.*

Ah-to-menō, the song of, 235.

Albert, Prince, Dr Buckland and, 167—reception of the Emperor Nicholas by, 177 *et seq.*—Murray's pamphlet on religious tenets of, 193 *et seq.*

Alison, Sir Archibald, criticism of ' The Prairie Bird ' by, 199 *et seq.*

Alleghanies, a journey to the, 130 *et seq.*

Andersen, Hans Christian, meeting of Murray with, 298—letter to Lady Murray from, *ib. et seq.*

Antelope hawking in Persia, 269.

Ardgowan, visits of the Murrays to, 30.

Arran, sport in, 49 *et seq.*

Art of public speaking, Lord Brougham on the, 65 *et seq.*

Ascot Tuesday, an, 181 *et seq.*

Ashburnham, Lord, the collection of MSS. of, 359—a splendid suit of armour belonging to, *ib.*—prices paid for MSS. of, 360.

Augustus Frederick, Prince, sponsor to Charles Murray, 4.

Azores, Murray's stay in the, 84.

Baden, Princess Mary of, romantic marriage of, 169 *et seq.*

Beckford, William, anecdote of, 44

—extraordinary gifts of, 43 *et seq.*—amusing story concerning, 45 *et seq.* — letter to Murray from, 201.

Bentley, Mr, publishes Murray's ' Travels,' 138.

Bright, Mr John, attitude of, regarding the Reform Bill of 1867, 300.

Brougham, Lord, friendship between Murray and, 48—letter to Lady Dunmore from, 64 *et seq.*—Samuel Rogers on the vagaries of, 149.

Buchanan, Sir Andrew, G.C.B., 145.

Buckland, Dr, and Prince Albert, 167.

Buffalo hunting in the Far West, 163.

Bulwer, Murray's criticism on the novels of, 271 *et seq.*

Bushire, bombardment of, 255.

Byron, Lord, remarks by Rogers on, 12, 34 *et seq.*, 350—criticism by Murray on, 274.

Cadzow Castle, occasion of Scott's ballad of, 48.

Cairo, an incident of superstition at, 365 *et seq.*

Cannes, Murray's stay at, 354 *et seq.* — the Rest Home endowed by Lady Murray at, 356.

Carlyle, letter to Murray from, 76 *et seq.*—lifelong intimacy between Murray and, 78.

Castletown, Dowager Lady, letters

from Murray to, 368 *et seq.*, 372 *et seq.*

Catlin, George, account of the Pawnees by, 124.

Chateaubriand, favourable opinion of Murray's 'Travels' held by, 137.

Clarendon, Lord, letter to Lord Stratford de Redcliffe from, 252 *et seq.*—his instructions to Murray during the difficulty with Persia, 254—defends Murray in the Persian imbroglio, 265—letter of Murray to, *ib.*—on the Spanish succession, 303—letter to Murray from, 304.

Clay, Henry, entertains Murray at Lexington, 97.

Cooper, Fenimore, Murray's meetings with, 88, 132—novels of Indian life by, *ib.*—letter to Murray from, 239 *et seq.*

Copenhagen, Murray offered appointment of British Minister at, 285.

Cowley, Earl, letter from Murray to, 263 *et seq.*

Crowe, Sir Joseph, life of Raphael by, 352.

Cuba, visit of Murray to, 128—Spanish administration of, 129.

Dalhousie, Earl of, letters to Murray from, 241 *et seq.*

Dalmeny, social gatherings at, 41.

Darwin, remarks by Murray on, 72.

David I., policy of, regarding feudal proprietors, 2.

Delawares, country of the, 130.

Denman, Chief-Justice, friendship between Murray and, 48.

Denmark, Murray on the war between Prussia and Austria and, 289.

Derby, Earl of, letter to Murray from, 327 *et seq.*

Douglas, Lord, Princess Mary of Baden's romantic attachment to, 169—story of the betrothal of, *ib. et seq.*—marriage of, 174—letter to Murray from, 175.

Doyle, Sir Francis Hastings, 140.

Dresden, appointment of Murray as British Minister at, 285.

Drummond, Prof. Henry, criticism by Murray of 'Natural Law in the Spiritual World' by, 368 *et seq.*

Dubuque, an incident at, 127 *et seq.*

Dundas, Mr, Lord Eldon and, 41 *et seq.*—amateur dentistry of, 42.

Dunmore, Countess of, letters from Samuel Rogers to, 5 *et seq.*, 8 *et seq.*, 31 *et seq.*, 80, 148 *et seq.*, 166 —letter from Lord Brougham to, 64 *et seq.*—death of, 208.

Edinburgh, gaiety of society in, at the beginning of this century, 39—literary activity of, *ib.*—stories of society of, 39 *et seq.*

Egypt, Murray Consul-General in, 210—success of Murray's administration in, 241.

Eldon, Lord Chancellor, pleasantries of, 41, 42.

Erskine, Henry, instances of the wit of, 39, 40.

Eton, Charles Murray at, 36.

Euphrates, a voyage by Murray on the, 270 *et seq.*

Falkirk Burghs, Murray's parliamentary candidature for, 79.

Fernando, Dom, of Portugal, description by Murray of, 304—proposed candidature for the Spanish throne by, 305 *et seq.*

Fincastle, Lady. See Dunmore, Countess of.

Fincastle, Lord, succeeds his father as Earl of Dunmore, 31—a practical joke by Charles Murray at the expense of, 37 *et seq.*

Fitzpatrick, Hon. Edythe, married to Sir Charles Murray, 287—letters from Murray to, 288 *et seq.*

Fletcher of Bearnish, anecdotes regarding, 29 *et seq.*

Fort Leavenworth, Murray's stay at, 101, 125.

Fort Lexington, visit of Murray to, 96—Murray's host at, 97.

Gamekeeper, a, of the old school, 49 *et seq.*

George IV., amusing incident on visit to Edinburgh of, 40—changes made on the apartments at Holyrood by, 41.

Girardin, Emile de, literary works of, 360—anecdote of, *ib. et seq.*

Gladstone, Mr, 'Church and State' by, 277—letter to Murray from, 286—attitude of, regarding the Reform Bill of 1867, 300.

Goethe, meeting of Murray with, 73—description by Murray of an interview with, *ib. et seq.*—autograph given to Murray by, 76.

Granville, Earl, letters from Murray to, 306 *et seq.*

Grey, Colonel George, letter to Murray from, 300 *et seq.*

Hadji Baba, a Bible annotated by, 336.

Hamilton, Duke of, old-fashioned manners of, 43—letter to Murray from, 169 *et seq.*

Hamilton, · Mr, of Dalzell, Lord Eldon and, 46.

Hampden, Dr, 143.

'Hassan,' Murray's novel entitled, 277 *et seq.*

Herbert, Hon. Sidney, 60.

Hope, Henry Beresford, friendship between Murray and, 53—Murray's rival for the parliamentary representation of Marylebone, 79.

'Horizons Célestes,' criticism by Murray of, 237.

Howden, Lord, letter to Murray from, 306.

Indians, the Red, manners of, 106 *et seq.*—character of, 107 *et seq.*, 132 *et seq.*—effects of the liquor traffic on, 125 *et seq.*—decay of, 136.

Iotan, story of the Indian chief, 105 *et seq.*

Irish in America, character of the, 127.

Journals, extracts from Murray's, 157 *et seq.*, 176 *et seq.*, 268 *et seq.*

Kinnaird, Mr, conversations of the Emperor Nicholas with, 180 *et seq.*

Kooshab, defeat of the Persians by the British at, 255.

Labouchere, Mr, remarks by Hon. Robert Lytton on, 318.

Lanarkshire, Murray's parliamentary candidature for, 152 *et seq.*

Landseer, Thomas, story of, 362.

Layard, Mr, attitude of, regarding the Persian war, 260.

Lehzen, Baroness, 160.

Lexington. See Fort Lexington.

Lichfield, parliamentary candidature by Murray for, 152 *et seq.*

Lisbon, appointment of Murray as British Minister at, 301—Murray's diplomatic service at, 303 *et seq.*

Louisville, description of, by Murray, 96.

Lytton, Hon. Robert, letters to Murray from, 313 *et seq.*, 323 *et seq.*, 341 *et seq.*—on the Spanish Academy of Science and Letters, 314—Madrid described by, 315—on the art of Velasquez, 316—on the acting of Rossi, *ib.*—criticism of 'The Prairie Bird' by, 317.

Lytton, Lord. See Lytton, Hon. Robert.

Macaulay, Lord, Murray's opinion of, as a writer, 275—as a politician, 277—anecdote of, 348.

Manning, Cardinal, letter to Murray from, 351 *et seq.*

'Marmion,' remarks by Samuel Rogers on, 10.

Martineau, Harriet, meeting of Murray with, 97—Murray's second meeting with, 227—intellectual characteristics of, *ib.*

Marylebone, Murray's parliamentary candidature for, 79.

Mazzini, outcry in London on behalf of, 190.

Meerza Hashem Khan, appointed British Agent at Shiraz, 247—is cause of the quarrel between Britain and Persia, 248.

Memlooks, massacre of the, 215 *et seq.*

Milton's ode "To Echo," Murray's translation into Latin verse of, 61.

Mohammed Ali, birthplace of, 212 —intellectual capacity of, *ib.*— incident in the career of, 213— energy and decision of, *ib.*—promoted by the Turkish Government, 214—appointed Brigadier-General, *ib.*—appointed governor of Egypt, *ib.*—a strong and sagacious ruler, 215—plot by the Memlooks against, *ib.*—massacre of the Memlooks by, 216 *et seq.*— Murray's opinion of, 221—internal administration founded by, 224—anecdotes regarding, 225 *et seq.* — Murray's lifelike portrait of, in 'Hassan,' 278.

Mohammerah, defeat of the Persians by the British at, 255.

Moore, Thomas, allusions by Rogers to, 9, 23.

Moray, Sir William, official name of, 3—families descended from, *ib.*

Morier, David, Bible annotated by Hadji Baba possessed by, 336.

Motley, John Lothrop, letter to Murray from, 294 *et. seq.*

Müller, Prof. Max, letter to Murray from, 343.

"Murmagh" or Moray, province of, 3.

Murray, George, Earl of Dunmore, 4—wife of, *ib.*—sons of, *ib.*

Murray, Hon. Cecil, tender solicitude of his father for, 340 *et seq.* —death of, 353.

Murray, Hon. Henry, letters from Sir Charles Murray to, 69 *et seq.*, 167 *et seq.*, 256 *et seq.*—letter to Murray from, 208 *et seq.*

Murray, John, Earl of Dunmore, becomes Duke of Athol, 4.

Murray, Lord Charles, titles of, 4.

Murray, Mr John, letter to Murray from, 349.

Murray, Sir Charles Augustus, birth of, 4—his sponsor, *ib.*—earliest historic allusion to, 5—description of Glen Finart by, 29 *et seq.* —goes to Eton, 36—incident that happened to, on a sea journey to London, 37—his skill in writing Latin verses, *ib.*—practical joke by, at the expense of his brother, 38—visit of, to Hamilton Palace, 43—his acquaintance with Sir Walter Scott, 48 —shooting experiences of, 49— at Oxford, 52—letters from P. Fraser Tytler to, 54 *et seq.*, 138 *et seq.*, 197 *et seq.*, 201 *et seq.*— friendship with Henry Hope, 56 —anecdotes of Newman by, *ib. et seq.*—friendship with Lord Edward Thynne, 58 *et seq.*— riding feat by, 59—a companion of Sidney Herbert, 60—his excellence as an athlete, *ib.*—scholarly tastes of, *ib.*—has Dean Tyler as tutor, 61—letter from Rogers to, 62—reads for the Bar, 64— letters to his brother from, 69 *et seq.*, 167 *et seq.*, 256 *et seq.*— splendid physique of, 71—remarks on Charles Darwin by, 72 —on the value of work, 73— active habits of, *ib.*—social interests of, *ib.*—meets Goethe at Weimar, *ib.*—letter from, descriptive of an interview with Goethe, *ib. et seq.*—letter from Carlyle to, 76 *et seq.*—his lifelong intimacy with Carlyle, 78 —unsuccessfully contests Falkirk Burghs and Marylebone, 79 —visits America, *ib.*—incident on the voyage to America, 81 *et seq.*—account of New York by, 86—verses to a child by, 87 —makes an expedition up the Hudson river, 88—meets Fenimore Cooper, *ib.*—panegyric on George Washington by, 89—letter from the President of the United States to, 90—hatred of slavery by, 92—remarks on the town of Washington by, 93 *et seq.*—revisits the Far West, 95 —his adventures among the Pawnees, 96 *et seq.*—meets Harriet Martineau, 97—entertained by Henry Clay, *ib.*—adopts Vernunft as a fellow-traveller, 98—his impressions of Pawnee braves, 100—is entertained by the Pawnee "nation," 102—engages in a buffalo-hunt, 103—his friendship with a Red Indian chief, 105—has unpleasant experiences in an Indian camp, 106 *et seq.*—description of the Pawnee tribe by, 110 *et seq.*—attacked on the plains, 114—lost in the wilderness, 115 *et seq.*—at Fort Leavenworth, 125—condemns the liquor traffic among the Red Indians, *ib. et seq.*—at St Louis, 126—on Irish lawlessness, 127—in New Orleans, 128—visits Cuba, *ib.*—at Philadelphia, 129—makes a journey to the Alleghanies, 130—at Lake Otsego, 131—meets Fenimore Cooper a second time, 132—romance of 'The Prairie Bird' by, 133, 194—'Travels in North America' by, *ib.*—dedicates his 'Travels' to the Queen, *ib.*—on American characteristics, 134—favourable reception of his 'Travels,' 137—Chateaubriand on the 'Travels' of, *ib.*—letters from Sir Charles Vaughan to, 140 *et seq.*—love-affair with Miss Wadsworth, 147—returns from America, 150—correspondence between Lord Stanley and, *ib. et seq.*—makes a third attempt to enter Parliament, 152 *et seq.*—observations by, regarding the early days of the Queen as a sovereign, 157 *et seq.*—his friendship with Lady Mary Stopford, 162—intermediary in the betrothal of Lord Douglas to Princess Mary of Baden, 169 *et seq.*—letters from Lieut.-Colonel Stepney-Cowell to, 171 *et seq.*—letter from Lord Douglas to, 175—extracts from journal of, on the visit of the Emperor Nicholas, 176 *et seq.*—on Government difficulties, 190 *et seq.*—literary acquaintances of, 193—publishes a pamphlet with reference to the

Queen's betrothal to Prince Albert, *ib.*—plot of 'The Prairie Bird' by, 195 *et seq.*—letter from William Beckford to, 201—literary facility of, 205—letter from Wordsworth to, 206—humorous poem by, 207—resigns the Mastership of the Household, *ib.*—appointed Secretary to the British Legation at Naples, *ib.*—appointed extra Groom-in-Waiting, *ib.*—letter from Capt. the Hon. H. Murray to, 208 *et seq.*—appointed Consul-General in Egypt, 210—description of Mohammed Ali by, *ib. et seq.*, 215 *et seq.*, 221 *et seq.*—on the massacre of the Memlooks, 221 *et seq.*—defence of Mohammed Ali by, 224 *et seq.*—anecdotes of Mohammed Ali by, 225 *et seq.*—interview with Harriet Martineau, 227—purchases the freedom of a slave, 228—letter from Lord Palmerston to, 229—letter to Lord Palmerston from, 230—letters to his second wife from, 232 *et seq.*, 288 *et seq.*, 325, 333 *et seq.*, 339 *et seq.*, 344 *et seq.*, 352, 355—translation of an Indian poem by, 235—marries Miss Wadsworth, 238—letter from Fenimore Cooper to, 239 *et seq.*—capable administration in Egypt of, 241—letters from the Earl of Dalhousie to, *ib. et seq.*—secures the first hippopotamus for the Zoological Society, 243 *et seq.*—appointed British Minister at Berne, 245—appointed Envoy to the Court of Persia, *ib.*—diplomatic work in Persia by, 248—the Shah of Persia and, 250—letter to Earl Cowley from, 263 *et seq.*—letter to Earl of Clarendon from, 265—on the Oriental character, 267—on the novels of Bulwer, 271 *et seq.*—description of a Persian rural scene by, 273—on Byron, 274—on Macaulay, 275, 277—on Tytler's 'History of Scotland,' 276—on Gladstone's 'Church and State,' 277—novel of 'Has-san' by, *ib.*—on the character of Sadr Azim, 278 *et seq.*—appointed British Minister at the Court of Saxony, 285—offered the appoint-ment of British Minister at the Court of Sweden, *ib.*—letter from Mr Gladstone to, 286—second marriage of, 287—on the war be-tween Denmark and Prussia, 289 —religious views of, 290 *et seq.*— on spiritualism, 292—letter from John Lothrop Motley to, 294 *et seq.*—receives the rank of K.C.B., 298 — leaves Denmark, *ib.* — meets Hans Christian Andersen, *ib.* — letters from Sir William Stirling - Maxwell to, 299, 320 *et seq.* — letter from Colonel George Grey to, 300 *et seq.*— appointed British Minister at Lisbon, 301—diplomatic duties at Lisbon of, 303 *et seq.*—letter from Lord Clarendon to, 304 *et seq.*—letter from Lord Howden to, 306—letters to Earl Granville from, *ib. et seq.* — letters from Hon. Robert Lytton to, 313 *et seq.*, 323 *et seq.*, 341 *et seq.*— letter from the Earl of Derby to, 327 *et seq.*—retires from diplo-matic life, 328—goes to reside at Kilburn, 329—letters from Hon. Mrs Norton to, 330 *et seq.*— letter from Dean Stanley to, 335 *et seq.*—home life of, 337 *et seq.* —letter in Latin to his grand-son, 340—letters to Mr Reginald Smith from, 341, 350 *et seq.*— revisits the United States, 343 —letter from Prof. Max Müller to, *ib.*—letter from Lord Acton to, 344 *et seq.*—reminiscences of Samuel Rogers by, 349 *et seq.*— letter from Mr John Murray to, 349—on modern Liberalism, 351 —letter from Cardinal Manning to, *ib.* — infirmities of old age come upon, 354—death of, 356 —character of, 357—memoranda left by, 358—extracts from a MS. volume by, 359 *et seq.*— translation of a poem of Sâdi's

by, 364—knowledge of Oriental languages possessed by, *ib.*, 366 —New Testament interpretations by, 367 *et seq.*—letters to Lady Castletown from, 368 *et seq.*, 372 —on dogma, 370—on everlast-ing punishment, 371—on Bishop Thirlwall's views, 374.

Murray, William, Earl of Tulli-bardine, 3.

Napier, Sir Charles, story of, 364 *et seq.*

Naples, appointment of Murray to the British Legation at, 207.

Napoleon III., attitude of, regard-ing the Spanish succession, 303.

New York, Murray's impressions of, 86—description of, by Feni-more Cooper, 240—story of a punctilious waiter in, 363.

Newman, John Henry, tutor to Murray at Oxford, 56 *et seq.*

Nicholas, Emperor, of Russia, ac-count by Murray of visit to England of, 176 *et seq.*—present given to Murray by, 186—leave-taking of, 188—personal acknow-ledgment to Murray by, *ib.*

Norton, Hon. Mrs, letters to Mur-ray from, 330 *et seq.*

Nuneham, an incident at, 206.

Obaysch, capture of the hippopota-mus named, 243.

Oliphant, Laurence, Murray's opin-ion of, 352.

Oliphant, Mrs, Life of Laurence Oliphant by, 352.

Orloff, Count, Murray meets, 178 —personal appearance of, 186 *et seq.*

Otoes, anecdote of a chief of the, 105.

Outram, General, defeats the Per-sians, 255.

Owen, Robert, the Educational In-stitution of, 48 *et seq.*

Oxford, Murray at, 52 *et seq.*

Palmerston, Lord, anecdote of, 191 —letter to Murray from, 229— letter from Murray to, 230—defence of Murray's Persian diplomacy by, 262.

Paris, state of, after Waterloo, 31 et seq.—treaty between Britain and Persia concluded at, 255.

Pawnees, the, adventures of Murray among, 96 et seq.—descriptions of, 100, 109 et seq.—extinction of, 135.

Peel, Sir Robert, as a politician, 189 et seq.

Persia, British policy regarding, 246, 272—ineptitude of the Shah of, 247—an insurrection in, ib. —Murray's diplomatic work in, 248 et seq.—a rural scene in, 273.

Philadelphia, favourable impression upon Murray of, 129.

'Prairie Bird,' publication of the, 133—characteristics of, 194 et seq.—favourable criticisms of, 197 et seq.

Public speaking, Lord Brougham on the art of, 65 et seq.

Radcliffe, Mrs, 11.

Redcliffe, Lord Stratford de, letter from the Earl of Clarendon to, 252 et seq.—prepares an ultimatum to Persia, 254.

Review, a royal, 183.

Rogers, Samuel, letters to Lady Susan Fincastle (Countess of Dunmore) from, 5 et seq., 8 et seq., 31 et seq., 80, 148 et seq., 166—friendship between the Fincastles and, 7—on London social affairs, 8 et seq.—on Byron's poems, 12—on Madame D'Arblay's novels, ib.—description of Patterdale by, 17—description of a journey to Edinburgh by, 18—description of a tour in Wales by, 25—a tour on the Continent described by, 26, 31 et seq.—on French patriotism, 33—on Lord Byron, 34 et seq. —letter to Murray from, 62— his patient revision of his literary work, 200—anecdotes of, 348 et seq.

Ross, Horatio, remarkable skill in shooting of, 337 et seq.

Russell, Lord John, letter to Murray from, 285—attitude of, regarding the Reform Bill of 1867, 300.

Sâdi, translation of a poem by, 364.

Sadr Azim, letters from the Shah to, 248 et seq., 250 et seq.— maligns Murray, 256—references by Murray to, 257, 259, 262— account of, by Murray, 278 et seq.

Sa-ni-tsa-rish, Murray's visit to the Pawnee chief called, 103—character of, 107 et seq.

Saxony, appointment of Murray as Minister at the Court of, 285— anecdote concerning King John of, 293.

Schleswig-Holstein difficulty, the, 289.

Scott, Sir Walter, acquaintance of Murray with, 48—ballad of Cadzow Castle by, ib.

Shah of Persia, the, ineptitude of, 247—letters of, 248 et seq., 250 et seq.

Shaw Stewart, Admiral Sir Houston, 30.

Shaw Stewart, Sir Michael, residence of, 30—daughters of, ib.

Slavery, the institution of, in America, 92—Murray's vehement condemnation of, 93.

Smith, Mr Reginald, letters from Murray to, 341, 350 et seq.

Smith, Rev. Sydney, anecdotes of, 28, 348—secret of the wit of, 348.

Solomon, Mr A., R.A., anecdote regarding, 362.

Spencer, William, ballad of Beth Gelert by, 24.

Spiritualism, Murray's opinion regarding, 292.

Stanley, Dean, letter to Murray from, 335 et seq.

Stanley, Lord, letter from Murray to, 150 et seq.—letter to Murray from, 151 et seq. See also Derby, Earl of.

Stepney-Cowell, Lieut.-Colonel, letters to Murray from, 171 et seq.

Stirling-Maxwell, Sir William,

Catalogue

of

Messrs Blackwood & Sons'

Publications

PHILOSOPHICAL CLASSICS FOR ENGLISH READERS.

EDITED BY WILLIAM KNIGHT, LL.D.,
Professor of Moral Philosophy in the University of St Andrews.

In crown 8vo Volumes, with Portraits, price 3s. 6d.

Contents of the Series.

DESCARTES, by Professor Mahaffy, Dublin.—BUTLER, by Rev. W. Lucas Collins, M.A.—BERKELEY, by Professor Campbell Fraser.—FICHTE, by Professor Adamson, Glasgow. — KANT, by Professor Wallace, Oxford.—HAMILTON, by Professor Veitch, Glasgow.—HEGEL, by the Master of Balliol.—LEIBNIZ, by J. Theodore Merz.—VICO by Professor Flint, Edinburgh.—HOBBES, by Professor Croom Robertson. — HUME , by the Editor. — SPINOZA, by the Very Rev. Principal Caird, Glasgow.— BACON: Part I. The Life, by Professor Nichol.—BACON: Part II. Philosophy, by the same Author.—LOCKE, by Professor Campbell Fraser.

FOREIGN CLASSICS FOR ENGLISH READERS.

EDITED BY MRS OLIPHANT.

In crown 8vo, 2s. 6d.

Contents of the Series.

DANTE, by the Editor. — VOLTAIRE, by General Sir E. B. Hamley, K.C.B. —PASCAL, by Principal Tulloch. — PETRARCH, by Henry Reeve, C.B.—GOETHE, by A. Hayward, Q.C.—MOLIÈRE, by the Editor and F. Tarver, M.A.—MONTAIGNE, by Rev. W. L. Collins, M.A.—RABELAIS, by Sir Walter Besant. — CALDERON, by E. J. Hasell.—SAINT SIMON, by Clifton W. Collins, M.A.—CERVANTES, by the Editor. — CORNEILLE AND RACINE, by Henry M. Trollope. — MADAME DE SÉVIGNÉ, by Miss Thackeray.—LA FONTAINE, AND OTHER FRENCH FABULISTS, by Rev. W. Lucas Collins, M.A.—SCHILLER, by James Sime, M.A., Author of 'Lessing, his Life and Writings.'—TASSO, by E. J. Hasell.—ROUSSEAU, by Henry Grey Graham. — ALFRED DE MUSSET, by C. F. Oliphant.

ANCIENT CLASSICS FOR ENGLISH READERS.

EDITED BY THE REV. W. LUCAS COLLINS, M.A.

CHEAP RE-ISSUE. In limp cloth, fcap. 8vo, price 1s. each.

Two Volumes will be issued Monthly in the following order:—

HOMER: ILIAD, . . The Editor. } *Ready.*	HESIOD AND THEOGNIS, J. Davies. } *Ready.*	
HOMER: ODYSSEY, . The Editor. }	PLAUTUS AND TERENCE, The Editor. }	
HERODOTUS, . . G. C. Swayne. } *Ready.*	TACITUS, ... W. B. Donne. } *Ready.*	
CÆSAR, . . Anthony Trollope. }	LUCIAN, ... The Editor. }	
VIRGIL, ... The Editor. } *Ready.*	PLATO, ... C. W. Collins. } *Ready.*	
HORACE, . Sir Theodore Martin. }	GREEK ANTHOLOGY, Lord Neaves. }	
ÆSCHYLUS, . Bishop Copleston. } *Ready.*	LIVY, ... The Editor. } *Ready.*	
XENOPHON, . . Sir Alex. Grant. }	OVID, ... Rev. A. Church. }	
CICERO, ... The Editor. } *Ready.*	CATULLUS, TIBULLUS, AND PROPERTIUS, . . . J. Davies. } 1898.	
SOPHOCLES, . . . C. W. Collins. }	DEMOSTHENES, . . W. J. Brodribb. } Jan.	
PLINY, . Church and Brodribb. } *Ready.*	ARISTOTLE, . . Sir Alex. Grant. } Feb.	
EURIPIDES, . . . W. B. Donne. }	THUCYDIDES, . . . The Editor. }	
JUVENAL, ... E. Walford. } *Ready.*	LUCRETIUS, . . W. H. Mallock. } March.	
ARISTOPHANES, . . The Editor. }	PINDAR, . . Rev. F. D. Morice. }	

CATALOGUE

OF

MESSRS BLACKWOOD & SONS'

PUBLICATIONS.

ALISON.
History of Europe. By Sir ARCHIBALD ALISON, Bart., D.C.L.
1. From the Commencement of the French Revolution to the Battle of Waterloo.
LIBRARY EDITION, 14 vols., with Portraits. Demy 8vo, £10, 10s.
ANOTHER EDITION, in 20 vols. crown 8vo, £6.
PEOPLE'S EDITION 13 vols. crown 8vo, £2, 11s.
2. Continuation to the Accession of Louis Napoleon.
LIBRARY EDITION, 8 vols. 8vo, £6, 7s. 6d.
PEOPLE'S EDITION, 8 vols. crown 8vo, 34s.
Epitome of Alison's History of Europe. Thirtieth Thousand, 7s. 6d.
Atlas to Alison's History of Europe. By A. Keith Johnston.
LIBRARY EDITION, demy 4to, £3, 3s.
PEOPLE'S EDITION, 31s. 6d.
Life of John Duke of Marlborough. With some Account of his Contemporaries, and of the War of the Succession. Third Edition. 2 vols. 8vo. Portraits and Maps, 30s.
Essays: Historical, Political, and Miscellaneous. 3 vols. demy 8vo, 45s.

ACROSS FRANCE IN A CARAVAN: BEING SOME ACCOUNT OF A JOURNEY FROM BORDEAUX TO GENOA IN THE "ESCARGOT," taken in the Winter 1889-90. By the Author of 'A Day of my Life at Eton.' With fifty Illustrations by John Wallace, after Sketches by the Author, and a Map. Cheap Edition, demy 8vo, 7s. 6d.

ACTA SANCTORUM HIBERNIÆ; Ex Codice Salmanticensi.
Nunc primum integre edita opera CAROLI DE SMEDT et JOSEPHI DE BACKER, e Soc. Jesu, Hagiographorum Bollandianorum; Auctore et Sumptus Largiente JOANNE PATRICIO MARCHIONE BOTHAE. In One handsome 4to Volume, bound in half roxburghe, £2, 2s.; in paper cover, 31s. 6d.

ADOLPHUS. Some Memories of Paris. By F. ADOLPHUS. Crown 8vo, 6s.

AFLALO. A Sketch of the Natural History (Vertebrates) of the British Islands. By F. G. AFLALO, F.R.G.S., F.Z.S., Author of 'A Sketch of the Natural History of Australia,' &c. With numerous Illustrations by Lodge and Bennett. In 1 vol. crown 8vo. [*In the press.*]

AIKMAN.
Manures and the Principles of Manuring. By C. M. AIKMAN, D.Sc., F.R.S.E., &c., Professor of Chemistry, Glasgow Veterinary College; Examiner in Chemistry, University of Glasgow, &c. Crown 8vo, 6s. 6d.
Farmyard Manure: Its Nature, Composition, and Treatment. Crown 8vo, 1s. 6d.

AIRD. Poetical Works of Thomas Aird. Fifth Edition, with
Memoir of the Author by the Rev. JARDINE WALLACE, and Portrait. Crown 8vo,
7s. 6d.

ALLARDYCE.
The City of Sunshine. By ALEXANDER ALLARDYCE, Author of
'Earlscourt,' &c. New Edition. Crown 8vo, 6s.
Balmoral : A Romance of the Queen's Country. New Edition.
Crown 8vo, 6s.

ALMOND. Sermons by a Lay Head-master. By HELY HUTCH-
INSON ALMOND, M.A. Oxon., Head-Master of Loretto School. Crown 8vo, 5s.

ANCIENT CLASSICS FOR ENGLISH READERS. Edited
by Rev. W. LUCAS COLLINS, M.A. Price 1s. each. *For List of Vols. see p. 2.*

ANDERSON. Daniel in the Critics' Den. A Reply to Dean
Farrar's 'Book of Daniel.' By ROBERT ANDERSON, LL.D., Barrister-at-Law,
Assistant Commissioner of Police of the Metropolis; Author of 'The Coming
Prince,' 'Human Destiny,' &c. Post 8vo, 4s. 6d.

AYTOUN.
Lays of the Scottish Cavaliers, and other Poems. By W.
EDMONDSTOUNE AYTOUN, D.C.L., Professor of Rhetoric and Belles-Lettres in the
University of Edinburgh. New Edition. Fcap. 8vo, 3s. 6d.
ANOTHER EDITION. Fcap. 8vo, 7s. 6d.
CHEAP EDITION. 1s. Cloth, 1s. 3d.
An Illustrated Edition of the Lays of the Scottish Cavaliers.
From designs by Sir NOEL PATON. Cheaper Edition. Small 4to, 10s. 6d.
Bothwell : a Poem. Third Edition. Fcap., 7s. 6d.
Poems and Ballads of Goethe. Translated by Professor
AYTOUN and Sir THEODORE MARTIN, K.C.B. Third Edition. Fcap., 6s.
The Ballads of Scotland. Edited by Professor AYTOUN.
Fourth Edition. 2 vols. fcap. 8vo, 12s.
Memoir of William E. Aytoun, D.C.L. By Sir THEODORE
MARTIN, K.C.B. With Portrait. Post 8vo, 12s.

BEDFORD & COLLINS. Annals of the Free Foresters, from
1856 to the Present Day. By W. K. R. BEDFORD, W. E. W. COLLINS, and other
Contributors. With 55 Portraits and 59 other Illustrations. Demy 8vo, 21s. *net.*

BELLAIRS. Gossips with Girls and Maidens, Betrothed and
Free. By LADY BELLAIRS. New Edition. Crown 8vo, 3s. 6d. Cloth, extra
gilt edges, 5s.

BELLESHEIM. History of the Catholic Church of Scotland.
From the Introduction of Christianity to the Present Day. By ALPHONS BEL-
LESHEIM, D.D., Canon of Aix-la-Chapelle. Translated, with Notes and Additions,
by D. OSWALD HUNTER BLAIR, O.S.B., Monk of Fort Augustus. Cheap Edition.
Complete in 4 vols. demy 8vo, with Maps. Price 21s. net.

BENTINCK. Racing Life of Lord George Cavendish Bentinck,
M.P., and other Reminiscences. By JOHN KENT, Private Trainer to the Good-
wood Stable. Edited by the Hon. FRANCIS LAWLEY. With Twenty-three full-
page Plates, and Facsimile Letter. Third Edition. Demy 8vo, 25s.

BEVERIDGE.
Culross and Tulliallan ; or, Perthshire on Forth. Its History
and Antiquities. With Elucidations of Scottish Life and Character from the
Burgh and Kirk-Session Records of that District. By DAVID BEVERIDGE. 2 vols.
8vo, with Illustrations, 42s.
Between the Ochils and the Forth ; or, From Stirling Bridge
to Aberdour. Crown 8vo, 6s.

BICKERDYKE. A Banished Beauty. By JOHN BICKERDYKE,
Author of 'Days in Thule, with Rod, Gun, and Camera,' 'The Book of the All-
Round Angler,' 'Curiosities of Ale and Beer,' &c. With Illustrations. Cheap
Edition. Crown 8vo, 2s.

BIRCH.

Examples of Stables, Hunting-Boxes, Kennels, Racing Estab-
lishments, &c. By JOHN BIRCH, Architect, Author of 'Country Architecture,'
&c. With 30 Plates. Royal 8vo, 7s.

Examples of Labourers' Cottages, &c. With Plans for Im-
proving the Dwellings of the Poor in Large Towns. With 34 Plates. Royal 8vo, 7s.

Picturesque Lodges. A Series of Designs for Gate Lodges,
Park Entrances, Keepers', Gardeners', Bailiffs', Grooms', Upper and Under Servants' Lodges, and other Rural Residences. With 16 Plates. 4to, 12s. 6d.

BLACK. Heligoland and the Islands of the North Sea. By
WILLIAM GEORGE BLACK. Crown 8vo, 4s.

BLACKIE.

The Wisdom of Goethe. By JOHN STUART BLACKIE, Emeritus
Professor of Greek in the University of Edinburgh. Fcap. 8vo. Cloth, extra
gilt, 6s.

John Stuart Blackie: A Biography. By ANNA M. STODDART.
With 3 Plates. Third Edition. 2 vols. demy 8vo, 21s.
POPULAR EDITION. With Portrait. Crown 8vo, 6s.

BLACKMORE.

The Maid of Sker. By R. D. BLACKMORE, Author of 'Lorna
Doone,' &c. New Edition. Crown 8vo, 6s. Cheaper Edition. Crown 8vo,
3s. 6d.

Dariel: A Romance of Surrey. With 14 Illustrations by
Chris. Hammond. Crown 8vo. 6s.

BLACKWOOD.

Annals of a Publishing House. William Blackwood and his
Sons; Their Magazine and Friends. By Mrs OLIPHANT. With Four Portraits.
Third Edition. Demy 8vo. Vols. I. and II. £2, 2s.

Blackwood's Magazine, from Commencement in 1817 to December 1897. Nos. 1 to 986, forming 161 Volumes.

Index to Blackwood's Magazine. Vols. 1 to 50. 8vo, 15s.

Tales from Blackwood. First Series. Price One Shilling each,
in Paper Cover. Sold separately at all Railway Bookstalls.
They may also be had bound in 12 vols., cloth, 18s. Half calf, richly gilt, 30s.
Or the 12 vols. in 6, roxburghe, 21s. Half red morocco, 28s.

Tales from Blackwood. Second Series. Complete in Twenty-
four Shilling Parts. Handsomely bound in 12 vols., cloth, 30s. In leather back,
roxburghe style, 37s. 6d. Half calf, gilt, 52s. 6d. Half morocco, 55s.

Tales from Blackwood. Third Series. Complete in Twelve
Shilling Parts. Handsomely bound in 6 vols., cloth, 15s.; and in 12 vols., cloth,
18s. The 6 vols. in roxburghe, 21s. Half calf, 25s. Half morocco, 28s.

Travel, Adventure, and Sport. From 'Blackwood's Magazine.'
Uniform with 'Tales from Blackwood.' In Twelve Parts, each price 1s. Handsomely bound in 6 vols., cloth, 15s. And in half calf, 25s.

6 *List of Books Published by*

BLACKWOOD.

New Educational Series. *See separate Catalogue.*
New Uniform Series of Novels (Copyright).
Crown 8vo, cloth. Price 3s. 6d. each. Now ready:—

THE MAID OF SKER. By R. D. Blackmore.
WENDERHOLME. By P. G. Hamerton.
THE STORY OF MARGRÉDEL. By D. Storrar Meldrum.
MISS MARJORIBANKS. By Mrs Oliphant.
THE PERPETUAL CURATE, and THE RECTOR. By the Same.
SALEM CHAPEL, and THE DOCTOR'S FAMILY. By the Same.
A SENSITIVE PLANT. By E. D. Gerard.
LADY LEE'S WIDOWHOOD. By General Sir E. B. Hamley.
KATIE STEWART, and other Stories. By Mrs Oliphant.
VALENTINE AND HIS BROTHER. By the Same.
SONS AND DAUGHTERS. By the Same.
MARMORNE. By P. G. Hamerton.

REATA. By E. D. Gerard.
BEGGAR MY NEIGHBOUR. By the Same.
THE WATERS OF HERCULES. By the Same.
FAIR TO SEE. By L. W. M. Lockhart.
MINE IS THINE. By the Same.
DOUBLES AND QUITS. By the Same.
ALTIORA PETO. By Laurence Oliphant
PICCADILLY. By the Same. With Illustrations.
LADY BABY. By D. Gerard.
THE BLACKSMITH OF VOE. By Paul Cushing.
THE DILEMMA. By the Author of 'The Battle of Dorking.'
MY TRIVIAL LIFE AND MISFORTUNE. By A Plain Woman.
POOR NELLIE. By the Same.

Standard Novels. Uniform in size and binding. Each complete in one Volume.

FLORIN SERIES, Illustrated Boards. Bound in Cloth, 2s. 6d.

TOM CRINGLE'S LOG. By Michael Scott.
THE CRUISE OF THE MIDGE. By the Same.
CYRIL THORNTON. By Captain Hamilton.
ANNALS OF THE PARISH. By John Galt.
THE PROVOST, &c. By the Same.
SIR ANDREW WYLIE. By the Same.
THE ENTAIL. By the Same.
MISS MOLLY. By Beatrice May Butt.
REGINALD DALTON. By J. G. Lockhart.

PEN OWEN. By Dean Hook.
ADAM BLAIR. By J. G. Lockhart.
LADY LEE'S WIDOWHOOD. By General Sir E. B. Hamley.
SALEM CHAPEL. By Mrs Oliphant.
THE PERPETUAL CURATE. By the Same.
MISS MARJORIBANKS. By the Same.
JOHN: A Love Story. By the Same.

SHILLING SERIES, Illustrated Cover. Bound in Cloth, 1s. 6d.

THE RECTOR, and THE DOCTOR'S FAMILY. By Mrs Oliphant.
THE LIFE OF MANSIE WAUCH. By D. M. Moir.
PENINSULAR SCENES AND SKETCHES. By F. Hardman.

SIR FRIZZLE PUMPKIN, NIGHTS AT MESS, &c.
THE SUBALTERN.
LIFE IN THE FAR WEST. By G. F. Ruxton.
VALERIUS: A Roman Story. By J. G. Lockhart.

BON GAULTIER'S BOOK OF BALLADS. Fifteenth Edition. With Illustrations by Doyle, Leech, and Crowquill. Fcap. 8vo, 5s.

BOWHILL. Questions and Answers in the Theory and Practice of Military Topography. By Major J. H. BOWHILL. In 1 vol. crown 8vo. With Atlas containing 34 working plans and diagrams. [*In the press.*

BRADDON. Thirty Years of Shikar. By Sir EDWARD BRADDON, K.C.M.G. With Illustrations by G. D. Giles, and Map of Oudh Forest Tracts and Nepal Terai. Demy 8vo, 18s.

BROUGHAM. Memoirs of the Life and Times of Henry Lord Brougham. Written by HIMSELF. 3 vols. 8vo, £2, 8s. The Volumes are sold separately, price 16s. each.

BROWN. The Forester: A Practical Treatise on the Planting and Tending of Forest-trees and the General Management of Woodlands. By JAMES BROWN, LL.D. Sixth Edition, Enlarged. Edited by JOHN NISBET, D.Œc., Author of 'British Forest Trees,' &c. In 2 vols. royal 8vo, with 350 Illustrations, 42s. net.

Also being issued in 15 Monthly parts, price 2s. 6d. net each.
[*Parts 1 to 11 ready.*

BROWN. A Manual of Botany, Anatomical and Physiological. For the Use of Students. By ROBERT BROWN, M.A., Ph.D. Crown 8vo, with numerous Illustrations, 12s. 6d.

BRUCE.

In Clover and Heather. Poems by WALLACE BRUCE. New
and Enlarged Edition. Crown 8vo, 3s. 6d.
A limited number of Copies of the First Edition, on large hand-made paper, 12s. 6d.

Here's a Hand. Addresses and Poems. Crown 8vo, 5s.
Large Paper Edition, limited to 100 copies, price 21s.

BUCHAN. Introductory Text-Book of Meteorology. By ALEX-
ANDER BUCHAN, LL.D., F.R.S.E., Secretary of the Scottish Meteorological
Society, &c. New Edition. Crown 8vo, with Coloured Charts and Engravings.
[*In preparation.*

BURBIDGE.

Domestic Floriculture, Window Gardening, and Floral Decora-
tions. Being Practical Directions for the Propagation, Culture, and Arrangement
of Plants and Flowers as Domestic Ornaments. By F. W. BURBIDGE. Second
Edition. Crown 8vo, with numerous Illustrations, 7s. 6d.

Cultivated Plants: Their Propagation and Improvement.
Including Natural and Artificial Hybridisation, Raising from Seed, Cuttings
and Layers, Grafting and Budding, as applied to the Families and Genera in
Cultivation. Crown 8vo, with numerous Illustrations, 12s. 6d.

BURGESS. The Viking Path: A Tale of the White Christ.
By J. J. HALDANE BURGESS, Author of 'Rasmie's Büddie,' 'Shetland Sketches,'
&c. Crown 8vo, 6s.

BURKE. The Flowering of the Almond Tree, and other Poems.
By CHRISTIAN BURKE. Pott 4to, 5s.

BURROWS.

Commentaries on the History of England, from the Earliest
Times to 1865. By MONTAGU BURROWS, Chichele Professor of Modern History
in the University of Oxford; Captain R.N.; F.S.A., &c.; "Officier de l'In-
struction Publique," France. Crown 8vo, 7s. 6d.

The History of the Foreign Policy of Great Britain. Demy
8vo, 12s.

BURTON.

The History of Scotland: From Agricola's Invasion to the
Extinction of the last Jacobite Insurrection. By JOHN HILL BURTON, D.C.L.,
Historiographer-Royal for Scotland. Cheaper Edition. In 8 vols. Crown 8vo,
3s. 6d. each.

History of the British Empire during the Reign of Queen
Anne. In 3 vols. 8vo. 36s.

The Scot Abroad. Third Edition. Crown 8vo, 10s. 6d.

The Book-Hunter. New Edition. With Portrait. Crown
8vo, 7s. 6d.

BUTCHER. Armenosa of Egypt. A Romance of the Arab
Conquest. By the Very Rev. Dean BUTCHER, D.D., F.S.A., Chaplain at Cairo.
Crown 8vo, 6s.

BUTE. The Altus of St Columba. With a Prose Paraphrase
and Notes. In paper cover, 2s. 6d.

BUTE, MACPHAIL, AND LONSDALE. The Arms of the
Royal and Parliamentary Burghs of Scotland. By JOHN, MARQUESS OF BUTE,
K.T., J. R. N. MACPHAIL, and H. W. LONSDALE. With 131 Engravings on
wood, and 11 other Illustrations. Crown 4to, £2, 2s. net.

BUTLER. The Ancient Church and Parish of Abernethy,
Perthshire. A Historical Study. By Rev. D. BUTLER, M.A., Minister of the
Parish. With Collotype Illustrations. In 1 vol. crown 4to. . [*In the press.*

BUTT.

Theatricals: An Interlude. By BEATRICE MAY BUTT. Crown
8vo, 6s.

Miss Molly. Cheap Edition, 2s.

Eugenie. Crown 8vo, 6s. 6d.

BUTT.
Elizabeth, and other Sketches. Crown 8vo, 6s.
Delicia. New Edition. Crown 8vo, 2s. 6d.

CAIRD. Sermons. By JOHN CAIRD, D.D., Principal of the
. University of Glasgow. Seventeenth Thousand. Fcap. 8vo, 5s.

CALDWELL. Schopenhauer's System in its Philosophical Significance (the Shaw Fellowship Lectures, 1893). By WILLIAM CALDWELL, M.A.,
D.Sc., Professor of Moral and Social Philosophy, Northwestern University,
U.S.A.; formerly Assistant to the Professor of Logic and Metaphysics, Edin.,
and Examiner in Philosophy in the University of St Andrews. Demy 8vo,
10s. 6d. net.

CALLWELL. The Effect of Maritime Command on Land
Campaigns since Waterloo. By Major C. .E. CALLWELL, R.A. With Plans.
Post 8vo, 6s. net.

CANTON. A Lost Epic, and other Poems. By WILLIAM
CANTON. Crown 8vo, 5s.

CARSTAIRS.
Human Nature in Rural India. By R. CARSTAIRS. Crown
8vo, 6s.
British Work in India. Crown 8vo, 6s.

CAUVIN. A Treasury of the English and German Languages.
Compiled from the best Authors and Lexicographers in both Languages. By
JOSEPH CAUVIN, LL.D. and Ph.D., of the University of Göttingen, &c. Crown
8vo, 7s. 6d.

CHARTERIS. Canonicity ; or, Early Testimonies to the Exist-
ence and Use of the Books of the New Testament. Based on Kirchhoffer's
'Quellensammlung.' Edited by A. H. CHARTERIS, D.D., Professor of Biblical
Criticism in the University of Edinburgh. 8vo, 18s.

CHENNELLS. Recollections of an Egyptian Princess. By
her English Governess (Miss E. CHENNELLS). Being a Record of Five Years'
Residence at the Court of Ismael Pasha, Khédive. Second Edition. With Three
Portraits. Post 8vo, 7s. 6d.

CHESNEY. The Dilemma. By General Sir GEORGE CHESNEY,
K.C.B., M.P., Author of 'The Battle of Dorking,' &c. New Edition. Crown
8vo, 3s. 6d.

CHRISTISON. Early Fortifications in Scotland: Motes, Camps,
and Forts. Being the Rhind Lectures in Archæology for 1893. By DAVID
CHRISTISON, M.D. With numerous Illustrations and Maps. In 1 vol. pott 4to.
                                                    [*In the press.*

CHRISTISON. Life of Sir Robert Christison, Bart., M.D.,
D.C.L. Oxon., Professor of Medical Jurisprudence in the University of Edin-
burgh. Edited by his SONS. In 2 vols. 8vo. Vol. I.—Autobiography. 16s.
Vol. II.—Memoirs. 16s.

CHURCH. Chapters in an Adventurous Life. Sir Richard
Church in Italy and Greece. By E. M. CHURCH. With Photogravure
Portrait. Demy 8vo, 10s. 6d.

CHURCH SERVICE SOCIETY.
A Book of Common Order : being Forms of Worship issued
by the Church Service Society. Seventh Edition, carefully revised. In 1 vol.
crown 8vo, cloth, 3s. 6d.; French morocco, 5s. Also in 2 vols. crown 8vo,
cloth, 4s.; French morocco, 6s. 6d.
Daily Offices for Morning and Evening Prayer throughout
the Week. Crown 8vo, 3s. 6d.

CHURCH SERVICE SOCIETY.
Order of Divine Service for Children. Issued by the Church Service Society. With Scottish Hymnal. Cloth, 3d.

CLOUSTON. Popular Tales and Fictions: their Migrations and Transformations. By W. A. CLOUSTON, Editor of 'Arabian Poetry for English Readers,' &c. 2 vols. post 8vo, roxburghe binding, 25s.

COCHRAN. A Handy Text-Book of Military Law. Compiled chiefly to assist Officers preparing for Examination; also for all Officers of the Regular and Auxiliary Forces. Comprising also a Synopsis of part of the Army Act. By Major F. COCHRAN, Hampshire Regiment Garrison Instructor, North British District. Crown 8vo, 7s. 6d.

COLQUHOUN. The Moor and the Loch. Containing Minute Instructions in all Highland Sports, with Wanderings over Crag and Corrie, Flood and Fell. By JOHN COLQUHOUN. Cheap Edition. With Illustrations. Demy 8vo, 10s. 6d.

COLVILE. Round the Black Man's Garden. By Lady Z. COLVILE, F.R.G.S. With 2 Maps and 50 Illustrations from Drawings by the Author and from Photographs. Demy 8vo, 16s.

CONDER. The Bible and the East. By Lieut.-Col. C. R. CONDER, R.E., LL.D., D.C.L., M.R.A.S., Author of 'Tent Work in Palestine,' &c. With Illustrations and a Map. Crown 8vo, 5s.

CONSTITUTION AND LAW OF THE CHURCH OF SCOTLAND. With an Introductory Note by the late Principal Tulloch. New Edition, Revised and Enlarged. Crown 8vo, 3s. 6d.

COTTERILL. Suggested Reforms in Public Schools. By C. C. COTTERILL, M.A. Crown 8vo, 3s. 6d.

COUNTY HISTORIES OF SCOTLAND. In demy 8vo volumes of about 350 pp. each. With Maps. Price 7s. 6d. net.
Fife and Kinross. By ÆNEAS J. G. MACKAY, LL.D., Sheriff of these Counties.
Dumfries and Galloway. By Sir HERBERT MAXWELL, Bart., M.P.
Moray and Nairn. By CHARLES RAMPINI, LL.D., Sheriff-Substitute of these Counties.
Inverness. By J. CAMERON LEES, D.D. [*Others in preparation.*

CRAWFORD. Saracinesca. By F. MARION CRAWFORD, Author of 'Mr Isaacs,' &c., &c. Cheap Edition. Crown 8vo, 3s. 6d.

CRAWFORD.
The Doctrine of Holy Scripture respecting the Atonement. By the late THOMAS J. CRAWFORD, D.D., Professor of Divinity in the University of Edinburgh. Fifth Edition. 8vo, 12s.
The Fatherhood of God, Considered in its General and Special Aspects. Third Edition, Revised and Enlarged. 8vo, 9s.
The Preaching of the Cross, and other Sermons. 8vo, 7s. 6d.
The Mysteries of Christianity. Crown 8vo, 7s. 6d.

CROSS. Impressions of Dante, and of the New World; with a Few Words on Bimetallism. By J. W. CROSS, Editor of 'George Eliot's Life, as related in her Letters and Journals.' Post 8vo, 6s.

CUMBERLAND. Sport on the Pamirs and Turkistan Steppes. By Major C. S. CUMBERLAND. With Map and Frontispiece. Demy 8vo, 10s. 6d.

CURSE OF INTELLECT. Third Edition. Fcap. 8vo, 2s. 6d. net.

CUSHING. The Blacksmith of Voe. By PAUL CUSHING, Author of 'The Bull i' th' Thorn,' 'Cut with his own Diamond.' Cheap Edition. Crown 8vo, 3s. 6d.

DARBISHIRE. Physical Maps for the use of History Students.
By BERNHARD V. DARBISHIRE, M.A., Trinity College, Oxford. Two Series:—
Ancient History (9 maps); Modern History (12 maps).   [*In the press.*

DAVIES. Norfolk Broads and Rivers; or, The Waterways,
Lagoons, and Decoys of East Anglia. By G. CHRISTOPHER DAVIES. Illustrated
with Seven full-page Plates. New and Cheaper Edition. Crown 8vo, 6s.

DE LA WARR. An Eastern Cruise in the 'Edeline.' By the
Countess DE LA WARR. In Illustrated Cover. 2s.

DESCARTES. The Method, Meditations, and Principles of Philo-
sophy of Descartes. Translated from the Original French and Latin. With a
New Introductory Essay, Historical and Critical, on the Cartesian Philosophy.
By Professor VEITCH, LL.D., Glasgow University. Eleventh Edition. 6s. 6d.

DOGS, OUR DOMESTICATED : Their Treatment in reference
to Food, Diseases, Habits, Punishment, Accomplishments. By 'MAGENTA.'
Crown 8vo, 2s. 6d.

DOUGLAS.
The Ethics of John Stuart Mill. By CHARLES DOUGLAS,
M.A., D.Sc., Lecturer in Moral Philosophy, and Assistant to the Professor of
Moral Philosophy in the University of Edinburgh. Post 8vo, 6s. net.
John Stuart Mill: A Study of his Philosophy. Crown 8vo,
4s. 6d. net.

DOUGLAS. Chinese Stories. By ROBERT K. DOUGLAS. With
numerous Illustrations by Parkinson, Forestier, and others. New and Cheaper
Edition. Small demy 8vo, 5s.

DOUGLAS. Iras: A Mystery. By THEO. DOUGLAS, Author of
'A Bride Elect.' Cheaper Edition, in Paper Cover specially designed by Womrath.
Crown 8vo, 1s. 6d.

DU CANE. The Odyssey of Homer, Books I.-XII. Translated
into English Verse. By Sir CHARLES DU CANE, K.C.M.G. 8vo, 10s. 6d.

DUDGEON. History of the Edinburgh or Queen's Regiment
Light Infantry Militia, now 3rd Battalion The Royal Scots; with an Account of
the Origin and Progress of the Militia, and a Brief Sketch of the Old Royal
Scots. By Major R. C. DUDGEON, Adjutant 3rd Battalion the Royal Scots.
Post 8vo, with Illustrations, 10s. 6d.

DUNSMORE. Manual of the Law of Scotland as to the Relations between Agricultural Tenants and the Landlords, Servants, Merchants, and
Bowers. By W. DUNSMORE. 8vo, 7s. 6d.

DZIEWICKI. Entombed in Flesh. By M. H. DZIEWICKI. In
1 vol. crown 8vo.   [*In the press.*

ELIOT.
George Eliot's Life, Related in Her Letters and Journals.
Arranged and Edited by her husband, J. W. CROSS. With Portrait and other
Illustrations. Third Edition. 3 vols. post 8vo, 42s.
George Eliot's Life. With Portrait and other Illustrations.
New Edition, in one volume. Crown 8vo, 7s. 6d.
Works of George Eliot (Standard Edition). 21 volumes,
crown 8vo. In buckram cloth, gilt top, 2s. 6d. per vol.; or in roxburghe
binding, 3s. 6d. per vol.
    ADAM BEDE. 2 vols.—THE MILL ON THE FLOSS. 2 vols.—FELIX HOLT, THE
    RADICAL. 2 vols.—ROMOLA. 2 vols.—SCENES OF CLERICAL LIFE. 2 vols.—
    MIDDLEMARCH. 3 vols.—DANIEL DERONDA. 3 vols.—SILAS MARNER. 1 vol.
    —JUBAL. 1 vol.—THE SPANISH GIPSY. 1 vol.—ESSAYS. 1 vol.—THEOPHRAS-
    TUS SUCH. · 1 vol.
Life and Works of George Eliot (Cabinet Edition). 24
volumes, crown 8vo, price £6. Also to be had handsomely bound in half and full
calf. The Volumes are sold separately, bound in cloth, price 5s. each.

ELIOT.

Novels by George Eliot. Cheap Edition. New issue in
Monthly Volumes. Printed on fine laid paper, and uniformly bound. In course
of publication.
> Adam Bede. 3s. 6d.—The Mill on the Floss. 3s. 6d.—Scenes of Clerical
> Life. 3s.—Silas Marner: the Weaver of Raveloe. 2s. 6d.—Felix Holt, the
> Radical. 3s. 6d.—Romola. 3s. 6d.—Middlemarch. 7s. 6d.—Daniel Deronda.
> 7s. 6d.

Essays. New Edition. Crown 8vo, 5s.

Impressions of Theophrastus Such. New Edition. Crown
8vo, 5s.

The Spanish Gypsy. New Edition. Crown 8vo, 5s.

The Legend of Jubal, and other Poems, Old and New.
New Edition. Crown 8vo, 5s.

Scenes of Clerical Life. Popular Edition. Royal 8vo, in
paper cover, price 6d.

Wise, Witty, and Tender Sayings, in Prose and Verse. Selected
from the Works of GEORGE ELIOT. New Edition. Fcap. 8vo, 3s. 6d.

ESSAYS ON SOCIAL SUBJECTS. Originally published in
the 'Saturday Review.' New Edition. First and Second Series. 2 vols. crown
8vo, 6s. each.

FAITHS OF THE WORLD, The. A Concise History of the
Great Religious Systems of the World. By various Authors. Crown 8vo, 5s.

FALKNER. The Lost Stradivarius. By J. MEADE FALKNER.
Second Edition. Crown 8vo, 6s.

FENNELL AND O'CALLAGHAN. A Prince of Tyrone. By
CHARLOTTE FENNELL and J. P. O'CALLAGHAN. Crown 8vo, 6s.

FERGUSON. Sir Samuel Ferguson in the Ireland of his Day.
By LADY FERGUSON, Author of 'The Irish before the Conquest,' 'Life of William
Reeves, D.D., Lord Bishop of Down, Connor, and Drumore,' &c., &c. With
Two Portraits. 2 vols. post 8vo, 21s.

FERRIER.

Philosophical Works of the late James F. Ferrier, B.A.
Oxon., Professor of Moral Philosophy and Political Economy, St Andrews.
New Edition. Edited by Sir ALEXANDER GRANT, Bart., D.C.L., and Professor
LUSHINGTON. 3 vols. crown 8vo, 34s. 6d.

Institutes of Metaphysic. Third Edition. 10s. 6d.

Lectures on the Early Greek Philosophy. 4th Edition. 10s. 6d.

Philosophical Remains, including the Lectures on Early
Greek Philosophy. New Edition. 2 vols. 24s.

FLINT.

Historical Philosophy in France and French Belgium and
Switzerland. By ROBERT FLINT, Corresponding Member of the Institute of
France, Hon. Member of the Royal Society of Palermo, Professor in the Univer-
sity of Edinburgh, &c. 8vo, 21s.

Agnosticism. Being the Croall Lecture for 1887-88.
[*In the press.*]

Theism. Being the Baird Lecture for 1876. Ninth Edition,
Revised. Crown 8vo, 7s. 6d.

Anti-Theistic Theories. Being the Baird Lecture for 1877.
Fifth Edition. Crown 8vo, 10s. 6d.

FOREIGN CLASSICS FOR ENGLISH READERS. Edited
by Mrs OLIPHANT. Price 2s. 6d. *For List of Volumes, see page 2.*

FOSTER. The Fallen City, and other Poems. By WILL FOSTER.
Crown 8vo, 6s.

FRANCILLON. Gods and Heroes; or, The Kingdom of Jupiter.
By R. E. FRANCILLON. With 8 Illustrations. Crown 8vo, 5s.

FRANCIS. Among the Untrodden Ways. By M. E. FRANCIS
(Mrs Francis Blundell), Author of 'In a North Country Village,' 'A Daughter of
the Soil,' 'Frieze and Fustian,' &c. Crown 8vo, 3s. 6d.

FRASER.
Philosophy of Theism. Being the Gifford Lectures delivered
before the University of Edinburgh in 1894-95. First Series. By ALEXANDER
CAMPBELL FRASER, D.C.L. Oxford; Emeritus Professor of Logic and Metaphysics in the University of Edinburgh. Post 8vo, 7s. 6d. net.
Philosophy of Theism. Being the Gifford Lectures delivered
before the University of Edinburgh in 1895-96. Second Series. Post 8vo,
7s. 6d. *net.*

FRASER. St Mary's of Old Montrose: A History of the Parish
of Maryton. By the Rev. WILLIAM RUXTON FRASER, M.A., F.S.A. Scot.,
Emeritus Minister of Maryton; Author of 'History of the Parish and Burgh of
Laurencekirk.' Crown 8vo, 3s. 6d.

FULLARTON.
Merlin: A Dramatic Poem. By RALPH MACLEOD FULLARTON.
Crown 8vo, 5s.
Tanhäuser. Crown 8vo, 6s.
Lallan Sangs and German Lyrics. Crown 8vo, 5s.

GALT.
Novels by JOHN GALT. With General Introduction and
Prefatory Notes by S. R. CROCKETT. The Text Revised and Edited by D.
STORRAR MELDRUM, Author of 'The Story of Margrédel.' With Photogravure
Illustrations from Drawings by John Wallace. Fcap. 8vo, 3s. net each vol.
ANNALS OF THE PARISH, and THE AYRSHIRE LEGATEES. 2 vols.—SIR ANDREW
WYLIE. 2 vols.—THE ENTAIL; or, The Lairds of Grippy. 2 vols.—THE PRO-
VOST, and THE LAST OF THE LAIRDS. 2 vols.
See also STANDARD NOVELS, *p. 6.*

GENERAL ASSEMBLY OF THE CHURCH OF SCOTLAND.
Scottish Hymnal, With Appendix Incorporated. Published
for use in Churches by Authority of the General Assembly. 1. Large type,
cloth, red edges, 2s. 6d.; French morocco, 4s. 2. Bourgeois type, limp cloth, 1s.;
French morocco, 2s. 3. Nonpareil type, cloth, red edges, 6d.; French morocco,
1s. 4d. 4. Paper covers, 3d. 5. Sunday-School Edition, paper covers, 1d.,
cloth, 2d. No. 1, bound with the Psalms and Paraphrases, French morocco, 8s.
No. 2, bound with the Psalms and Paraphrases, cloth, 2s.; French morocco, 3s.
Prayers for Social and Family Worship. Prepared by a
Special Committee of the General Assembly of the Church of Scotland. Entirely
New Edition, Revised and Enlarged. Fcap. 8vo, red edges, 2s.
Prayers for Family Worship. A Selection of Four Weeks'
Prayers. New Edition. Authorised by the General Assembly of the Church of
Scotland. Fcap. 8vo, red edges, 1s. 6d.
One Hundred Prayers. Prepared by the Committee on Aids
to Devotion. 16mo, cloth limp, 6d.
Morning and Evening Prayers for Affixing to Bibles. Prepared
by the Committee on Aids to Devotion. 1d. for 6, or 1s. per 100.

GERARD.
Reata: What's in a Name. By E. D. GERARD. Cheap
Edition. Crown 8vo, 3s. 6d.
Beggar my Neighbour. Cheap Edition. Crown 8vo, 3s. 6d.
The Waters of Hercules. Cheap Edition. Crown 8vo, 3s. 6d.
A Sensitive Plant. Crown 8vo, 3s. 6d.

GERARD.

A Foreigner. An Anglo-German Study. By E. GERARD.
Crown 8vo, 6s.

The Land beyond the Forest. Facts, Figures, and Fancies
from Transylvania. With Maps and Illustrations. 2 vols. post 8vo, 25s.

Bis : Some Tales Retold. Crown 8vo, 6s.

A Secret Mission. 2 vols. crown 8vo, 17s.

An Electric Shock, and other Stories. Crown 8vo, 6s.

GERARD.

A Spotless Reputation. By DOROTHEA GERARD. Third
Edition. Crown 8vo, 6s.

The Wrong Man. Second Edition. Crown 8vo, 6s.

Lady Baby. Cheap Edition. Crown 8vo, 3s. 6d.

Recha. Second Edition. Crown 8vo, 6s.

The Rich Miss Riddell. Second Edition. Crown 8vo, 6s.

GERARD. Stonyhurst Latin Grammar. By Rev. JOHN GERARD.
Second Edition. Fcap. 8vo, 3s.

GORDON CUMMING.

At Home in Fiji. By C. F. GORDON CUMMING. Fourth
Edition, post 8vo. With Illustrations and Map. 7s. 6d.

A Lady's Cruise in a French Man-of-War. New and Cheaper
Edition. 8vo. With Illustrations and Map. 12s. 6d.

Fire-Fountains. The Kingdom of Hawaii : Its Volcanoes,
and the History of its Missions. With Map and Illustrations. 2 vols. 8vo, 25s.

Wanderings in China. New and Cheaper Edition. 8vo, with
Illustrations, 10s.

Granite Crags : The Yō-semité Region of California. Illustrated with 8 Engravings. New and Cheaper Edition. 8vo, 8s. 6d.

GRAHAM. Manual of the Elections (Scot.) (Corrupt and Illegal
Practices) Act, 1890. With Analysis, Relative Act of Sederunt, Appendix con-
taining the Corrupt Practices Acts of 1883 and 1885, and Copious Index. By J.
EDWARD GRAHAM, Advocate. 8vo, 4s. 6d.

GRAND.

A Domestic Experiment. By SARAH GRAND, Author of
'The Heavenly Twins,' 'Ideala : A Study from Life.' Crown 8vo, 6s.

Singularly Deluded. Crown 8vo, 6s.

GRANT. Bush-Life in Queensland. By A. C. GRANT. New
Edition. Crown 8vo, 6s.

GRIER.

In Furthest Ind. The Narrative of Mr EDWARD CARLYON of
Ellswether, in the County of Northampton, and late of the Honourable East India
Company's Service, Gentleman. Wrote by his own hand in the year of grace 1697.
Edited, with a few Explanatory Notes, by SYDNEY C. GRIER. Post 8vo, 6s.

His Excellency's English Governess. Crown 8vo, 6s.

An Uncrowned King : A Romance of High Politics. Second
Edition. Crown 8vo, 6s.

Peace with Honour. Crown 8vo, 6s.

GUTHRIE - SMITH. Crispus : A Drama. By H. GUTHRIE-
SMITH. Fcap. 4to, 5s.

HAGGARD. Under Crescent and Star. By Lieut.-Col. ANDREW
HAGGARD, D.S.O., Author of 'Dodo and I,' 'Tempest Torn,' &c. With a
Portrait. Second Edition. Crown 8vo, 6s.

HALDANE. Subtropical Cultivations and Climates. A Handy
Book for Planters, Colonists, and Settlers. By R. C. HALDANE. Post 8vo, 9s.

HAMERTON.

Wenderholme : A Story of Lancashire and Yorkshire Life. By P. G. HAMERTON, Author of 'A Painter's Camp.' New Edition. Crown 8vo, 3s. 6d.

Marmorne. New Edition. Crown 8vo, 3s. 6d.

HAMILTON.

Lectures on Metaphysics. By Sir WILLIAM HAMILTON, Bart., Professor of Logic and Metaphysics in the University of Edinburgh. Edited by the Rev. H. L. MANSEL, B.D., LL.D., Dean of St Paul's; and JOHN VEITCH, M.A., LL.D., Professor of Logic and Rhetoric, Glasgow. Seventh Edition. 2 vols. 8vo, 24s.

Lectures on Logic. Edited by the SAME. Third Edition, Revised. 2 vols., 24s.

Discussions on Philosophy and Literature, Education and University Reform. Third Edition. 8vo, 21s.

Memoir of Sir William Hamilton, Bart., Professor of Logic and Metaphysics in the University of Edinburgh. By Professor VEITCH, of the University of Glasgow. 8vo, with Portrait, 18s.

Sir William Hamilton : The Man and his Philosophy. Two Lectures delivered before the Edinburgh Philosophical Institution, January and February 1883. By Professor VEITCH. Crown 8vo, 2s.

HAMLEY.

The Operations of War Explained and Illustrated. By General Sir EDWARD BRUCE HAMLEY, K.C.B., K.C.M.G. Fifth Edition, Revised throughout. 4to, with numerous Illustrations, 30s.

National Defence ; Articles and Speeches. Post 8vo, 6s.

Shakespeare's Funeral, and other Papers. Post 8vo, 7s. 6d.

Thomas Carlyle : An Essay. Second Edition. Crown 8vo, 2s. 6d.

On Outposts. Second Edition. 8vo, 2s.

Wellington's Career ; A Military and Political Summary. Crown 8vo, 2s.

Lady Lee's Widowhood. New Edition. Crown 8vo, 3s. 6d. Cheaper Edition, 2s. 6d.

Our Poor Relations. A Philozoic Essay. With Illustrations, chiefly by Ernest Griset. Crown 8vo, cloth gilt, 3s. 6d.

The Life of General Sir Edward Bruce Hamley, K.C.B., K.C.M.G. By ALEXANDER INNES SHAND. With two Photogravure Portraits and other Illustrations. Cheaper Edition. With a Statement by Mr EDWARD HAMLEY. 2 vols. demy 8vo, 10s. 6d.

HANNAY. The Later Renaissance. By DAVID HANNAY. Being the second volume of 'Periods of European Literature.' Edited by Professor Saintsbury. In 1 vol. crown 8vo. [*In the press.*

HARE. Down the Village Street : Scenes in a West Country Hamlet. By CHRISTOPHER HARE. Second Edition. Crown 8vo, 6s.

HARRADEN.

In Varying Moods : Short Stories. By BEATRICE HARRADEN, Author of 'Ships that Pass in the Night.' Twelfth Edition Crown 8vo, 3s. 6d.

Hilda Strafford, and The Remittance Man. Two Californian Stories. Tenth Edition. Crown 8vo, 3s. 6d.

Untold Tales of the Past. With 40 Illustrations by H. R. Millar. Square crown 8vo, gilt top, 6s.

HARRIS.

From Batum to Baghdad, *viâ* Tiflis, Tabriz, and Persian Kurdistan. By WALTER B. HARRIS, F.R.G.S., Author of 'The Land of an African Sultan; Travels in Morocco,' &c. With numerous Illustrations and 2 Maps. Demy 8vo, 12s.

HARRIS.
Tafilet. The Narrative of a Journey of Exploration to the
Atlas Mountains and the Oases of the North-West Sahara. With Illustrations
by Maurice Romberg from Sketches and Photographs by the Author, and Two
Maps. Demy 8vo, 12s.

A Journey through the Yemen, and some General Remarks
upon that Country. With 3 Maps and numerous Illustrations by Forestier and
Wallace from Sketches and Photographs taken by the Author. Demy 8vo, 16s.

Danovitch, and other Stories. Crown 8vo, 6s.

HAWKER. The Prose Works of Rev. R. S. HAWKER, Vicar of
Morwenstow. Including 'Footprints of Former Men in Far Cornwall.' Re-edited,
with Sketches never before published. With a Frontispiece. Crown 8vo, 3s. 6d.

HAY. The Works of the Right Rev. Dr George Hay, Bishop of
Edinburgh. Edited under the Supervision of the Right Rev. Bishop STRAIN.
With Memoir and Portrait of the Author. 5 vols. crown 8vo, bound in extra
cloth, £1, 1s. The following Volumes may be had separately—viz. :
  The Devout Christian Instructed in the Law of Christ from the Written
  Word. 2 vols., 8s.—The Pious Christian Instructed in the Nature and Practice
  of the Principal Exercises of Piety. 1 vol., 3s.

HEATLEY.
The Horse-Owner's Safeguard. A Handy Medical Guide for
every Man who owns a Horse. By G. S. HEATLEY, M.R.C.V.S. Crown 8vo, 5s.

The Stock-Owner's Guide. A Handy Medical Treatise for
every Man who owns an Ox or a Cow. Crown 8vo, 4s. 6d.

HEDDERWICK. Lays of Middle Age ; and other Poems. By
JAMES HEDDERWICK, LL.D., Author of 'Backward Glances.' Price 3s. 6d.

HEMANS.
The Poetical Works of Mrs Hemans. Copyright Editions.
Royal 8vo, 5s. The Same with Engravings, cloth, gilt edges, 7s. 6d.

Select Poems of Mrs Hemans. Fcap., cloth, gilt edges, 3s.

HERKLESS. Cardinal Beaton : Priest and Politician. By
JOHN HERKLESS, Professor of Church History, St Andrews. With a Portrait.
Post 8vo, 7s. 6d.

HEWISON. The Isle of Bute in the Olden Time. With Illus-
trations, Maps, and Plans. By JAMES KING HEWISON, M.A., F.S.A. (Scot.),
Minister of Rothesay. Vol. I., Celtic Saints and Heroes. Crown 4to, 15s. net.
Vol. II., The Royal Stewards and the Brandanes. Crown 4to, 15s. net.

HIBBEN. Inductive Logic. By JOHN GRIER HIBBEN, Ph.D.,
Assistant Professor of Logic in Princeton University, U.S.A. Crown 8vo,
3s. 6d. net.

HILDEBRAND. The Early Relations between Britain and
Scandinavia. Being the Rhind Lectures in Archæology for 1896. By Dr HANS
HILDEBRAND, Royal Antiquary of Sweden. With Illustrations. In 1 vol.
post 8vo. [*In the press.*]

HOME PRAYERS. By Ministers of the Church of Scotland
and Members of the Church Service Society. Second Edition. Fcap. 8vo, 3s.

HORNBY. Admiral of the Fleet Sir Geoffrey Phipps Hornby,
G.C.B. A Biography. By Mrs FRED. EGERTON. With Three Portraits. Demy
8vo, 16s.

HUTCHINSON. Hints on the Game of Golf. By HORACE G.
HUTCHINSON. Ninth Edition, Enlarged. Fcap. 8vo, cloth, 1s.

HYSLOP. The Elements of Ethics. By JAMES H. HYSLOP,
Ph.D., Instructor in Ethics, Columbia College, New York, Author of 'The
Elements of Logic.' Post 8vo, 7s. 6d. net.

IDDESLEIGH. Life, Letters, and Diaries of Sir Stafford North-
cote, First Earl of Iddesleigh. By ANDREW LANG. With Three Portraits and a
View of Pynes. Third Edition. 2 vols. post 8vo, 31s. 6d.
  POPULAR EDITION. With Portrait and View of Pynes. Post 8vo, 7s. 6d.

INDEX GEOGRAPHICUS: Being a List, alphabetically ar-
ranged, of the Principal Places on the Globe, with the Countries and Subdivisions
of the Countries in which they are situated, and their Latitudes and Longitudes.
Imperial 8vo, pp. 676, 21s.

JEAN JAMBON.   Our Trip to Blunderland ; or, Grand Excursion to Blundertown and Back.   By JEAN JAMBON.   With Sixty Illustrations
designed by CHARLES DOYLE, engraved by DALZIEL.   Fourth Thousand.   Cloth,
gilt edges, 6s. 6d.   Cheap Edition, cloth, 3s. 6d.   Boards, 2s. 6d.

JEBB.   A Strange Career.   The Life and Adventures of JOHN
GLADWYN JEBB.   By his Widow.   With an Introduction by H. RIDER HAGGARD,
and an Electrogravure Portrait of Mr Jebb.   Third Edition.   Demy 8vo, 10s. 6d.
CHEAP EDITION.   With Illustrations by John Wallace.   Crown 8vo, 3s. 6d.

  Some Unconventional People.   By Mrs GLADWYN JEBB,
Author of 'Life and Adventures of J. G. Jebb.'   With Illustrations.   Crown
8vo, 3s. 6d.

JERNINGHAM.
  Reminiscences of an Attaché.   By HUBERT E. H. JERNINGHAM.
Second Edition.   Crown 8vo, 5s

  Diane de Breteuille.   A Love Story.   Crown 8vo, 2s. 6d.

JOHNSTON.
  The Chemistry of Common Life.   By Professor J. F. W.
JOHNSTON.   New Edition, Revised.   By ARTHUR HERBERT CHURCH, M.A. Oxon.;
Author of 'Food : its Sources, Constituents, and Uses,' &c.   With Maps and 102
Engravings.   Crown 8vo, 7s. 6d.

  Elements of Agricultural Chemistry.   An entirely New
Edition from the Edition by Sir CHARLES A. CAMERON, M.D., F.R.C.S.I., &c.
Revised and brought down to date by C. M. AIKMAN, M.A., B.Sc., F.R.S.E.,
Professor of Chemistry, Glasgow Veterinary College.   17th Edition.   Crown 8vo,
6s. 6d.

  Catechism of Agricultural Chemistry.   An entirely New
Edition from the Edition by Sir CHARLES A. CAMERON.   Revised and Enlarged
by C. M. AIKMAN, M.A., &c.   95th Thousand.   With numerous Illustrations.
Crown 8vo, 1s.

JOHNSTON.   Agricultural Holdings (Scotland) Acts, 1883 and
1889 ; and the Ground Game Act, 1880.   With Notes, and Summary of Procedure,
&c.   By CHRISTOPHER N. JOHNSTON, M.A., Advocate.   Demy 8vo, 5s.

JOKAI.   Timar's Two Worlds.   By MAURUS JOKAI.   Authorised
Translation by Mrs HEGAN KENNARD.   Cheap Edition.   Crown 8vo, 6s.

KEBBEL.   The Old and the New : English Country Life.   By
T. E. KEBBEL, M.A., Author of 'The Agricultural Labourers,' 'Essays in History
and Politics,' 'Life of Lord Beaconsfield.'   Crown 8vo, 5s.

KERR.   St Andrews in 1645-46.   By D. R. KERR.   Crown
8vo, 2s. 6d.

KINGLAKE.
  History of the Invasion of the Crimea.   By A. W. KINGLAKE.
Cabinet Edition, Revised.   With an Index to the Complete Work.   Illustrated
with Maps and Plans.   Complete in 9 vols., crown 8vo, at 6s. each.

  —— Abridged Edition for Military Students.   Revised by
Lieut.-Col. Sir GEORGE SYDENHAM CLARKE, K.C.M.G., R.E.   In 1 vol. demy 8vo.
[In the press.

  History of the Invasion of the Crimea.   Demy 8vo.   Vol. VI.
Winter Troubles.   With a Map, 16s.   Vols. VII. and VIII.   From the Morrow of
Inkerman to the Death of Lord Raglan   With an Index to the Whole Work.
With Maps and Plans.   28s.

  Eothen.   A New Edition, uniform with the Cabinet Edition
of the 'History of the Invasion of the Crimea.'   6s.
    CHEAPER EDITION.   With Portrait and Biographical Sketch of the Author.
Crown 8vo, 3s. 6d.   Popular Edition, in paper cover, 1s net.

KIRBY. In Haunts of Wild Game: A Hunter-Naturalist's Wanderings from Kahlamba to Libombo. By FREDERICK VAUGHAN KIRBY, F.Z.S. (Maqaqamba). With numerous Illustrations by Charles Whymper, and a Map. Large demy 8vo, 25s.

KNEIPP. My Water-Cure. As Tested through more than Thirty Years, and Described for the Healing of Diseases and the Preservation of Health. By SEBASTIAN KNEIPP, Parish Priest of Wörishofen (Bavaria). With a Portrait and other Illustrations. Authorised English Translation from the Thirtieth German Edition, by A. de F. Cheap Edition. With an Appendix, containing the Latest Developments of Pfarrer Kneipp's System, and a Preface by E. Gerard. Crown 8vo, 3s. 6d.

KNOLLYS. The Elements of Field-Artillery. Designed for the Use of Infantry and Cavalry Officers. By HENRY KNOLLYS, Colonel Royal Artillery; Author of 'From Sedan to Saarbrück,' Editor of 'Incidents in the Sepoy War,' &c. With Engravings. Crown 8vo, 7s. 6d.

LANG.

Life, Letters, and Diaries of Sir Stafford Northcote, First Earl of Iddesleigh. By ANDREW LANG. With Three Portraits and a View of Pynes. Third Edition. 2 vols. post 8vo, 31s. 6d.
POPULAR EDITION. With Portrait and View of Pynes. Post 8vo, 7s. 6d.

The Highlands of Scotland in 1750. From Manuscript 104 in the King's Library, British Museum. With an Introduction. In 1 vol. crown 8vo. [*In the press.*]

LANG. The Expansion of the Christian Life. The Duff Lecture for 1897. By the Rev. J. MARSHALL LANG, D.D. Crown 8vo, 5s.

LEES. A Handbook of the Sheriff and Justice of Peace Small Debt Courts. With Notes, References, and Forms. By J. M. LEES, Advocate, Sheriff of Stirling, Dumbarton, and Clackmannan. 8vo, 7s. 6d.

LINDSAY.

Recent Advances in Theistic Philosophy of Religion. By Rev. JAMES LINDSAY, M.A., B.D., B.Sc., F.R.S.E., F.G.S., Minister of the Parish of St Andrew's, Kilmarnock. Demy 8vo, 12s. 6d. net.

The Progressiveness of Modern Christian Thought. Crown 8vo, 6s.

Essays, Literary and Philosophical. Crown 8vo, 3s. 6d.

The Significance of the Old Testament for Modern Theology. Crown 8vo, 1s. net.

The Teaching Function of the Modern Pulpit. Crown 8vo, 1s. net.

LOCKHART.

Doubles and Quits. By LAURENCE W. M. LOCKHART. New Edition. Crown 8vo, 3s. 6d.

Fair to See. New Edition. Crown 8vo, 3s. 6d.

Mine is Thine. New Edition. Crown 8vo, 3s. 6d.

LOCKHART.

The Church of Scotland in the Thirteenth Century. The Life and Times of David de Bernham of St Andrews (Bishop), A.D. 1239 to 1253. With List of Churches dedicated by him, and Dates. By WILLIAM LOCKHART, A.M., D.D., F.S.A. Scot., Minister of Colinton Parish. 2d Edition. 8vo, 6s.

Dies Tristes: Sermons for Seasons of Sorrow. Crown 8vo, 6s.

LORIMER.

The Institutes of Law: A Treatise of the Principles of Jurisprudence as determined by Nature. By the late JAMES LORIMER, Professor of Public Law and of the Law of Nature and Nations in the University of Edinburgh. New Edition, Revised and much Enlarged. 8vo, 18s.

LORIMER.

The Institutes of the Law of Nations. A Treatise of the Jural Relation of Separate Political Communities. In 2 vols. 8vo. Volume I., price 16s. Volume II., price 20s.

LUGARD. The Rise of our East African Empire : Early Efforts in Uganda and Nyassaland. By F. D. LUGARD, Captain Norfolk Regiment. With 130 Illustrations from Drawings and Photographs under the personal superintendence of the Author, and 14 specially prepared Maps. In 2 vols. large demy 8vo, 42s.

M'CHESNEY.

Miriam Cromwell, Royalist : A Romance of the Great Rebellion. By DORA GREENWELL M'CHESNEY. Crown 8vo, 6s.

Kathleen Clare : Her Book, 1637-41. With Frontispiece, and five full-page Illustrations by James A. Shearman. Crown 8vo, 6s.

M'COMBIE. Cattle and Cattle-Breeders. By WILLIAM M'COMBIE, Tillyfour. New Edition, Enlarged, with Memoir of the Author by JAMES MACDONALD, F.R.S.E., Secretary Highland and Agricultural Society of Scotland. Crown 8vo, 3s. 6d.

M'CRIE.

Works of the Rev. Thomas M'Crie, D.D. Uniform Edition. 4 vols. crown 8vo, 24s.

Life of John Knox. Crown 8vo, 6s. Another Edition, 3s. 6d.

Life of Andrew Melville. Crown 8vo, 6s.

History of the Progress and Suppression of the Reformation in Italy in the Sixteenth Century. Crown 8vo, 4s.

History of the Progress and Suppression of the Reformation in Spain in the Sixteenth Century. Crown 8vo, 3s. 6d.

M'CRIE. The Public Worship of Presbyterian Scotland. Historically treated. With copious Notes, Appendices, and Index. The Fourteenth Series of the Cunningham Lectures. By the Rev. CHARLES G. M'CRIE, D.D. Demy 8vo, 10s. 6d.

MACDONALD. A Manual of the Criminal Law (Scotland) Procedure Act, 1887. By NORMAN DORAN MACDONALD. Revised by the LORD JUSTICE-CLERK. 8vo, 10s. 6d.

MACDONALD AND SINCLAIR. History of Polled Aberdeen and Angus Cattle. Giving an Account of the Origin, Improvement, and Characteristics of the Breed. By JAMES MACDONALD and JAMES SINCLAIR. Illustrated with numerous Animal Portraits. Post 8vo, 12s. 6d.

MACDOUGALL AND DODDS. A Manual of the Local Government (Scotland) Act, 1894. With Introduction, Explanatory Notes, and Copious Index. By J. PATTEN MACDOUGALL, Legal Secretary to the Lord Advocate, and J. M. DODDS. Tenth Thousand, Revised. Crown 8vo, 2s. 6d. net.

MACINTYRE. Hindu - Koh : Wanderings and Wild Sports on and beyond the Himalayas. By Major-General DONALD MACINTYRE, V.C., late Prince of Wales' Own Goorkhas, F.R.G.S. *Dedicated to H.R.H. The Prince of Wales.* New and Cheaper Edition, Revised, with numerous Illustrations. Post 8vo, 3s. 6d.

MACKAY.

Elements of Modern Geography. By the Rev. ALEXANDER MACKAY, LL.D., F.R.G.S. 55th Thousand, Revised to the present time. Crown 8vo, pp. 300, 3s.

The Intermediate Geography. Intended as an Intermediate Book between the Author's 'Outlines of Geography' and 'Elements of Geography.' Eighteenth Edition, Revised. Fcap. 8vo, pp. 238, 2s.

Outlines of Modern Geography. 191st Thousand, Revised to the present time. Fcap. 8vo, pp. 128, 1s.

Elements of Physiography. New Edition. Rewritten and Enlarged. With numerous Illustrations. Crown 8vo. [*In the press.*

MACKENZIE. Studies in Roman Law. With Comparative Views of the Laws of France, England, and Scotland. By Lord MACKENZIE, one of the Judges of the Court of Session in Scotland. Sixth Edition, Edited by JOHN KIRKPATRICK, M.A., LL.B., Advocate, Professor of History in the University of Edinburgh. 8vo, 12s.

MACPHERSON. Glimpses of Church and Social Life in the Highlands in Olden Times. By ALEXANDER MACPHERSON, F.S.A. Scot. With 6 Photogravure Portraits and other full-page Illustrations. Small 4to, 25s.

M'PHERSON. Golf and Golfers. Past and Present. By J. GORDON M'PHERSON, Ph.D., F.R.S.E. With an Introduction by the Right Hon. A. J. BALFOUR, and a Portrait of the Author. Fcap. 8vo, 1s. 6d.

MACRAE. A Handbook of Deer-Stalking. By ALEXANDER MACRAE, late Forester to Lord Henry Bentinck. With Introduction by Horatio Ross, Esq. Fcap. 8vo, with 2 Photographs from Life. 3s. 6d.

MAIN. Three Hundred English Sonnets. Chosen and Edited by DAVID M. MAIN. New Edition. Fcap. 8vo, 3s. 6d.

MAIR. A Digest of Laws and Decisions, Ecclesiastical and Civil, relating to the Constitution, Practice, and Affairs of the Church of Scotland. With Notes and Forms of Procedure. By the Rev. WILLIAM MAIR, D.D., Minister of the Parish of Earlston. New Edition, Revised. Crown 8vo, 9s. net.

MARCHMONT AND THE HUMES OF POLWARTH. By One of their Descendants. With numerous Portraits and other Illustrations. Crown 4to, 21s. net.

MARSHMAN. History of India. From the Earliest Period to the present time. By JOHN CLARK MARSHMAN, C.S.I. Third and Cheaper Edition. Post 8vo, with Map, 6s.

MARTIN.
The Æneid of Virgil. Books I.-VI. Translated by Sir THEODORE MARTIN, K.C.B. Post 8vo, 7s. 6d.
Goethe's Faust. Part I. Translated into English Verse. Second Edition, crown 8vo, 6s. Ninth Edition, fcap. 8vo, 3s. 6d.
Goethe's Faust. Part II. Translated into English Verse. Second Edition, Revised. Fcap. 8vo, 6s.
The Works of Horace. Translated into English Verse, with Life and Notes. 2 vols. New Edition. Crown 8vo, 21s.
Poems and Ballads of Heinrich Heine. Done into English Verse. Third Edition. Small crown 8vo, 5s.
The Song of the Bell, and other Translations from Schiller, Goethe, Uhland, and Others. Crown 8vo, 7s. 6d.
Madonna Pia : A Tragedy ; and Three Other Dramas. Crown 8vo, 7s. 6d.
Catullus. With Life and Notes. Second Edition, Revised and Corrected. Post 8vo, 7s. 6d.
The 'Vita Nuova' of Dante. Translated, with an Introduction and Notes. Third Edition. Small crown 8vo, 5s.
Aladdin : A Dramatic Poem. By ADAM OEHLENSCHLAEGER. Fcap. 8vo, 5s.
Correggio : A Tragedy. By OEHLENSCHLAEGER. With Notes. Fcap. 8vo, 3s.

MARTIN. On some of Shakespeare's Female Characters. By HELENA FAUCIT, Lady MARTIN. Dedicated by permission to Her Most Gracious Majesty the Queen. Fifth Edition. With a Portrait by Lehmann. Demy 8vo, 7s. 6d.

MARWICK. Observations on the Law and Practice in regard to Municipal Elections and the Conduct of the Business of Town Councils and Commissioners of Police in Scotland. By Sir JAMES D. MARWICK, LL.D. Town-Clerk of Glasgow. Royal 8vo, 30s.

MATHESON.
Can the Old Faith Live with the New? or, The Problem of Evolution and Revelation. By the Rev. GEORGE MATHESON, D.D. Third Edition. Crown 8vo, 7s. 6d.
The Psalmist and the Scientist; or, Modern Value of the Religious Sentiment. Third Edition. Crown 8vo, 5s.
Spiritual Development of St Paul. Fourth Edition. Cr. 8vo, 5s.
The Distinctive Messages of the Old Religions. Second Edition. Crown 8vo, 5s.
Sacred Songs. New and Cheaper Edition. Crown 8vo, 2s. 6d.

MATHIESON. The Supremacy and Sufficiency of Jesus Christ our Lord, as set forth in the Epistle to the Hebrews. By J. E. MATHIESON, Superintendent of Mildmay Conference Hall, 1880 to 1890. Second Edition. Crown 8vo, 3s. 6d.

MAURICE. The Balance of Military Power in Europe. An Examination of the War Resources of Great Britain and the Continental States. By Colonel MAURICE, R.A., Professor of Military Art and History at the Royal Staff College. Crown 8vo, with a Map, 6s.

MAXWELL.
A Duke of Britain. A Romance of the Fourth Century. By Sir HERBERT MAXWELL, Bart., M.P., F.S.A., &c., Author of 'Passages in the Life of Sir Lucian Elphin.' Fourth Edition. Crown 8vo, 6s.
Life and Times of the Rt. Hon. William Henry Smith, M.P. With Portraits and numerous Illustrations by Herbert Railton, G. L. Seymour, and Others. 2 vols. demy 8vo, 25s.
    POPULAR EDITION. With a Portrait and other Illustrations. Crown 8vo, 3s. 6d.
Scottish Land-Names: Their Origin and Meaning. Being the Rhind Lectures in Archæology for 1893. Post 8vo, 6s.
Meridiana: Noontide Essays. Post 8vo, 7s. 6d.
Post Meridiana: Afternoon Essays. Post 8vo, 6s.
Dumfries and Galloway. Being one of the Volumes of the County Histories of Scotland. With Four Maps. Demy 8vo, 7s. 6d. net.

MELDRUM.
The Story of Margrédel: Being a Fireside History of a Fifeshire Family. By D. STORRAR MELDRUM. Cheap Edition. Crown 8vo, 3s. 6d.
Grey Mantle and Gold Fringe. Crown 8vo, 6s.

MELLONE. Studies in Philosophical Criticism and Construction. By SYDNEY HERBERT MELLONE, M.A. Lond., D.Sc. Edin. Post 8vo, 10s. 6d. net.

MERZ. A History of European Thought in the Nineteenth Century. By JOHN THEODORE MERZ. Vol. I., post 8vo, 10s. 6d. net.

MICHIE.
The Larch: Being a Practical Treatise on its Culture and General Management. By CHRISTOPHER Y. MICHIE, Forester, Cullen House. Crown 8vo, with Illustrations. New and Cheaper Edition, Enlarged, 5s.
The Practice of Forestry. Crown 8vo, with Illustrations. 6s.

MIDDLETON. The Story of Alastair Bhan Comyn; or, The Tragedy of Dunphail. A Tale of Tradition and Romance. By the Lady MIDDLETON. Square 8vo, 10s. Cheaper Edition, 5s.

MIDDLETON. Latin Verse Unseens. By G. MIDDLETON, M.A., Lecturer in Latin, Aberdeen University; late Scholar of Emmanuel College. Cambridge; Joint-Author of 'Student's Companion to Latin Authors.' Crown 8vo, 1s. 6d.

MILLER. The Dream of Mr H——, the Herbalist. By HUGH MILLER, F.R.S.E., late H.M. Geological Survey, Author of 'Landscape Geology.' With a Photogravure Frontispiece. Crown 8vo, 2s. 6d.

MILLS. Greek Verse Unseens. By T. R. MILLS, M.A., late Lecturer in Greek, Aberdeen University; formerly Scholar of Wadham College, Oxford; Joint-Author of 'Student's Companion to Latin Authors. In 1 vol. crown 8vo.   [*In the press.*

MINTO.

A Manual of English Prose Literature, Biographical and
Critical: designed mainly to show Characteristics of Style. By W. MINTO,
M.A., Hon. LL.D. of St Andrews; Professor of Logic in the University of Aber-
deen. Third Edition, Revised. Crown 8vo, 7s. 6d.

Characteristics of English Poets, from Chaucer to Shirley.
New Edition, Revised. Crown 8vo, 7s. 6d.

Plain Principles of Prose Composition. Crown 8vo, 1s. 6d.

The Literature of the Georgian Era. Edited, with a Biographical Introduction, by Professor KNIGHT, St Andrews. Post 8vo, 6s.

MOIR.

Life of Mansie Wauch, Tailor in Dalkeith. By D. M. MOIR.
With CRUIKSHANK's Illustrations. Cheaper Edition. Crown 8vo, 2s. 6d.
Another Edition, without Illustrations, fcap. 8vo, 1s. 6d.

Domestic Verses. Centenary Edition. With a Portrait. Crown
8vo, 3s. 6d.

MOLE. For the Sake of a Slandered Woman. By MARION
MOLE. Fcap. 8vo, 2s. 6d. net.

MOMERIE.

Defects of Modern Christianity, and other Sermons. By Rev.
ALFRED WILLIAMS MOMERIE, M.A., D.Sc., LL.D. Fifth Edition. Crown 8vo, 5s.

The Basis of Religion. Being an Examination of Natural
Religion. Third Edition. Crown 8vo, 2s. 6d.

The Origin of Evil, and other Sermons. Eighth Edition,
Enlarged. Crown 8vo, 5s.

Personality. The Beginning and End of Metaphysics, and a Necessary Assumption in all Positive Philosophy. Fifth Ed., Revised. Cr. 8vo, 3s.

Agnosticism. Fourth Edition, Revised. Crown 8vo, 5s.

Preaching and Hearing; and other Sermons. Fourth Edition,
Enlarged. Crown 8vo, 5s.

Belief in God. Third Edition. Crown 8vo, 3s.

Inspiration; and other Sermons. Second Edition, Enlarged.
Crown 8vo, 5s.

Church and Creed. Third Edition. Crown 8vo, 4s. 6d.

The Future of Religion, and other Essays. Second Edition.
Crown 8vo, 3s. 6d.

The English Church and the Romish Schism. Second Edition.
Crown 8vo, 2s. 6d.

MONCREIFF.

The Provost-Marshal. A Romance of the Middle Shires. By
the Hon. FREDERICK MONCREIFF. Crown 8vo, 6s.

The X Jewel. A Romance of the Days of James VI. Cr. 8vo, 6s.

MONTAGUE. Military Topography. Illustrated by Practical
Examples of a Practical Subject. By Major-General W. E. MONTAGUE, C.B.,
P.S.C., late Garrison Instructor Intelligence Department, Author of 'Campaign-
ing in South Africa.' With Forty-one Diagrams. Crown 8vo, 5s.

MONTALEMBERT. Memoir of Count de Montalembert. A
Chapter of Recent French History. By Mrs OLIPHANT, Author of the 'Life of
Edward Irving,' &c. 2 vols. crown 8vo, £1, 4s.

MORISON.

Doorside Ditties. By JEANIE MORISON. With a Frontispiece. Crown 8vo, 3s. 6d.

Æolus. A Romance in Lyrics. Crown 8vo, 3s.

There as Here. Crown 8vo, 3s.
  ₊ A limited impression on hand-made paper, bound in vellum, 7s. 6d.

Selections from Poems. Crown 8vo, 4s. 6d.

Sordello. An Outline Analysis of Mr Browning's Poem.
Crown 8vo, 3s.

MORISON.
Of "Fifine at the Fair," "Christmas Eve and Easter Day,
and other of Mr Browning's Poems. Crown 8vo, 3s.
The Purpose of the Ages. Crown 8vo, 9s.
Gordon : An Our-day Idyll. Crown 8vo, 3s.
Saint Isadora, and other Poems. Crown 8vo, 1s. 6d.
Snatches of Song. Paper, 1s. 6d. ; cloth, 3s.
Pontius Pilate. Paper, 1s. 6d. ; cloth, 3s.
Mill o' Forres. Crown 8vo, 1s.
Ane Booke of Ballades. Fcap. 4to, 1s.

MUNRO. The Lost Pibroch, and other Sheiling Stories. By
NEIL MUNRO. Crown 8vo, 6s.

MUNRO.
Rambles and Studies in Bosnia-Herzegovina and Dalmatia.
With an Account of the Proceedings of the Congress of Archæologists and
Anthropologists held at Sarajevo in 1894. By ROBERT MUNRO, M.A., M.D.,
F.R.S.E., Author of 'The Lake-Dwellings of Europe,' &c. With numerous Illus-
trations. Demy 8vo, 12s. 6d. net.
Prehistoric Problems. With numerous Illustrations. Demy
8vo, 10s. net.

MUNRO. On Valuation of Property. By WILLIAM MUNRO,
M.A., Her Majesty's Assessor of Railways and Canals for Scotland. Second
Edition, Revised and Enlarged. 8vo, 3s. 6d.

MURDOCH. Manual of the Law of Insolvency and Bankruptcy:
Comprehending a Summary of the Law of Insolvency, Notour Bankruptcy,
Composition-Contracts, Trust-Deeds, Cessios, and Sequestrations; and the
Winding-up of Joint-Stock Companies in Scotland; with Annotations on the
various Insolvency and Bankruptcy Statutes; and with Forms of Procedure
applicable to these Subjects. By JAMES MURDOCH, Member of the Faculty of
Procurators in Glasgow. Fifth Edition, Revised and Enlarged. 8vo, 12s. net.

MURRAY. A Popular Manual of Finance. By SYDNEY J.
MURRAY. In 1 vol. crown 8vo. [In the press.

MYERS. A Manual of Classical Geography. By JOHN L.
MYERS, M.A., Fellow of Magdalene College; Lecturer and Tutor, Christ Church,
Oxford. In 1 vol. crown 8vo. [In the press.

MY TRIVIAL LIFE AND MISFORTUNE: A Gossip with
no Plot in Particular. By A PLAIN WOMAN. Cheap Edition. Crown 8vo, 3s. 6d.
By the SAME AUTHOR.
POOR NELLIE. Cheap Edition. Crown 8vo, 3s. 6d.

NAPIER. The Construction of the Wonderful Canon of Loga-
rithms. By JOHN NAPIER of Merchiston. Translated, with Notes, and a
Catalogue of Napier's Works, by WILLIAM RAE MACDONALD. Small 4to, 15s.
A few large-paper copies on Whatman paper, 30s.

NEAVES. Songs and Verses, Social and Scientific. By An Old
Contributor to 'Maga.' By the Hon. Lord NEAVES. Fifth Edition. Fcap.
8vo, 4s.

NICHOLSON.
A Manual of Zoology, for the Use of Students. With a
General Introduction on the Principles of Zoology. By HENRY ALLEYNE
NICHOLSON, M.D., D.Sc., F.L.S., F.G.S., Regius Professor of Natural History in
the University of Aberdeen. Seventh Edition, Rewritten and Enlarged. Post
8vo, pp. 956, with 555 Engravings on Wood, 18s.
Text-Book of Zoology, for Junior Students. Fifth Edition,
Rewritten and Enlarged. Crown 8vo, with 358 Engravings on Wood, 10s. 6d.
Introductory Text-Book of Zoology. By PROFESSOR H. A.
NICHOLSON and ALEXANDER BROWN, M.A., M.B., D.Sc., Lecturer on Zoology in
the University of Aberdeen. New Edition, Revised and Enlarged. [In the press.

NICHOLSON.

A Manual of Palæontology, for the Use of Students. With a
General Introduction on the Principles of Palæontology. By Professor H.
ALLEYNE NICHOLSON and RICHARD LYDEKKER, B.A. Third Edition, entirely
Rewritten and greatly Enlarged. 2 vols. 8vo, £3, 3s.

The Ancient Life-History of the Earth. An Outline of the
Principles and Leading Facts of Palæontological Science. Crown 8vo, with 276
Engravings, 10s. 6d.

On the "Tabulate Corals" of the Palæozoic Period, with
Critical Descriptions of Illustrative Species. Illustrated with 15 Lithographed
Plates and numerous Engravings. Super-royal 8vo, 21s.

Synopsis of the Classification of the Animal Kingdom. 8vo,
with 106 Illustrations, 6s.

On the Structure and Affinities of the Genus Monticulipora
and its Sub-Genera, with Critical Descriptions of Illustrative Species. Illustrated
with numerous Engravings on Wood and Lithographed Plates. Super-royal
8vo, 18s.

NICHOLSON.

Thoth. A Romance. By JOSEPH SHIELD NICHOLSON, M.A.,
D.Sc., Professor of Commercial and Political Economy and Mercantile Law in
the University of Edinburgh. Third Edition. Crown 8vo, 4s. 6d.

A Dreamer of Dreams. A Modern Romance. Second Edi-
tion. Crown 8vo, 6s.

NICOLSON AND MURE. A Handbook to the Local Govern-
ment (Scotland) Act, 1889. With Introduction, Explanatory Notes, and Index.
By J. BADENACH NICOLSON, Advocate, Counsel to the Scotch Education
Department, and W. J. MURE, Advocate, Legal Secretary to the Lord Advocate
for Scotland. Ninth Reprint. 8vo, 5s.

OLIPHANT.

Masollam : A Problem of the Period. A Novel. By LAURENCE
OLIPHANT. 3 vols. post 8vo, 25s. 6d.

Scientific Religion ; or, Higher Possibilities of Life and
Practice through the Operation of Natural Forces. Second Edition. 8vo, 16s.

Altiora Peto. Cheap Edition. Crown 8vo, boards, 2s. 6d. ;
cloth, 3s. 6d. Illustrated Edition. Crown 8vo, cloth, 6s.

Piccadilly. With Illustrations by Richard Doyle. New Edi-
tion, 3s. 6d. Cheap Edition, boards, 2s. 6d.

Traits and Travesties ; Social and Political. Post 8vo, 10s. 6d.

Episodes in a Life of Adventure ; or, Moss from a Rolling
Stone. Cheaper Edition. Post 8vo, 3s. 6d.

Haifa : Life in Modern Palestine. Second Edition. 8vo, 7s. 6d.

The Land of Gilead. With Excursions in the Lebanon.
With Illustrations and Maps. Demy 8vo, 21s.

Memoir of the Life of Laurence Oliphant, and of Alice
Oliphant, his Wife. By Mrs M. O. W. OLIPHANT. Seventh Edition. 2 vols.
post 8vo, with Portraits. 21s.
POPULAR EDITION. With a New Preface. Post 8vo, with Portraits. 7s. 6d.

OLIPHANT.

Annals of a Publishing House. William Blackwood and his
Sons; Their Magazine and Friends. By Mrs OLIPHANT. With Four Portraits.
Third Edition. Demy 8vo. Vols. I. and II. £2, 2s.

Who was Lost and is Found. Second Edition. Crown
8vo, 6s.

Miss Marjoribanks. New Edition. Crown 8vo, 3s. 6d.

The Perpetual Curate, and The Rector. New Edition. Crown
8vo, 3s. 6d.

OLIPHANT.
Salem Chapel, and The Doctor's Family. New Edition.
Crown 8vo, 3s. 6d
Chronicles of Carlingford. 3 vols. crown 8vo, in uniform
binding, gilt top, 3s. 6d. each.
Katie Stewart, and other Stories. New Edition. Crown 8vo,
cloth, 3s. 6d.
Katie Stewart. Illustrated boards, 2s. 6d.
Valentine and his Brother. New Edition. Crown 8vo, 3s. 6d.
Sons and Daughters. Crown 8vo, 3s. 6d.
Two Stories of the Seen and the Unseen. The Open Door
—Old Lady Mary. Paper covers, 1s.
OLIPHANT. Notes of a Pilgrimage to Jerusalem and the Holy
Land. By F. R. OLIPHANT. Crown 8vo, 3s. 6d.
OSWALD. By Fell and Fjord; or, Scenes and Studies in Ice-
land. By E. J. OSWALD. Post 8vo, with Illustrations. 7s. 6d.

PAGE.
Introductory Text-Book of Geology. By DAVID PAGE, LL.D.,
Professor of Geology in the Durham University of Physical Science, Newcastle.
With Engravings and Glossarial Index. New Edition. Revised by Professor
LAPWORTH of Mason Science College, Birmingham. [*In preparation.*
Advanced Text-Book of Geology, Descriptive and Industrial.
With Engravings, and Glossary of Scientific Terms. New Edition. Revised by
Professor LAPWORTH. [*In preparation.*
Introductory Text-Book of Physical Geography. With Sketch-
Maps and Illustrations. Edited by Professor LAPWORTH, LL.D., F.G.S., &c.,
Mason Science College, Birmingham. Thirteenth Edition, Revised and Enlarged.
2s. 6d.
Advanced Text-Book of Physical Geography. Third Edition.
Revised and Enlarged by Professor LAPWORTH. With Engravings. 5s.
PATERSON. A Manual of Agricultural Botany. From the
German of Dr A. B. FRANK, Professor in the Royal Agricultural College, Berlin.
Translated by JOHN W. PATERSON, B.Sc., Free Life Member of the High-
land and Agricultural Society of Scotland, and of the Royal Agricultural Society
of England. With over 100 Illustrations. In 1 vol. crown 8vo. [*In the press.*
PATON.
Spindrift. By Sir J. NOEL PATON. Fcap., cloth, 5s.
Poems by a Painter. Fcap., cloth, 5s.
PATRICK. The Apology of Origen in Reply to Celsus. A Chap-
ter in the History of Apologetics. By the Rev. J. PATRICK, D.D. Post 8vo, 7s. 6d.
PAUL. History of the Royal Company of Archers, the Queen's
Body-Guard for Scotland. By JAMES BALFOUR PAUL, Advocate of the Scottish
Bar. Crown 4to, with Portraits and other Illustrations. £2, 2s.
PEILE. Lawn Tennis as a Game of Skill. By Lieut.-Col. S. C.
F. PEILE, B.S.C. Revised Edition, with new Scoring Rules. Fcap. 8vo, cloth, 1s.
PETTIGREW. The Handy Book of Bees, and their Profitable
Management. By A. PETTIGREW. Fifth Edition, Enlarged, with Engravings.
Crown 8vo, 3s. 6d.
PFLEIDERER. Philosophy and Development of Religion.
Being the Edinburgh Gifford Lectures for 1894. By OTTO PFLEIDERER, D.D.
Professor of Theology at Berlin University. In 2 vols. post 8vo, 15s. net.
PHILLIPS. The Knight's Tale. By F. EMILY PHILLIPS, Author
of 'The Education of Antonia.' Crown 8vo, 3s. 6d.
PHILOSOPHICAL CLASSICS FOR ENGLISH READERS.
Edited by WILLIAM KNIGHT, LL.D., Professor of Moral Philosophy, University
of St Andrews. In crown 8vo volumes, with Portraits, price 3s. 6d.
[*For List of Volumes, see page 2.*

POLLARD. A Study in Municipal Government: The Corpora-
tion of Berlin. By JAMES POLLARD, C.A., Chairman of the Edinburgh Public
Health Committee, and Secretary of the Edinburgh Chamber of Commerce.
Second Edition, Revised. Crown 8vo, 3s. 6d.

POLLOK. The Course of Time: A Poem. By ROBERT POLLOK,
A.M. Cottage Edition, 32mo, 8d. The Same, cloth, gilt edges, 1s. 6d. Another
Edition, with Illustrations by Birket Foster and others, fcap., cloth, 3s. 6d., or
with edges gilt, 4s.

PORT ROYAL LOGIC. Translated from the French; with
Introduction, Notes, and Appendix. By THOMAS SPENCER BAYNES, LL.D., Professor in the University of St Andrews. Tenth Edition, 12mo, 4s.

POTTS AND DARNELL.
Aditus Faciliores: An Easy Latin Construing Book, with
Complete Vocabulary By A. W. POTTS, M.A., LL.D., and the Rev. C. DARNELL,
M.A., Head-Master of Cargilfield Preparatory School Edinburgh. Tenth Edition,
fcap. 8vo, 3s. 6d.

Aditus Faciliores Graeci. An Easy Greek Construing Book,
with Complete Vocabulary. Fifth Edition, Revised. Fcap. 8vo, 3s.

POTTS. School Sermons. By the late ALEXANDER WM. POTTS,
LL.D., First Head-Master of Fettes College. With a Memoir and Portrait.
Crown 8vo, 7s. 6d.

PRINGLE. The Live Stock of the Farm. By ROBERT O.
PRINGLE. Third Edition. Revised and Edited by JAMES MACDONALD. Crown
8vo, 7s. 6d.

PUBLIC GENERAL STATUTES AFFECTING SCOTLAND
from 1707 to 1847, with Chronological Table and Index. 3 vols. large 8vo, £3, 3s.

PUBLIC GENERAL STATUTES AFFECTING SCOTLAND,
COLLECTION OF. Published Annually, with General Index.

RAMSAY. Scotland and Scotsmen in the Eighteenth Century.
Edited from the MSS. of JOHN RAMSAY, Esq. of Ochtertyre, by ALEXANDER
ALLARDYCE, Author of 'Memoir of Admiral Lord Keith, K.B.,' &c. 2 vols.
8vo, 31s. 6d.

RANJITSINHJI. The Jubilee Book of Cricket. By PRINCE
RANJITSINHJI.
ÉDITION DE LUXE. Limited to 350 Copies, printed on hand-made paper, and
handsomely bound in buckram. Crown 4to, with 22 Photogravures and 85
full-page Plates. Each copy signed by Prince Ranjitsinhji. Price £5, 5s. net.
FINE PAPER EDITION. Medium 8vo, with Photogravure Frontispiece and 106
full-page Plates on art paper. 25s. net.
POPULAR EDITION. With 107 full-page Illustrations. Fifth Edition. Large
crown 8vo, 6s.

RANKIN.
A Handbook of the Church of Scotland. By JAMES RANKIN,
D.D., Minister of Muthill; Author of 'Character Studies in the Old Testament,
&c. An entirely New and much Enlarged Edition. Crown 8vo, with 2 Maps,
7s. 6d.

The First Saints. Post 8vo, 7s. 6d.

The Creed in Scotland. An Exposition of the Apostles'
Creed. With Extracts from Archbishop Hamilton's Catechism of 1552, John
Calvin's Catechism of 1556, and a Catena of Ancient Latin and other Hymns.
Post 8vo, 7s. 6d.

The Worthy Communicant. A Guide to the Devout Observance of the Lord's Supper. Limp cloth, 1s. 3d.

The Young Churchman. Lessons on the Creed, the Com-
mandments, the Means of Grace, and the Church. Limp cloth, 1s. 3d.

First Communion Lessons. 25th Edition. Paper Cover, 2d.

RANKINE. A Hero of the Dark Continent. Memoir of Rev.
Wm. Affleck Scott, M.A., M.B., C.M., Church of Scotland Missionary at Blantyre,
British Central Africa. By W. HENRY RANKINE, B.D., Minister at Titwood.
With a Portrait and other Illustrations. Cheap Edition. Crown 8vo, 2s.

ROBERTSON. The Early Religion of Israel. As set forth by
Biblical Writers and Modern Critical Historians. Being the Baird Lecture for
1888-89. By JAMES ROBERTSON, D.D., Professor of Oriental Languages in the
University of Glasgow. Fourth Edition. Crown 8vo, 10s. 6d.

ROBERTSON.
Orellana, and other Poems. By J. LOGIE ROBERTSON,
M.A. Fcap. 8vo. Printed on hand-made paper. 6s.

A History of English Literature. For Secondary Schools.
With an Introduction by Professor MASSON, Edinburgh University. Cr. 8vo, 3s.

English Verse for Junior Classes. In Two Parts. Part I.—
Chaucer to Coleridge. Part II.—Nineteenth Century Poets. Crown 8vo, each
1s. 6d. net.

Outlines of English Literature for Young Scholars. With
Illustrative Specimens. Crown 8vo, 1s. 6d.

ROBINSON. Wild Traits in Tame Animals. Being some
Familiar Studies in Evolution. By LOUIS ROBINSON, M.D. With Illustrations
by STEPHEN T. DADD. Demy 8vo, 10s. 6d. net.

RODGER. Aberdeen Doctors at Home and Abroad. The Story
of a Medical School. By ELLA HILL BURTON RODGER. Demy 8vo, 10s. 6d.

ROSCOE. Rambles with a Fishing-Rod. By E. S. ROSCOE.
Crown 8vo, 4s. 6d.

ROSS AND SOMERVILLE. Beggars on Horseback : A Riding
Tour in North Wales. By MARTIN ROSS and E. Œ. SOMERVILLE. With Illustrations by E. Œ. SOMERVILLE. Crown 8vo, 3s. 6d.

RUTLAND.
Notes of an Irish Tour in 1846. By the DUKE OF RUTLAND,
G.C.B. (Lord JOHN MANNERS). New Edition. Crown 8vo, 2s. 6d.

Correspondence between the Right Honble. William Pitt
and Charles Duke of Rutland, Lord - Lieutenant of Ireland, 1781-1787. With
Introductory Note by JOHN DUKE OF RUTLAND. 8vo, 7s. 6d.

RUTLAND.
Gems of German Poetry. Translated by the DUCHESS OF
RUTLAND (Lady JOHN MANNERS). [*New Edition in preparation.*

Impressions of Bad-Homburg. Comprising a Short Account
of the Women's Associations of Germany under the Red Cross. Crown 8vo, 1s. 6d.

Some Personal Recollections of the Later Years of the Earl
of Beaconsfield, K.G. Sixth Edition. 6d.

Employment of Women in the Public Service. 6d.

Some of the Advantages of Easily Accessible Reading and
Recreation Rooms and Free Libraries. With Remarks on Starting and Maintaining them. Second Edition. Crown 8vo, 1s.

A Sequel to Rich Men's Dwellings, and other Occasional
Papers. Crown 8vo, 2s. 6d.

Encouraging Experiences of Reading and Recreation Rooms,
Aims of Guilds, Nottingham Social Guide, Existing Institutions, &c., &c.
Crown 8vo, 1s.

SAINTSBURY. The Flourishing of Romance and the Rise of
Allegory (12th and 13th Centuries). By GEORGE SAINTSBURY, M.A., Professor of
Rhetoric and English Literature in Edinburgh University. Being the first vol-
ume issued of "PERIODS OF EUROPEAN LITERATURE." Edited by Professor
SAINTSBURY. Crown 8vo, 5s. net.

SCHEFFEL. The Trumpeter. A Romance of the Rhine. By
JOSEPH VICTOR VON SCHEFFEL. Translated from the Two Hundredth German
Edition by JESSIE BECK and LOUISA LORIMER. With an Introduction by Sir
THEODORE MARTIN, K.C.B. Long 8vo, 3s. 6d.

SCHILLER. Wallenstein. A Dramatic Poem. By FRIEDRICH
VON SCHILLER. Translated by C. G. N. LOCKHART. Fcap. 8vo, 7s. 6d

SCOTT. Tom Cringle's Log. By MICHAEL SCOTT. New Edition.
With 19 Full-page Illustrations. Crown 8vo, 3s. 6d.

SCOUGAL. Prisons and their Inmates; or, Scenes from a
Silent World. By FRANCIS SCOUGAL. Crown 8vo, boards, 2s.

SELKIRK. Poems. By J. B. SELKIRK, Author of 'Ethics and
Æsthetics of Modern Poetry,' 'Bible Truths with Shakespearian Parallels,' &c.
New and Enlarged Edition. Crown 8vo, printed on antique paper, 6s.

SELLAR'S Manual of the Acts relating to Education in Scotland. By J. EDWARD GRAHAM, B.A. Oxon., Advocate. Ninth Edition. Demy
8vo, 12s. 6d.

SETH.
Scottish Philosophy. A Comparison of the Scottish and
German Answers to Hume. Balfour Philosophical Lectures, University of
Edinburgh. By ANDREW SETH, LL.D., Professor of Logic and Metaphysics in
Edinburgh University. Second Edition. Crown 8vo, 5s.

Hegelianism and Personality. Balfour Philosophical Lectures.
Second Series. Second Edition. Crown 8vo, 5s.

Man's Place in the Cosmos, and other Essays. Post 8vo,
7s. 6d. net.

Two Lectures on Theism. Delivered on the occasion of the
Sesquicentennial Celebration of Princeton University. Crown 8vo, 2s. 6d.

SETH. A Study of Ethical Principles. By JAMES SETH, M.A.,
Professor of Philosophy in Cornell University, U.S.A. New Edition, Revised.
In 1 vol. post 8vo. [*In the press.*

SHADWELL. The Life of Colin Campbell, Lord Clyde. Illustrated by Extracts from his Diary and Correspondence. By Lieutenant-General
SHADWELL C.B. With Portrait, Maps, and Plans. 2 vols. 8vo, 36s.

SHAND.
The Life of General Sir Edward Bruce Hamley, K.C.B.,
K.C.M.G. By ALEX. INNES SHAND, Author of 'Kilcarra,' 'Against Time,' &c.
With two Photogravure Portraits and other Illustrations. Cheaper Edition, with
a Statement by Mr Edward Hamley. 2 vols. demy 8vo, 10s. 6d.

Letters from the West of Ireland. Reprinted from the
'Times.' Crown 8vo, 5s.

SHARPE. Letters from and to Charles Kirkpatrick Sharpe.
Edited by ALEXANDER ALLARDYCE, Author of 'Memoir of Admiral Lord Keith,
K.B.,' &c. With a Memoir by the Rev. W. K. R. BEDFORD. In 2 vols. 8vo.
Illustrated with Etchings and other Engravings. £2, 12s. 6d.

SIM. Margaret Sim's Cookery. With an Introduction by L. B.
WALFORD, Author of 'Mr Smith: A Part of his Life,' &c. Crown 8vo, 5s.

SIMPSON. The Wild Rabbit in a New Aspect; or, Rabbit-
Warrens that Pay. A book for Landowners, Sportsmen, Land Agents, Farmers,
Gamekeepers, and Allotment Holders. A Record of Recent Experiments con-
ducted on the Estate of the Right Hon. the Earl of Wharncliffe at Wortley Hall.
By J. SIMPSON. Second Edition, Enlarged. Small crown 8vo, 5s.

SIMPSON. Side-Lights on Siberia. With an Account of a
Journey on the Great Siberian Iron Road. By J. Y. SIMPSON. With numerous
Illustrations. In 1 vol. demy 8vo. [*In the press.*

SINCLAIR. Audrey Craven. By MAY SINCLAIR. Second
Edition. Crown 8vo, 6s.

SKELTON.
The Table-Talk of Shirley. By JOHN SKELTON, Advocate,
C.B., LL.D., Author of 'The Essays of Shirley.' With a Frontispiece. Sixth
Edition, Revised and Enlarged. Post 8vo, 7s. 6d.

The Table-Talk of Shirley. Second Series. Summers and
Winters at Balmawhapple. With Illustrations. Two Volumes. Second Edition.
Post 8vo, 10s. net.

SKELTON.
   Maitland of Lethington; and the Scotland of Mary Stuart.
   A History. Limited Edition, with Portraits. Demy 8vo, 2 vols., 28s. net.
   The Handbook of Public Health. A New Edition, Revised by
   JAMES PATTEN MACDOUGALL, Advocate, Legal Member of the Local Government
   Board for Scotland, Joint-Author of 'The Parish Council Guide for Scotland,'
   and ABIJAH MURRAY, Chief Clerk of the Local Government Board for Scotland.
   In Two Parts. Crown 8vo. Part I.—The Public Health (Scotland) Act, 1897,
   with Notes. Part II.—Circulars of the Local Government Board, &c. The
   Parts will be issued separately, and also complete in one Volume.
   The Local Government (Scotland) Act in Relation to Public
   Health. A Handy Guide for County and District Councillors, Medical Officers,
   Sanitary Inspectors, and Members of Parochial Boards. Second Edition. With
   a new Preface on appointment of Sanitary Officers. Crown 8vo, 2s.

SKRINE. **Columba : A Drama.** By JOHN HUNTLEY SKRINE,
   Warden of Glenalmond ; Author of 'A Memory of Edward Thring.' Fcap. 4to, 6s.

SMITH.
   Thorndale ; or, The Conflict of Opinions. By WILLIAM SMITH,
   Author of 'A Discourse on Ethics,' &c. New Edition. Crown 8vo, 10s. 6d.
   Gravenhurst ; or, Thoughts on Good and Evil Second Edi-
   tion. With Memoir and Portrait of the Author. Crown 8vo, 8s.
   The Story of William and Lucy Smith. Edited by GEORGE
   MERRIAM. Large post 8vo, 12s. 6d.

SMITH. **Memoir of the Families of M'Combie and Thoms,**
   originally M'Intosh and M'Thomas. Compiled from History and Tradition. By
   WILLIAM M'COMBIE SMITH. With Illustrations. 8vo, 7s. 6d.

SMITH. **Greek Testament Lessons for Colleges, Schools, and**
   Private Students, consisting chiefly of the Sermon on the Mount and the Parables
   of our Lord. With Notes and Essays. By the Rev. J. HUNTER SMITH, M.A.,
   King Edward's School, Birmingham. Crown 8vo, 6s.

SMITH. **The Secretary for Scotland.** Being a Statement of the
   Powers and Duties of the new Scottish Office. With a Short Historical Intro-
   duction, and numerous references to important Administrative Documents. By
   W. C. SMITH, LL.B., Advocate. 8vo, 6s.

"SON OF THE MARSHES, A."
   From Spring to Fall ; or, When Life Stirs. By "A SON OF
   THE MARSHES." Cheap Uniform Edition. Crown 8vo, 3s. 6d.
   Within an Hour of London Town : Among Wild Birds and
   their Haunts. Edited by J. A. OWEN. Cheap Uniform Edition. Crown 8vo,
   3s. 6d.
   With the Woodlanders and by the Tide. Cheap Uniform
   Edition. Crown 8vo, 3s. 6d.
   On Surrey Hills. Cheap Uniform Edition. Crown 8vo, 3s. 6d.
   Annals of a Fishing Village. Cheap Uniform Edition. Crown
   8vo, 3s. 6d.

SORLEY. **The Ethics of Naturalism.** Being the Shaw Fellowship Lectures, 1884. By W. R. SORLEY, M.A., Fellow of Trinity College, Cambridge, Professor of Moral Philosophy in the University of Aberdeen. Crown
   8vo, 6s.

SPROTT. **The Worship and Offices of the Church of Scotland.**
   By GEORGE W. SPROTT, D.D., Minister of North Berwick. Crown 8vo, 6s.

STATISTICAL ACCOUNT OF SCOTLAND. Complete, with
   Index. 15 vols. 8vo, £16, 16s.

STEEVENS.
   The Land of the Dollar. By G. W. STEEVENS, Author of
   'Naval Policy,' &c. Crown 8vo, 6s.
   With the Conquering Turk. With 4 Maps. Demy 8vo, 10s. 6d.

STEPHENS.

The Book of the Farm ; detailing the Labours of the Farmer,
Farm-Steward, Ploughman, Shepherd, Hedger, Farm-Labourer, Field-Worker,
and Cattle-man. Illustrated with numerous Portraits of Animals and Engravings
of Implements, and Plans of Farm Buildings. Fourth Edition. Revised, and
in great part Re-written, by JAMES MACDONALD, F.R.S.E., Secretary Highland
and Agricultural Society of Scotland. Complete in Six Divisional Volumes,
bound in cloth, each 10s. 6d., or handsomely bound, in 3 volumes, with leather
back and gilt top, £3, 3s.
   *** Also being issued in 20 monthly Parts, price 2s. 6d. net each.
      [Parts I.-VII. ready.

Catechism of Practical Agriculture. 22d Thousand. Revised
by JAMES MACDONALD, F.R.S.E. With numerous Illustrations. Crown 8vo, 1s.

The Book of Farm Implements and Machines. By J. SLIGHT
and R. SCOTT BURN, Engineers. Edited by HENRY STEPHENS. Large 8vo, £2, 2s.

STEVENSON. British Fungi. (Hymenomycetes.) By Rev.
JOHN STEVENSON, Author of 'Mycologia Scotica,' Hon. Sec. Cryptogamic Society
of Scotland. Vols. I. and II., post 8vo, with Illustrations, price 12s. 6d. net each.

STEWART. Advice to Purchasers of Horses. By JOHN
STEWART, V.S. New Edition. 2s. 6d.

STODDART.

John Stuart Blackie: A Biography. By ANNA M. STODDART.
With 3 Plates. Third Edition. 2 vols. demy 8vo, 21s.
   POPULAR EDITION, with Portrait. Crown 8vo, 6s.

Sir Philip Sidney : Servant of God. Illustrated by MARGARET
L. HUGGINS. With a New Portrait of Sir Philip Sidney. Small 4to, with a
specially designed Cover. 5s.

STORMONTH.

Dictionary of the English Language, Pronouncing, Etymological, and Explanatory. By the Rev. JAMES STORMONTH. Revised by the
Rev. P. H. PHELP. Library Edition. New and Cheaper Edition, with Supplement. Imperial 8vo, handsomely bound in half morocco, 18s. net.

Etymological and Pronouncing Dictionary of the English
Language. Including a very Copious Selection of Scientific Terms. For use in
Schools and Colleges, and as a Book of General Reference. The Pronunciation
carefully revised by the Rev. P. H. PHELP, M.A. Cantab. Thirteenth Edition,
with Supplement. Crown 8vo, pp. 800. 7s. 6d.

The School Dictionary. New Edition, Revised.
      [In preparation.

STORY. The Apostolic Ministry in the Scottish Church (The
Baird Lecture for 1897). By ROBERT HERBERT STORY, D.D. (Edin.), F.S.A.
Scot., Professor of Ecclesiastical History in the University of Glasgow; Principal
Clerk of the General Assembly ; and Chaplain to the Queen. Crown 8vo, 7s. 6d.

STORY.

Nero ; A Historical Play. By W. W. STORY, Author of
'Roba di Roma.' Fcap. 8vo, 6s.

Vallombrosa. Post 8vo, 5s.

Poems. 2 vols., 7s. 6d.

Fiammetta. A Summer Idyl. Crown 8vo, 7s. 6d.

Conversations in a Studio. 2 vols. crown 8vo, 12s. 6d.

Excursions in Art and Letters. Crown 8vo, 7s. 6d.

A Poet's Portfolio : Later Readings. 18mo, 3s. 6d.

STRACHEY. Talk at a Country House. Fact and Fiction.
By Sir EDWARD STRACHEY, Bart. With a Portrait of the Author. Crown 8vo,
4s. 6d. net.

STURGIS. Little Comedies, Old and New. By JULIAN STURGIS.
Crown 8vo, 7s. 6d.

SUTHERLAND. Handbook of Hardy Herbaceous and Alpine
Flowers, for General Garden Decoration. Containing Descriptions of upwards
of 1000 Species of Ornamental Hardy Perennial and Alpine Plants; along with
Concise and Plain Instructions for their Propagation and Culture. By WILLIAM
SUTHERLAND, Landscape Gardener; formerly Manager of the Herbaceous Depart-
ment at Kew. Crown 8vo, 7s. 6d.

TAYLOR. The Story of my Life. By the late Colonel
MEADOWS TAYLOR, Author of 'The Confessions of a Thug,' &c., &c. Edited by
his Daughter. New and Cheaper Edition, being the Fourth. Crown 8vo, 6s.

THOMAS. The Woodland Life. By EDWARD THOMAS. With a
Frontispiece. Square 8vo, 6s.

THOMSON.
The Diversions of a Prime Minister. By Basil Thomson.
With a Map, numerous Illustrations by J. W. Cawston and others, and Repro-
ductions of Rare Plates from Early Voyages of Sixteenth and Seventeenth Centuries. Small demy 8vo, 15s.

South Sea Yarns. With 10 Full-page Illustrations. Cheaper
Edition. Crown 8vo, 3s. 6d.

THOMSON.
Handy Book of the Flower-Garden: Being Practical Direc-
tions for the Propagation, Culture, and Arrangement of Plants in Flower-
Gardens all the year round. With Engraved Plans. By DAVID THOMSON,
Gardener to his Grace the Duke of Buccleuch, K.T., at Drumlanrig. Fourth
and Cheaper Edition. Crown 8vo, 5s.

The Handy Book of Fruit-Culture under Glass: Being a
series of Elaborate Practical Treatises on the Cultivation and Forcing of Pines,
Vines, Peaches, Figs, Melons, Strawberries, and Cucumbers. With Engravings
of Hothouses, &c. Second Edition, Revised and Enlarged. Crown 8vo, 7s. 6d.

THOMSON. A Practical Treatise on the Cultivation of the
Grape Vine. By WILLIAM THOMSON, Tweed Vineyards. Tenth Edition. 8vo, 5s.

THOMSON. Cookery for the Sick and Convalescent. With
Directions for the Preparation of Poultices, Fomentations, &c. By BARBARA
THOMSON. Fcap. 8vo, 1s. 6d.

THORBURN. Asiatic Neighbours. By S. S. THORBURN, Bengal
Civil Service, Author of 'Bannú; or, Our Afghan Frontier,' 'David Leslie:
A Story of the Afghan Frontier,' 'Mussalmans and Money-Lenders in the Pan-
jab.' With Two Maps. Demy 8vo, 10s. 6d. net.

THORNTON. Opposites. A Series of Essays on the Unpopular
Sides of Popular Questions. By LEWIS THORNTON. 8vo, 12s. 6d.

TIELE. Elements of the Science of Religion. Part I.—Morpho-
logical. Being the Gifford Lectures delivered before the University of Edinburgh
in 1896. By C. P. TIELE, Theol. D., Litt. D. (Bonon.), Hon. M.R.A.S., &c., Professor of the Science of Religion in the University of Leiden. In 2 vols. Vol. I.
post 8vo, 7s. 6d. *net.*

TOKE. French Historical Unseens. For Army Classes. By
N. E. TOKE, B.A. In 1 vol. crown 8vo. [*In the press.*

TRANSACTIONS OF THE HIGHLAND AND AGRICUL-
TURAL SOCIETY OF SCOTLAND. Published annually, price 5s.

TRAVERS.
Mona Maclean, Medical Student. A Novel. By GRAHAM
TRAVERS. Twelfth Edition. Crown 8vo, 6s.

Fellow Travellers. Fourth Edition. Crown 8vo, 6s.

TRYON. Life of Vice-Admiral Sir George Tryon, K.C.B. By
Rear-Admiral C. C. PENROSE FITZGERALD. With Two Portraits and numerous
Illustrations. Second Edition. Demy 8vo, 21s.

TULLOCH.
Rational Theology and Christian Philosophy in England in
the Seventeenth Century. By JOHN TULLOCH, D.D., Principal of St Mary's College in the University of St Andrews, and one of her Majesty's Chaplains in
Ordinary in Scotland. Second Edition. 2 vols. 8vo, 16s.

TULLOCH.
Modern Theories in Philosophy and Religion. 8vo, 15s.
Luther, and other Leaders of the Reformation. Third Edi-
tion, Enlarged. Crown 8vo, 3s. 6d.
Memoir of Principal Tulloch, D.D., LL.D. By Mrs OLIPHANT,
Author of 'Life of Edward Irving.' Third and Cheaper Edition. 8vo, with
Portrait, 7s. 6d.
TWEEDIE. The Arabian Horse: His Country and People.
By Major-General W. TWEEDIE, C.S.I., Bengal Staff Corps; for many years
H.B.M.'s Consul-General, Baghdad, and Political Resident for the Government
of India in Turkish Arabia. In one vol. royal 4to, with Seven Coloured Plates
and other Illustrations, and a Map of the Country. Price £3, 3s. net.
TYLER. The Whence and the Whither of Man. A Brief His-
tory of his Origin and Development through Conformity to Environment. The
Morse Lectures of 1895. By JOHN M. TYLER, Professor of Biology, Amherst College, U.S.A. Post 8vo, 6s. net.

VEITCH.
Memoir of John Veitch, LL.D., Professor of Logic and Rhetoric,
University of Glasgow. By MARY R. L. BRYCE. With Portrait and 3 Photo-
gravure Plates. Demy 8vo, 7s. 6d.
Border Essays. By JOHN VEITCH, LL.D., Professor of Logic
and Rhetoric, University of Glasgow. Crown 8vo, 4s. 6d. net.
The History and Poetry of the Scottish Border: their Main
Features and Relations. New and Enlarged Edition. 2 vols. demy 8vo, 16s.
Institutes of Logic. Post 8vo, 12s. 6d.
The Feeling for Nature in Scottish Poetry. From the Ear-
liest Times to the Present Day. 2 vols. fcap. 8vo, in roxburghe binding, 15s.
Merlin and other Poems. Fcap. 8vo, 4s. 6d.
Knowing and Being. Essays in Philosophy. First Series.
Crown 8vo, 5s.
Dualism and Monism; and other Essays. Essays in Phil-
osophy. Second Series. With an Introduction by R. M. Wenley. Crown 8vo,
4s. 6d. net.
VIRGIL. The Æneid of Virgil. Translated in English Blank
Verse by G. K. RICKARDS, M.A., and Lord RAVENSWORTH. 2 vols. fcap. 8vo, 10s.

WACE. Christianity and Agnosticism. Reviews of some Recent
Attacks on the Christian Faith. By HENRY WACE, D.D., Principal of King's
College, London; Preacher of Lincoln's Inn; Chaplain to the Queen. Second
Edition. Post 8vo, 10s. 6d. net.
WADDELL. An Old Kirk Chronicle: Being a History of Auld-
hame, Tyninghame, and Whitekirk, in East Lothian. From Session Records,
1615 to 1850. By Rev. P. HATELY WADDELL, B.D., Minister of the United
Parish. Small Paper Edition, 200 Copies. Price £1. Large Paper Edition, 50
Copies. Price £1, 10s.
WALDO. The Ban of the Gubbe. By CEDRIC DANE WALDO.
Crown 8vo, 2s. 6d.
WALFORD. Four Biographies from 'Blackwood': Jane Taylor,
Hannah More, Elizabeth Fry, Mary Somerville. By L. B. WALFORD. Crown
8vo, 5s.
WARREN'S (SAMUEL) WORKS:—
Diary of a Late Physician. Cloth, 2s. 6d.; boards, 2s
Ten Thousand A-Year. Cloth, 3s. 6d.; boards, 2s. 6d.
Now and Then. The Lily and the Bee. Intellectual and
Moral Development of the Present Age. 4s. 6d.
Essays: Critical, Imaginative, and Juridical. 5s.

WENLEY.
Socrates and Christ: A Study in the Philosophy of Religion.
By R. M. WENLEY, M.A., D.Sc., D.Phil., Professor of Philosophy in the University of Michigan, U.S.A. Crown 8vo, 6s.
Aspects of Pessimism. Crown 8vo, 6s.

WHITE.
The Eighteen Christian Centuries. By the Rev. JAMES WHITE. Seventh Edition. Post 8vo, with Index, 6s.
History of France, from the Earliest Times. Sixth Thousand.
Post 8vo, with Index, 6s.

WHITE.
Archæological Sketches in Scotland—Kintyre and Knapdale.
By Colonel T. P. WHITE, R.E., of the Ordnance Survey. With numerous Illustrations. 2 vols, folio, £4, 4s. Vol. I., Kintyre, sold separately, £2, 2s.
The Ordnance Survey of the United Kingdom. A Popular Account. Crown 8vo, 5s.

WILKES. Latin Historical Unseens. For Army Classes. By L. C. VAUGHAN WILKES, M.A. In 1 vol. crown 8vo. [*In the press.*

WILLIAMSON. The Horticultural Handbook and Exhibitor's Guide. A Treatise on Cultivating, Exhibiting, and Judging Plants, Flowers, Fruits, and Vegetables. By W. WILLIAMSON, Gardener. Revised by MALCOLM DUNN, Gardener to his Grace the Duke of Buccleuch and Queensberry, Dalkeith Park. New and Cheaper Edition, enlarged. Crown 8vo, paper cover, 2s.; cloth, 2s. 6d.

WILLIAMSON, Poems of Nature and Life. By DAVID R. WILLIAMSON, Minister of Kirkmaiden. Fcap. 8vo, 3s.

WILLS. Behind an Eastern Veil. A Plain Tale of Events occurring in the Experience of a Lady who had a unique opportunity of observing the Inner Life of Ladies of the Upper Class in Persia. By C. J. WILLS, Author of 'In the Land of the Lion and Sun,' 'Persia as it is,' &c., &c. Cheaper Edition. Demy 8vo, 5s.

WILSON.
Works of Professor Wilson. Edited by his Son-in-Law, Professor FERRIER. 12 vols. crown 8vo, £2, 8s.
Christopher in his Sporting-Jacket. 2 vols., 8s.
Isle of Palms, City of the Plague, and other Poems. 4s.
Lights and Shadows of Scottish Life, and other Tales. 4s.
Essays, Critical and Imaginative. 4 vols., 16s.
The Noctes Ambrosianæ. 4 vols., 16s.
Homer and his Translators, and the Greek Drama. Crown 8vo, 4s.

WORSLEY.
Homer's Odyssey. Translated into English Verse in the Spenserian Stanza. By PHILIP STANHOPE WORSLEY, M.A. New and Cheaper Edition. Post 8vo, 7s. 6d. net.
Homer's Iliad. Translated by P. S. Worsley and Prof. Conington. 2 vols. crown 8vo, 21s.

YATE. England and Russia Face to Face in Asia. A Record of Travel with the Afghan Boundary Commission. By Captain A. C. YATE, Bombay Staff Corps. 8vo, with Maps and Illustrations, 21s.

YATE. Northern Afghanistan; or, Letters from the Afghan Boundary Commission. By Colonel C. E. YATE, C.S.I., C.M.G., Bombay Staff Corps, F.R.G.S. 8vo, with Maps, 18s.

YULE. Fortification: For the use of Officers in the Army, and Readers of Military History. By Colonel Sir HENRY YULE, Bengal Engineers. 8vo, with Numerous Illustrations, 10s.

12/97.

www.ingramcontent.com/pod-product-compliance
Lightning Source LLC
Chambersburg PA
CBHW030954110726
47900CB00004B/1261